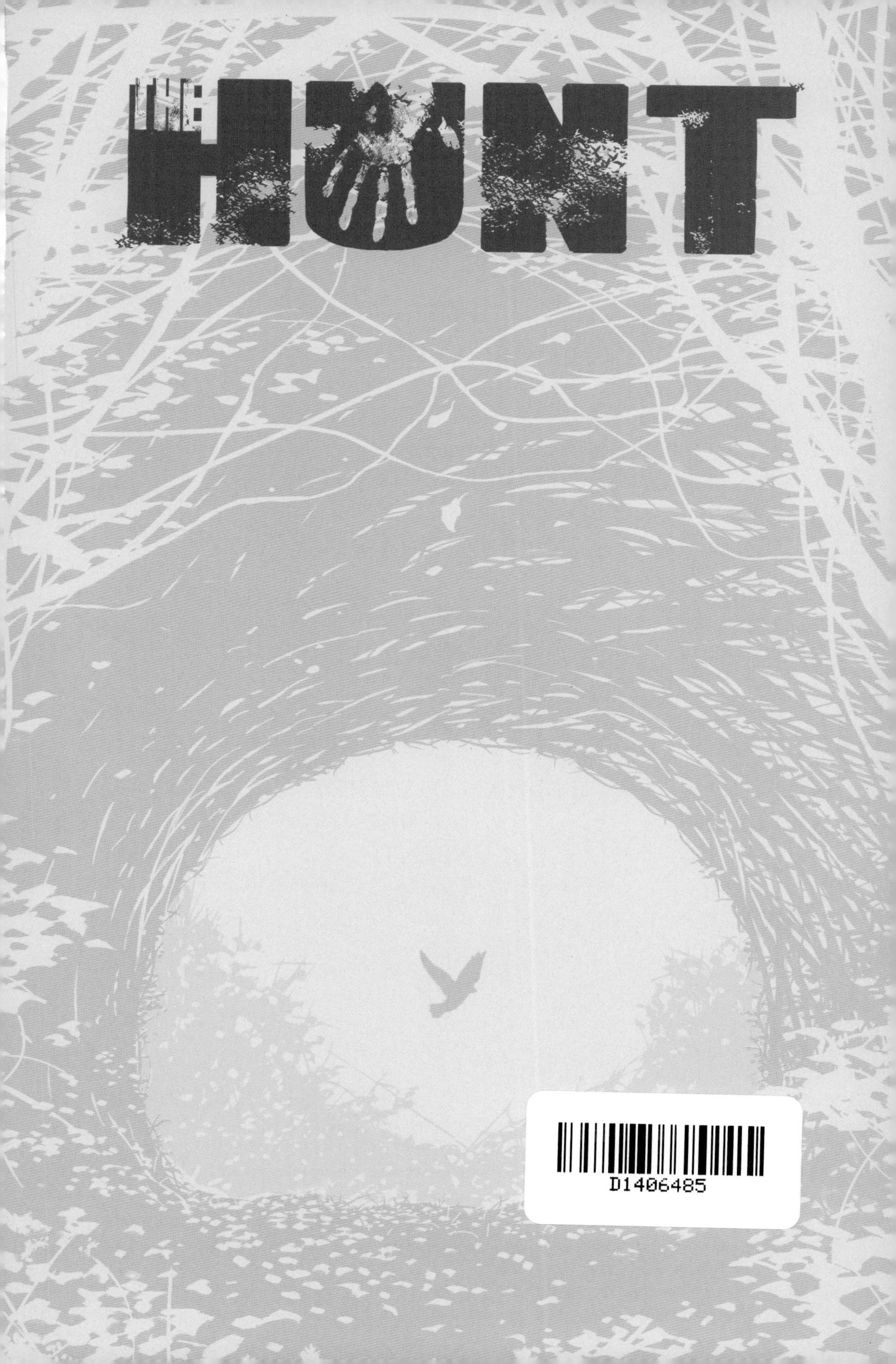
THE HUNT

image® COMICS PRESENTS

Created, Written and Illustrated by
COLIN LORIMER

Colored by
JOANA LAFUENTE

Lettered by
JIM CAMPBELL

Covers by
COLIN LORIMER & JOANA LAFUENTE

Logo design by
COLIN LORIMER & JASON KEVITT

A

Shadowline®
PRODUCTION

LAURA TAVISHATI
Editor

MARC LOMBARDI
Communications

JIM VALENTINO
Publisher

IMAGE COMICS, INC.
Robert Kirkman—Chief Operating Officer
Erik Larsen—Chief Financial Officer
Todd McFarlane—President
Marc Silvestri—Chief Executive Officer
Jim Valentino—Vice-President

Eric Stephenson—Publisher
Corey Murphy—Director of Sales
Jeff Boison—Director of Publishing Planning & Book Trade Sales
Chris Ross—Director of Digital Sales
Kat Salazar—Director of PR & Marketing
Branwyn Bigglestone—Controller
Susan Korpela—Accounts Manager
Drew Gill—Art Director
Brett Warnock—Production Manager
Meredith Wallace—Print Manager
Briah Skelly—Publicist
Aly Hoffman— Conventions & Events Coordinator
Sasha Head—Sales & Marketing Production Designer
David Brothers—Branding Manager
Melissa Gifford—Content Manager
Erika Schnatz—Production Artist
Ryan Brewer—Production Artist
Shanna Matuszak—Production Artist
Tricia Ramos—Production Artist
Vincent Kukua—Production Artist
Jeff Stang—Direct Market Sales Representative
Emilio Bautista—Digital Sales Associate
Leanna Caunter—Accounting Assistant
Chloe Ramos-Peterson—Library Market Sales Representative
IMAGECOMICS.COM

First printing. April 2017.   ISBN: 978-1-5343-0062-0.

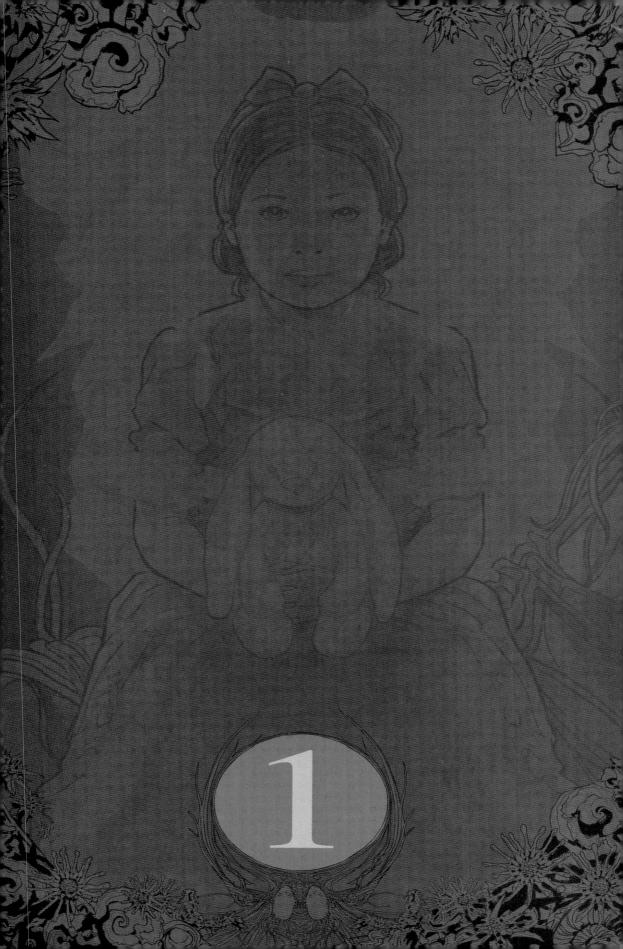

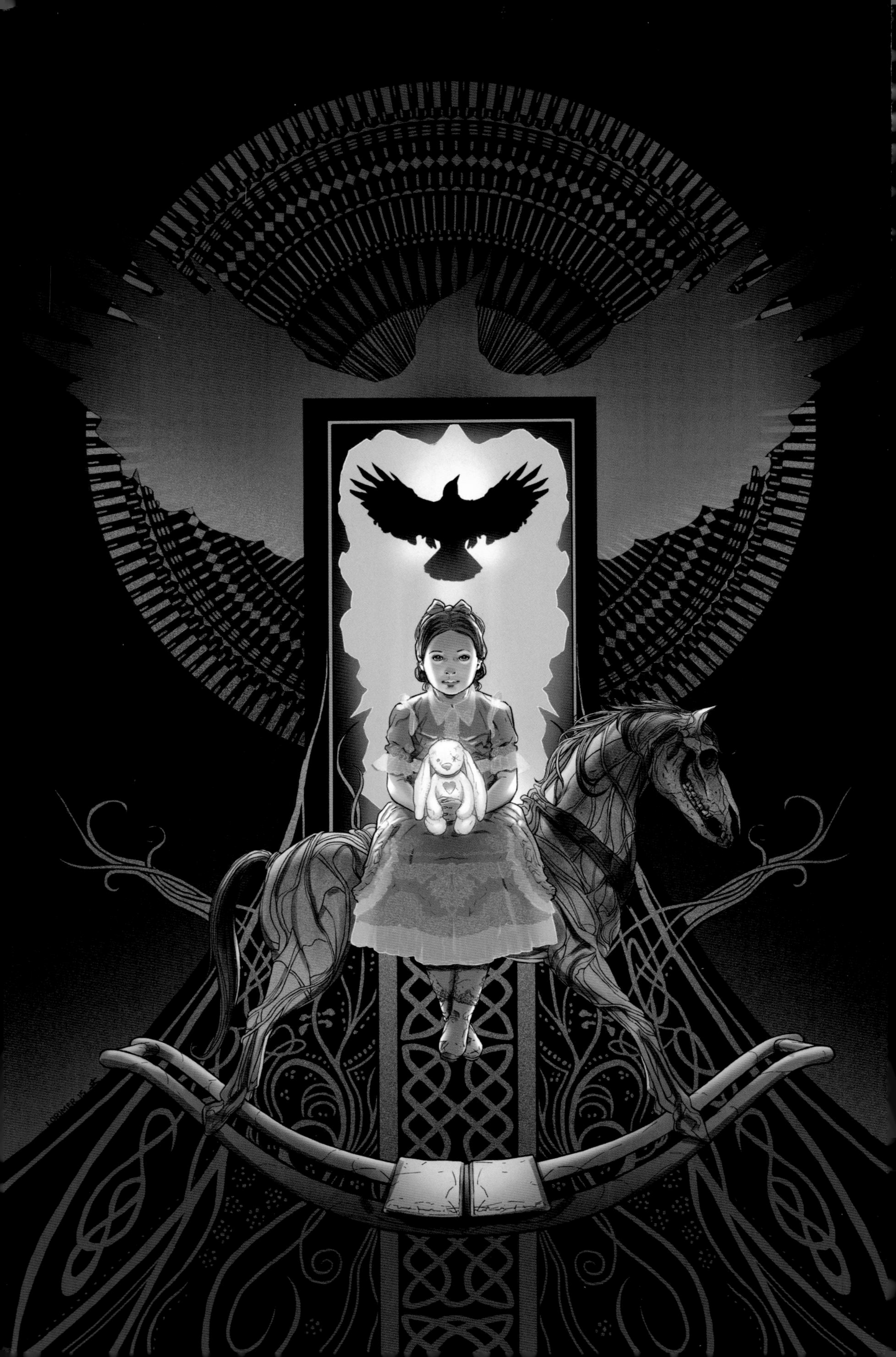

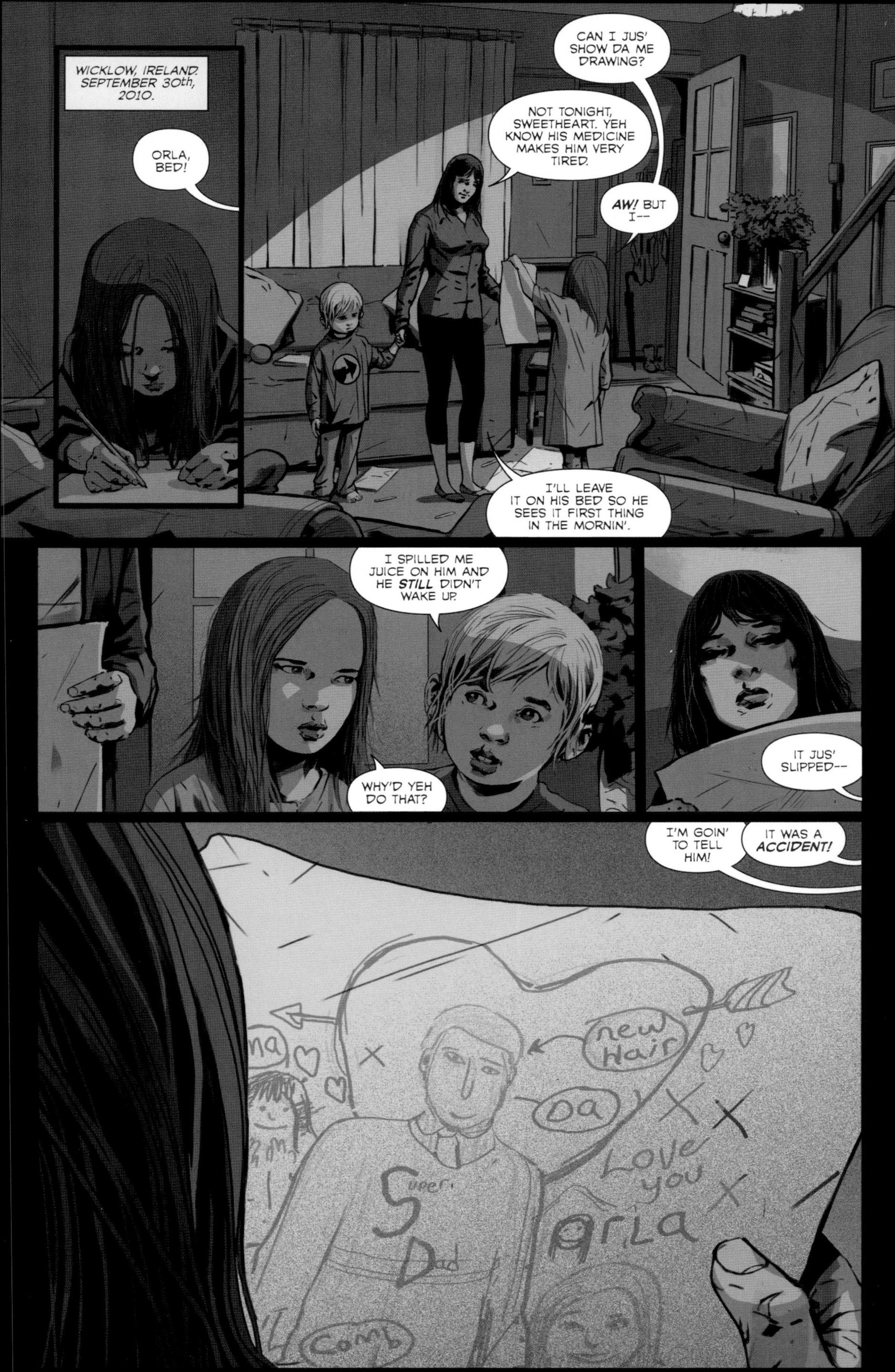
WICKLOW, IRELAND. SEPTEMBER 30th, 2010.
ORLA, BED!
CAN I JUS' SHOW DA ME DRAWING?
NOT TONIGHT, SWEETHEART. YEH KNOW HIS MEDICINE MAKES HIM VERY TIRED.
AW! BUT I--
I'LL LEAVE IT ON HIS BED SO HE SEES IT FIRST THING IN THE MORNIN'.
I SPILLED ME JUICE ON HIM AND HE STILL DIDN'T WAKE UP.
WHY'D YEH DO THAT?
IT JUS' SLIPPED--
I'M GOIN' TO TELL HIM!
IT WAS A ACCIDENT!
new Hair
Da
Love you
Super
Dad
Comb

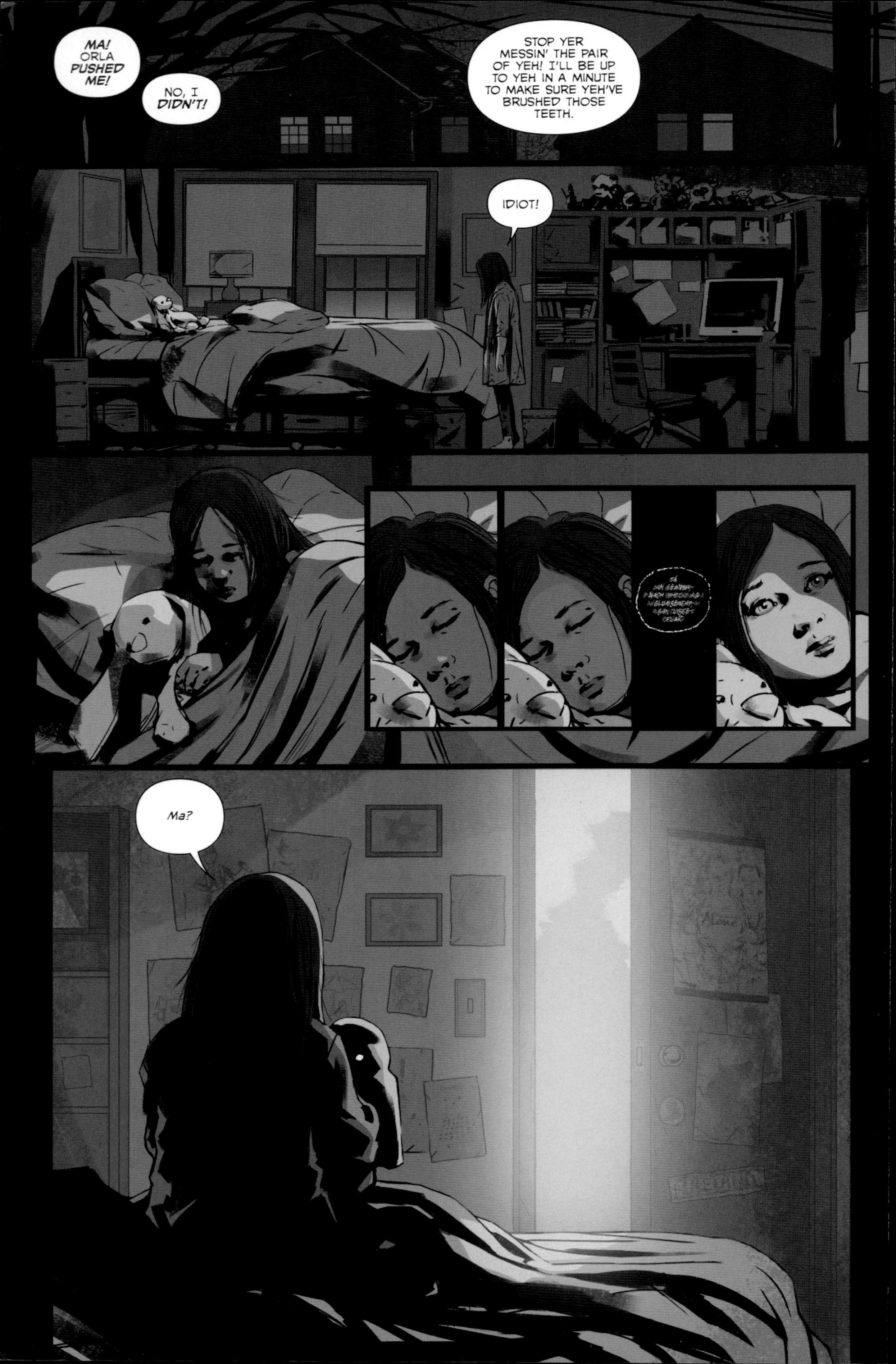
MA! ORLA PUSHED ME!
NO, I DIDN'T!
STOP YER MESSIN' THE PAIR OF YEH! I'LL BE UP TO YEH IN A MINUTE TO MAKE SURE YEH'VE BRUSHED THOSE TEETH.
IDIOT!
Ma?

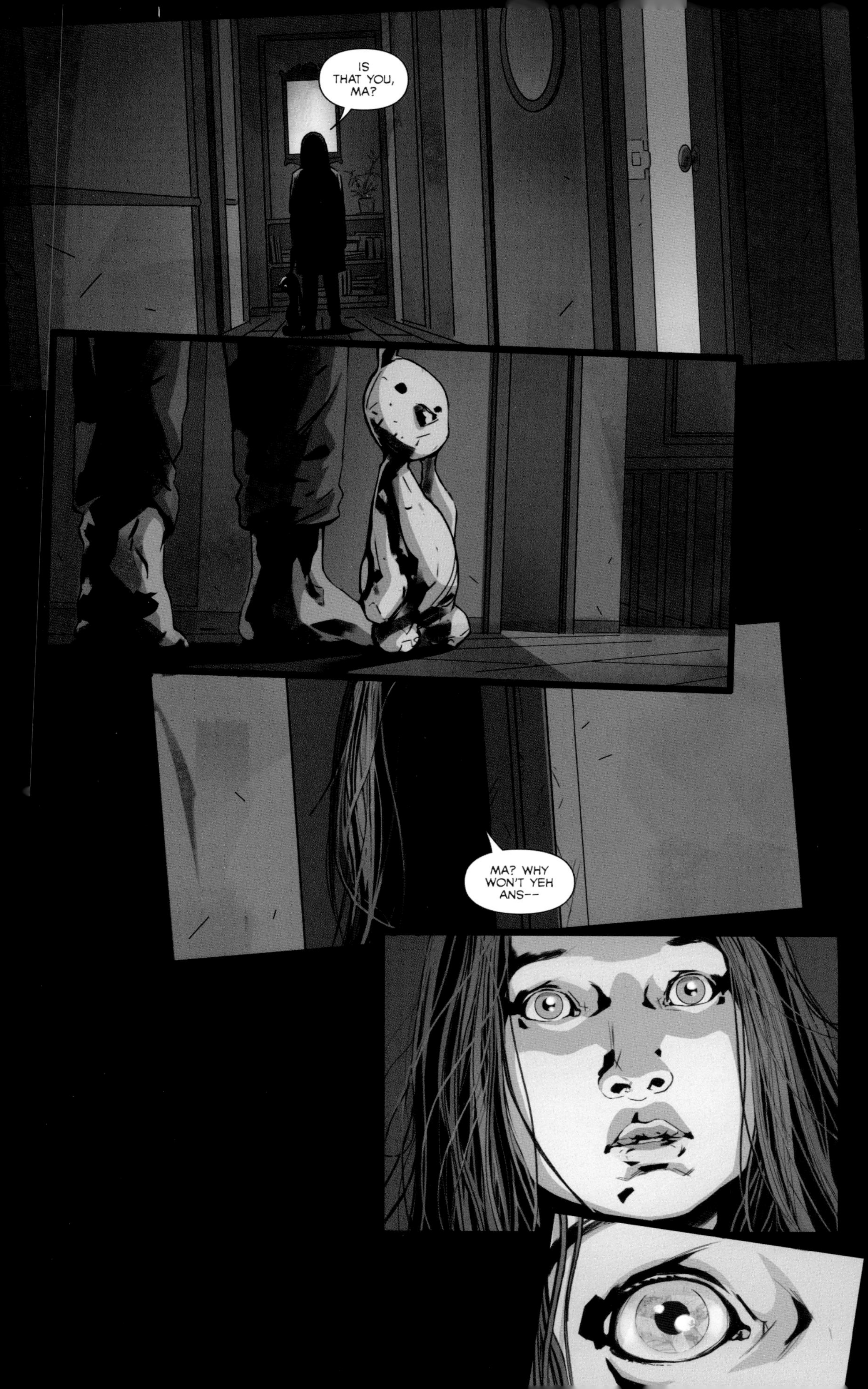

IS THAT YOU, MA?
MA? WHY WON'T YEH ANS--

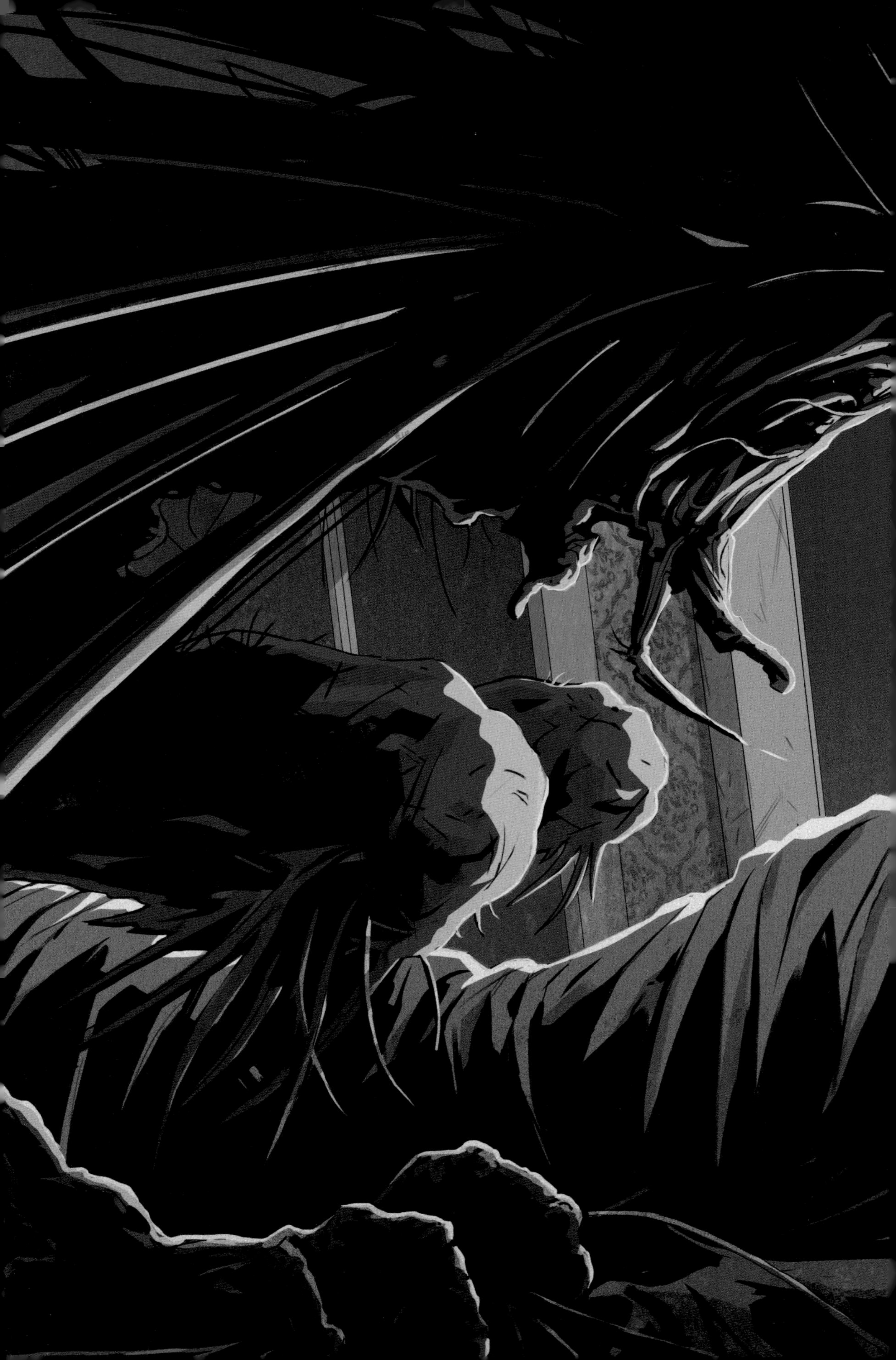

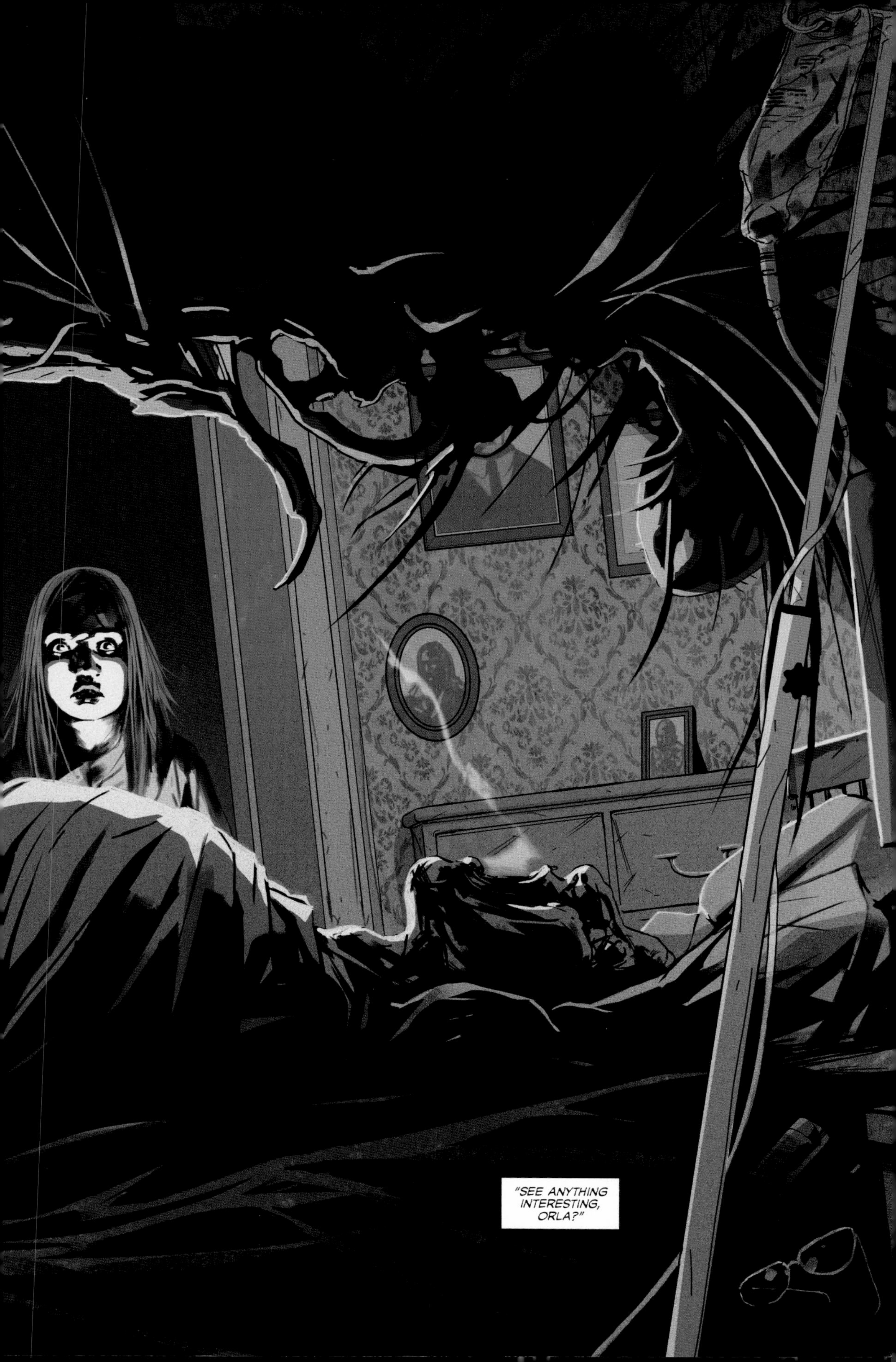
"SEE ANYTHING INTERESTING, ORLA?"

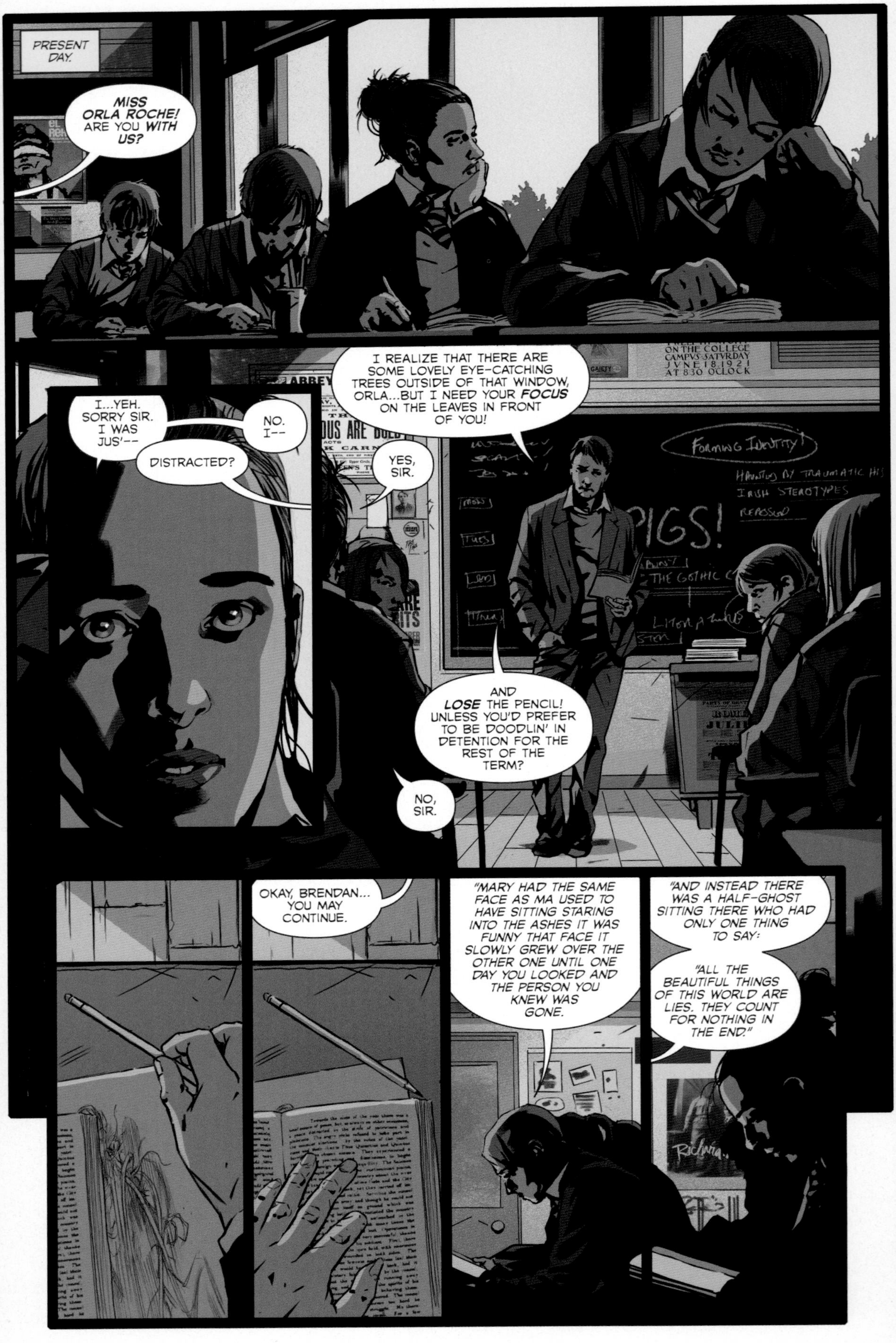
PRESENT DAY.
MISS ORLA ROCHE! ARE YOU WITH US?
I REALIZE THAT THERE ARE SOME LOVELY EYE-CATCHING TREES OUTSIDE OF THAT WINDOW, ORLA...BUT I NEED YOUR FOCUS ON THE LEAVES IN FRONT OF YOU!
I...YEH. SORRY SIR. I WAS JUS'--
NO. I--
DISTRACTED?
YES, SIR.
AND LOSE THE PENCIL! UNLESS YOU'D PREFER TO BE DOODLIN' IN DETENTION FOR THE REST OF THE TERM?
NO, SIR.
FORMING IDENTITY
IRISH STEROTYPES
PIGS!
THE GOTHIC
ON THE COLLEGE CAMPVS-SATVRDAY JVNE 18 1921 AT 830 OCLOCK
OKAY, BRENDAN... YOU MAY CONTINUE.
"MARY HAD THE SAME FACE AS MA USED TO HAVE SITTING STARING INTO THE ASHES IT WAS FUNNY THAT FACE IT SLOWLY GREW OVER THE OTHER ONE UNTIL ONE DAY YOU LOOKED AND THE PERSON YOU KNEW WAS GONE.
"AND INSTEAD THERE WAS A HALF-GHOST SITTING THERE WHO HAD ONLY ONE THING TO SAY:
"ALL THE BEAUTIFUL THINGS OF THIS WORLD ARE LIES. THEY COUNT FOR NOTHING IN THE END."

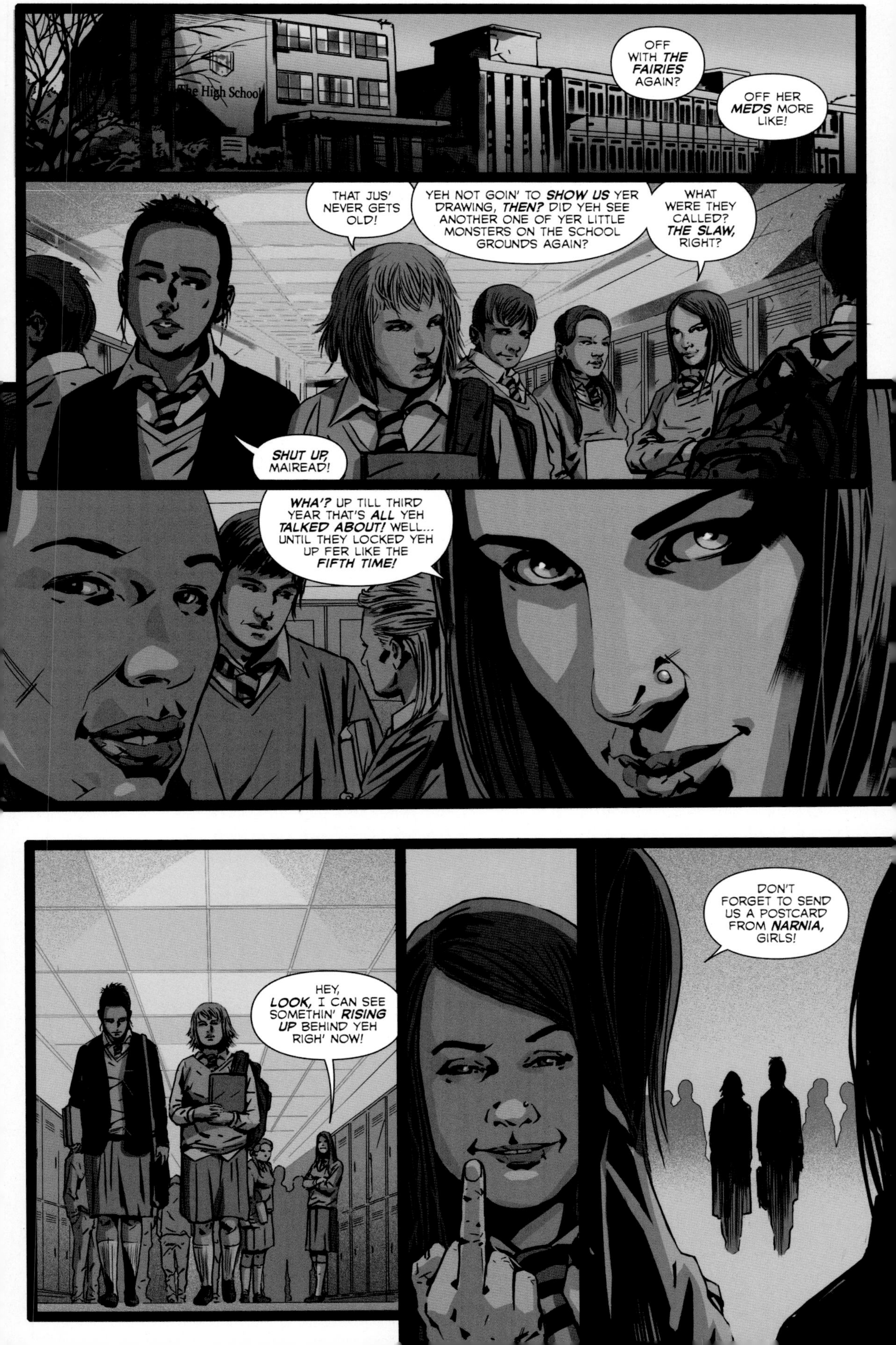
The High School
OFF WITH THE FAIRIES AGAIN?
OFF HER MEDS MORE LIKE!
THAT JUS' NEVER GETS OLD!
YEH NOT GOIN' TO SHOW US YER DRAWING, THEN? DID YEH SEE ANOTHER ONE OF YER LITTLE MONSTERS ON THE SCHOOL GROUNDS AGAIN?
WHAT WERE THEY CALLED? THE SLAW, RIGHT?
SHUT UP, MAIREAD!
WHA'? UP TILL THIRD YEAR THAT'S ALL YEH TALKED ABOUT! WELL... UNTIL THEY LOCKED YEH UP FER LIKE THE FIFTH TIME!
HEY, LOOK, I CAN SEE SOMETHIN' RISING UP BEHIND YEH RIGH' NOW!
DON'T FORGET TO SEND US A POSTCARD FROM NARNIA, GIRLS!

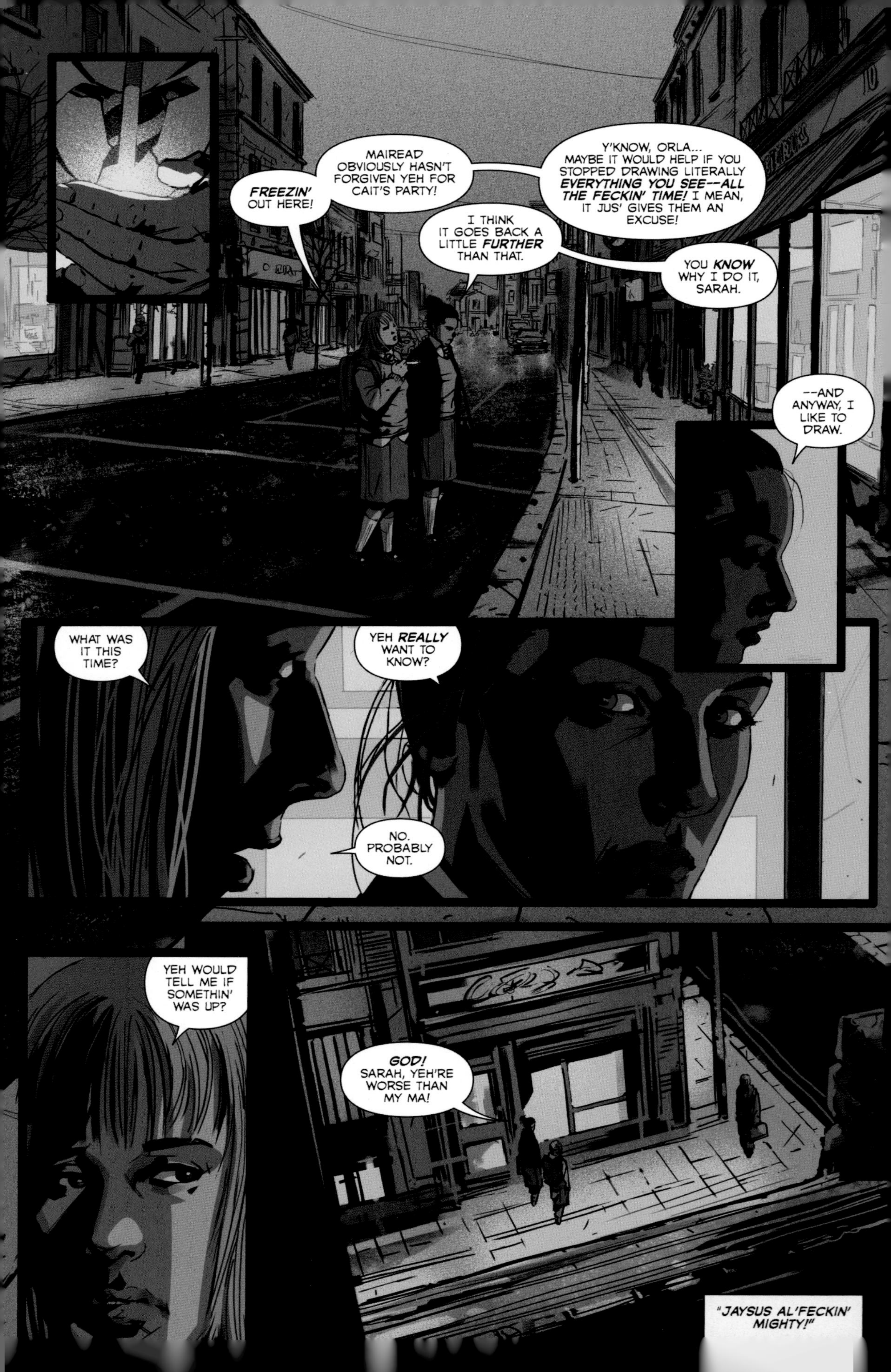
FREEZIN' OUT HERE!
MAIREAD OBVIOUSLY HASN'T FORGIVEN YEH FOR CAIT'S PARTY!
Y'KNOW, ORLA... MAYBE IT WOULD HELP IF YOU STOPPED DRAWING LITERALLY EVERYTHING YOU SEE--ALL THE FECKIN' TIME! I MEAN, IT JUS' GIVES THEM AN EXCUSE!
I THINK IT GOES BACK A LITTLE FURTHER THAN THAT.
YOU KNOW WHY I DO IT, SARAH.
--AND ANYWAY, I LIKE TO DRAW.
WHAT WAS IT THIS TIME?
YEH REALLY WANT TO KNOW?
NO. PROBABLY NOT.
YEH WOULD TELL ME IF SOMETHIN' WAS UP?
GOD! SARAH, YEH'RE WORSE THAN MY MA!
"JAYSUS AL'FECKIN' MIGHTY!"

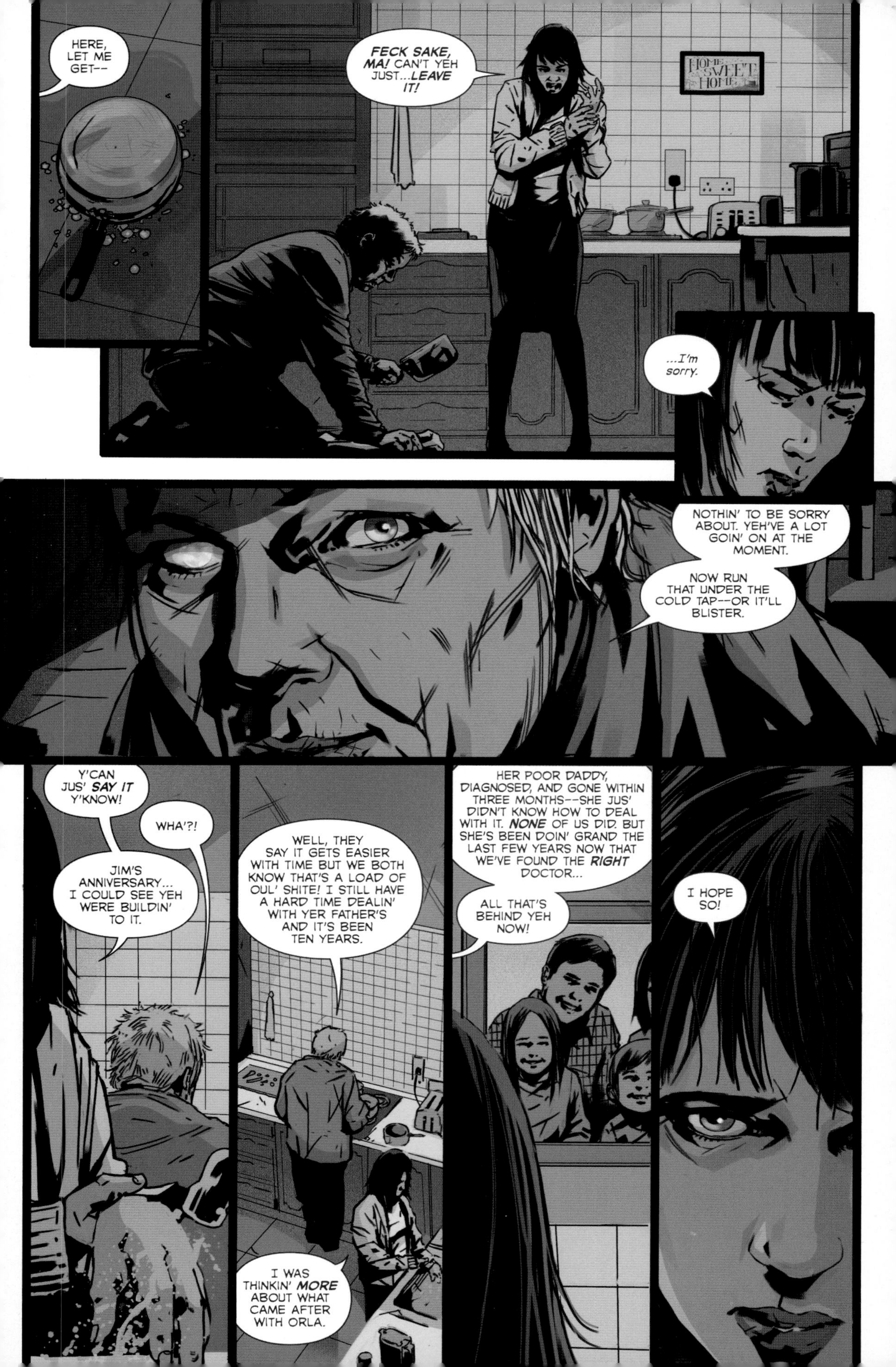
HERE, LET ME GET--
FECK SAKE, MA! CAN'T YEH JUST...LEAVE IT!
HOME SWEET HOME
...I'm sorry.
NOTHIN' TO BE SORRY ABOUT. YEH'VE A LOT GOIN' ON AT THE MOMENT.
NOW RUN THAT UNDER THE COLD TAP--OR IT'LL BLISTER.
Y'CAN JUS' SAY IT Y'KNOW!
WHA'?!
JIM'S ANNIVERSARY... I COULD SEE YEH WERE BUILDIN' TO IT.
WELL, THEY SAY IT GETS EASIER WITH TIME BUT WE BOTH KNOW THAT'S A LOAD OF OUL' SHITE! I STILL HAVE A HARD TIME DEALIN' WITH YER FATHER'S AND IT'S BEEN TEN YEARS.
I WAS THINKIN' MORE ABOUT WHAT CAME AFTER WITH ORLA.
HER POOR DADDY, DIAGNOSED, AND GONE WITHIN THREE MONTHS--SHE JUS' DIDN'T KNOW HOW TO DEAL WITH IT. NONE OF US DID. BUT SHE'S BEEN DOIN' GRAND THE LAST FEW YEARS NOW THAT WE'VE FOUND THE RIGHT DOCTOR...
ALL THAT'S BEHIND YEH NOW!
I HOPE SO!

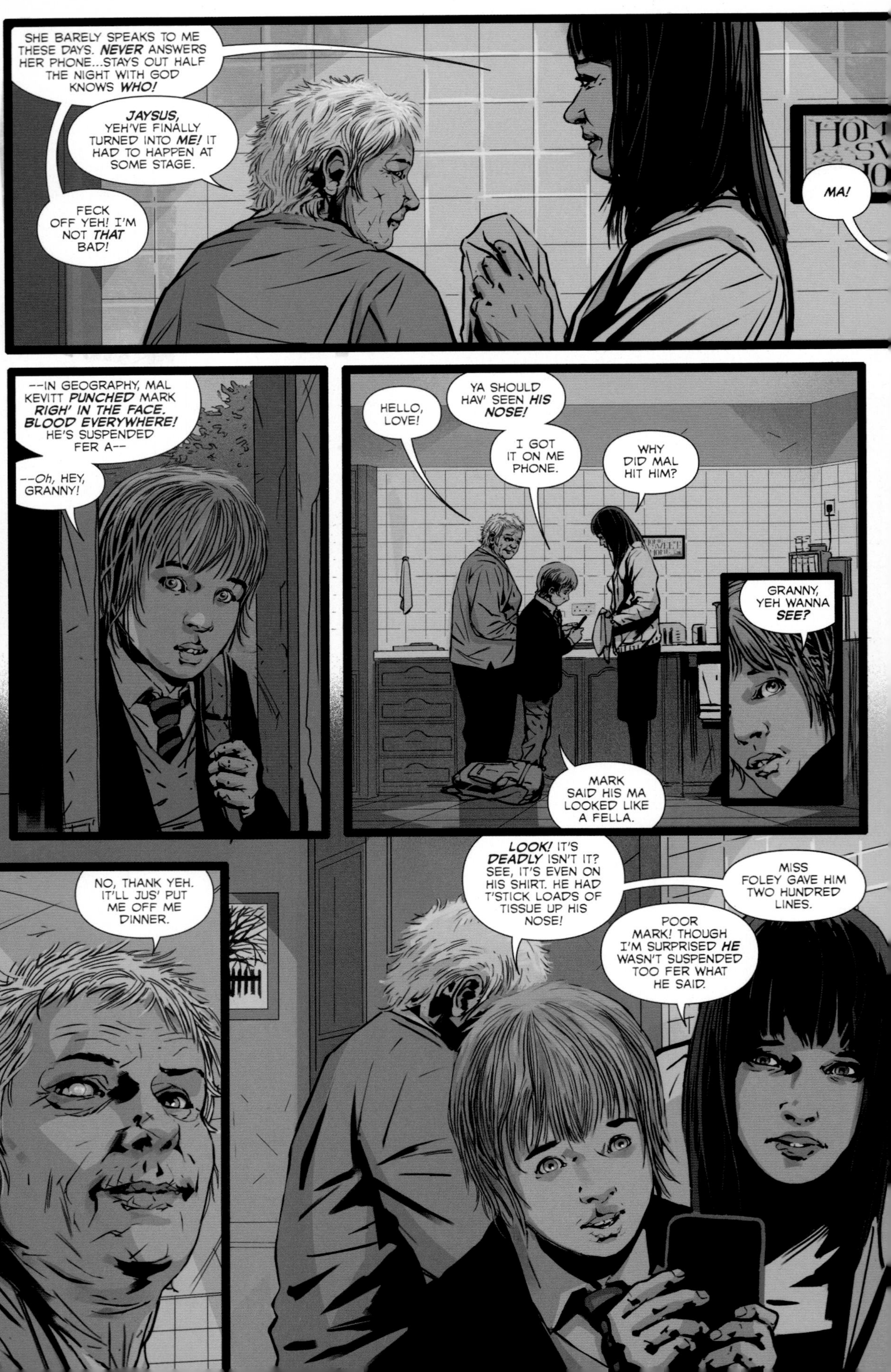
SHE BARELY SPEAKS TO ME THESE DAYS. **NEVER** ANSWERS HER PHONE...STAYS OUT HALF THE NIGHT WITH GOD KNOWS **WHO!**
JAYSUS, YEH'VE FINALLY TURNED INTO **ME!** IT HAD TO HAPPEN AT SOME STAGE.
FECK OFF YEH! I'M NOT **THAT** BAD!
MA!
--IN GEOGRAPHY, MAL KEVITT **PUNCHED** MARK **RIGH' IN THE FACE. BLOOD EVERYWHERE!** HE'S SUSPENDED FER A--
--*Oh,* HEY, GRANNY!
HELLO, LOVE!
YA SHOULD HAV' SEEN **HIS NOSE!**
I GOT IT ON ME PHONE.
WHY DID MAL HIT HIM?
GRANNY, YEH WANNA **SEE?**
MARK SAID HIS MA LOOKED LIKE A FELLA.
NO, THANK YEH. IT'LL JUS' PUT ME OFF ME DINNER.
LOOK! IT'S **DEADLY** ISN'T IT? SEE, IT'S EVEN ON HIS SHIRT. HE HAD T'STICK LOADS OF TISSUE UP HIS NOSE!
MISS FOLEY GAVE HIM TWO HUNDRED LINES.
POOR MARK! THOUGH I'M SURPRISED **HE** WASN'T SUSPENDED TOO FER WHAT HE SAID.

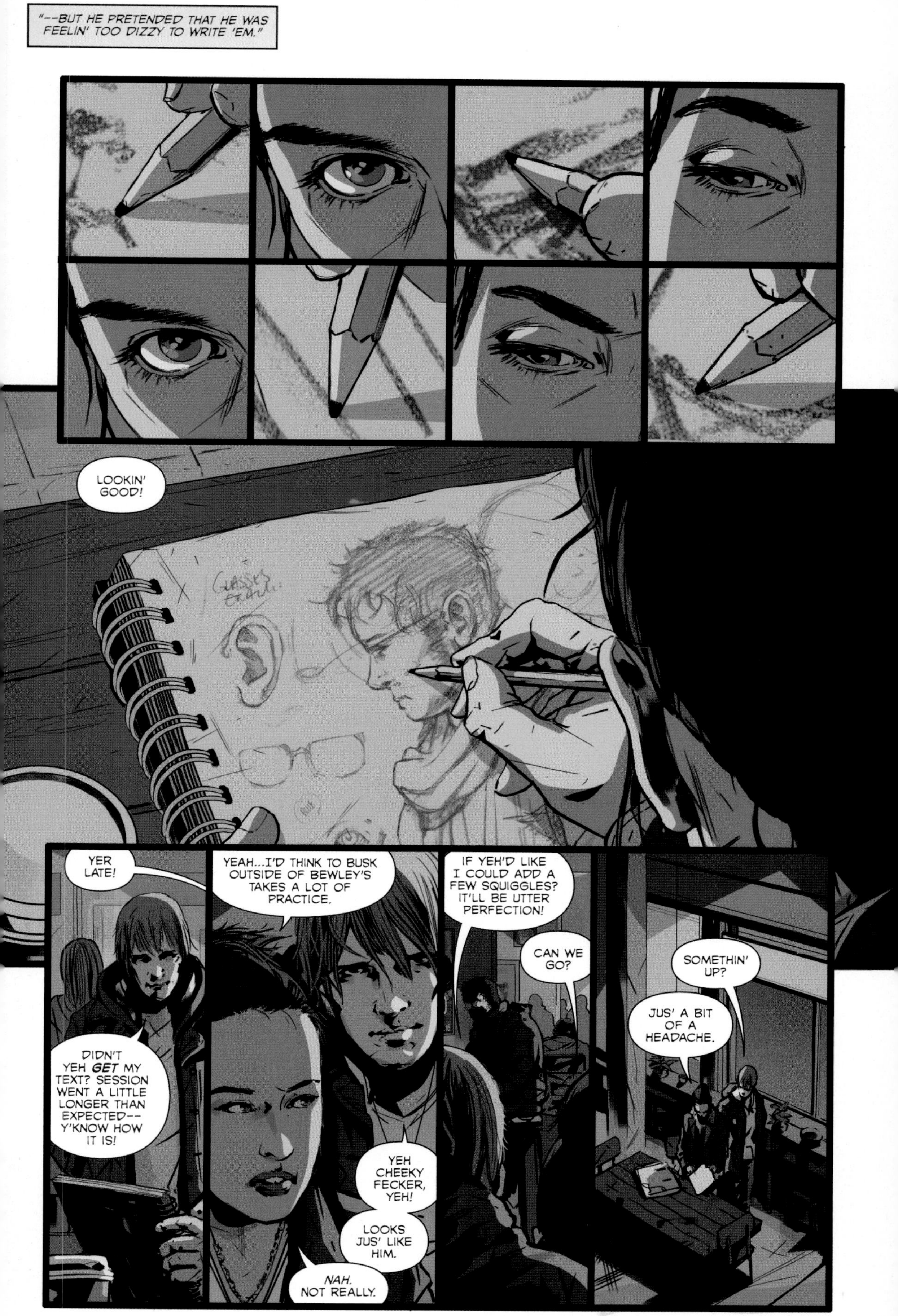
"--BUT HE PRETENDED THAT HE WAS FEELIN' TOO DIZZY TO WRITE 'EM."
LOOKIN' GOOD!
YER LATE!
DIDN'T YEH **GET** MY TEXT? SESSION WENT A LITTLE LONGER THAN EXPECTED-- Y'KNOW HOW IT IS!
YEAH...I'D THINK TO BUSK OUTSIDE OF BEWLEY'S TAKES A LOT OF PRACTICE.
YEH CHEEKY FECKER, YEH!
LOOKS JUS' LIKE HIM.
NAH. NOT REALLY.
IF YEH'D LIKE I COULD ADD A FEW SQUIGGLES? IT'LL BE UTTER PERFECTION!
CAN WE GO?
SOMETHIN' UP?
JUS' A BIT OF A HEADACHE.

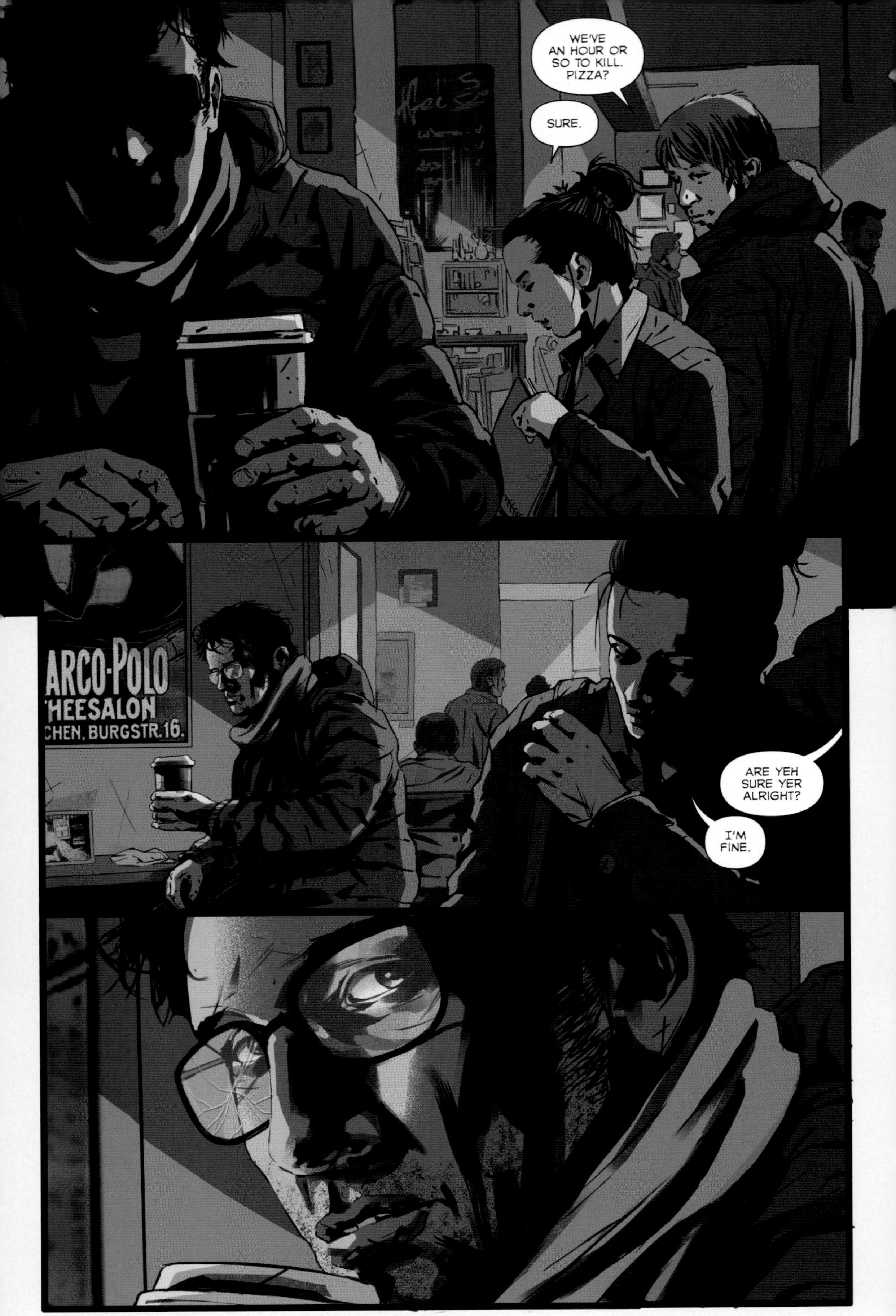
WE'VE AN HOUR OR SO TO KILL. PIZZA?
SURE.
ARCO-POLO
THEESALON
CHEN, BURGSTR. 16.
ARE YEH SURE YER ALRIGHT?
I'M FINE.

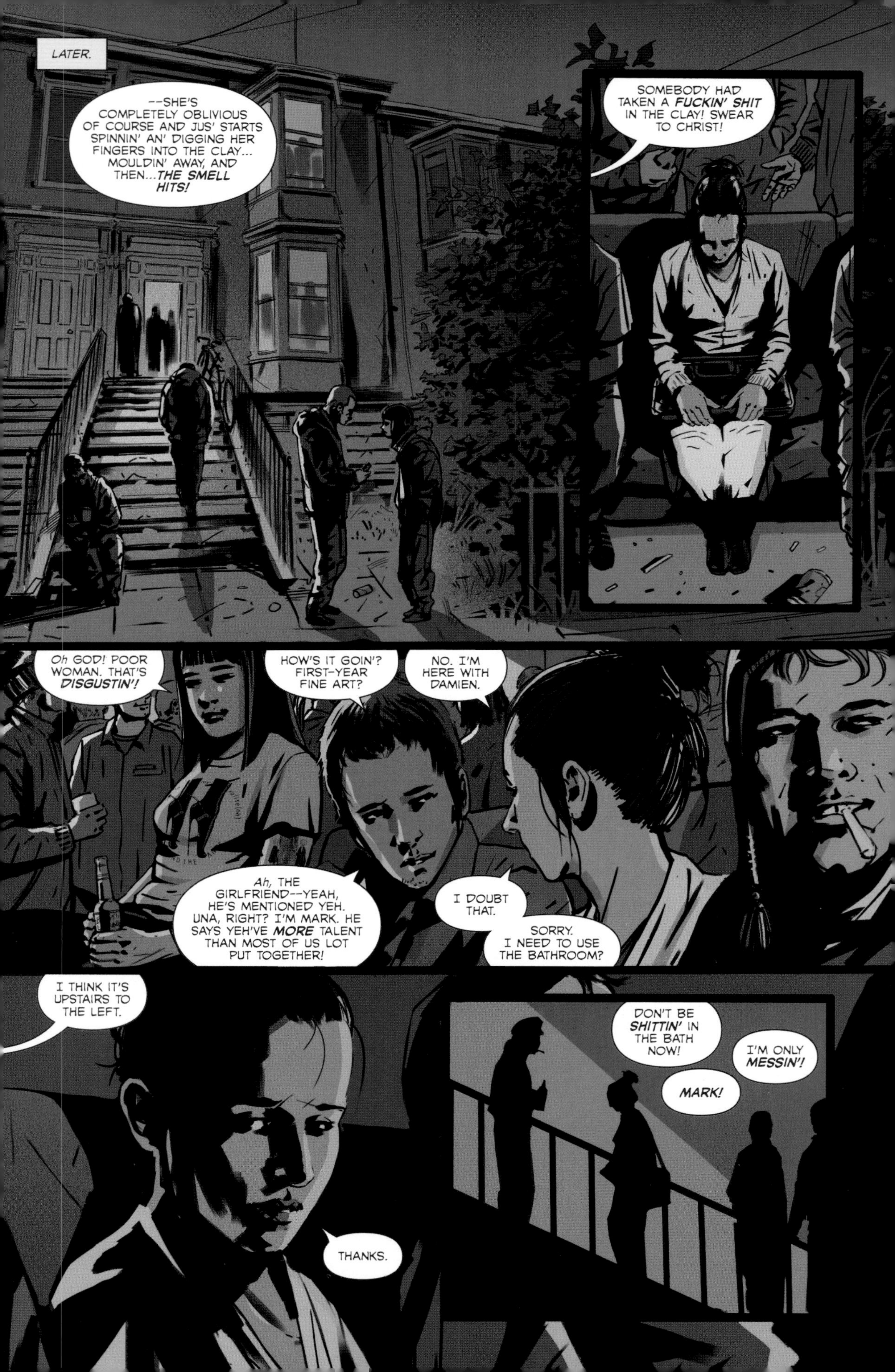
LATER.
--SHE'S COMPLETELY OBLIVIOUS OF COURSE AND JUS' STARTS SPINNIN' AN' DIGGING HER FINGERS INTO THE CLAY... MOULDIN' AWAY, AND THEN...THE SMELL HITS!
SOMEBODY HAD TAKEN A FUCKIN' SHIT IN THE CLAY! SWEAR TO CHRIST!
Oh GOD! POOR WOMAN. THAT'S DISGUSTIN'!
HOW'S IT GOIN'? FIRST-YEAR FINE ART?
NO. I'M HERE WITH DAMIEN.
Ah, THE GIRLFRIEND--YEAH, HE'S MENTIONED YEH. UNA, RIGHT? I'M MARK. HE SAYS YEH'VE MORE TALENT THAN MOST OF US LOT PUT TOGETHER!
I DOUBT THAT.
SORRY. I NEED TO USE THE BATHROOM?
I THINK IT'S UPSTAIRS TO THE LEFT.
THANKS.
DON'T BE SHITTIN' IN THE BATH NOW!
MARK!
I'M ONLY MESSIN'!

Mairead Lynch
2 hrs.

Comment   Share

56

Kate O'Neill that 1s stuk so far
up her own arse.Unreal
Like Reply 3

Amy Hughes "searching looking
4 love" lol
Like Reply 2

Noreen Kelly its all a act. pity u
bien stuck in class with that yoke
Like Reply 2

Jacinta O'Brien is she still sucking
on ghost dick?
Like Reply 4

Noel Ryan Nah.Monster cock

Comment   Share

Liam Morton jaysis!Im in love!!!!!
Like Reply 3

Sean Hovan HOT AF!!!!
Like Reply 1

Jane Murphy lookin gud girl
Like Reply 1

Mary Foley GODDESS!!
Like Reply 1

on ghost dick?
Like Reply 4

Noel Ryan Nah.Monster cock
right?
Like Reply 7

 Ciara Doherty HA!! remember
this one https:www.pic?v= md
qlMMKqtyOQ
Like Reply 32

Jane Kevitt LOL
Like Reply 1

Jay McCann thats deadly!!
Like Reply 1

Marie Smith SHARED!

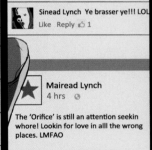

Like Reply 1

Sinead Lynch Ye brasser ye!!! LOL
Like Reply 1

Mairead Lynch
4 hrs.

The 'Orifice' is still an attention seekin
whore! Lookin for love in alll the wrong
places. LMFAO

CUNT

Noel Ryan Nah.Monster cock
right?
Like Reply 7

Ciara Doherty HA!! remember
this one http   www.pic?v=
lMMKq

Like Re

ane Kev

ike Repl

CUNT SPOTTING

Like   Comment   Share

35

STILL MISSING

HER DAD!

Missing: Orla Roche,11, was last seen at
her family home in Bray, County Wicklow.
Orla had recently lost her father to cancer.

"STOP YER
PULLING!"

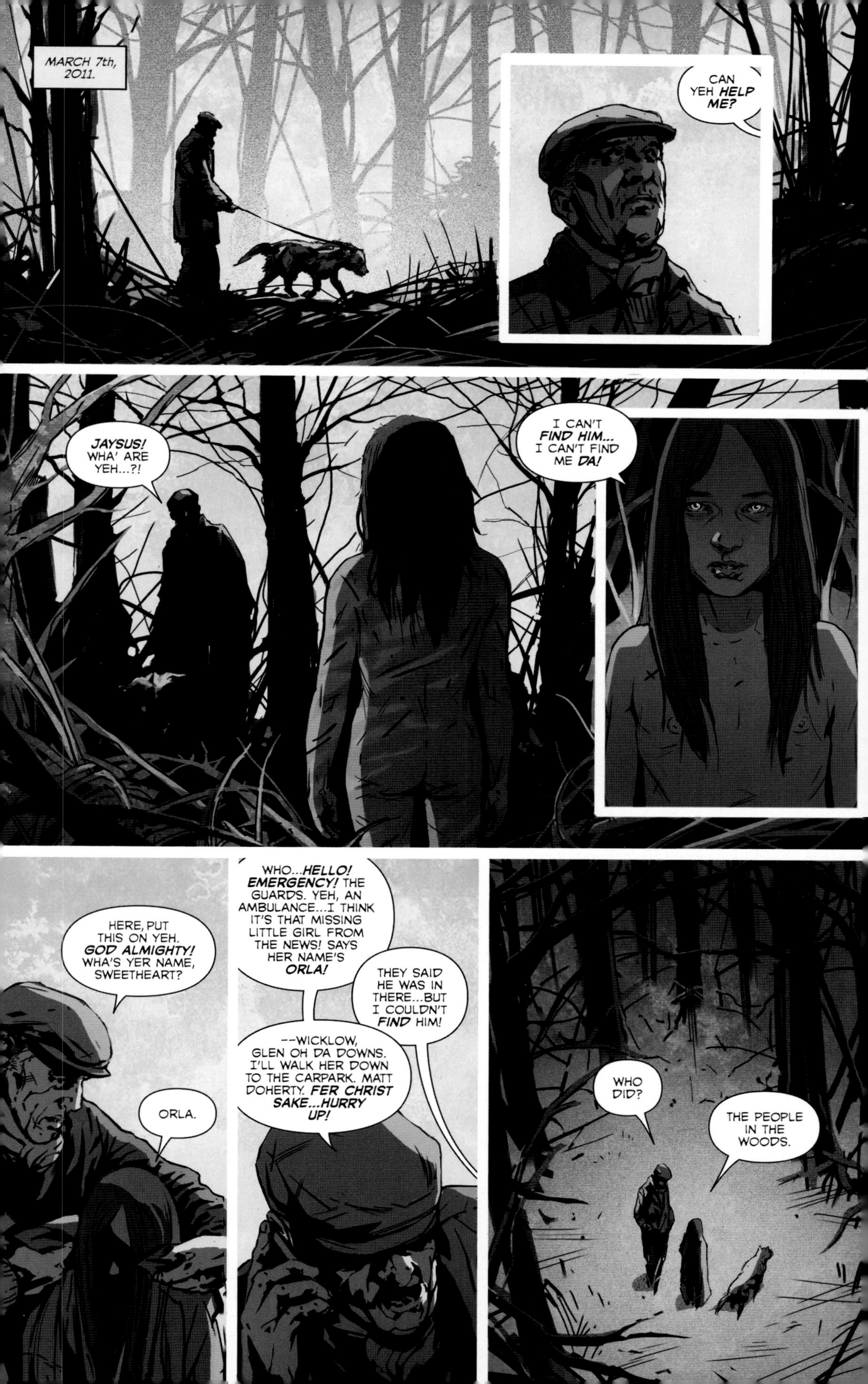
MARCH 7th, 2011.
CAN YEH HELP ME?
JAYSUS! WHA' ARE YEH...?!
I CAN'T FIND HIM... I CAN'T FIND ME DA!
HERE, PUT THIS ON YEH. GOD ALMIGHTY! WHA'S YER NAME, SWEETHEART?
ORLA.
WHO...HELLO! EMERGENCY! THE GUARDS. YEH, AN AMBULANCE...I THINK IT'S THAT MISSING LITTLE GIRL FROM THE NEWS! SAYS HER NAME'S ORLA!
THEY SAID HE WAS IN THERE...BUT I COULDN'T FIND HIM!
--WICKLOW, GLEN OH DA DOWNS. I'LL WALK HER DOWN TO THE CARPARK. MATT DOHERTY. FER CHRIST SAKE...HURRY UP!
WHO DID?
THE PEOPLE IN THE WOODS.

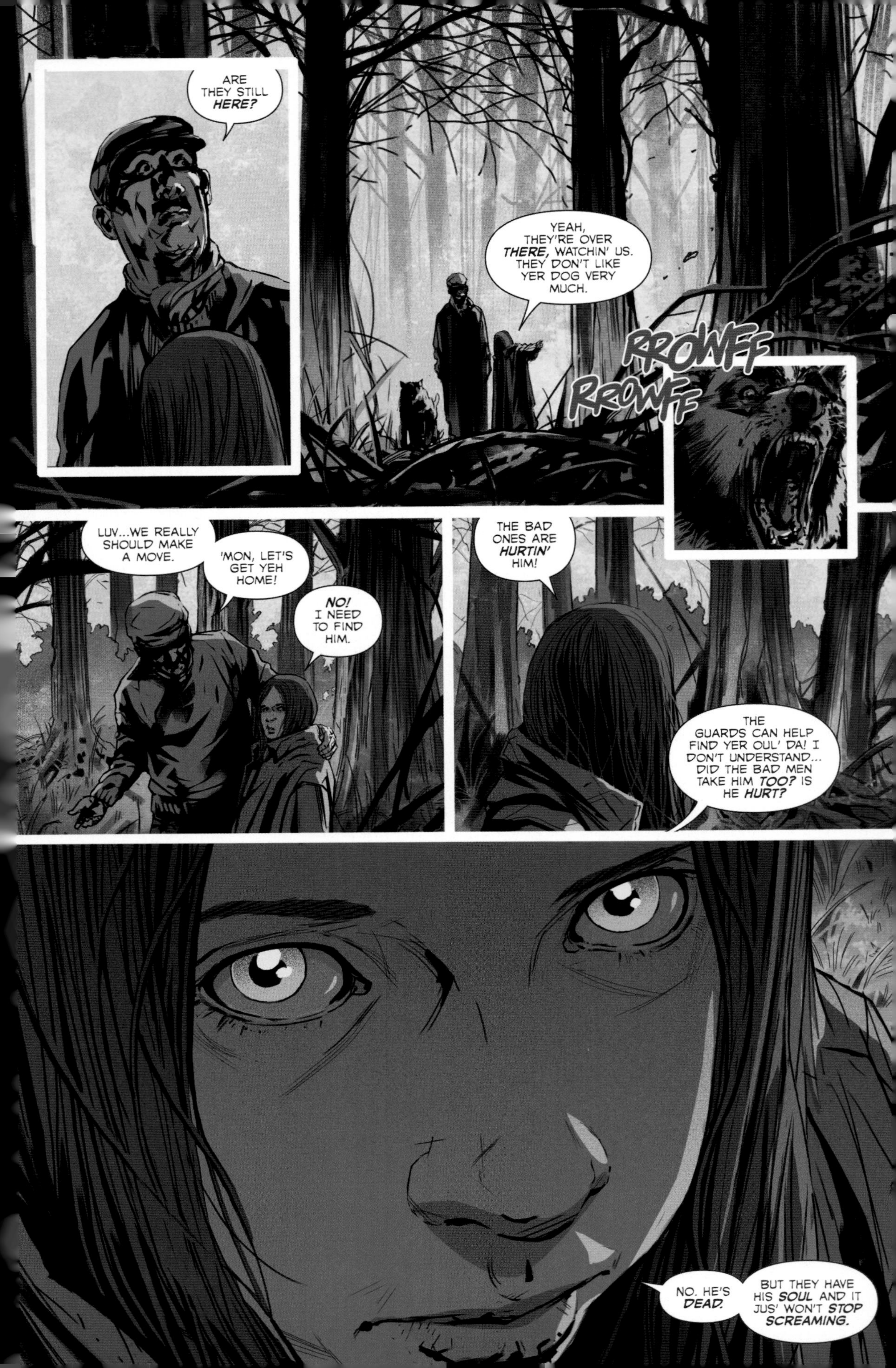
ARE THEY STILL HERE?
YEAH, THEY'RE OVER THERE, WATCHIN' US. THEY DON'T LIKE YER DOG VERY MUCH.
RROWFF
RROWFF
LUV...WE REALLY SHOULD MAKE A MOVE.
'MON, LET'S GET YEH HOME!
NO! I NEED TO FIND HIM.
THE BAD ONES ARE HURTIN' HIM!
THE GUARDS CAN HELP FIND YER OUL' DA! I DON'T UNDERSTAND... DID THE BAD MEN TAKE HIM TOO? IS HE HURT?
NO. HE'S DEAD.
BUT THEY HAVE HIS SOUL AND IT JUS' WON'T STOP SCREAMING.

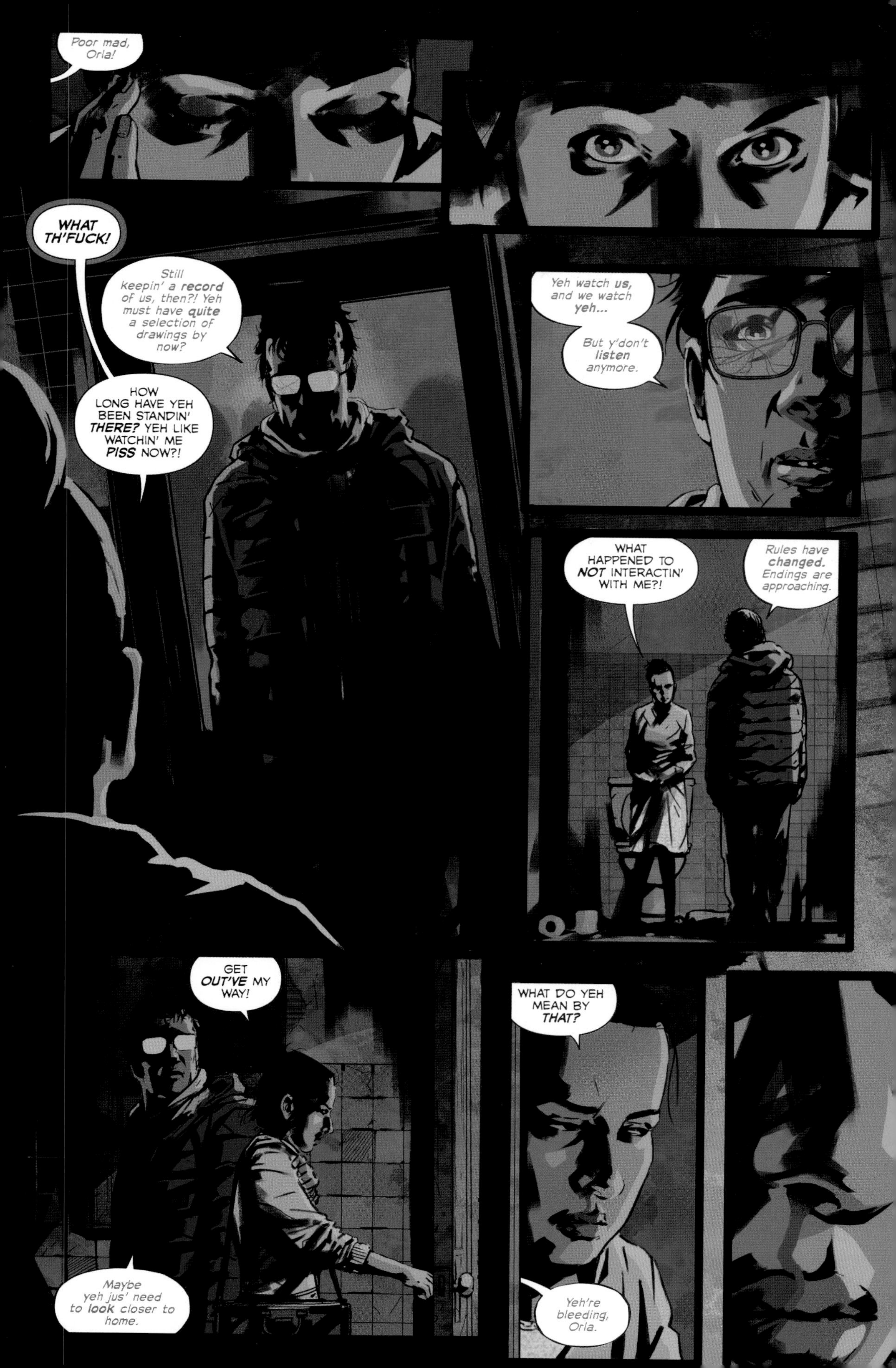
Poor mad, Orla!
WHAT TH'FUCK!
Still keepin' a record of us, then?! Yeh must have quite a selection of drawings by now?
HOW LONG HAVE YEH BEEN STANDIN' THERE? YEH LIKE WATCHIN' ME PISS NOW?!
Yeh watch us, and we watch yeh...
But y'don't listen anymore.
WHAT HAPPENED TO NOT INTERACTIN' WITH ME?!
Rules have changed. Endings are approaching.
GET OUT'VE MY WAY!
Maybe yeh jus' need to look closer to home.
WHAT DO YEH MEAN BY THAT?
Yeh're bleeding, Orla.

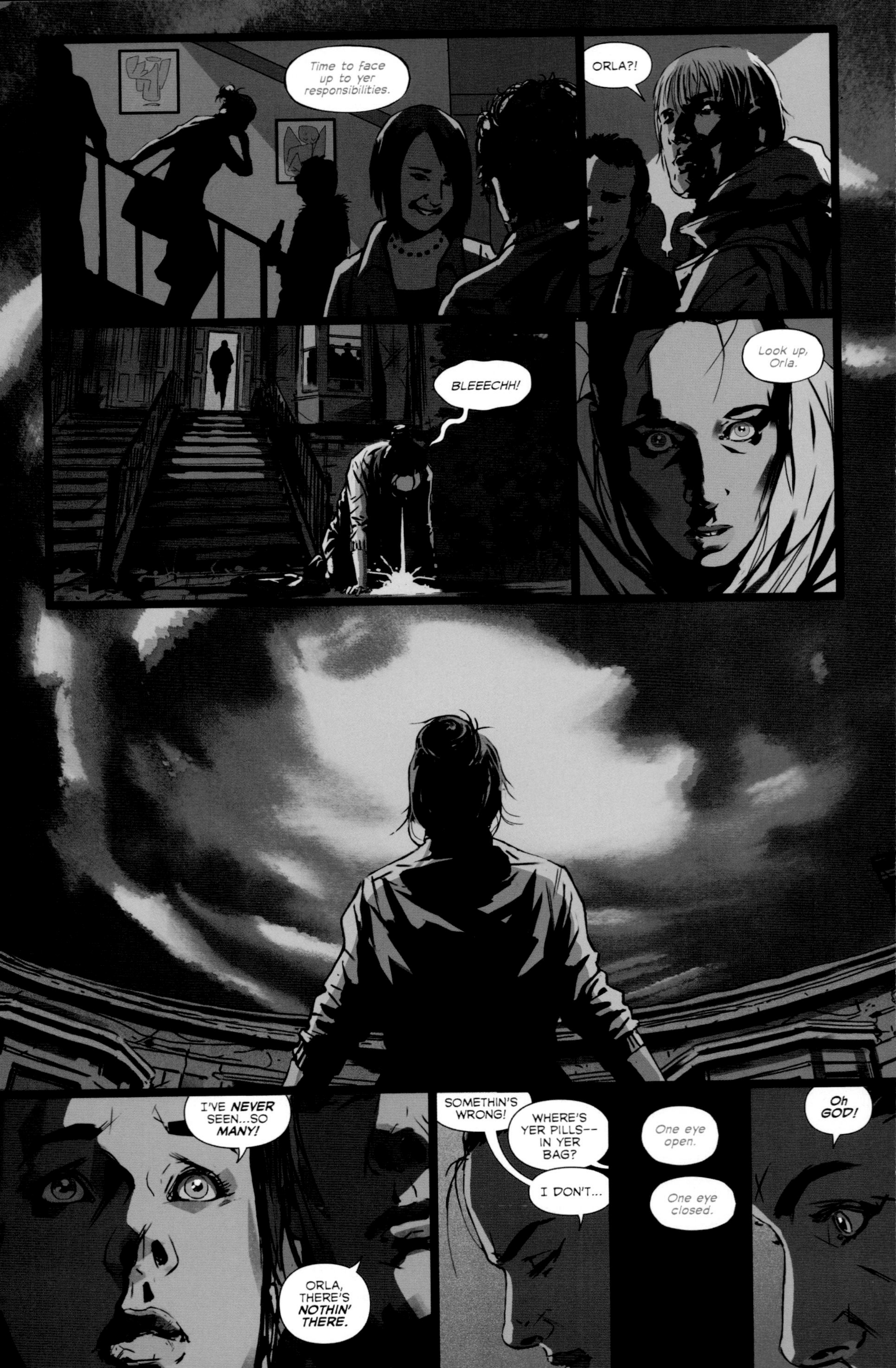
Time to face up to yer responsibilities.
ORLA?!
BLEEECHH!
Look up, Orla.
I'VE NEVER SEEN...SO MANY!
ORLA, THERE'S NOTHIN' THERE.
SOMETHIN'S WRONG!
WHERE'S YER PILLS-- IN YER BAG?
I DON'T...
One eye open.
One eye closed.
Oh GOD!

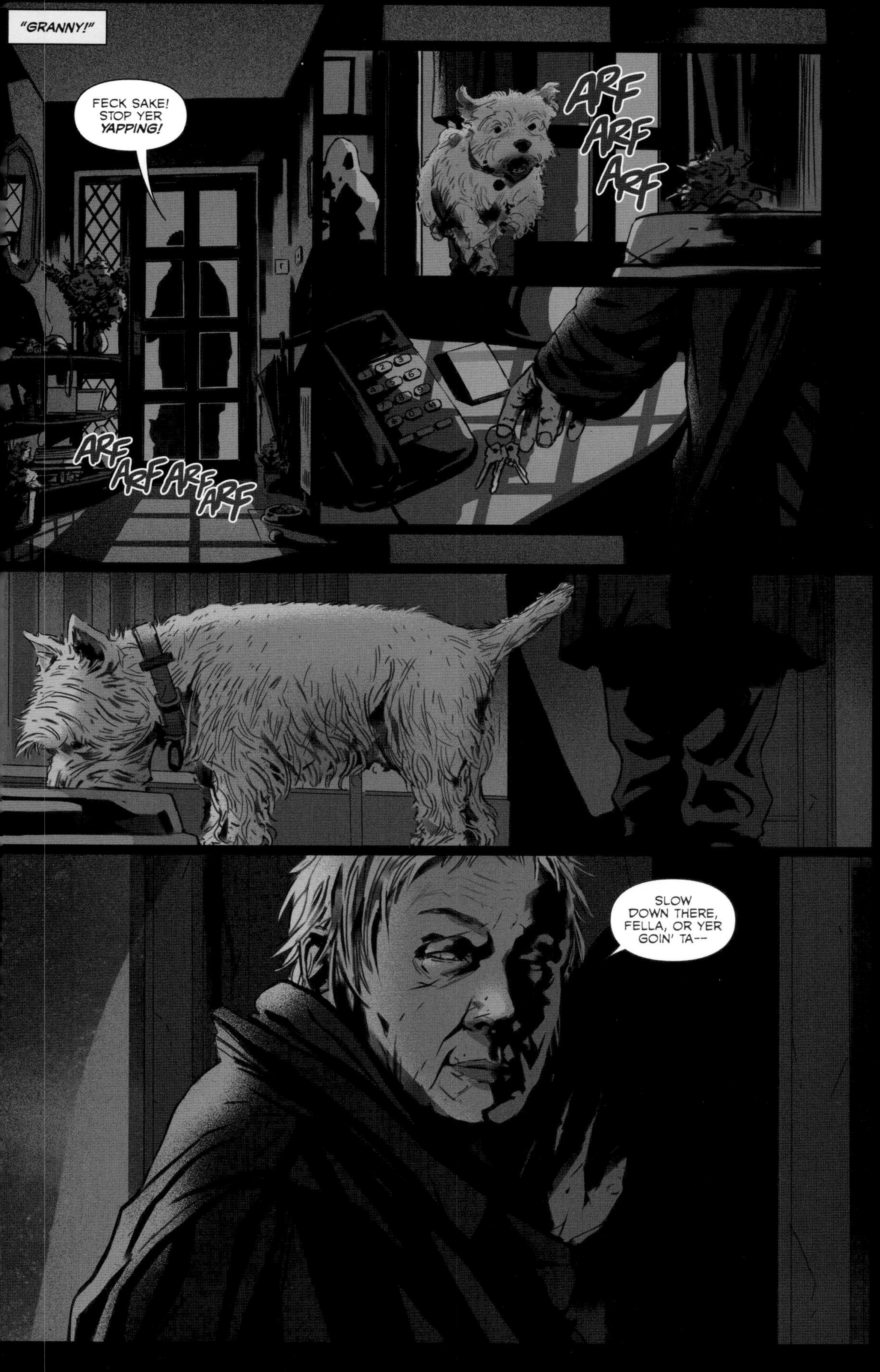
"GRANNY!"
FECK SAKE! STOP YER YAPPING!
ARF ARF ARF
ARF ARF ARF ARF
SLOW DOWN THERE, FELLA, OR YER GOIN' TA--

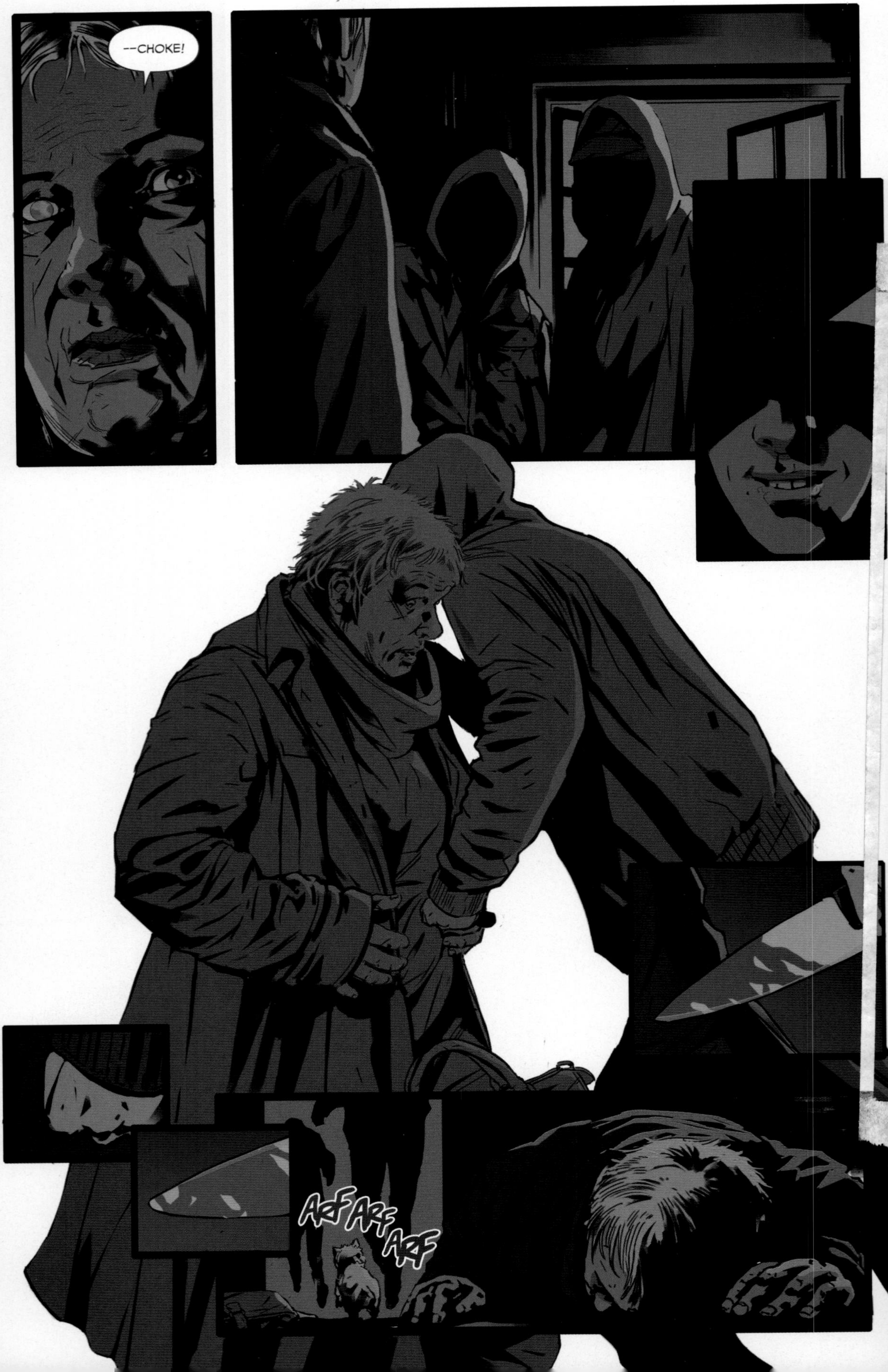
--CHOKE!
ARF ARF ARF

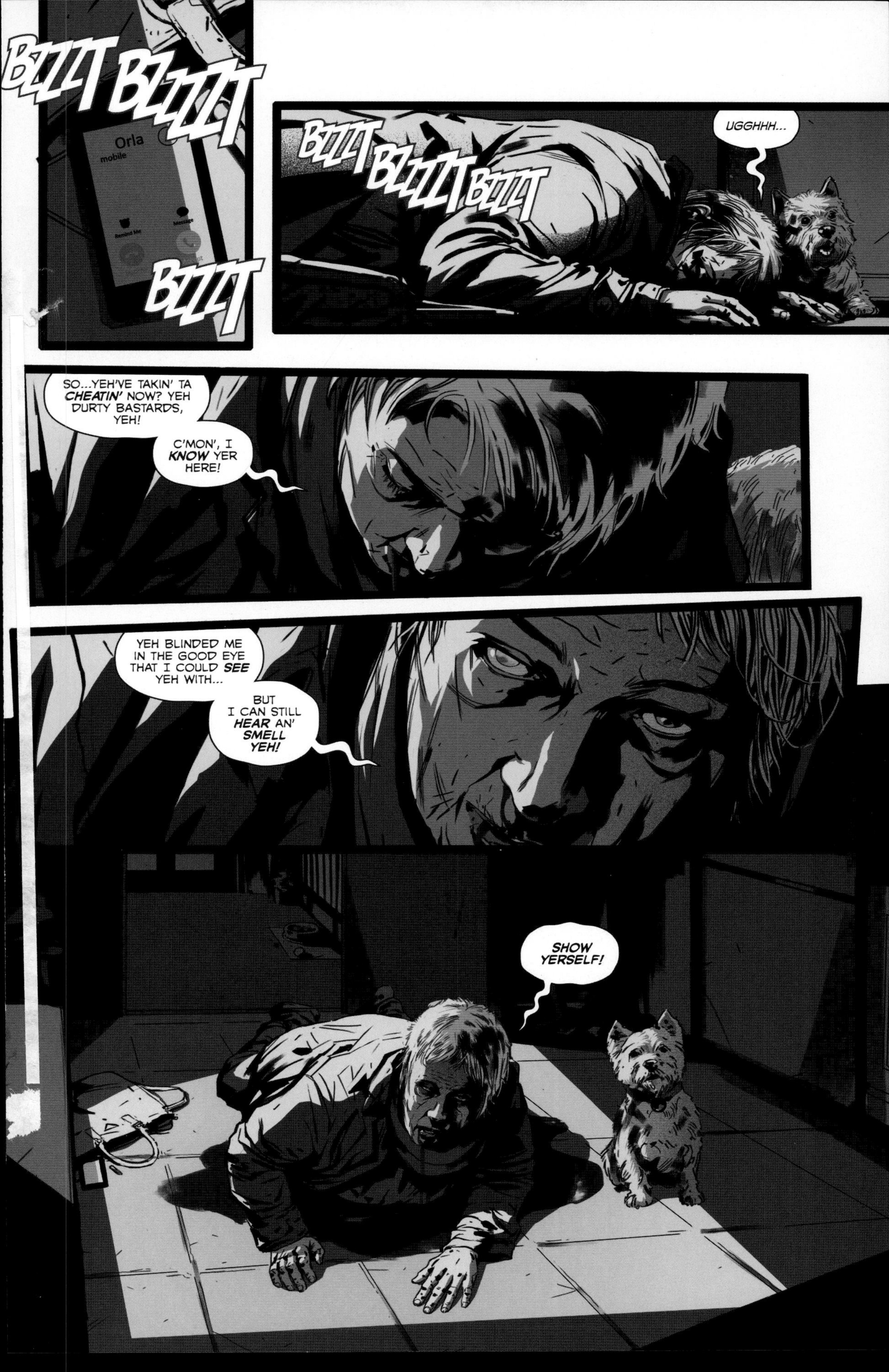
BZZZT BZZZZT
Orla
mobile
Remind Me
Message
BZZZT
BZZZT BZZZZT BZZZT
UGGHHH...
SO...YEH'VE TAKIN' TA CHEATIN' NOW? YEH DURTY BASTARDS, YEH!
C'MON', I KNOW YER HERE!
YEH BLINDED ME IN THE GOOD EYE THAT I COULD SEE YEH WITH...
BUT I CAN STILL HEAR AN' SMELL YEH!
SHOW YERSELF!

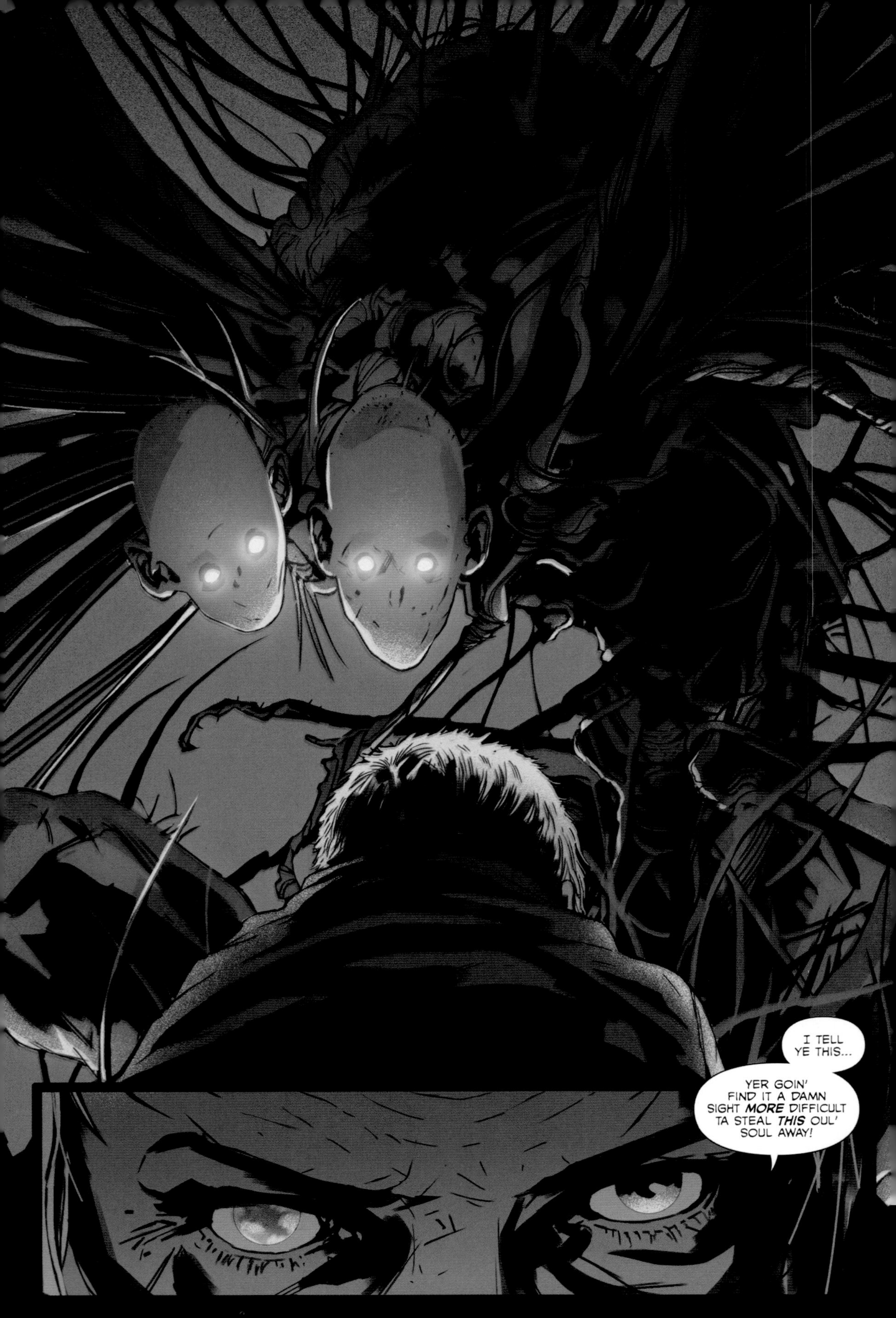
I TELL YE THIS...
YER GOIN' FIND IT A DAMN SIGHT MORE DIFFICULT TA STEAL THIS OUL' SOUL AWAY!

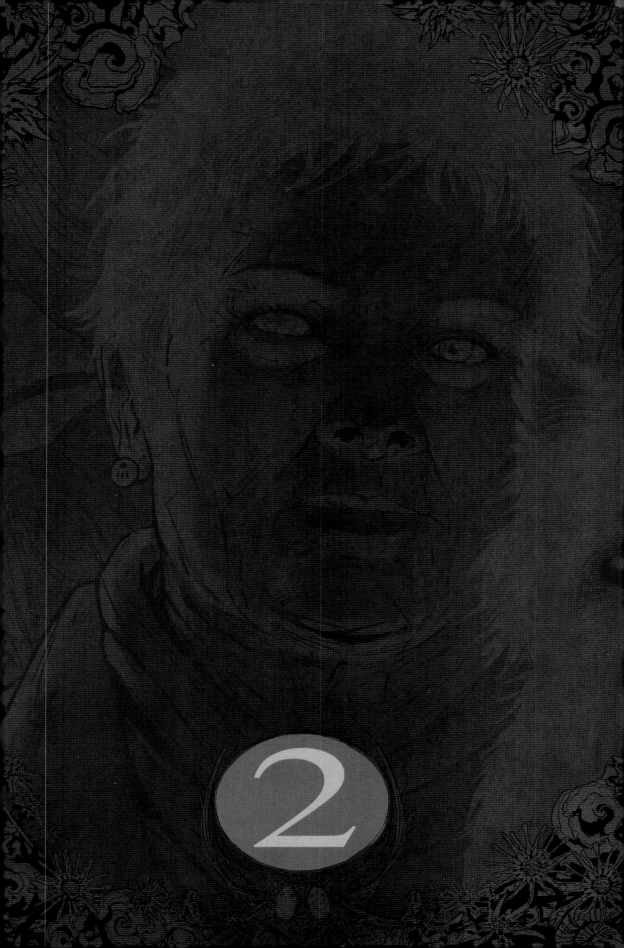

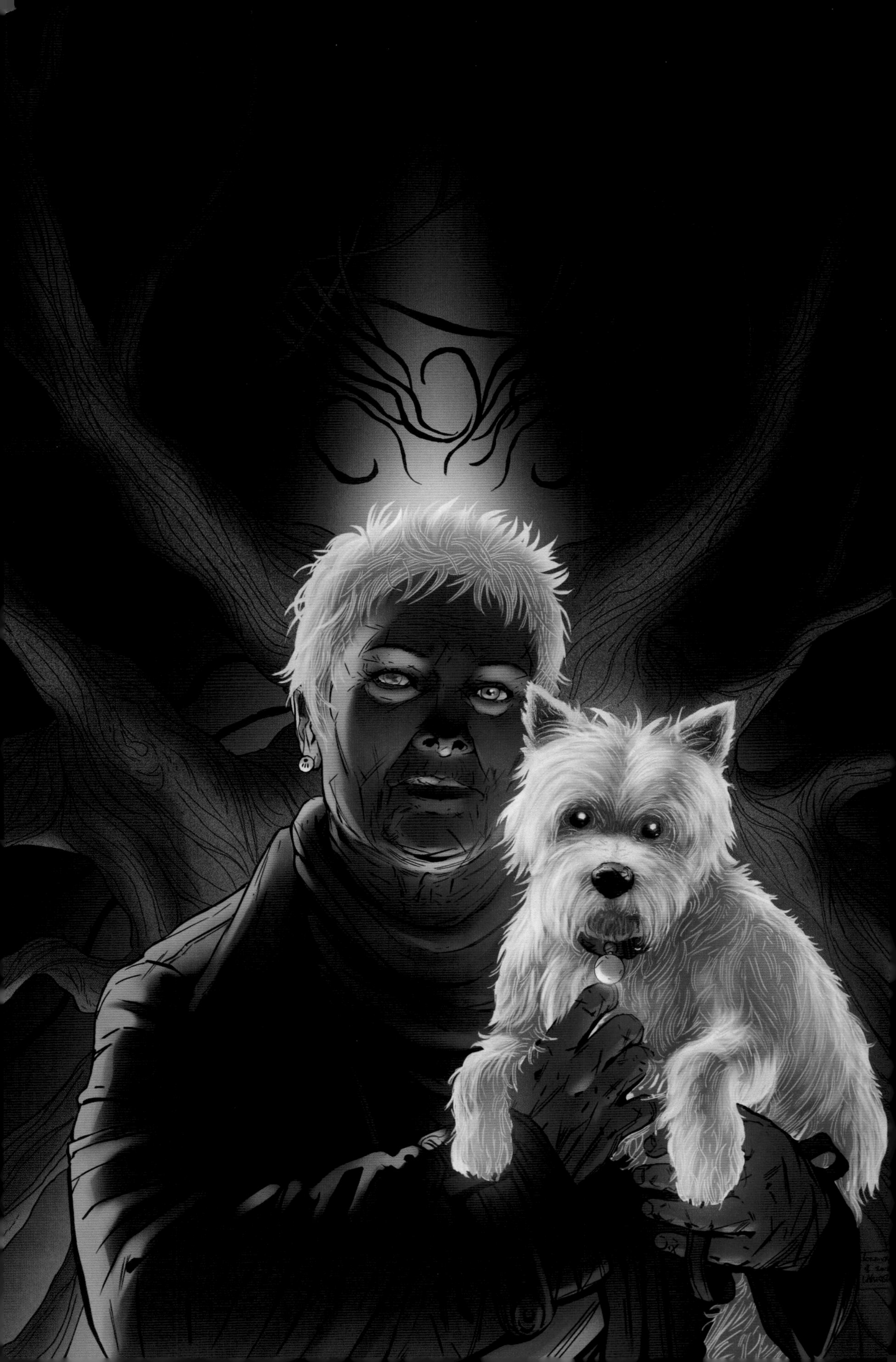

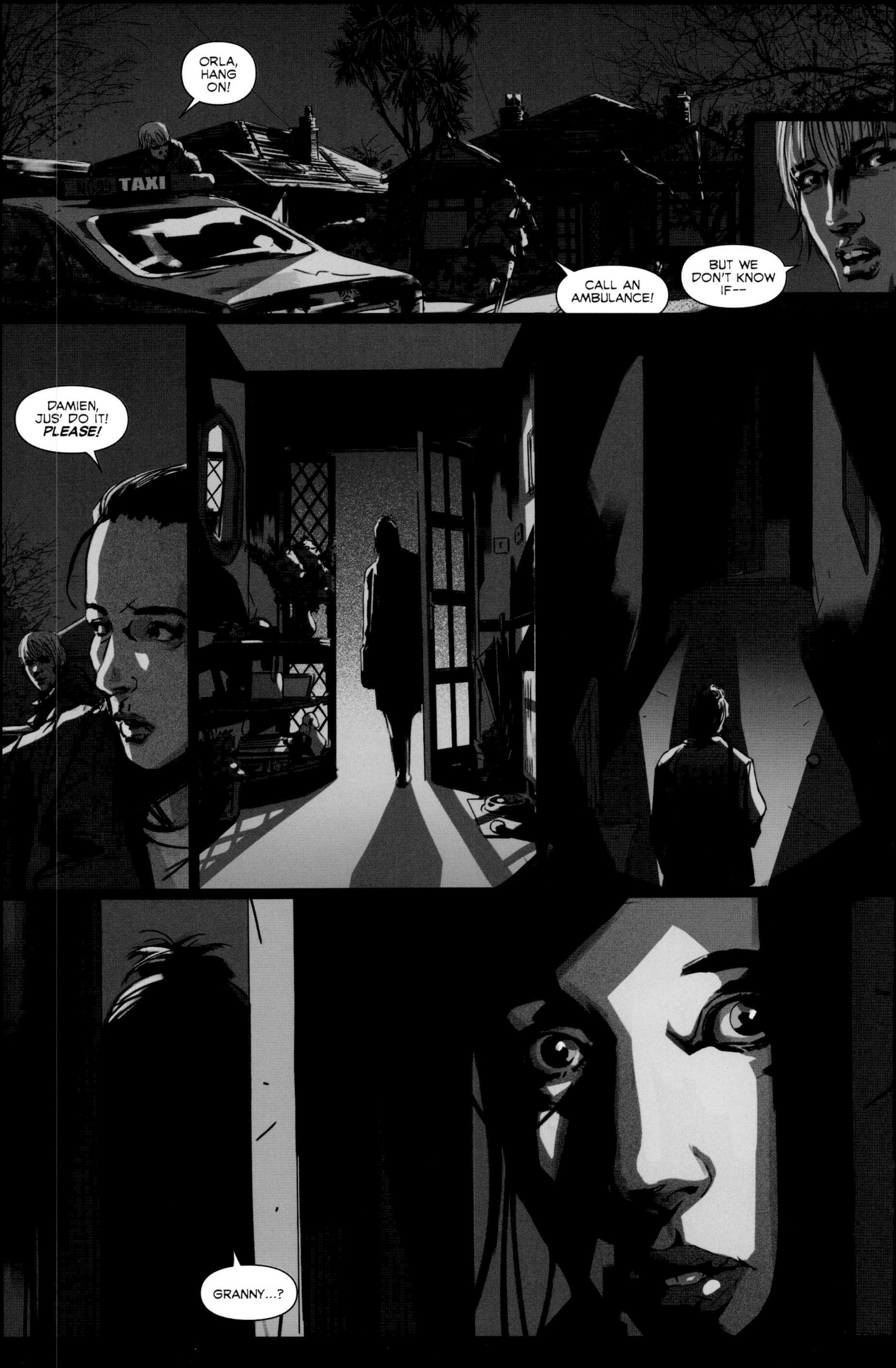
ORLA, HANG ON!
CALL AN AMBULANCE!
BUT WE DON'T KNOW IF--
DAMIEN, JUS' DO IT! PLEASE!
GRANNY...?

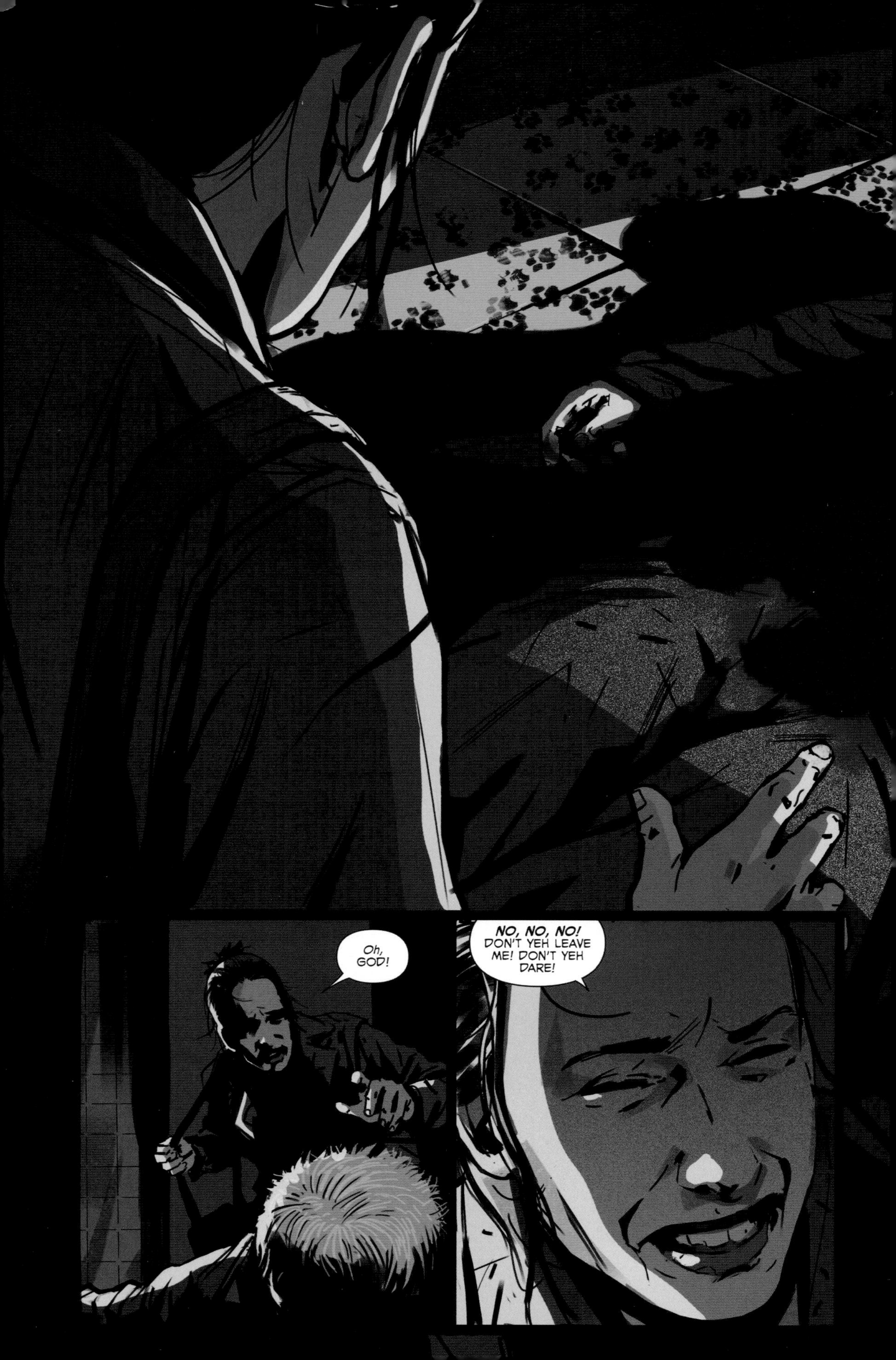

Oh, GOD!
NO, NO, NO! DON'T YEH LEAVE ME! DON'T YEH DARE!

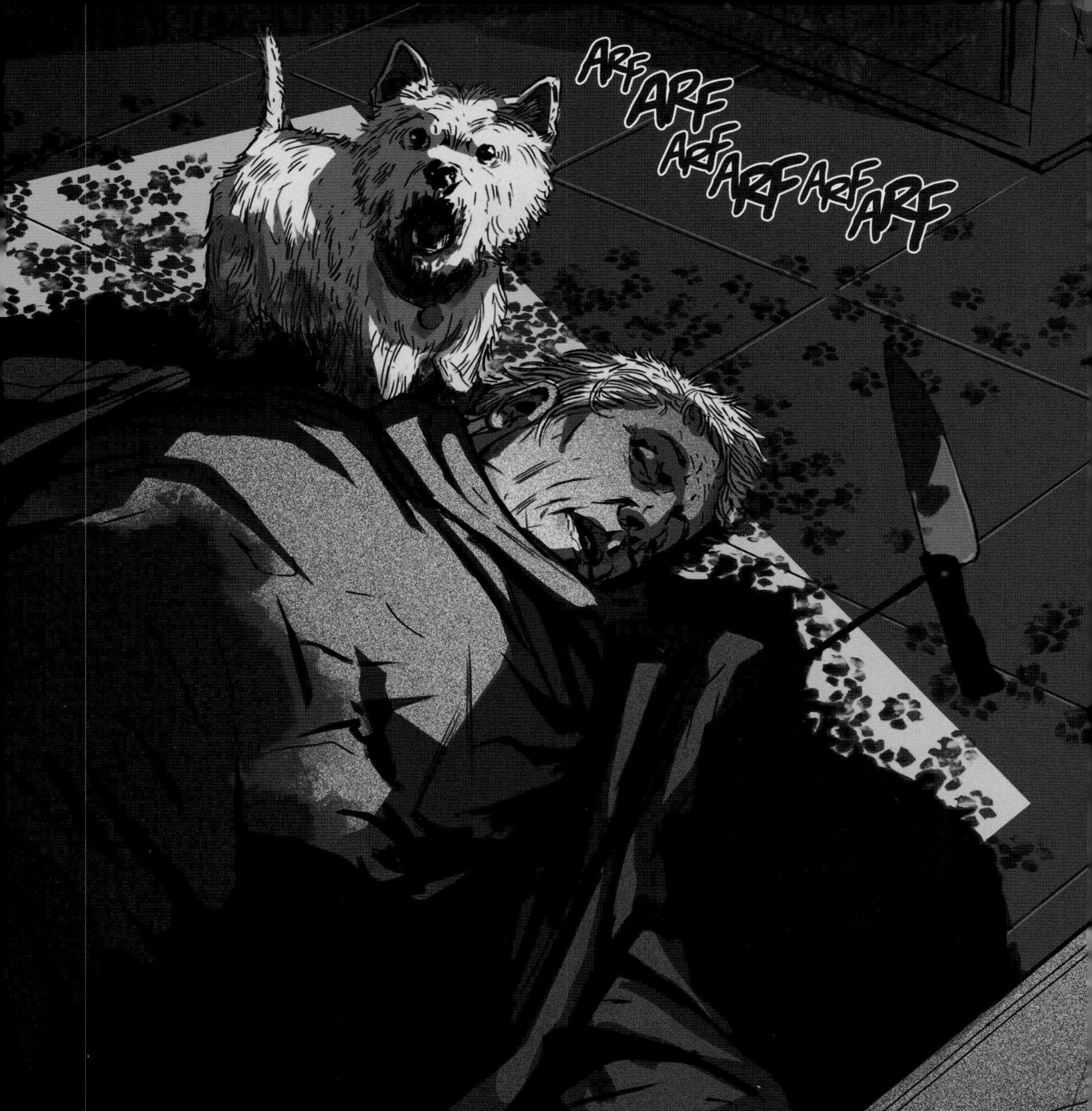
ARF ARF
ARF ARF ARF ARF

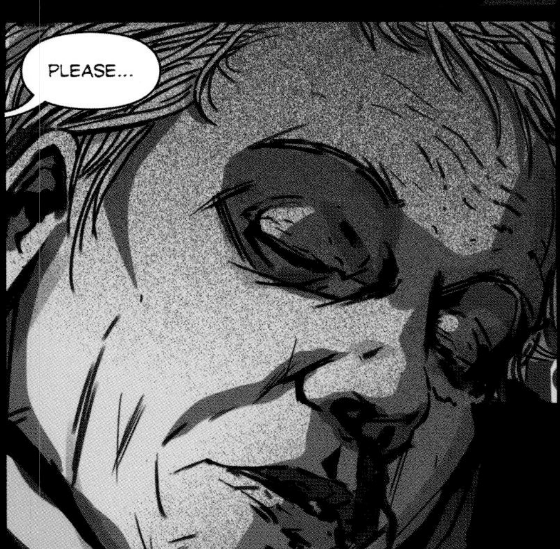
PLEASE...

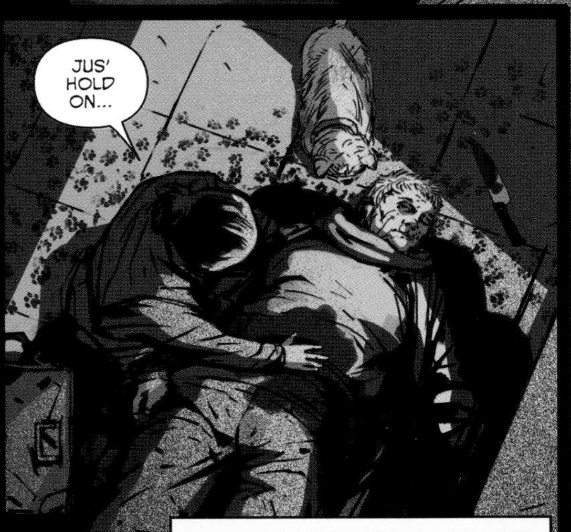
JUS' HOLD ON...
"WHOLE FAMILY'S FUCKIN' MAD! SURE HAVE YE **SEEN** THE ONE-EYED OUL' GRANNY! FUCKIN' OUL' WITCH!"

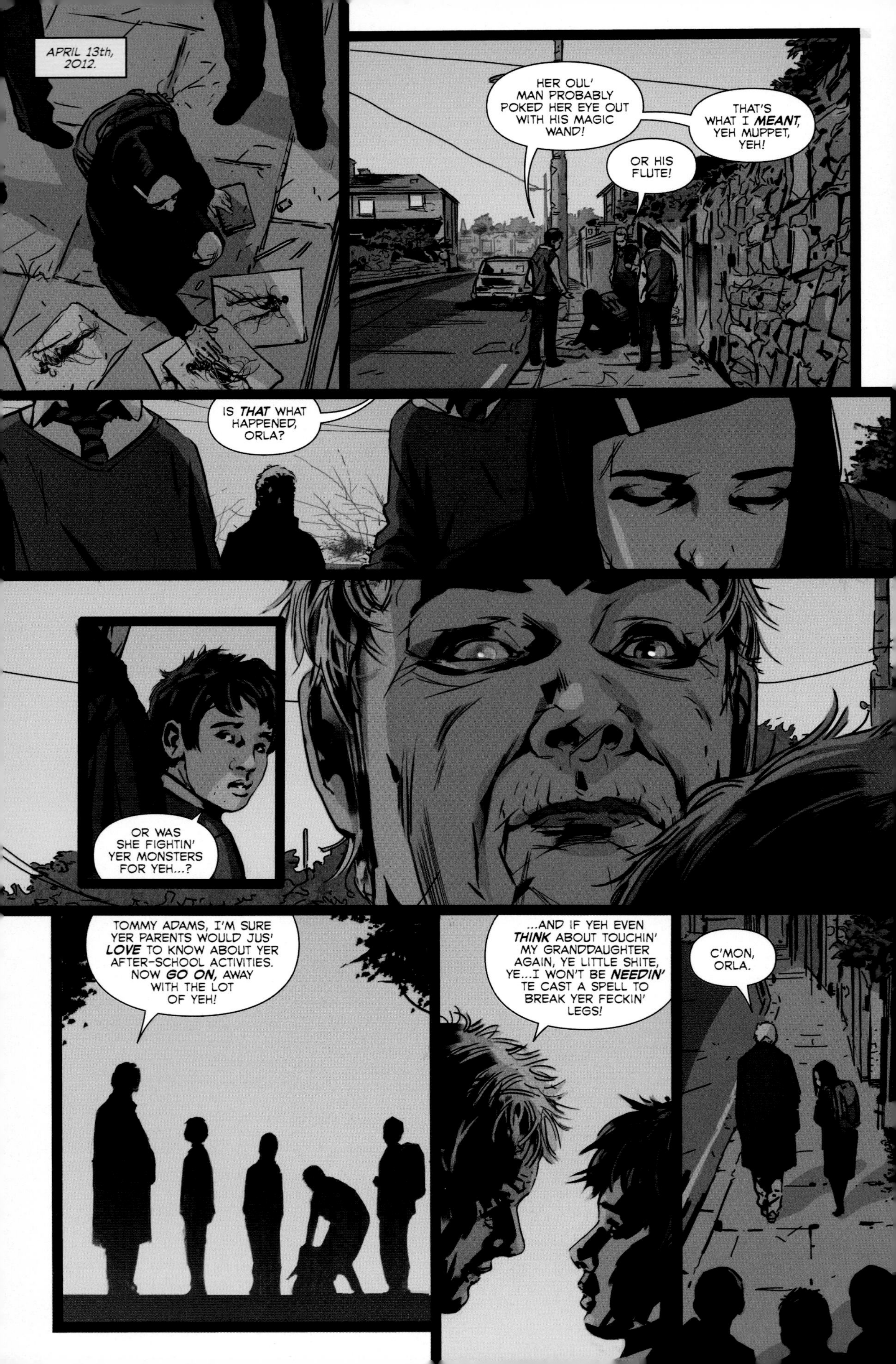
APRIL 13th, 2012.
HER OUL' MAN PROBABLY POKED HER EYE OUT WITH HIS MAGIC WAND!
THAT'S WHAT I MEANT, YEH MUPPET, YEH!
OR HIS FLUTE!
IS THAT WHAT HAPPENED, ORLA?
OR WAS SHE FIGHTIN' YER MONSTERS FOR YEH...?
TOMMY ADAMS, I'M SURE YER PARENTS WOULD JUS' LOVE TO KNOW ABOUT YER AFTER-SCHOOL ACTIVITIES. NOW GO ON, AWAY WITH THE LOT OF YEH!
...AND IF YEH EVEN THINK ABOUT TOUCHIN' MY GRANDDAUGHTER AGAIN, YE LITTLE SHITE, YE...I WON'T BE NEEDIN' TE CAST A SPELL TO BREAK YER FECKIN' LEGS!
C'MON, ORLA.

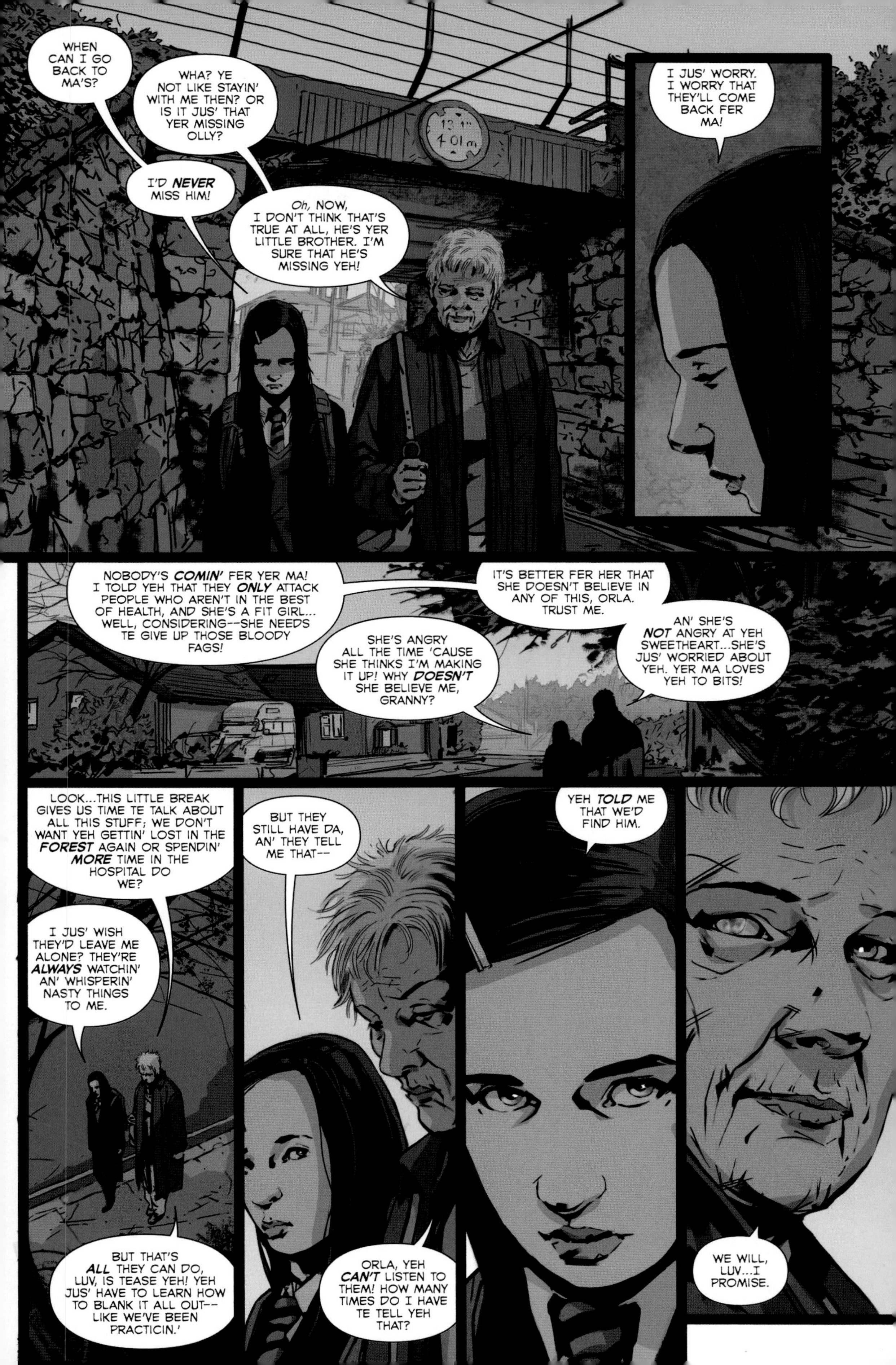
WHEN CAN I GO BACK TO MA'S?
WHA? YE NOT LIKE STAYIN' WITH ME THEN? OR IS IT JUS' THAT YER MISSING OLLY?
I'D NEVER MISS HIM!
Oh, NOW, I DON'T THINK THAT'S TRUE AT ALL, HE'S YER LITTLE BROTHER. I'M SURE THAT HE'S MISSING YEH!
I JUS' WORRY. I WORRY THAT THEY'LL COME BACK FER MA!
NOBODY'S COMIN' FER YER MA! I TOLD YEH THAT THEY ONLY ATTACK PEOPLE WHO AREN'T IN THE BEST OF HEALTH, AND SHE'S A FIT GIRL... WELL, CONSIDERING--SHE NEEDS TE GIVE UP THOSE BLOODY FAGS!
SHE'S ANGRY ALL THE TIME 'CAUSE SHE THINKS I'M MAKING IT UP! WHY DOESN'T SHE BELIEVE ME, GRANNY?
IT'S BETTER FER HER THAT SHE DOESN'T BELIEVE IN ANY OF THIS, ORLA. TRUST ME.
AN' SHE'S NOT ANGRY AT YEH SWEETHEART...SHE'S JUS' WORRIED ABOUT YEH. YER MA LOVES YEH TO BITS!
LOOK...THIS LITTLE BREAK GIVES US TIME TE TALK ABOUT ALL THIS STUFF; WE DON'T WANT YEH GETTIN' LOST IN THE FOREST AGAIN OR SPENDIN' MORE TIME IN THE HOSPITAL DO WE?
I JUS' WISH THEY'D LEAVE ME ALONE? THEY'RE ALWAYS WATCHIN' AN' WHISPERIN' NASTY THINGS TO ME.
BUT THAT'S ALL THEY CAN DO, LUV, IS TEASE YEH! YEH JUS' HAVE TO LEARN HOW TO BLANK IT ALL OUT-- LIKE WE'VE BEEN PRACTICIN.'
BUT THEY STILL HAVE DA, AN' THEY TELL ME THAT--
ORLA, YEH CAN'T LISTEN TO THEM! HOW MANY TIMES DO I HAVE TE TELL YEH THAT?
YEH TOLD ME THAT WE'D FIND HIM.
WE WILL, LUV...I PROMISE.

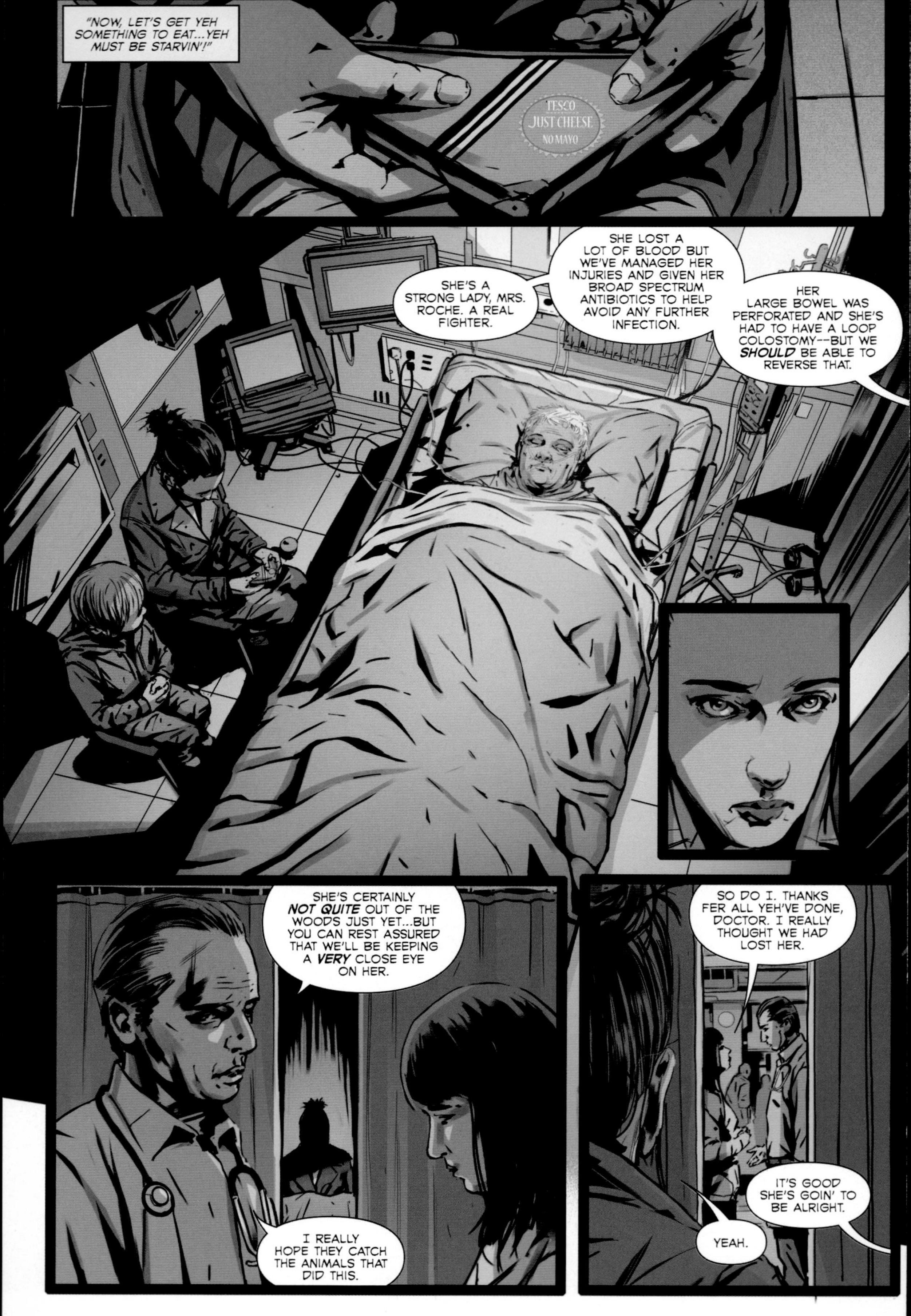
"NOW, LET'S GET YEH SOMETHING TO EAT...YEH MUST BE STARVIN'!"
TESCO JUST CHEESE NO MAYO
SHE'S A STRONG LADY, MRS. ROCHE. A REAL FIGHTER.
SHE LOST A LOT OF BLOOD BUT WE'VE MANAGED HER INJURIES AND GIVEN HER BROAD SPECTRUM ANTIBIOTICS TO HELP AVOID ANY FURTHER INFECTION.
HER LARGE BOWEL WAS PERFORATED AND SHE'S HAD TO HAVE A LOOP COLOSTOMY--BUT WE SHOULD BE ABLE TO REVERSE THAT.
SHE'S CERTAINLY NOT QUITE OUT OF THE WOODS JUST YET...BUT YOU CAN REST ASSURED THAT WE'LL BE KEEPING A VERY CLOSE EYE ON HER.
I REALLY HOPE THEY CATCH THE ANIMALS THAT DID THIS.
SO DO I. THANKS FER ALL YEH'VE DONE, DOCTOR. I REALLY THOUGHT WE HAD LOST HER.
IT'S GOOD SHE'S GOIN' TO BE ALRIGHT.
YEAH.

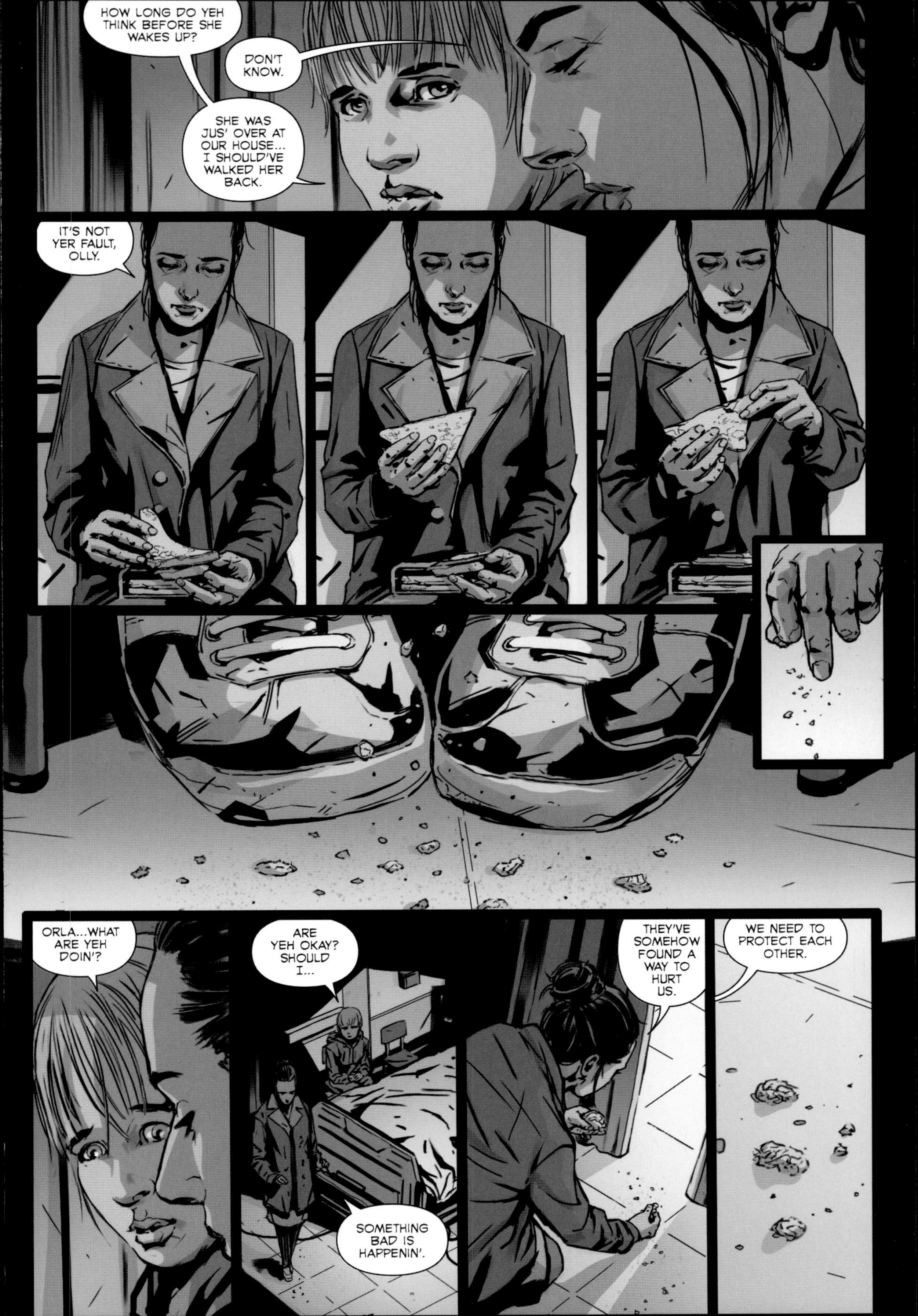
HOW LONG DO YEH THINK BEFORE SHE WAKES UP?
DON'T KNOW.
SHE WAS JUS' OVER AT OUR HOUSE... I SHOULD'VE WALKED HER BACK.
IT'S NOT YER FAULT, OLLY.
ORLA...WHAT ARE YEH DOIN'?
ARE YEH OKAY? SHOULD I...
SOMETHING BAD IS HAPPENIN'.
THEY'VE SOMEHOW FOUND A WAY TO HURT US.
WE NEED TO PROTECT EACH OTHER.

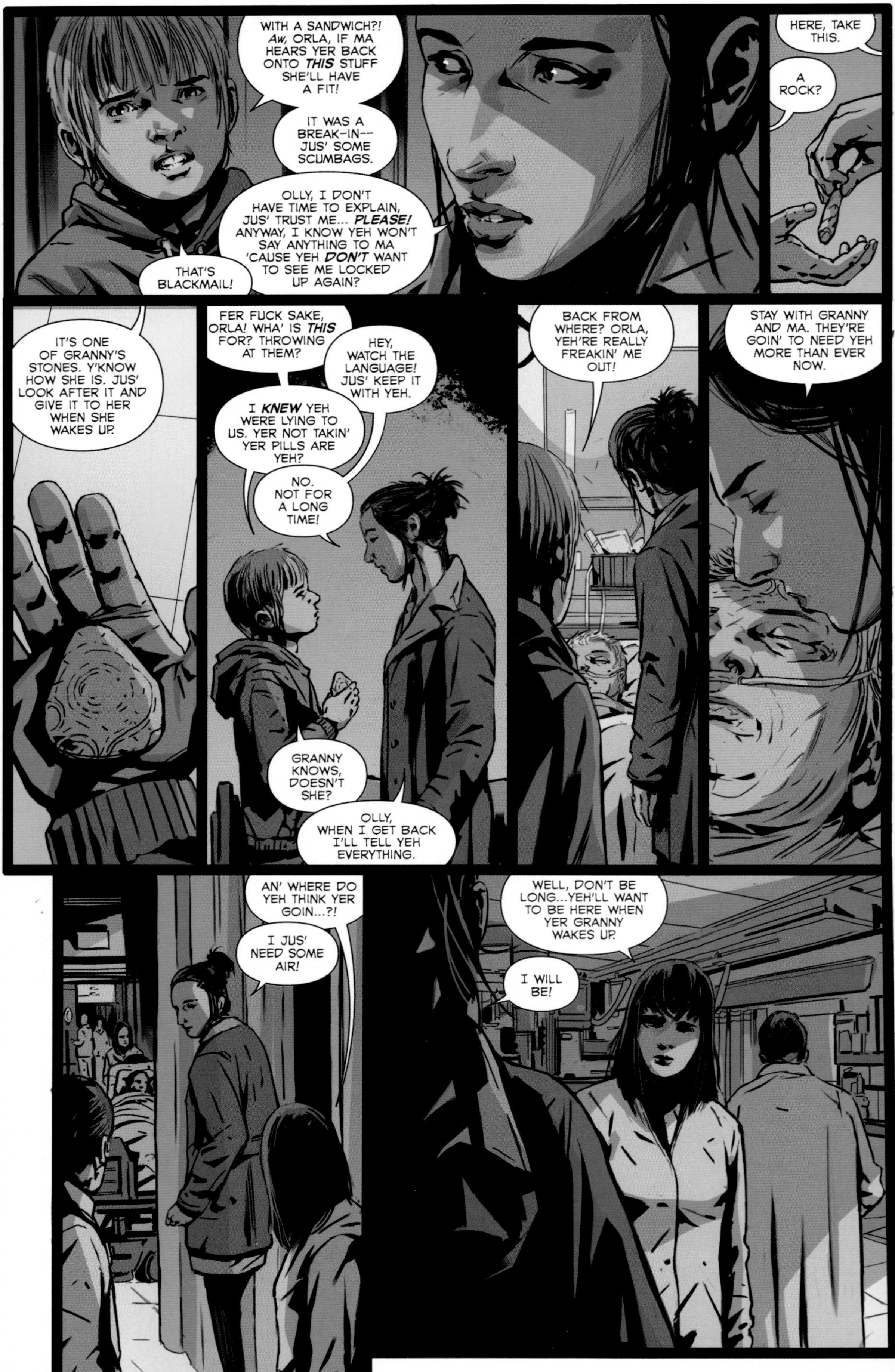

WITH A SANDWICH?! Aw, ORLA, IF MA HEARS YER BACK ONTO THIS STUFF SHE'LL HAVE A FIT!
IT WAS A BREAK-IN-- JUS' SOME SCUMBAGS.
OLLY, I DON'T HAVE TIME TO EXPLAIN, JUS' TRUST ME... PLEASE! ANYWAY, I KNOW YEH WON'T SAY ANYTHING TO MA 'CAUSE YEH DON'T WANT TO SEE ME LOCKED UP AGAIN?
THAT'S BLACKMAIL!
HERE, TAKE THIS.
A ROCK?
IT'S ONE OF GRANNY'S STONES. Y'KNOW HOW SHE IS. JUS' LOOK AFTER IT AND GIVE IT TO HER WHEN SHE WAKES UP.
FER FUCK SAKE, ORLA! WHA' IS THIS FOR? THROWING AT THEM?
HEY, WATCH THE LANGUAGE! JUS' KEEP IT WITH YEH.
I KNEW YEH WERE LYING TO US. YER NOT TAKIN' YER PILLS ARE YEH?
NO. NOT FOR A LONG TIME!
GRANNY KNOWS, DOESN'T SHE?
OLLY, WHEN I GET BACK I'LL TELL YEH EVERYTHING.
BACK FROM WHERE? ORLA, YEH'RE REALLY FREAKIN' ME OUT!
STAY WITH GRANNY AND MA. THEY'RE GOIN' TO NEED YEH MORE THAN EVER NOW.
AN' WHERE DO YEH THINK YER GOIN...?!
I JUS' NEED SOME AIR!
WELL, DON'T BE LONG...YEH'LL WANT TO BE HERE WHEN YER GRANNY WAKES UP.
I WILL BE!

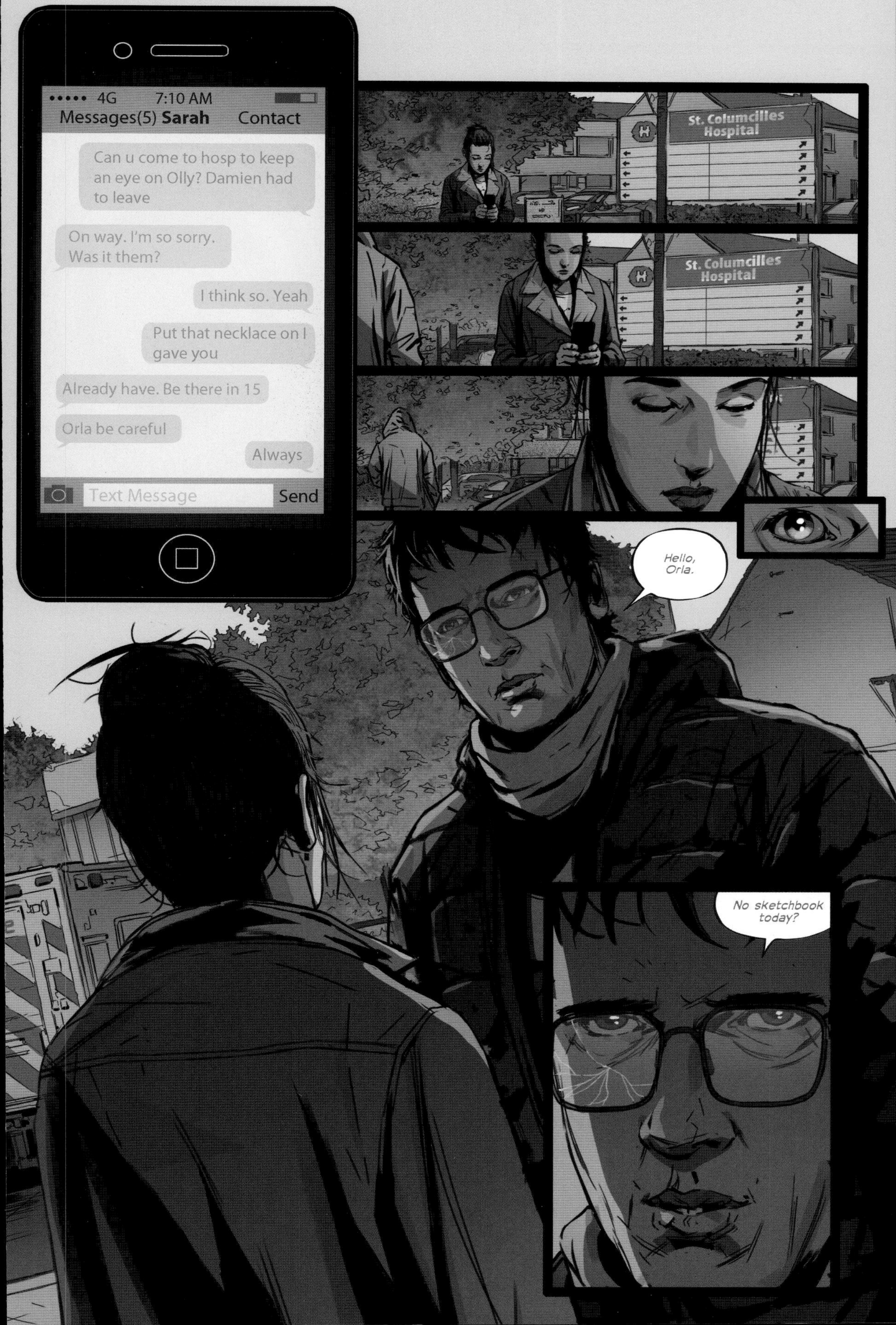

4G 7:10 AM
Messages(5) Sarah Contact
Can u come to hosp to keep an eye on Olly? Damien had to leave
On way. I'm so sorry. Was it them?
I think so. Yeah
Put that necklace on I gave you
Already have. Be there in 15
Orla be careful
Always
Text Message
Send
St. Columcilles Hospital
St. Columcilles Hospital
Hello, Orla.
No sketchbook today?

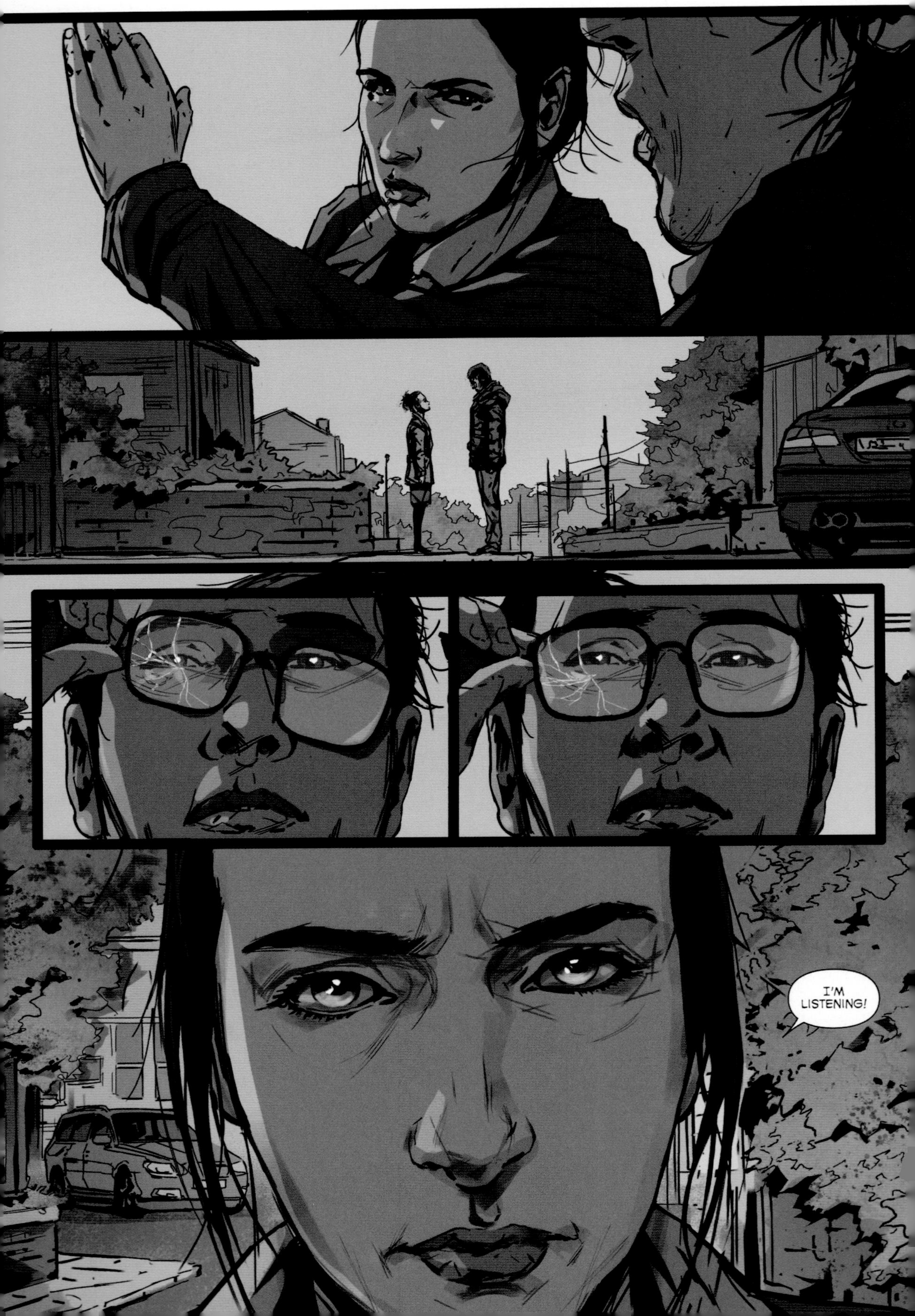
I'M LISTENING!

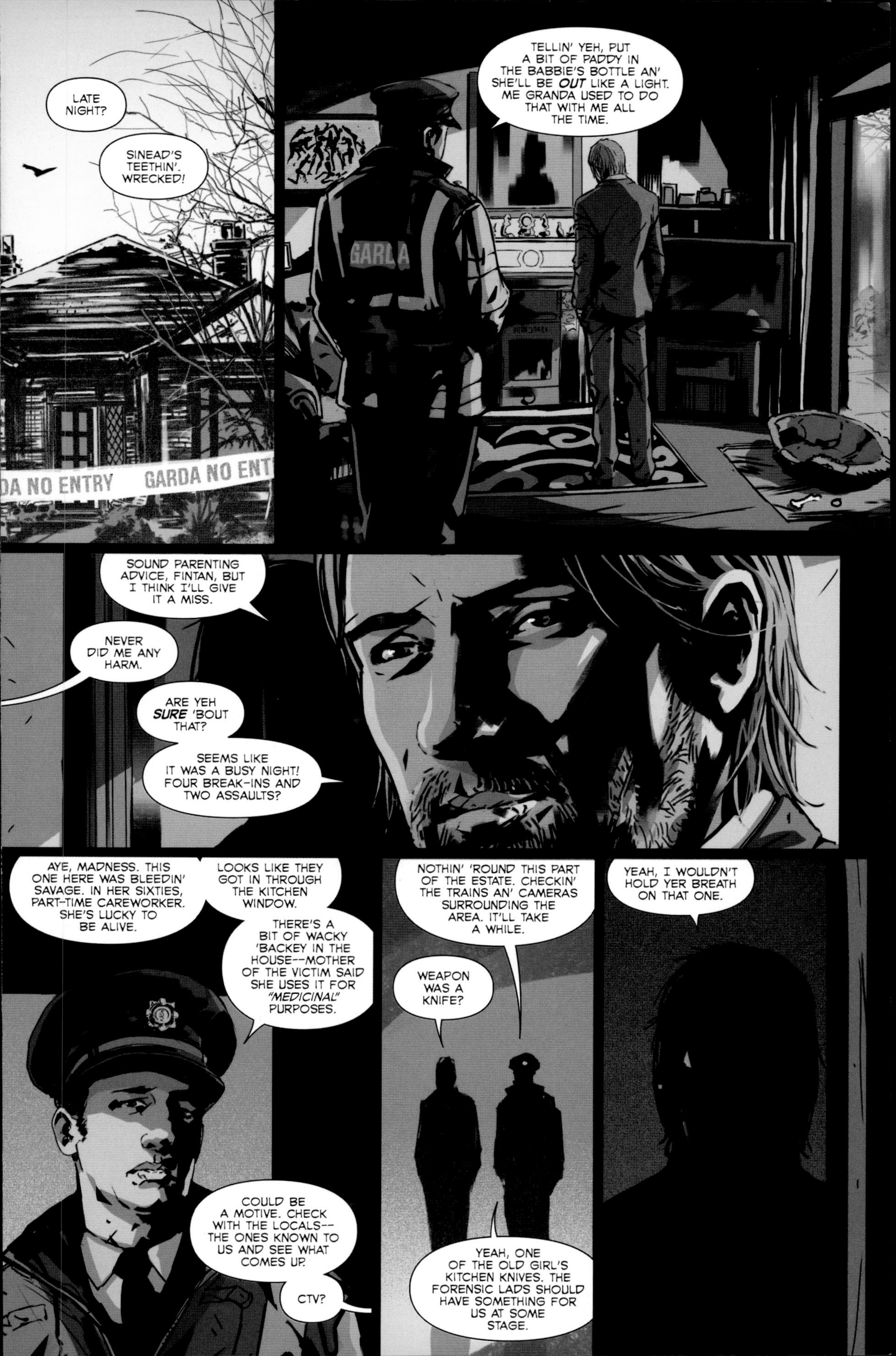
LATE NIGHT?
SINEAD'S TEETHIN'. WRECKED!
GARDA NO ENTRY
GARDA
TELLIN' YEH, PUT A BIT OF PADDY IN THE BABBIE'S BOTTLE AN' SHE'LL BE OUT LIKE A LIGHT. ME GRANDA USED TO DO THAT WITH ME ALL THE TIME.
SOUND PARENTING ADVICE, FINTAN, BUT I THINK I'LL GIVE IT A MISS.
NEVER DID ME ANY HARM.
ARE YEH SURE 'BOUT THAT?
SEEMS LIKE IT WAS A BUSY NIGHT! FOUR BREAK-INS AND TWO ASSAULTS?
AYE, MADNESS. THIS ONE HERE WAS BLEEDIN' SAVAGE. IN HER SIXTIES, PART-TIME CAREWORKER. SHE'S LUCKY TO BE ALIVE.
LOOKS LIKE THEY GOT IN THROUGH THE KITCHEN WINDOW.
THERE'S A BIT OF WACKY 'BACKEY IN THE HOUSE--MOTHER OF THE VICTIM SAID SHE USES IT FOR "MEDICINAL" PURPOSES.
COULD BE A MOTIVE. CHECK WITH THE LOCALS--THE ONES KNOWN TO US AND SEE WHAT COMES UP.
CTV?
NOTHIN' 'ROUND THIS PART OF THE ESTATE. CHECKIN' THE TRAINS AN' CAMERAS SURROUNDING THE AREA. IT'LL TAKE A WHILE.
WEAPON WAS A KNIFE?
YEAH, ONE OF THE OLD GIRL'S KITCHEN KNIVES. THE FORENSIC LADS SHOULD HAVE SOMETHING FOR US AT SOME STAGE.
YEAH, I WOULDN'T HOLD YER BREATH ON THAT ONE.

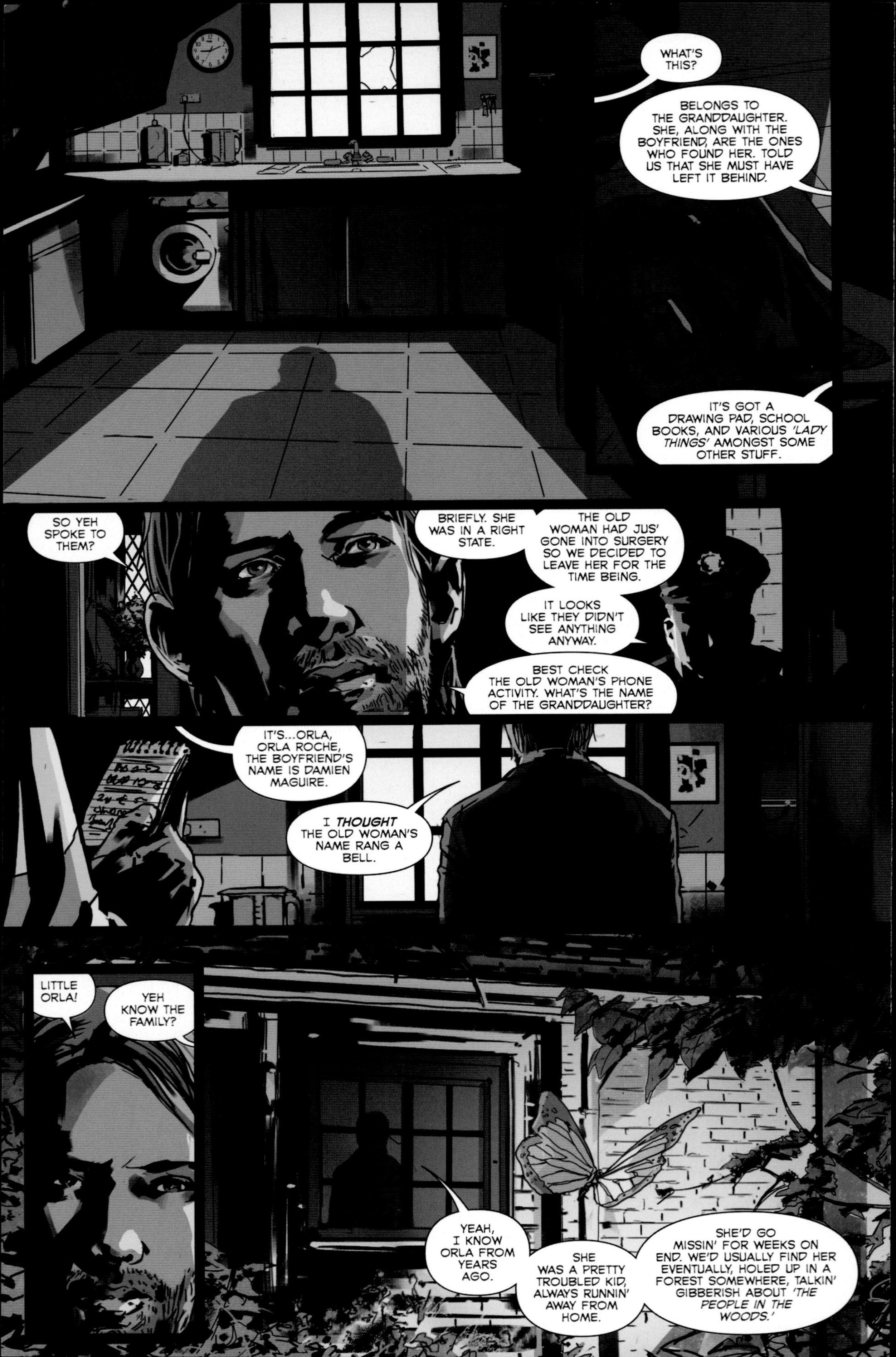
WHAT'S THIS?
BELONGS TO THE GRANDDAUGHTER. SHE, ALONG WITH THE BOYFRIEND, ARE THE ONES WHO FOUND HER. TOLD US THAT SHE MUST HAVE LEFT IT BEHIND.
IT'S GOT A DRAWING PAD, SCHOOL BOOKS, AND VARIOUS *'LADY THINGS'* AMONGST SOME OTHER STUFF.
SO YEH SPOKE TO THEM?
BRIEFLY. SHE WAS IN A RIGHT STATE.
THE OLD WOMAN HAD JUS' GONE INTO SURGERY SO WE DECIDED TO LEAVE HER FOR THE TIME BEING.
IT LOOKS LIKE THEY *DIDN'T* SEE ANYTHING ANYWAY.
BEST CHECK THE OLD WOMAN'S PHONE ACTIVITY. WHAT'S THE NAME OF THE GRANDDAUGHTER?
IT'S...ORLA, ORLA ROCHE, THE BOYFRIEND'S NAME IS DAMIEN MAGUIRE.
I ***THOUGHT*** THE OLD WOMAN'S NAME RANG A BELL.
LITTLE ORLA!
YEH KNOW THE FAMILY?
YEAH, I KNOW ORLA FROM YEARS AGO.
SHE WAS A PRETTY TROUBLED KID, ALWAYS RUNNIN' AWAY FROM HOME.
SHE'D GO MISSIN' FOR WEEKS ON END. WE'D USUALLY FIND HER EVENTUALLY, HOLED UP IN A FOREST SOMEWHERE, TALKIN' GIBBERISH ABOUT *'THE PEOPLE IN THE WOODS.'*

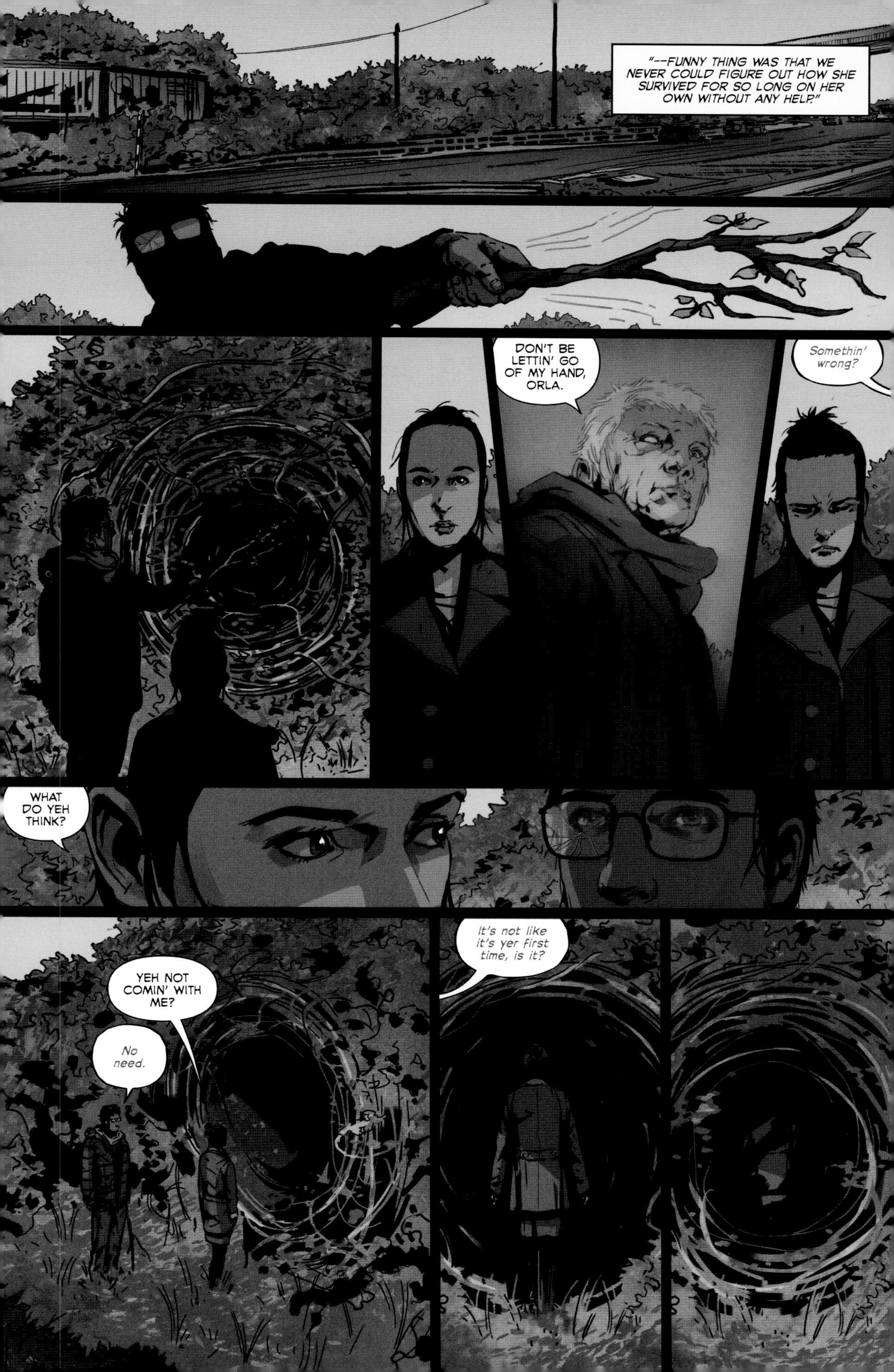

"--FUNNY THING WAS THAT WE NEVER COULD FIGURE OUT HOW SHE SURVIVED FOR SO LONG ON HER OWN WITHOUT ANY HELP."
DON'T BE LETTIN' GO OF MY HAND, ORLA.
Somethin' wrong?
WHAT DO YEH THINK?
YEH NOT COMIN' WITH ME?
No need.
It's not like it's yer first time, is it?

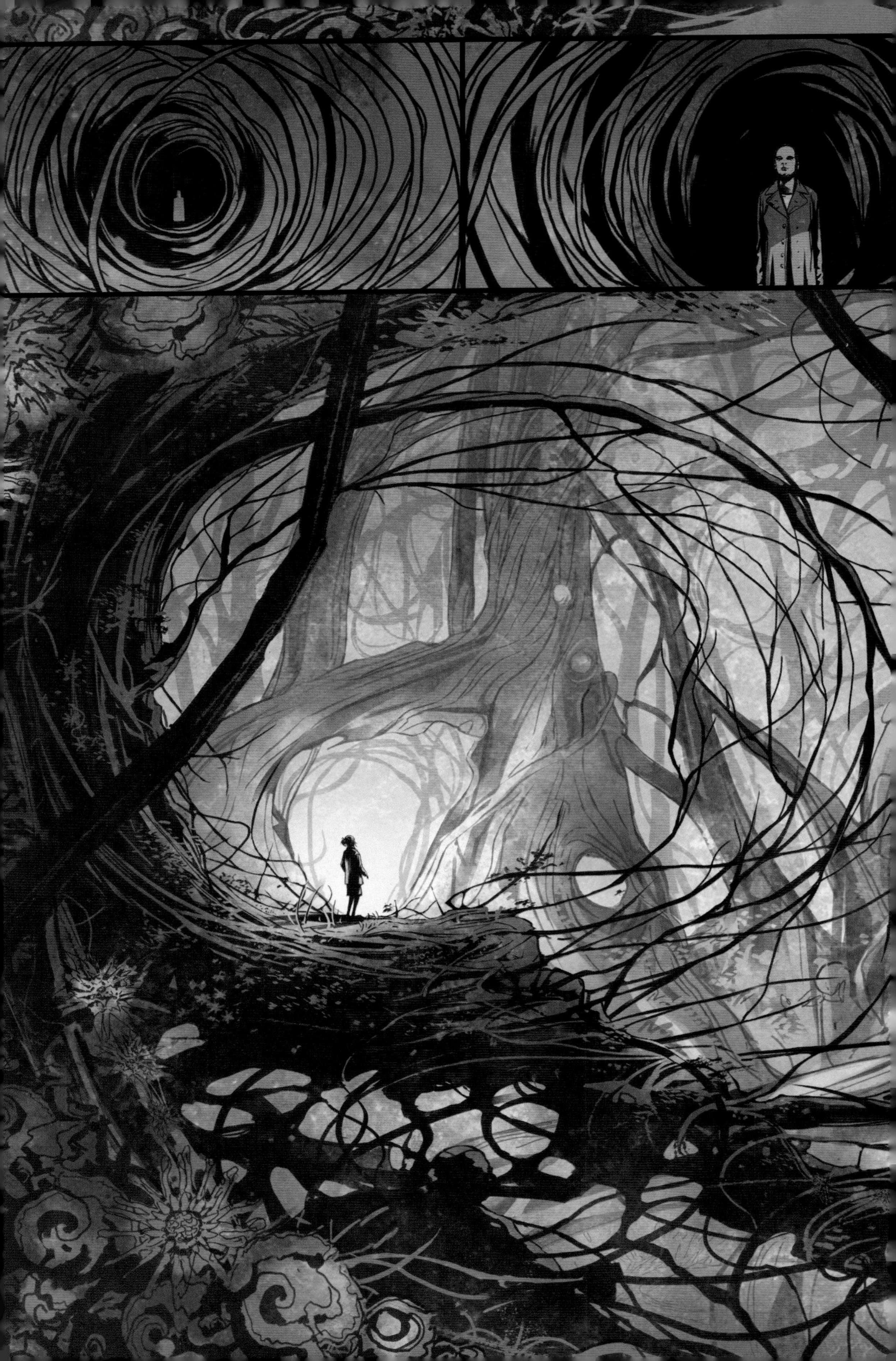

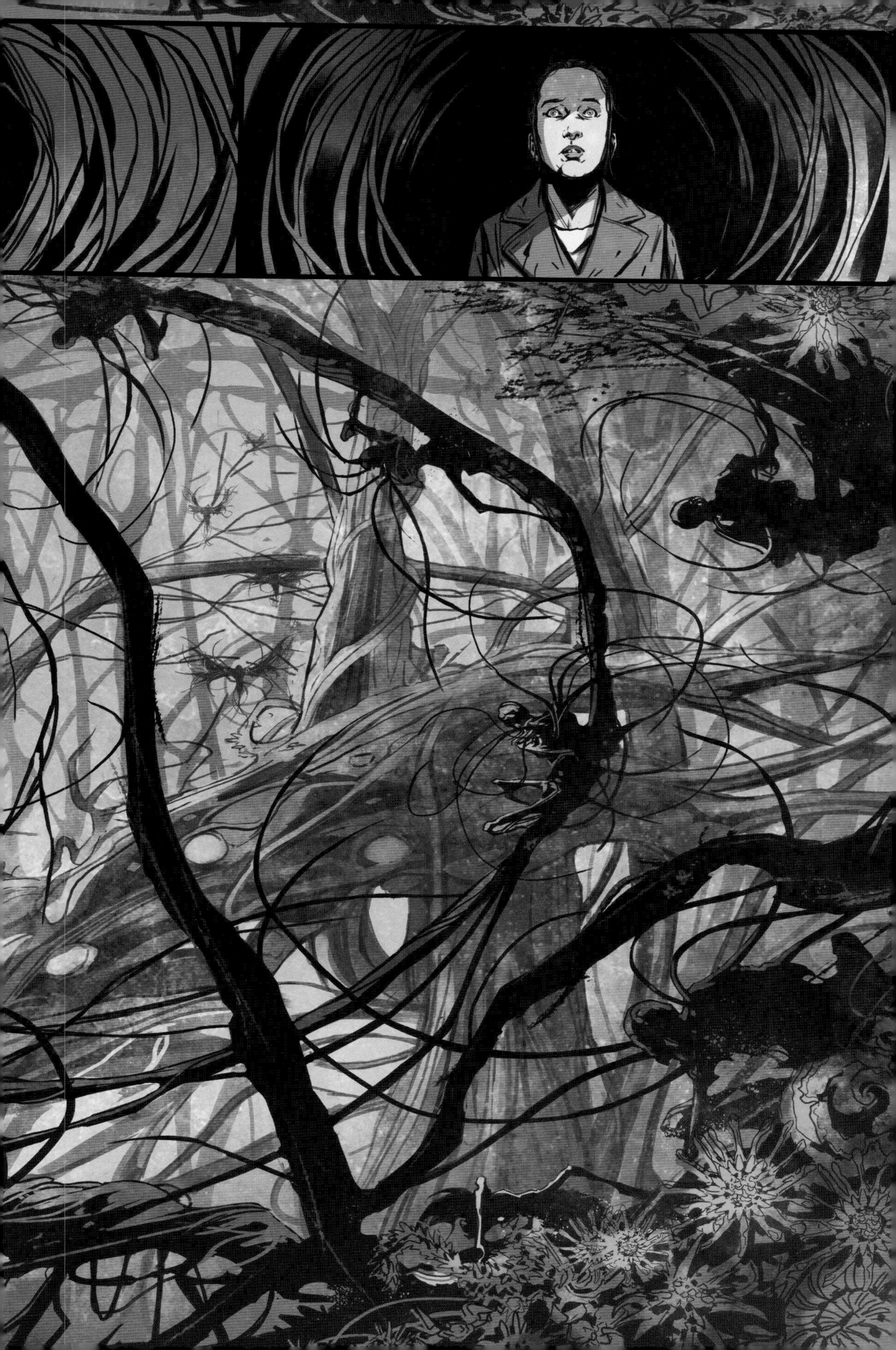

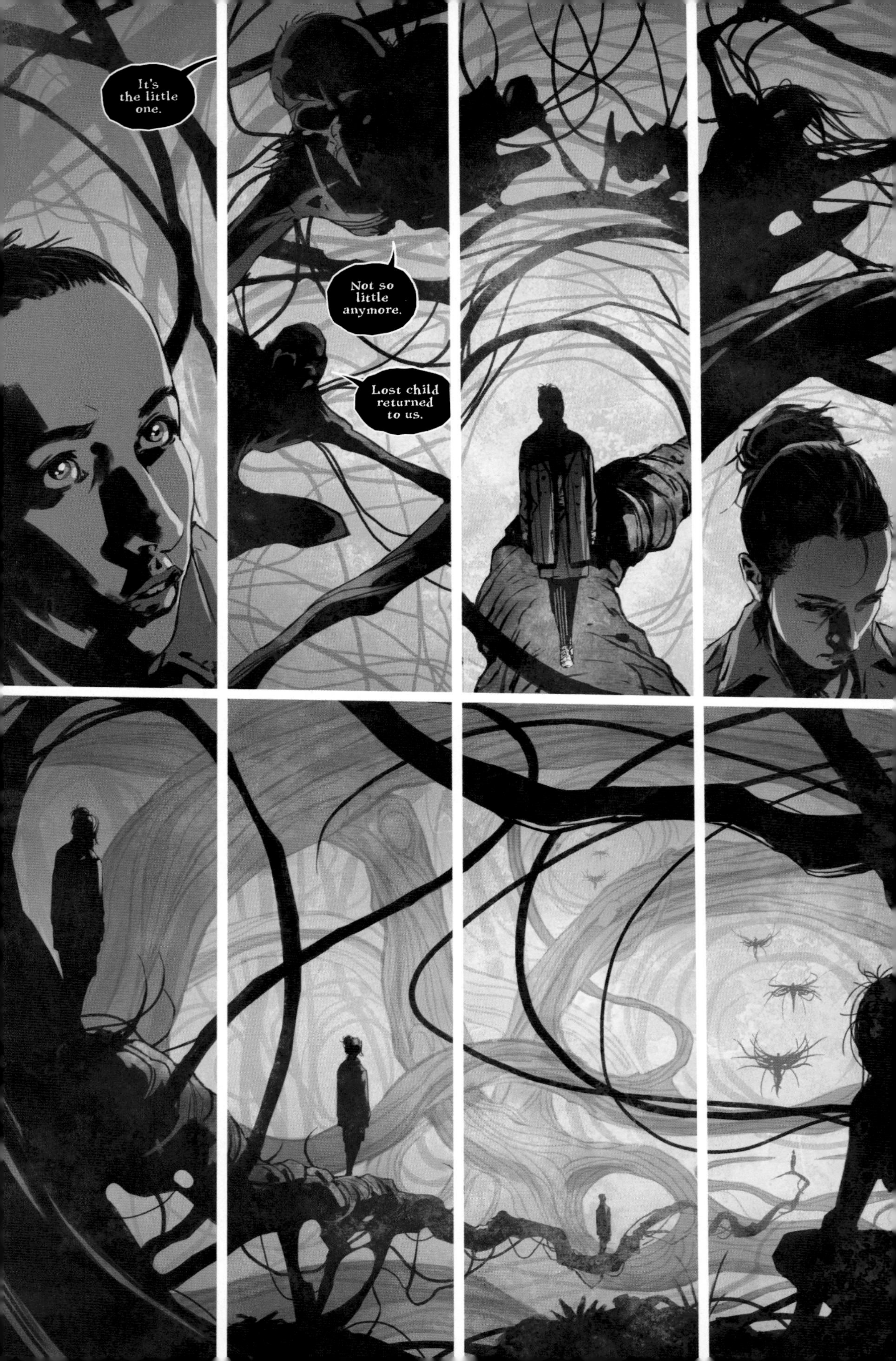
It's the little one.
Not so little anymore.
Lost child returned to us.

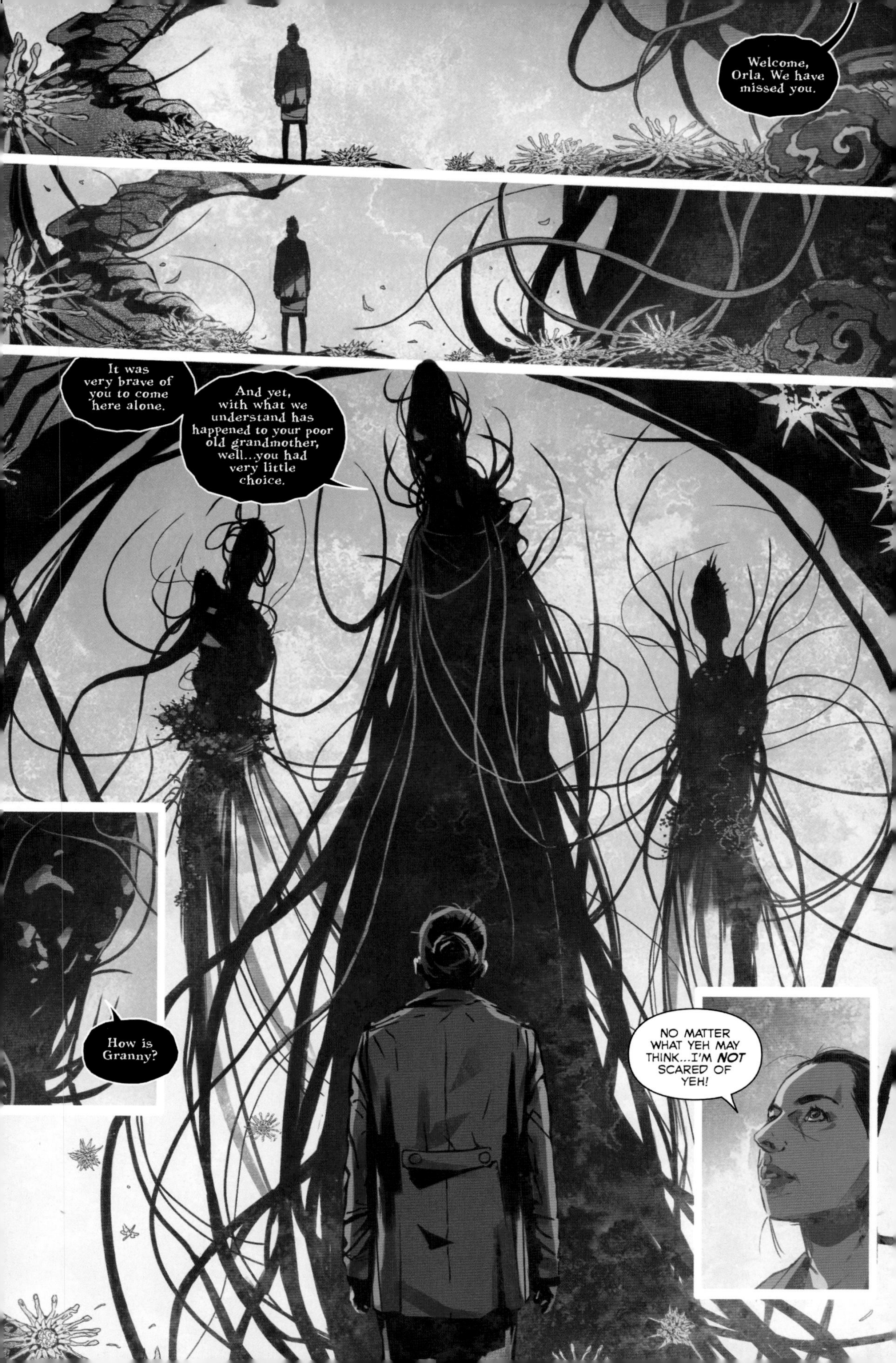
Welcome, Orla. We have missed you.
It was very brave of you to come here alone.
And yet, with what we understand has happened to your poor old grandmother, well...you had very little choice.
How is Granny?
NO MATTER WHAT YEH MAY THINK...I'M ***NOT*** SCARED OF YEH!

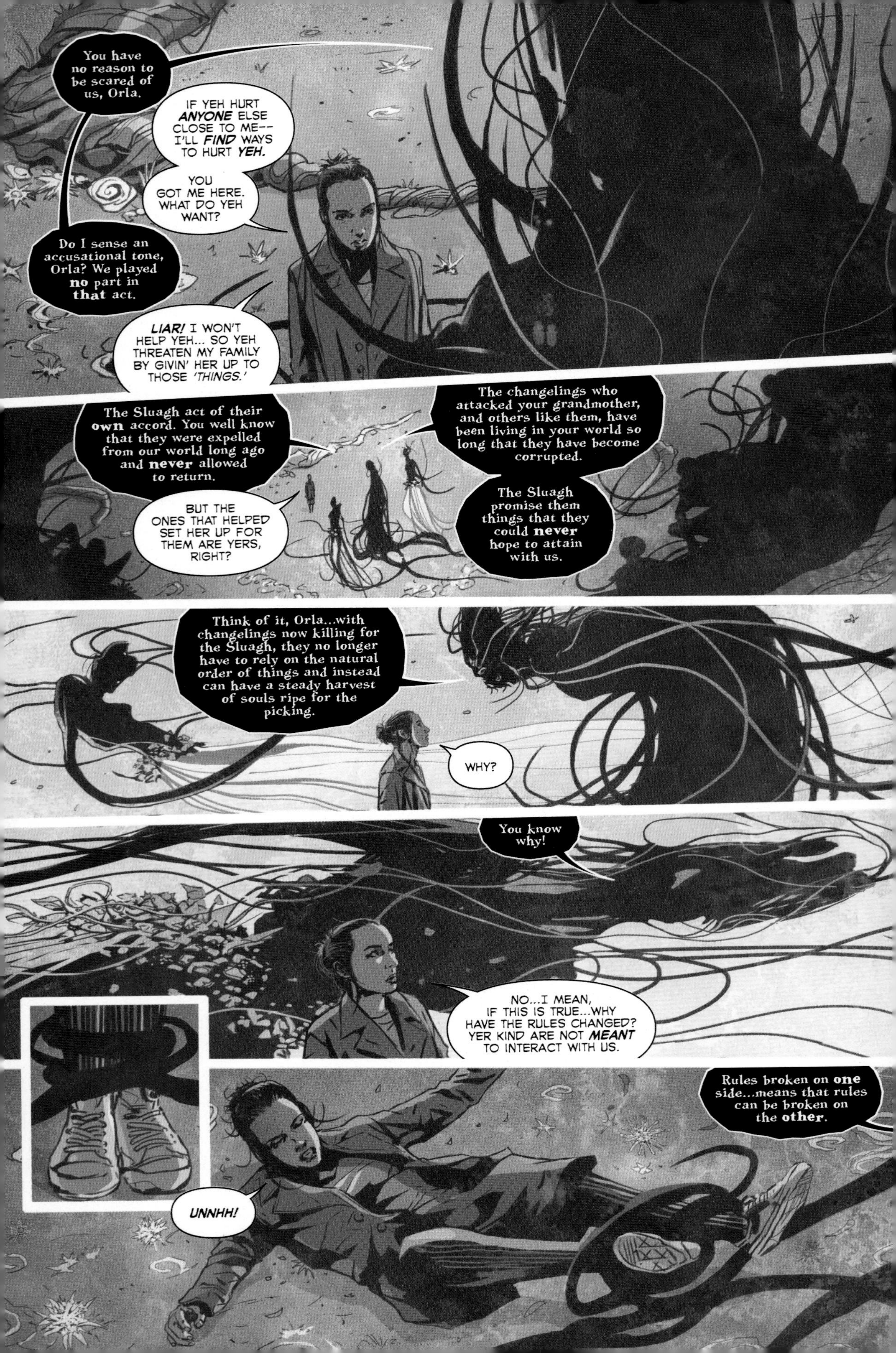
You have no reason to be scared of us, Orla.
IF YEH HURT ANYONE ELSE CLOSE TO ME-- I'LL FIND WAYS TO HURT YEH.
YOU GOT ME HERE. WHAT DO YEH WANT?
Do I sense an accusational tone, Orla? We played no part in that act.
LIAR! I WON'T HELP YEH... SO YEH THREATEN MY FAMILY BY GIVIN' HER UP TO THOSE 'THINGS.'
The Sluagh act of their own accord. You well know that they were expelled from our world long ago and never allowed to return.
BUT THE ONES THAT HELPED SET HER UP FOR THEM ARE YERS, RIGHT?
The changelings who attacked your grandmother, and others like them, have been living in your world so long that they have become corrupted.
The Sluagh promise them things that they could never hope to attain with us.
Think of it, Orla...with changelings now killing for the Sluagh, they no longer have to rely on the natural order of things and instead can have a steady harvest of souls ripe for the picking.
WHY?
You know why!
NO...I MEAN, IF THIS IS TRUE...WHY HAVE THE RULES CHANGED? YER KIND ARE NOT MEANT TO INTERACT WITH US.
Rules broken on one side...means that rules can be broken on the other.
UNNHH!

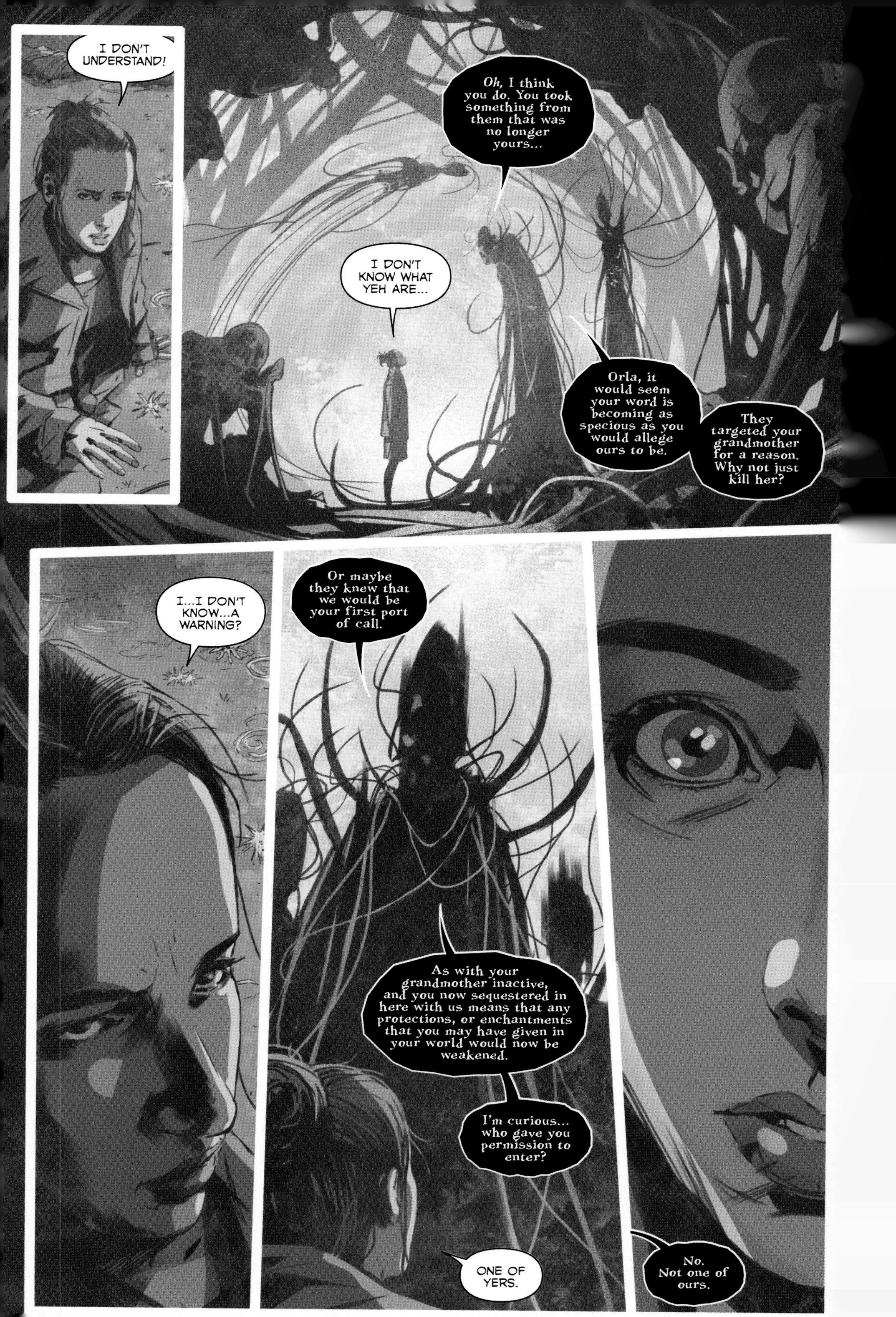

I DON'T UNDERSTAND!
Oh, I think you do. You took something from them that was no longer yours...
I DON'T KNOW WHAT YEH ARE...
Orla, it would seem your word is becoming as specious as you would allege ours to be.
They targeted your grandmother for a reason. Why not just kill her?
I...I DON'T KNOW...A WARNING?
Or maybe they knew that we would be your first port of call.
As with your grandmother inactive, and you now sequestered in here with us means that any protections, or enchantments that you may have given in your world would now be weakened.
I'm curious... who gave you permission to enter?
ONE OF YERS.
No. Not one of ours.

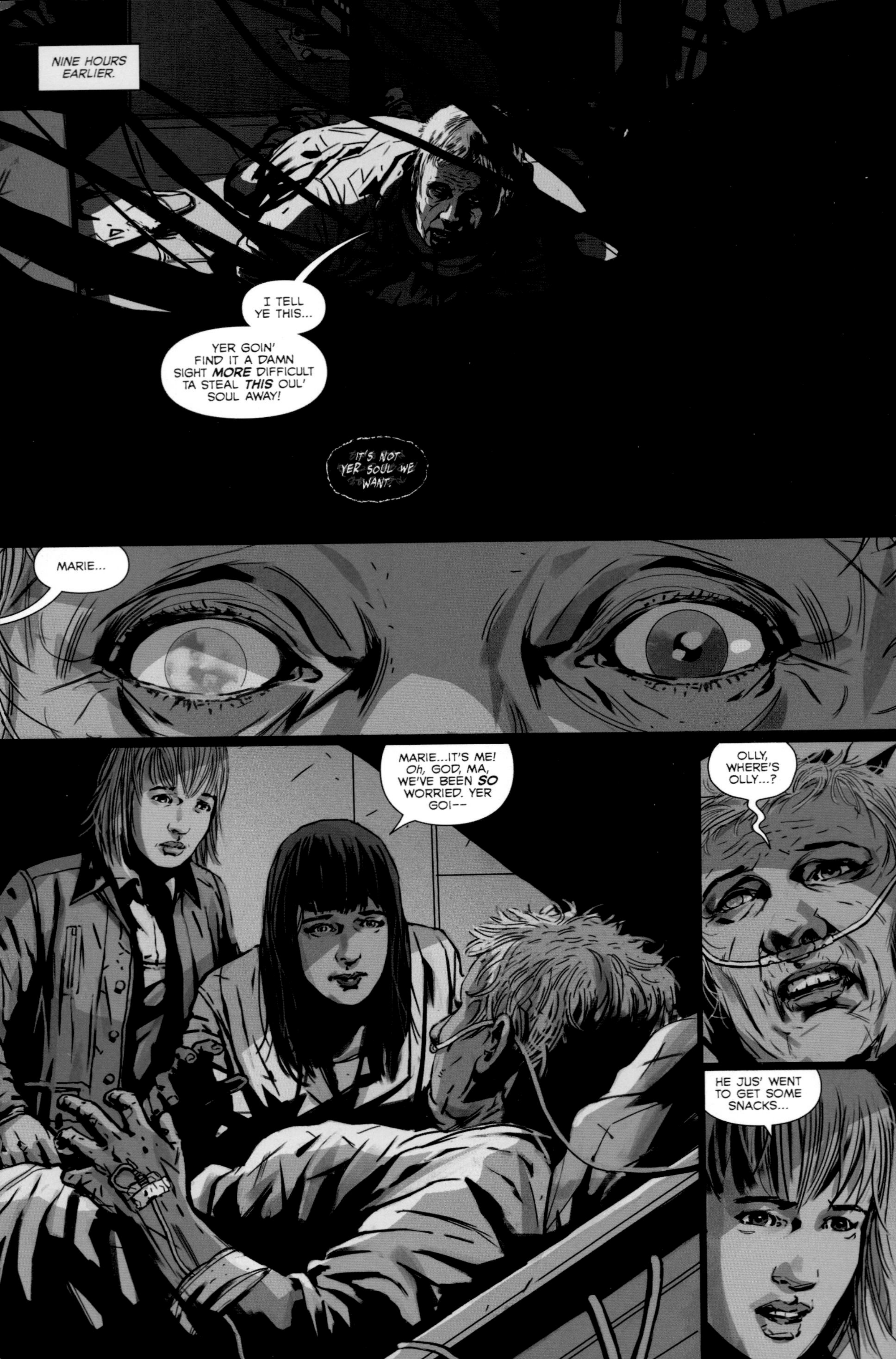
NINE HOURS EARLIER.
I TELL YE THIS...
YER GOIN' FIND IT A DAMN SIGHT MORE DIFFICULT TA STEAL THIS OUL' SOUL AWAY!
IT'S NOT YER SOUL WE WANT.
MARIE...
MARIE...IT'S ME! Oh, GOD, MA, WE'VE BEEN SO WORRIED. YER GOI--
OLLY, WHERE'S OLLY...?
HE JUS' WENT TO GET SOME SNACKS...

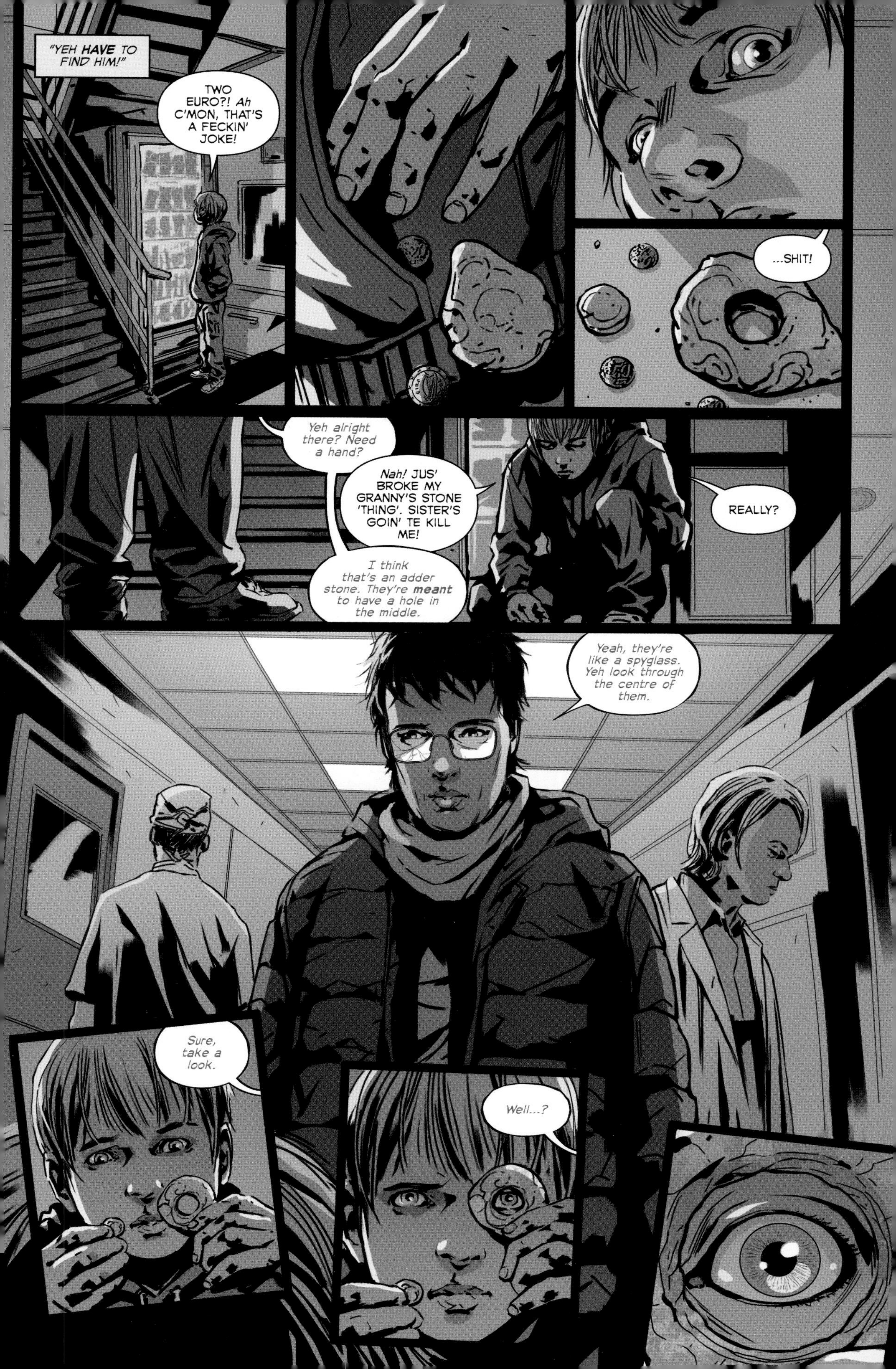
"YEH **HAVE** TO FIND HIM!"
TWO EURO?! *Ah* C'MON, THAT'S A FECKIN' JOKE!
...SHIT!
Yeh alright there? Need a hand?
Nah! JUS' BROKE MY GRANNY'S STONE 'THING'. SISTER'S GOIN' TE KILL ME!
I think that's an adder stone. They're ***meant*** *to have a hole in the middle.*
REALLY?
Yeah, they're like a spyglass. Yeh look through the centre of them.
Sure, take a look.
Well...?

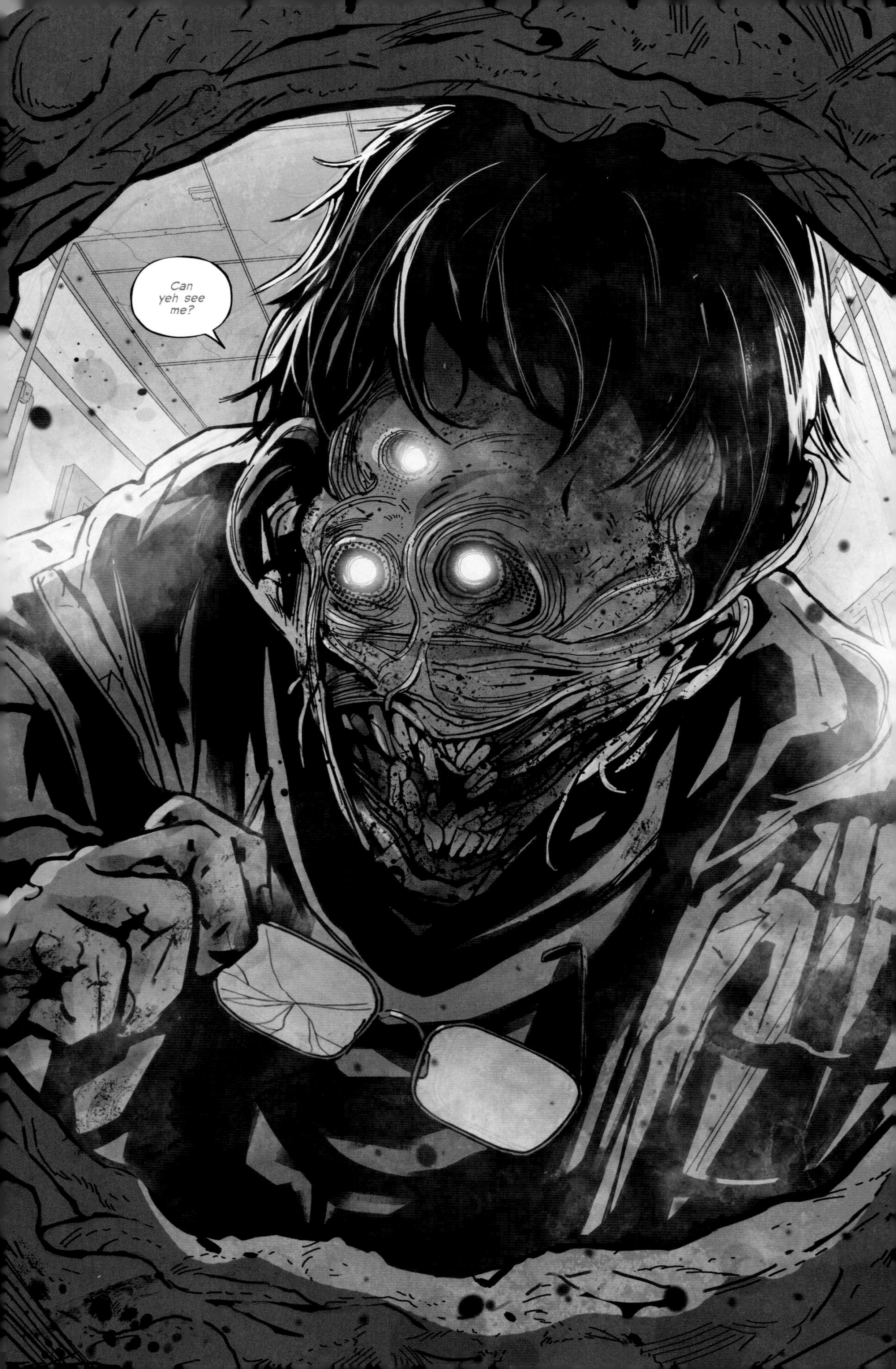
Can yeh see me?

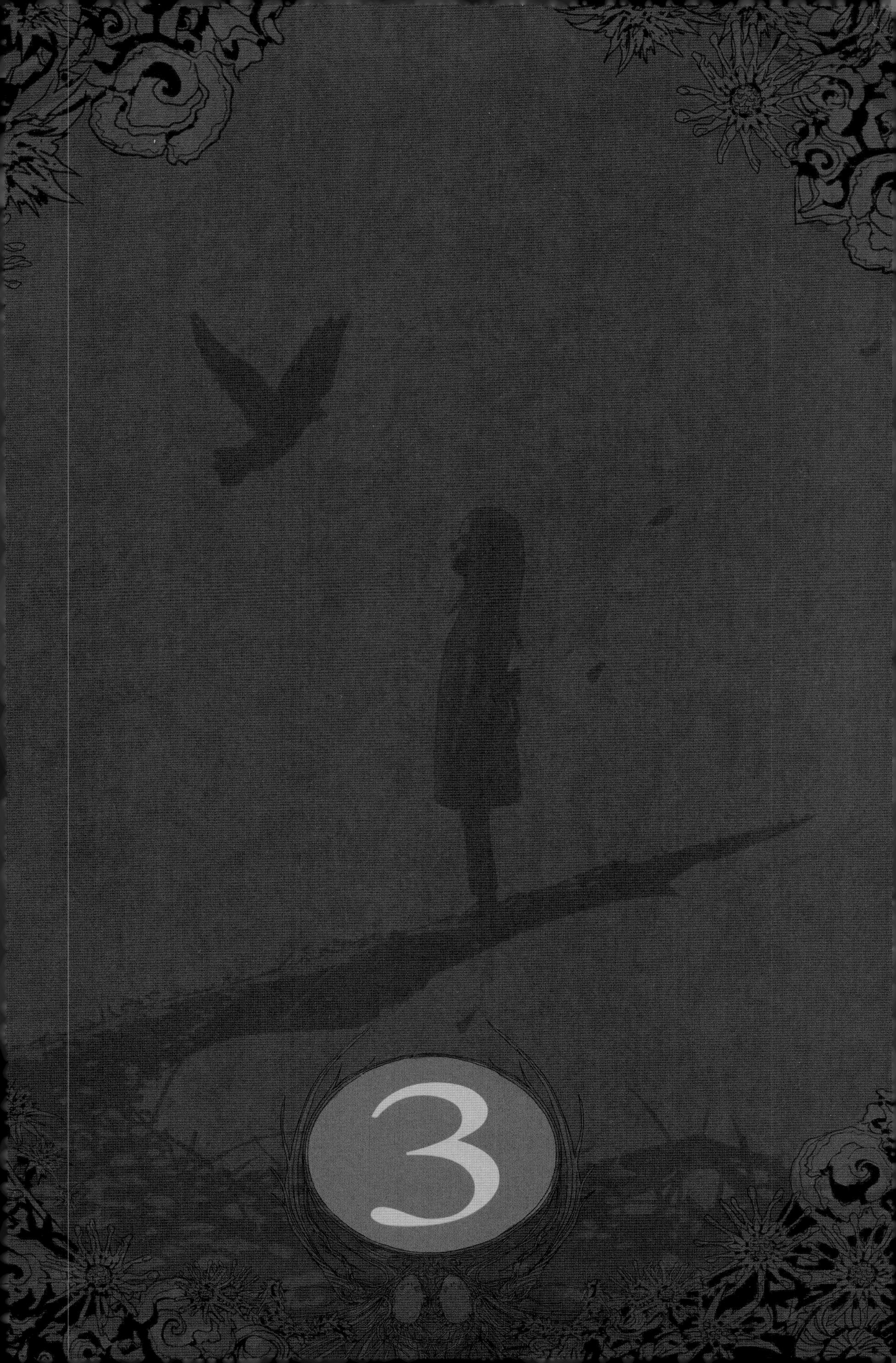
3

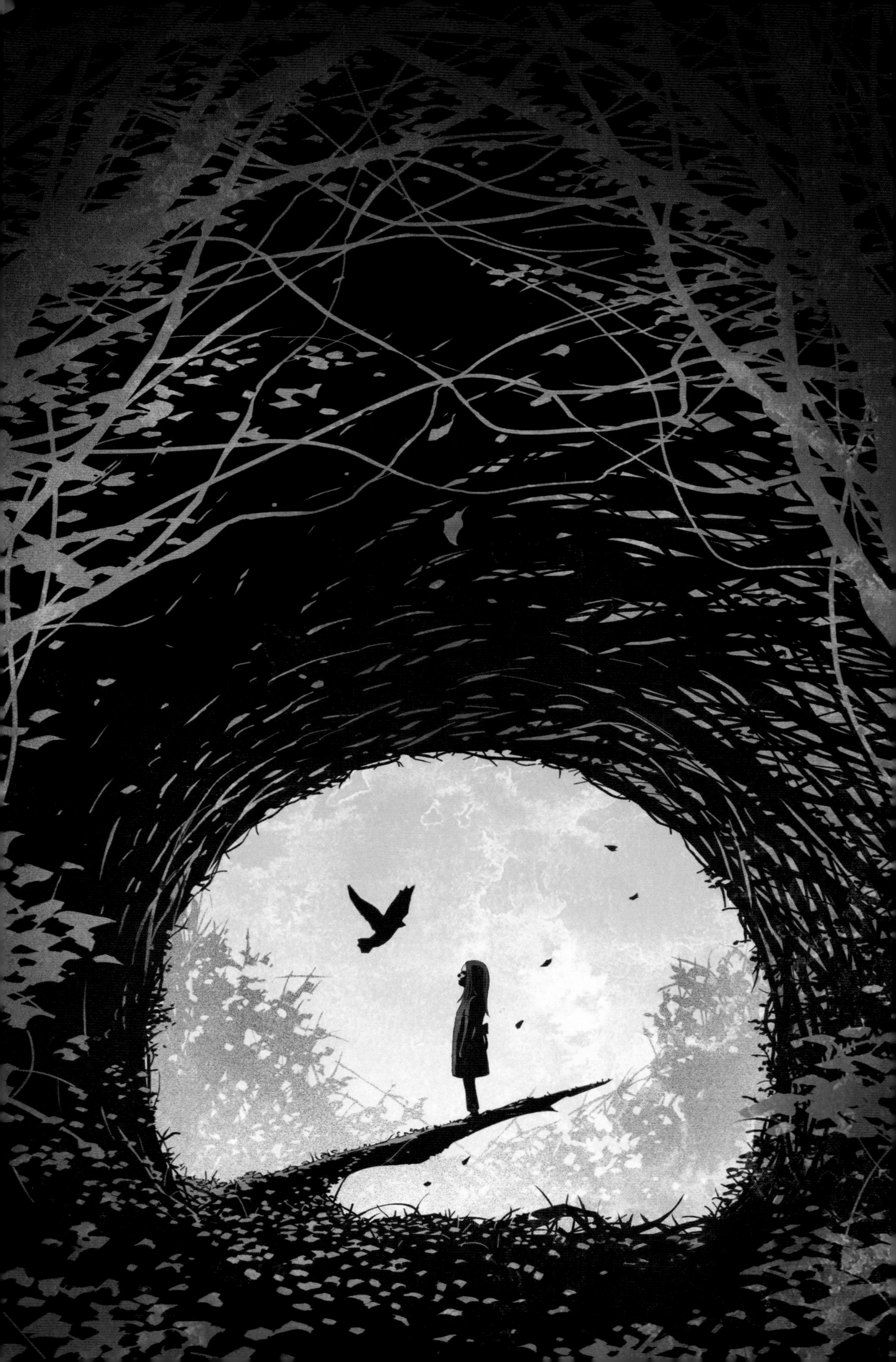

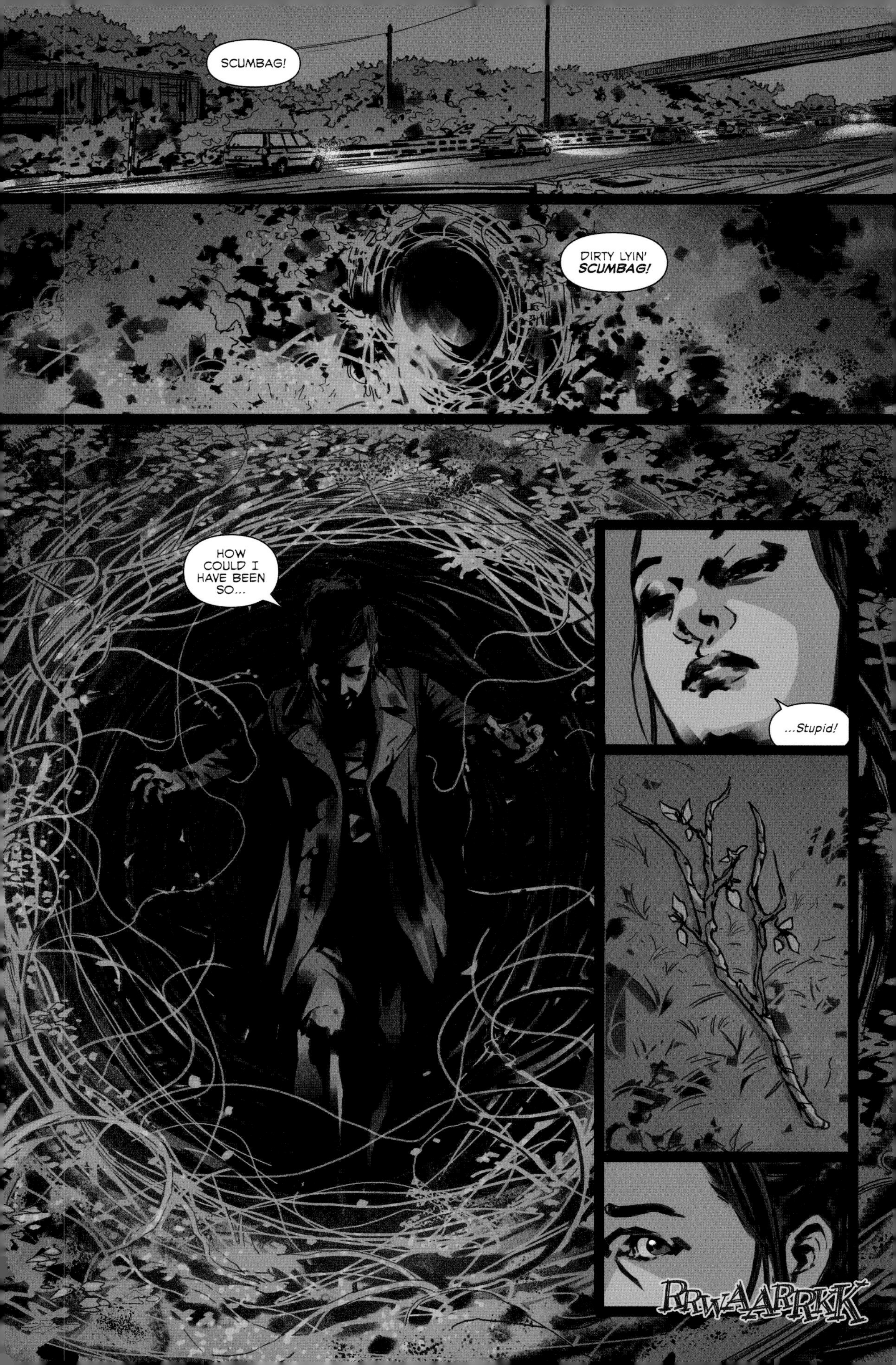
SCUMBAG!
DIRTY LYIN' SCUMBAG!
HOW COULD I HAVE BEEN SO...
...Stupid!
RRWAARRKK

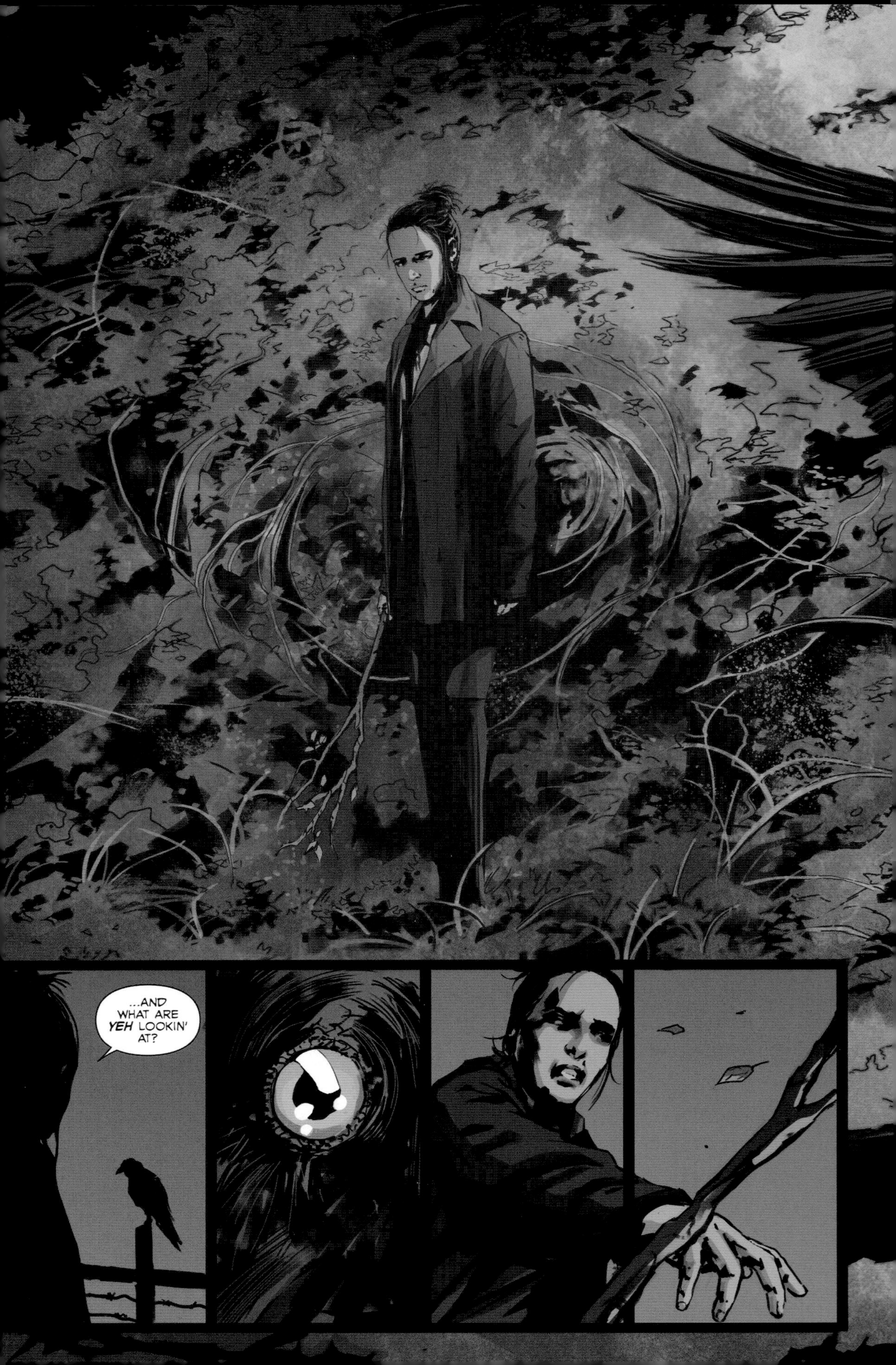
...AND
WHAT ARE
YEH LOOKIN'
AT?

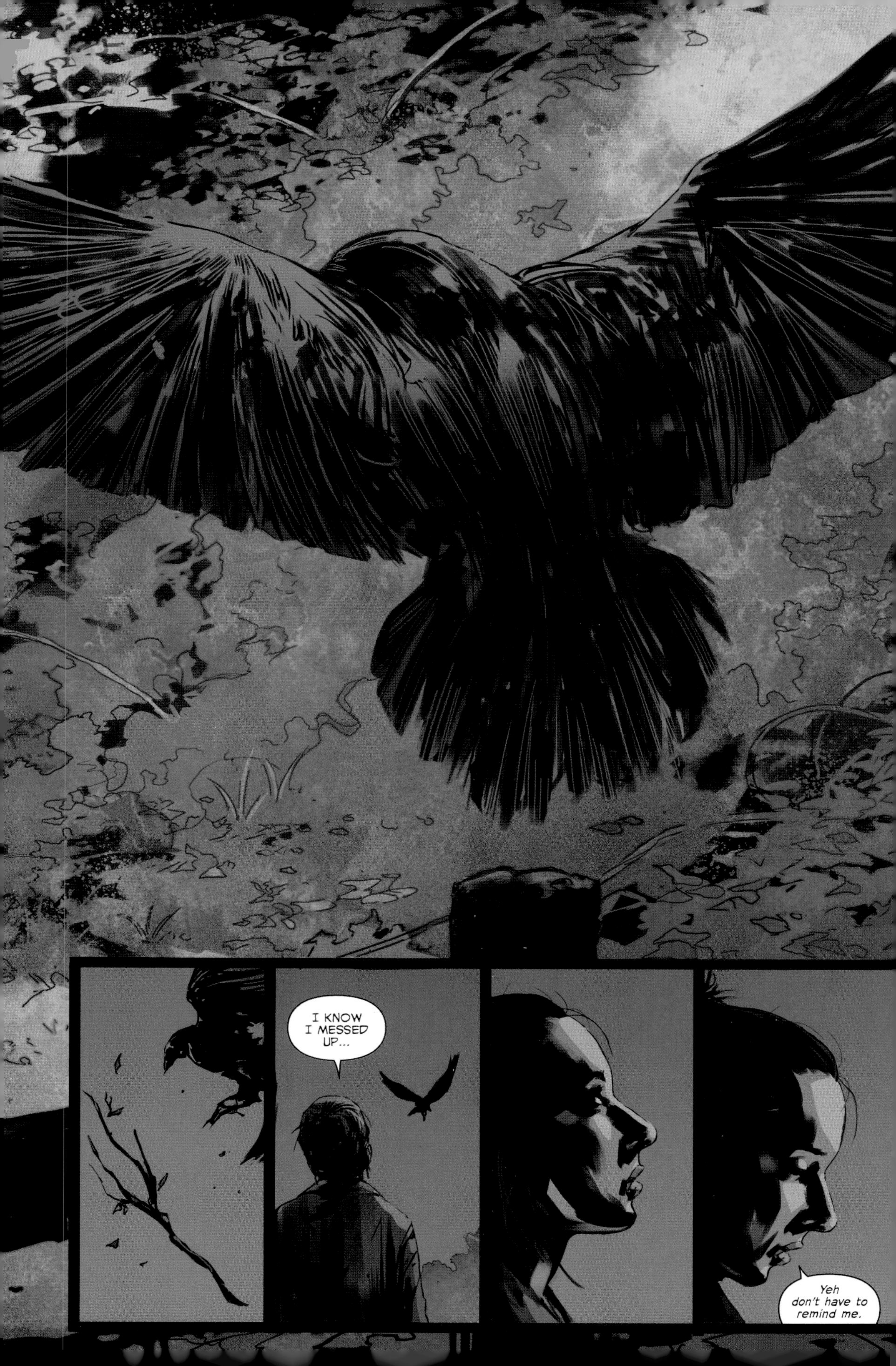
I KNOW I MESSED UP...
Yeh don't have to remind me.

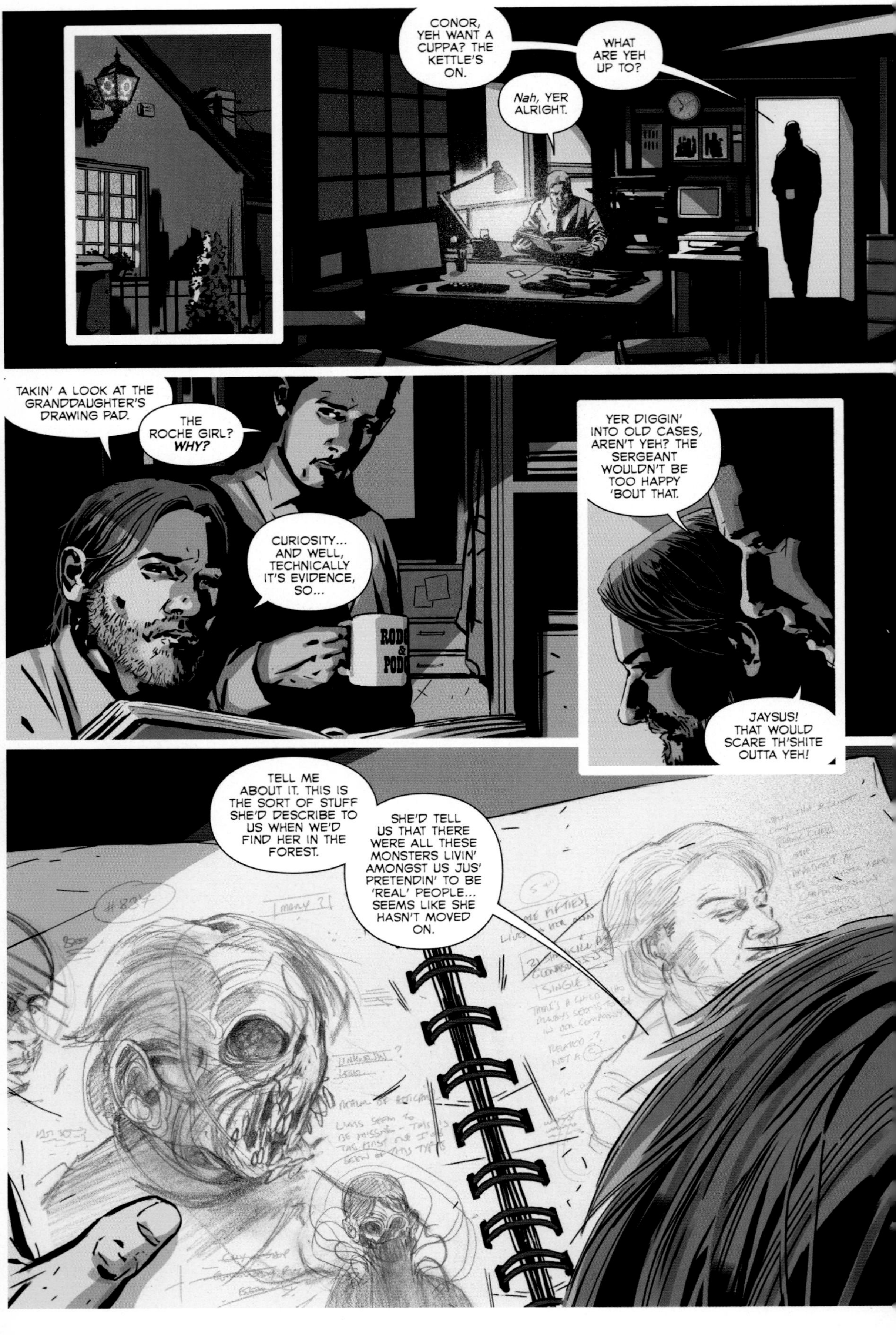
CONOR, YEH WANT A CUPPA? THE KETTLE'S ON.
WHAT ARE YEH UP TO?
Nah, YER ALRIGHT.
TAKIN' A LOOK AT THE GRANDDAUGHTER'S DRAWING PAD.
THE ROCHE GIRL? ***WHY?***
CURIOSITY... AND WELL, TECHNICALLY IT'S EVIDENCE, SO...
YER DIGGIN' INTO OLD CASES, AREN'T YEH? THE SERGEANT WOULDN'T BE TOO HAPPY 'BOUT THAT.
JAYSUS! THAT WOULD SCARE TH'SHITE OUTTA YEH!
TELL ME ABOUT IT. THIS IS THE SORT OF STUFF SHE'D DESCRIBE TO US WHEN WE'D FIND HER IN THE FOREST.
SHE'D TELL US THAT THERE WERE ALL THESE MONSTERS LIVIN' AMONGST US JUS' PRETENDIN' TO BE 'REAL' PEOPLE... SEEMS LIKE SHE HASN'T MOVED ON.

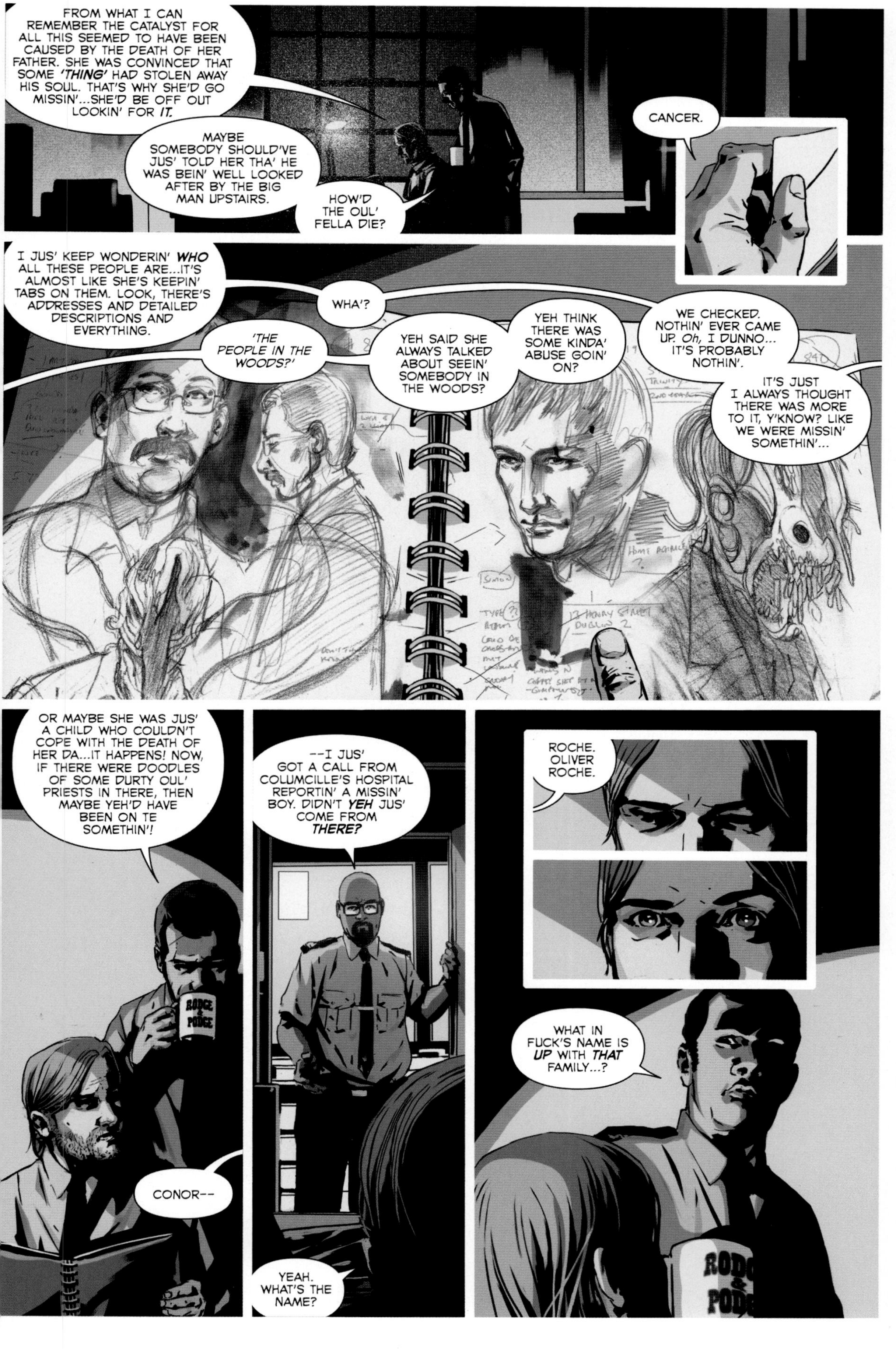

FROM WHAT I CAN REMEMBER THE CATALYST FOR ALL THIS SEEMED TO HAVE BEEN CAUSED BY THE DEATH OF HER FATHER. SHE WAS CONVINCED THAT SOME 'THING' HAD STOLEN AWAY HIS SOUL. THAT'S WHY SHE'D GO MISSIN'...SHE'D BE OFF OUT LOOKIN' FOR IT.
MAYBE SOMEBODY SHOULD'VE JUS' TOLD HER THA' HE WAS BEIN' WELL LOOKED AFTER BY THE BIG MAN UPSTAIRS.
HOW'D THE OUL' FELLA DIE?
CANCER.
I JUS' KEEP WONDERIN' WHO ALL THESE PEOPLE ARE...IT'S ALMOST LIKE SHE'S KEEPIN' TABS ON THEM. LOOK, THERE'S ADDRESSES AND DETAILED DESCRIPTIONS AND EVERYTHING.
WHA'?
'THE PEOPLE IN THE WOODS?'
YEH SAID SHE ALWAYS TALKED ABOUT SEEIN' SOMEBODY IN THE WOODS?
YEH THINK THERE WAS SOME KINDA' ABUSE GOIN' ON?
WE CHECKED. NOTHIN' EVER CAME UP. Oh, I DUNNO... IT'S PROBABLY NOTHIN'.
IT'S JUST I ALWAYS THOUGHT THERE WAS MORE TO IT, Y'KNOW? LIKE WE WERE MISSIN' SOMETHIN'...
OR MAYBE SHE WAS JUS' A CHILD WHO COULDN'T COPE WITH THE DEATH OF HER DA...IT HAPPENS! NOW, IF THERE WERE DOODLES OF SOME DURTY OUL' PRIESTS IN THERE, THEN MAYBE YEH'D HAVE BEEN ON TE SOMETHIN'!
CONOR--
--I JUS' GOT A CALL FROM COLUMCILLE'S HOSPITAL REPORTIN' A MISSIN' BOY. DIDN'T YEH JUS' COME FROM THERE?
YEAH. WHAT'S THE NAME?
ROCHE. OLIVER ROCHE.
WHAT IN FUCK'S NAME IS UP WITH THAT FAMILY...?

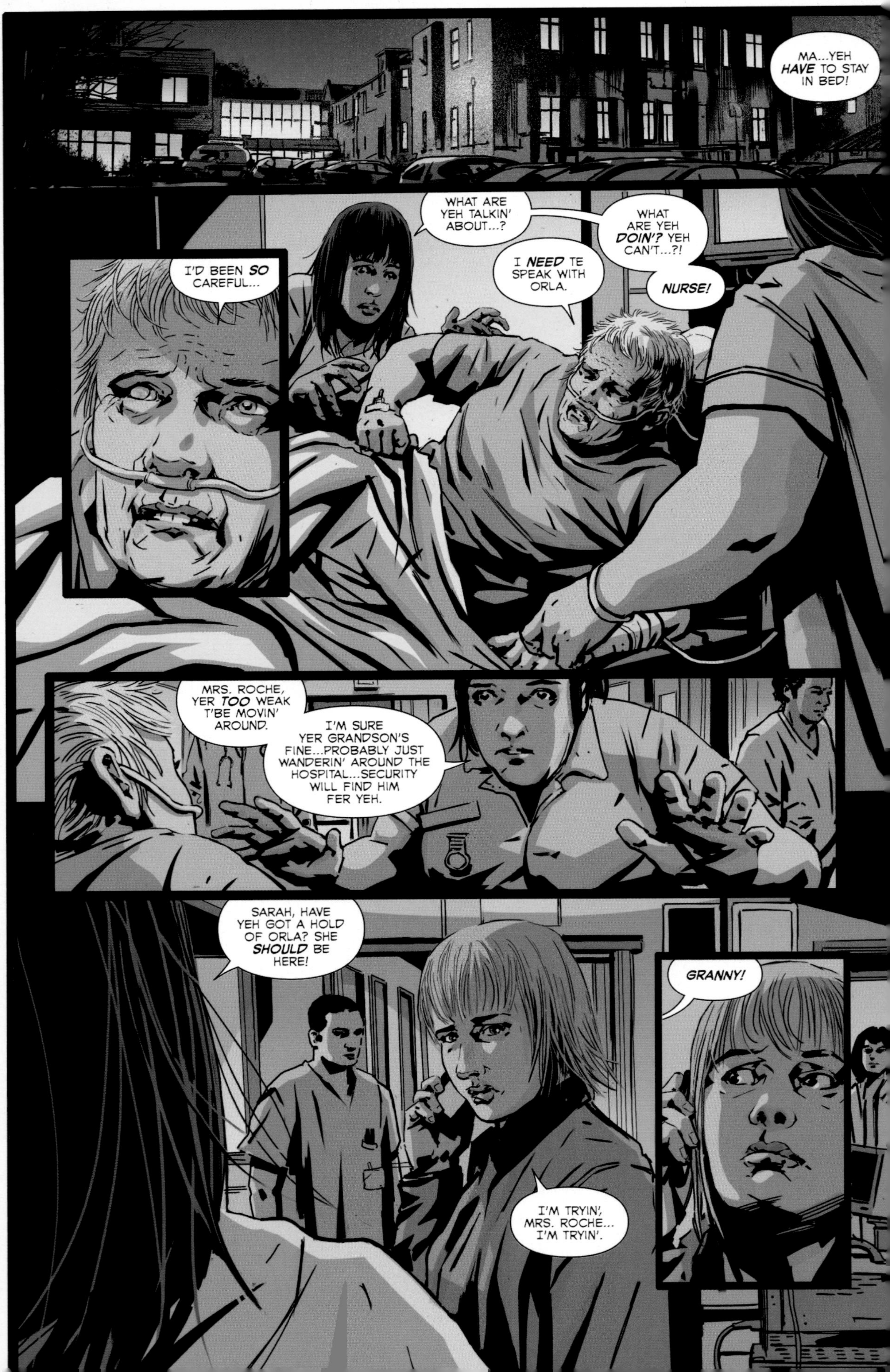
MA...YEH HAVE TO STAY IN BED!
I'D BEEN SO CAREFUL...
WHAT ARE YEH TALKIN' ABOUT...?
WHAT ARE YEH DOIN'? YEH CAN'T...?!
I NEED TE SPEAK WITH ORLA.
NURSE!
MRS. ROCHE, YER TOO WEAK T'BE MOVIN' AROUND.
I'M SURE YER GRANDSON'S FINE...PROBABLY JUST WANDERIN' AROUND THE HOSPITAL...SECURITY WILL FIND HIM FER YEH.
SARAH, HAVE YEH GOT A HOLD OF ORLA? SHE SHOULD BE HERE!
GRANNY!
I'M TRYIN', MRS. ROCHE... I'M TRYIN'.

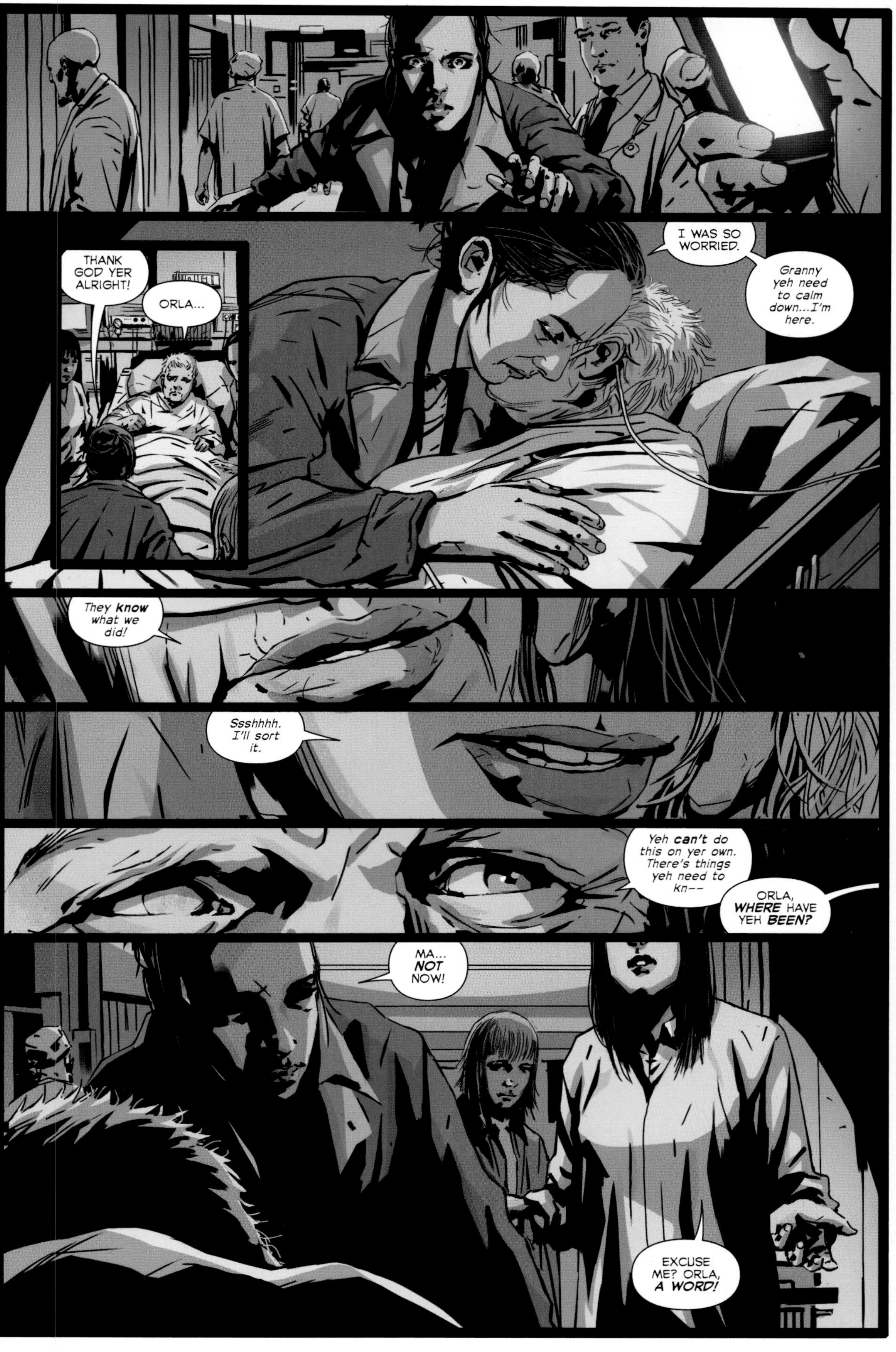
THANK GOD YER ALRIGHT!
ORLA...
I WAS SO WORRIED.
Granny yeh need to calm down...I'm here.
They **know** what we did!
Ssshhhh. I'll sort it.
Yeh **can't** do this on yer own. There's things yeh need to kn--
ORLA, ***WHERE*** HAVE YEH ***BEEN?***
MA... ***NOT*** NOW!
EXCUSE ME? ORLA, ***A WORD!***

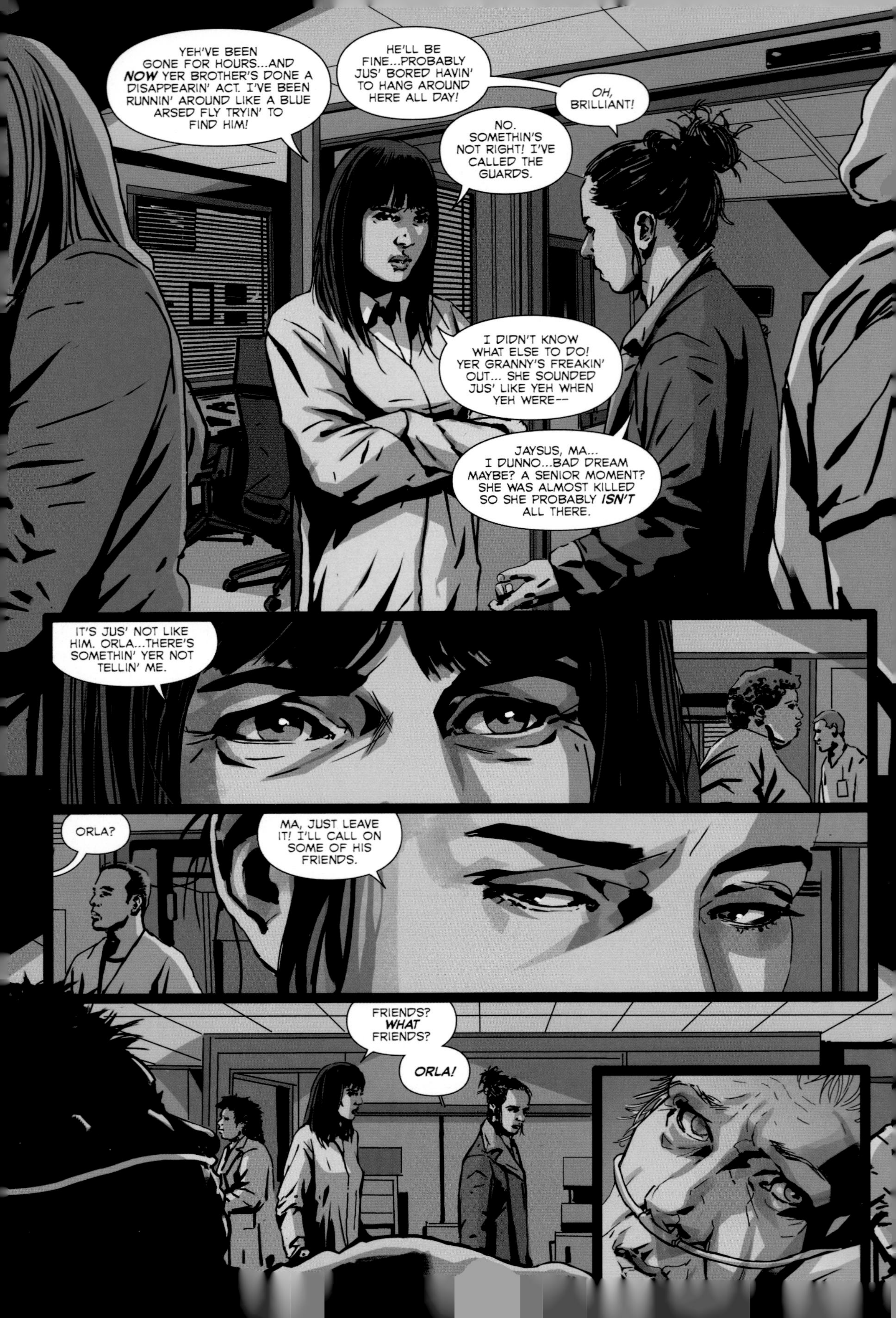
YEH'VE BEEN GONE FOR HOURS...AND NOW YER BROTHER'S DONE A DISAPPEARIN' ACT. I'VE BEEN RUNNIN' AROUND LIKE A BLUE ARSED FLY TRYIN' TO FIND HIM!
HE'LL BE FINE...PROBABLY JUS' BORED HAVIN' TO HANG AROUND HERE ALL DAY!
OH, BRILLIANT!
NO. SOMETHIN'S NOT RIGHT! I'VE CALLED THE GUARDS.
I DIDN'T KNOW WHAT ELSE TO DO! YER GRANNY'S FREAKIN' OUT... SHE SOUNDED JUS' LIKE YEH WHEN YEH WERE--
JAYSUS, MA... I DUNNO...BAD DREAM MAYBE? A SENIOR MOMENT? SHE WAS ALMOST KILLED SO SHE PROBABLY ISN'T ALL THERE.
IT'S JUS' NOT LIKE HIM. ORLA...THERE'S SOMETHIN' YER NOT TELLIN' ME.
ORLA?
MA, JUST LEAVE IT! I'LL CALL ON SOME OF HIS FRIENDS.
FRIENDS? WHAT FRIENDS?
ORLA!

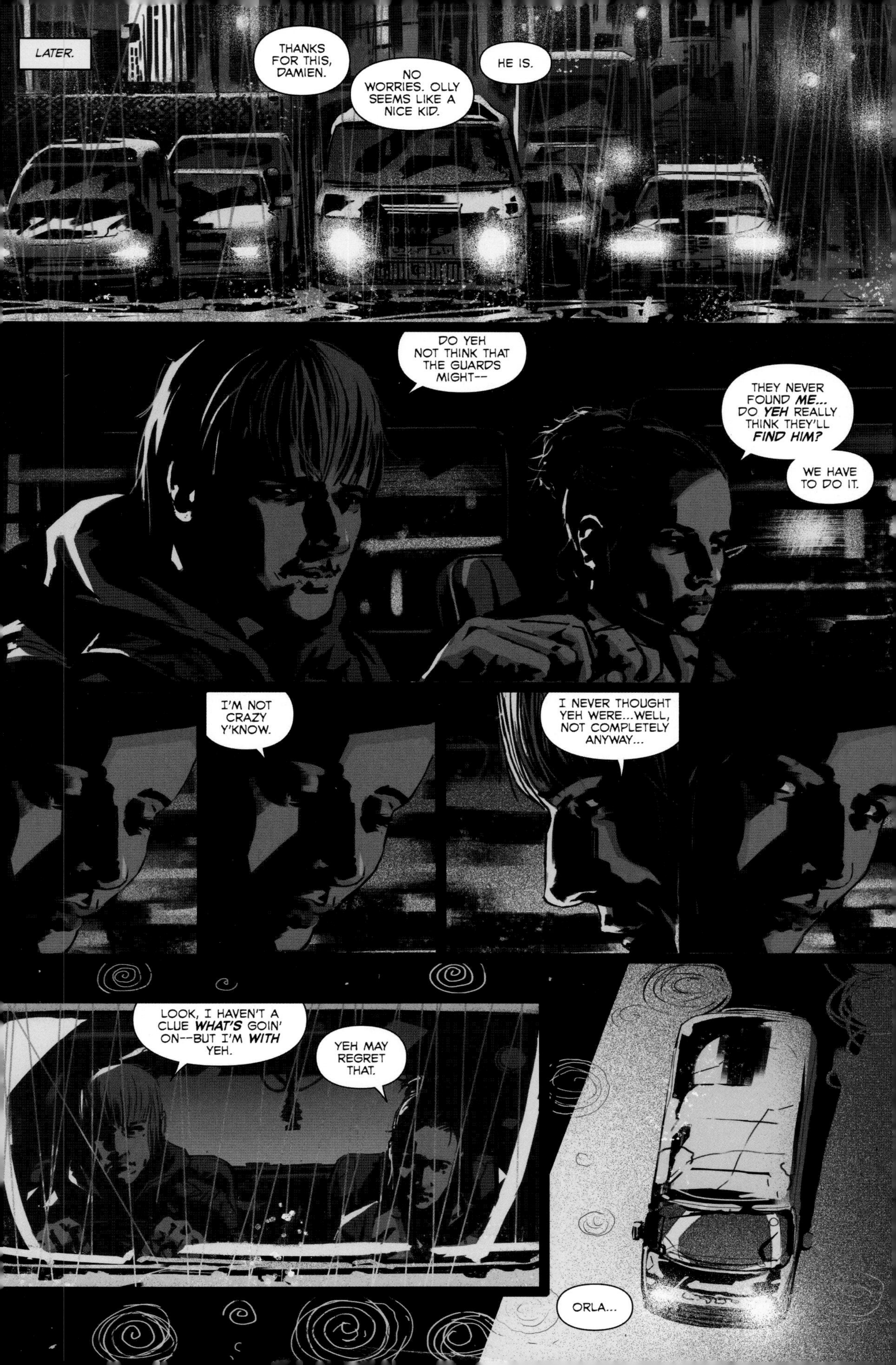
LATER.
THANKS FOR THIS, DAMIEN.
NO WORRIES. OLLY SEEMS LIKE A NICE KID.
HE IS.
DO YEH NOT THINK THAT THE GUARDS MIGHT--
THEY NEVER FOUND ME... DO YEH REALLY THINK THEY'LL FIND HIM?
WE HAVE TO DO IT.
I'M NOT CRAZY Y'KNOW.
I NEVER THOUGHT YEH WERE...WELL, NOT COMPLETELY ANYWAY...
LOOK, I HAVEN'T A CLUE WHAT'S GOIN' ON--BUT I'M WITH YEH.
YEH MAY REGRET THAT.
ORLA...

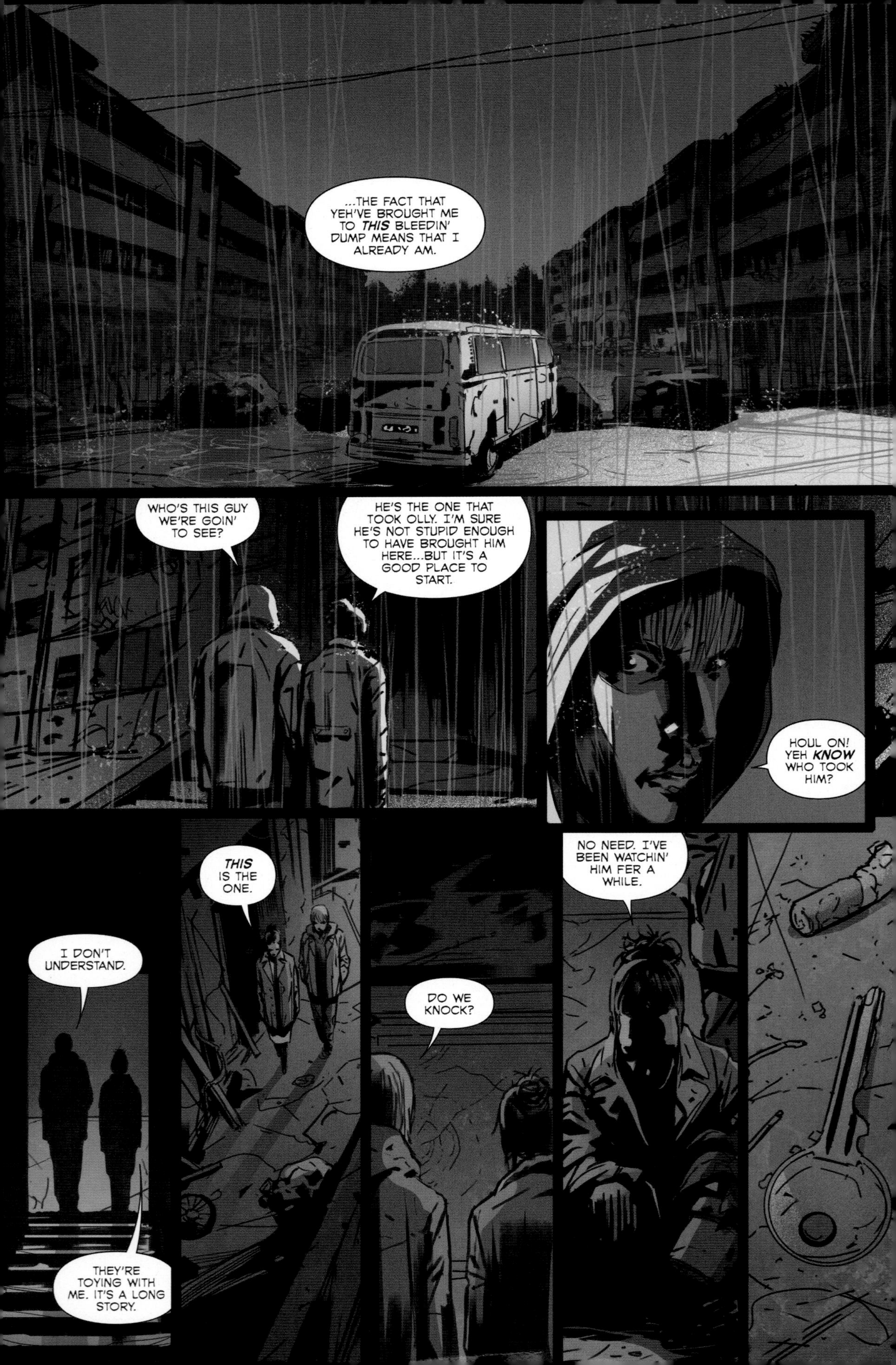
...THE FACT THAT YEH'VE BROUGHT ME TO *THIS* BLEEDIN' DUMP MEANS THAT I ALREADY AM.
WHO'S THIS GUY WE'RE GOIN' TO SEE?
HE'S THE ONE THAT TOOK OLLY. I'M SURE HE'S NOT STUPID ENOUGH TO HAVE BROUGHT HIM HERE...BUT IT'S A GOOD PLACE TO START.
HOUL ON! YEH *KNOW* WHO TOOK HIM?
I DON'T UNDERSTAND.
THEY'RE TOYING WITH ME. IT'S A LONG STORY.
THIS IS THE ONE.
DO WE KNOCK?
NO NEED. I'VE BEEN WATCHIN' HIM FER A WHILE.

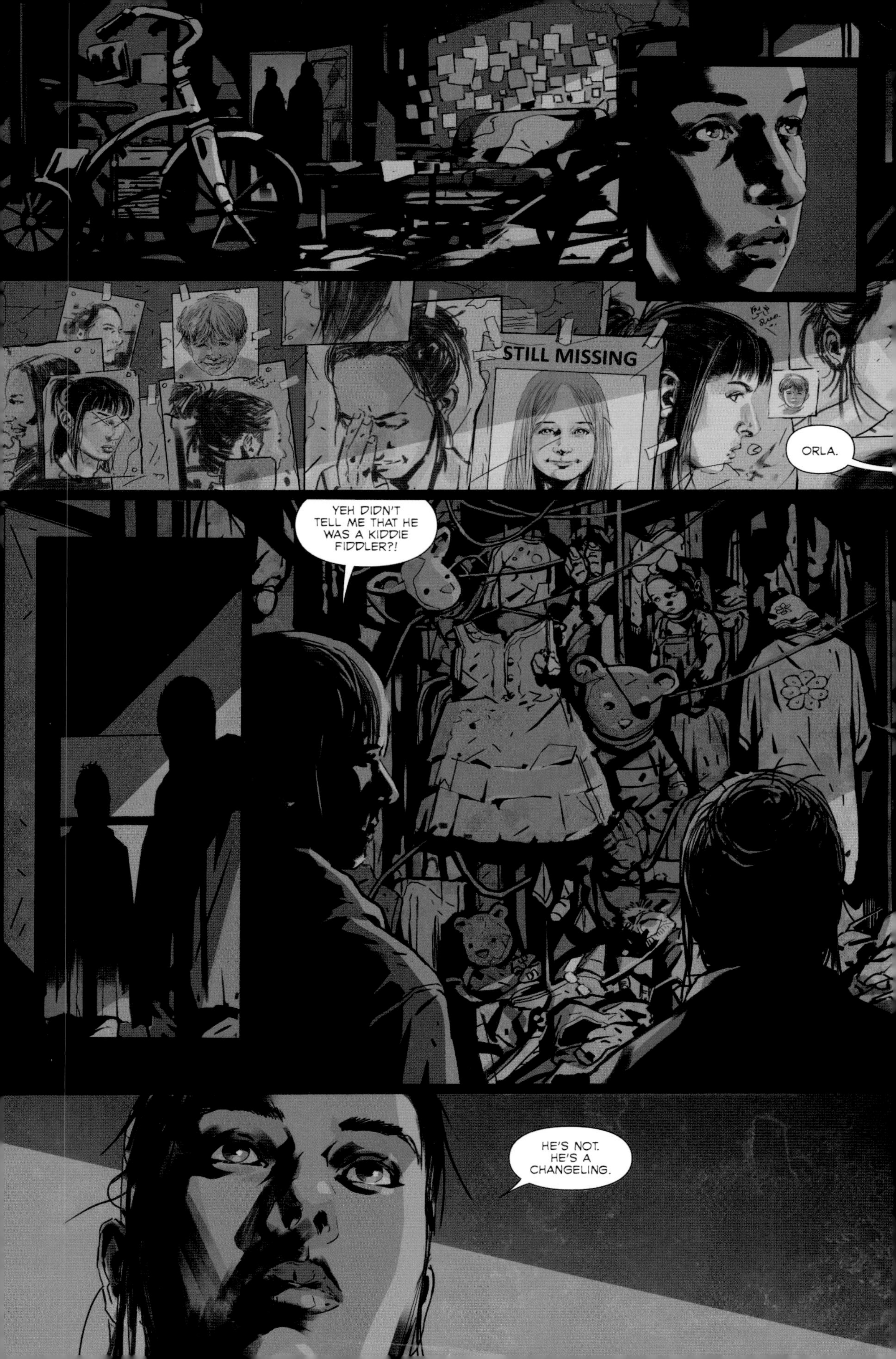
STILL MISSING
ORLA.
YEH DIDN'T TELL ME THAT HE WAS A KIDDIE FIDDLER?!
HE'S NOT. HE'S A CHANGELING.

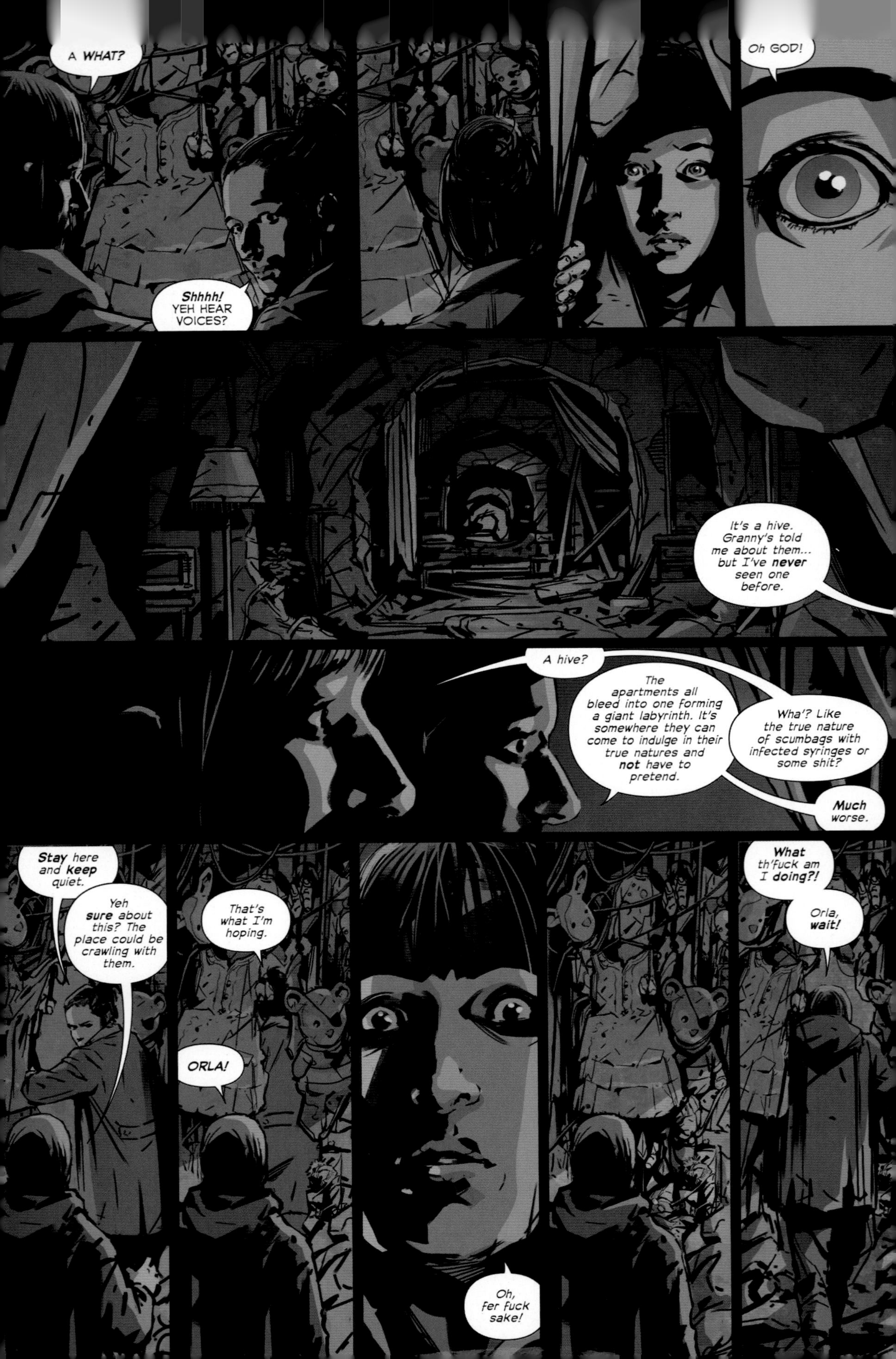

A WHAT?
Shhhh! YEH HEAR VOICES?
Oh GOD!
It's a hive. Granny's told me about them... but I've never seen one before.
A hive?
The apartments all bleed into one forming a giant labyrinth. It's somewhere they can come to indulge in their true natures and not have to pretend.
Wha'? Like the true nature of scumbags with infected syringes or some shit?
Much worse.
Stay here and keep quiet.
Yeh sure about this? The place could be crawling with them.
That's what I'm hoping.
ORLA!
Oh, fer fuck sake!
What th'fuck am I doing?!
Orla, wait!

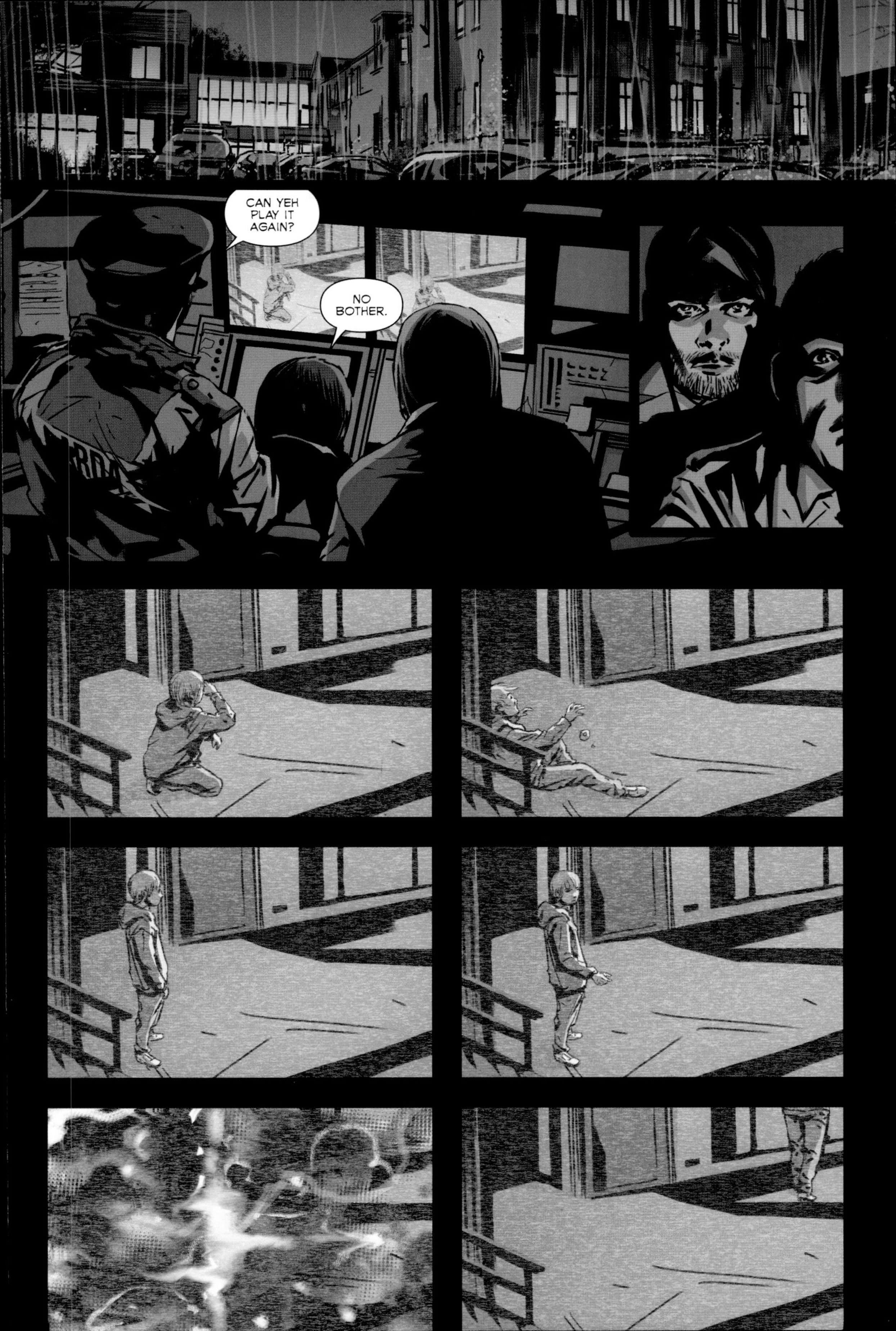
CAN YEH PLAY IT AGAIN?
NO BOTHER.

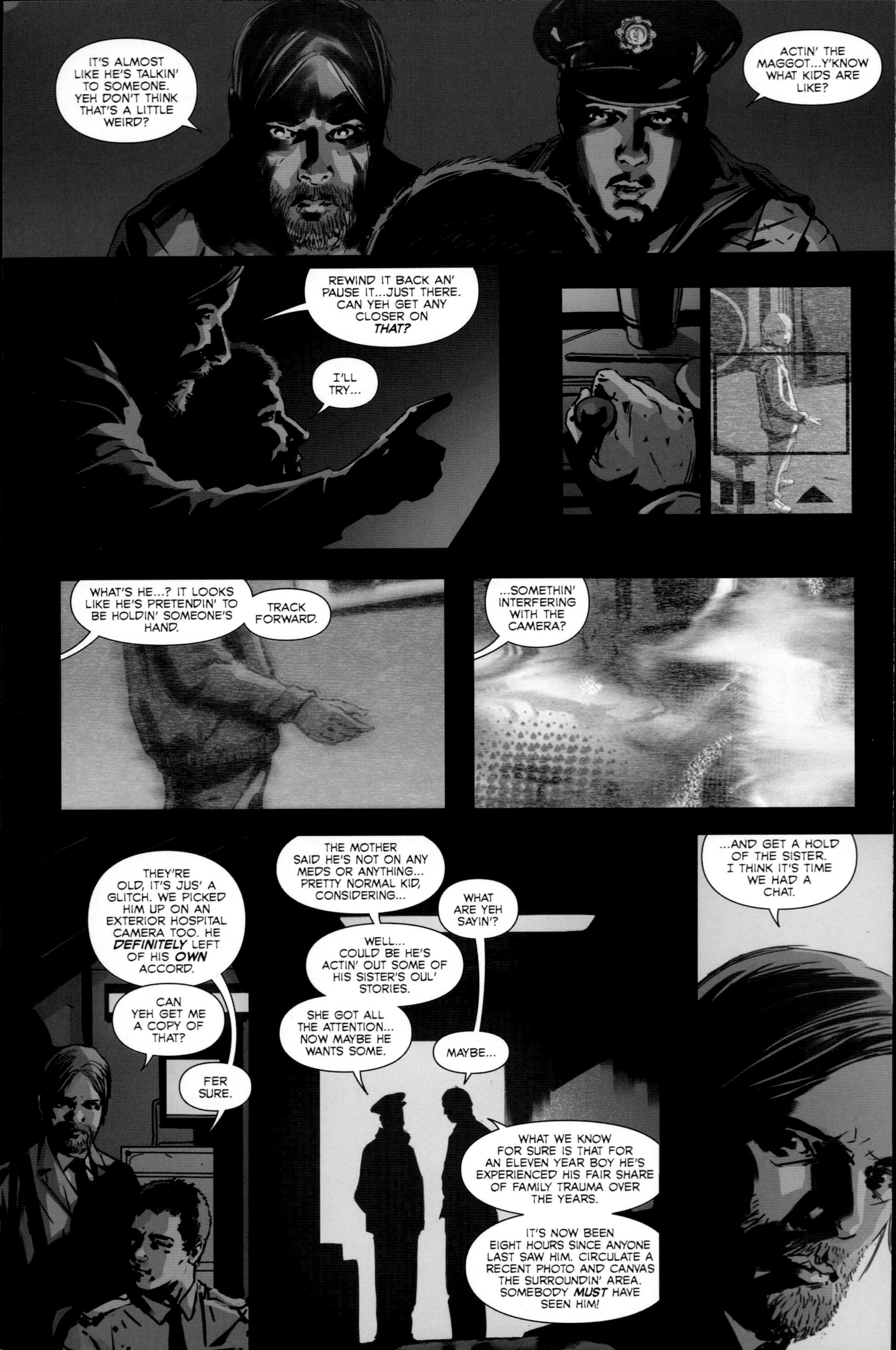
IT'S ALMOST LIKE HE'S TALKIN' TO SOMEONE. YEH DON'T THINK THAT'S A LITTLE WEIRD?
ACTIN' THE MAGGOT...Y'KNOW WHAT KIDS ARE LIKE?
REWIND IT BACK AN' PAUSE IT...JUST THERE. CAN YEH GET ANY CLOSER ON THAT?
I'LL TRY...
WHAT'S HE...? IT LOOKS LIKE HE'S PRETENDIN' TO BE HOLDIN' SOMEONE'S HAND.
TRACK FORWARD.
...SOMETHIN' INTERFERING WITH THE CAMERA?
THEY'RE OLD, IT'S JUS' A GLITCH. WE PICKED HIM UP ON AN EXTERIOR HOSPITAL CAMERA TOO. HE DEFINITELY LEFT OF HIS OWN ACCORD.
CAN YEH GET ME A COPY OF THAT?
FER SURE.
THE MOTHER SAID HE'S NOT ON ANY MEDS OR ANYTHING... PRETTY NORMAL KID, CONSIDERING...
WHAT ARE YEH SAYIN'?
WELL... COULD BE HE'S ACTIN' OUT SOME OF HIS SISTER'S OUL' STORIES.
SHE GOT ALL THE ATTENTION... NOW MAYBE HE WANTS SOME.
MAYBE...
WHAT WE KNOW FOR SURE IS THAT FOR AN ELEVEN YEAR BOY HE'S EXPERIENCED HIS FAIR SHARE OF FAMILY TRAUMA OVER THE YEARS.
IT'S NOW BEEN EIGHT HOURS SINCE ANYONE LAST SAW HIM. CIRCULATE A RECENT PHOTO AND CANVAS THE SURROUNDIN' AREA. SOMEBODY MUST HAVE SEEN HIM!
...AND GET A HOLD OF THE SISTER. I THINK IT'S TIME WE HAD A CHAT.

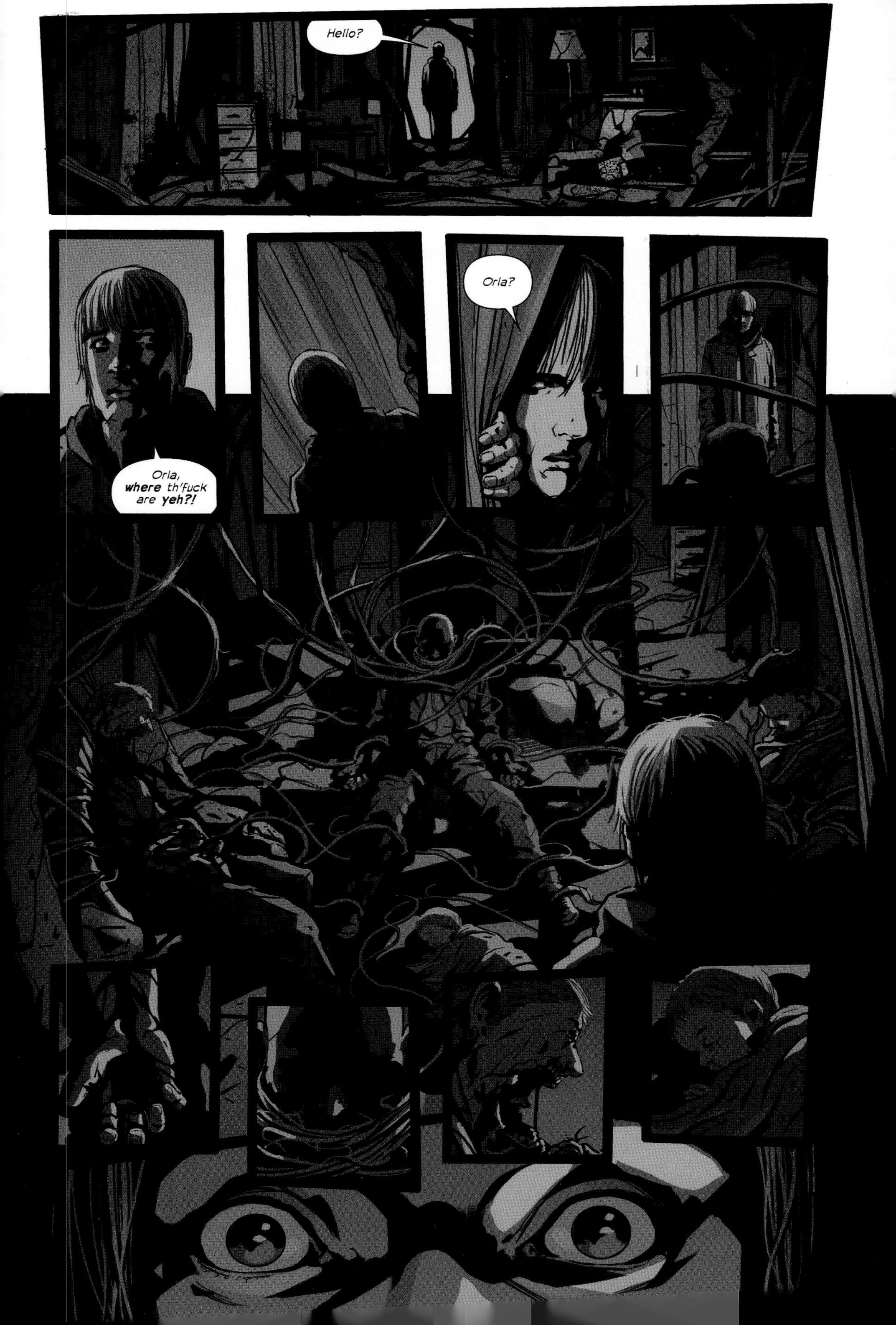
Hello?
Orla,
where th'fuck
are yeh?!
Orla?

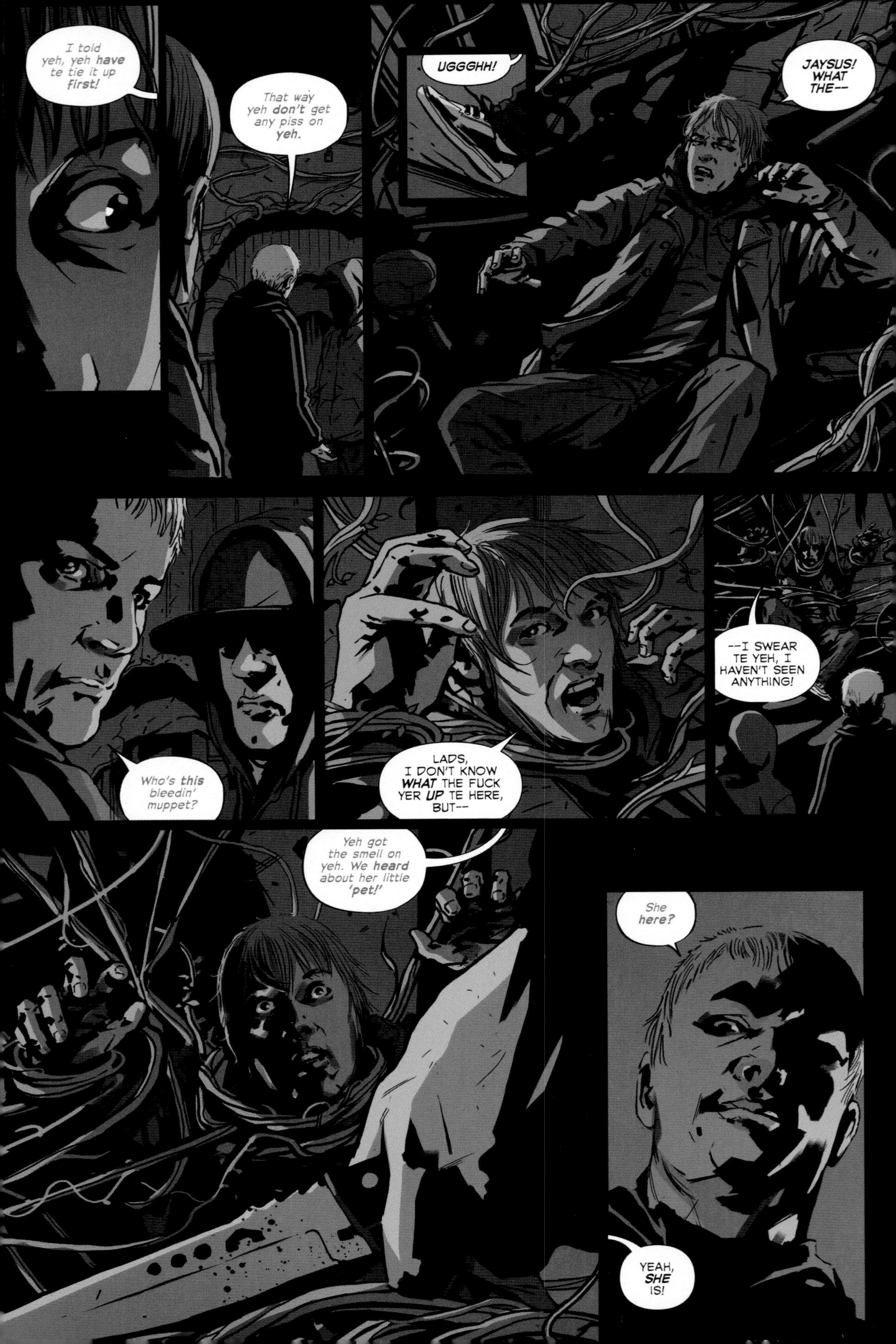
I told yeh, yeh **have** te tie it up **first!**
That way yeh **don't** get any piss on **yeh.**
UGGGHH!
JAYSUS! WHAT THE--
Who's **this** bleedin' muppet?
LADS, I DON'T KNOW **WHAT** THE FUCK YER **UP** TE HERE, BUT--
--I SWEAR TE YEH, I HAVEN'T SEEN ANYTHING!
Yeh got the smell on yeh. **We heard** about her little **'pet!'**
She **here?**
YEAH, **SHE** IS!

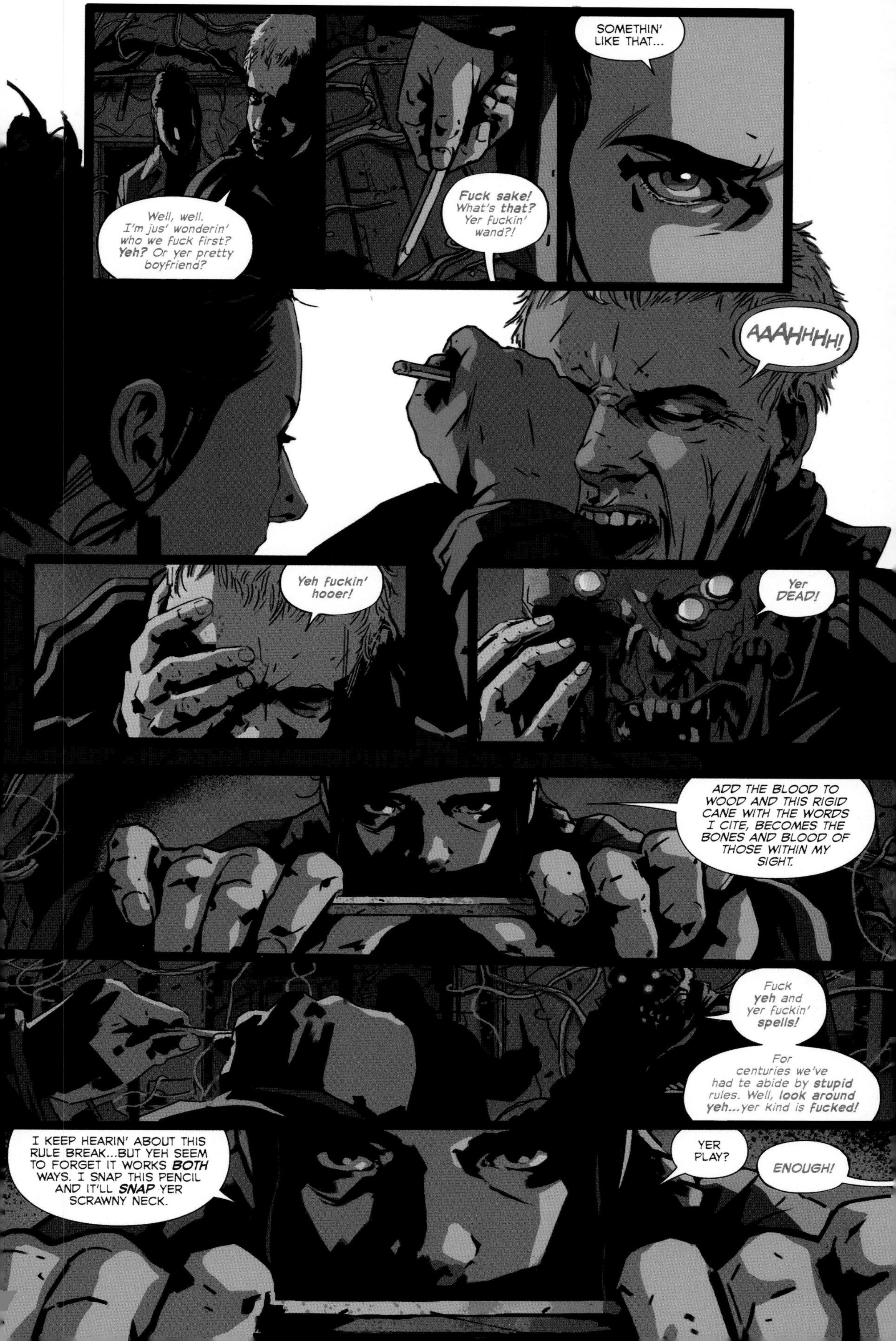
Well, well. I'm jus' wonderin' who we fuck first? Yeh? Or yer pretty boyfriend?
Fuck sake! What's that? Yer fuckin' wand?!
SOMETHIN' LIKE THAT...
AAAHHHH!
Yeh fuckin' hooer!
Yer DEAD!
ADD THE BLOOD TO WOOD AND THIS RIGID CANE WITH THE WORDS I CITE, BECOMES THE BONES AND BLOOD OF THOSE WITHIN MY SIGHT.
Fuck yeh and yer fuckin' spells!
For centuries we've had te abide by stupid rules. Well, look around yeh...yer kind is fucked!
I KEEP HEARIN' ABOUT THIS RULE BREAK...BUT YEH SEEM TO FORGET IT WORKS BOTH WAYS. I SNAP THIS PENCIL AND IT'LL SNAP YER SCRAWNY NECK.
YER PLAY?
ENOUGH!

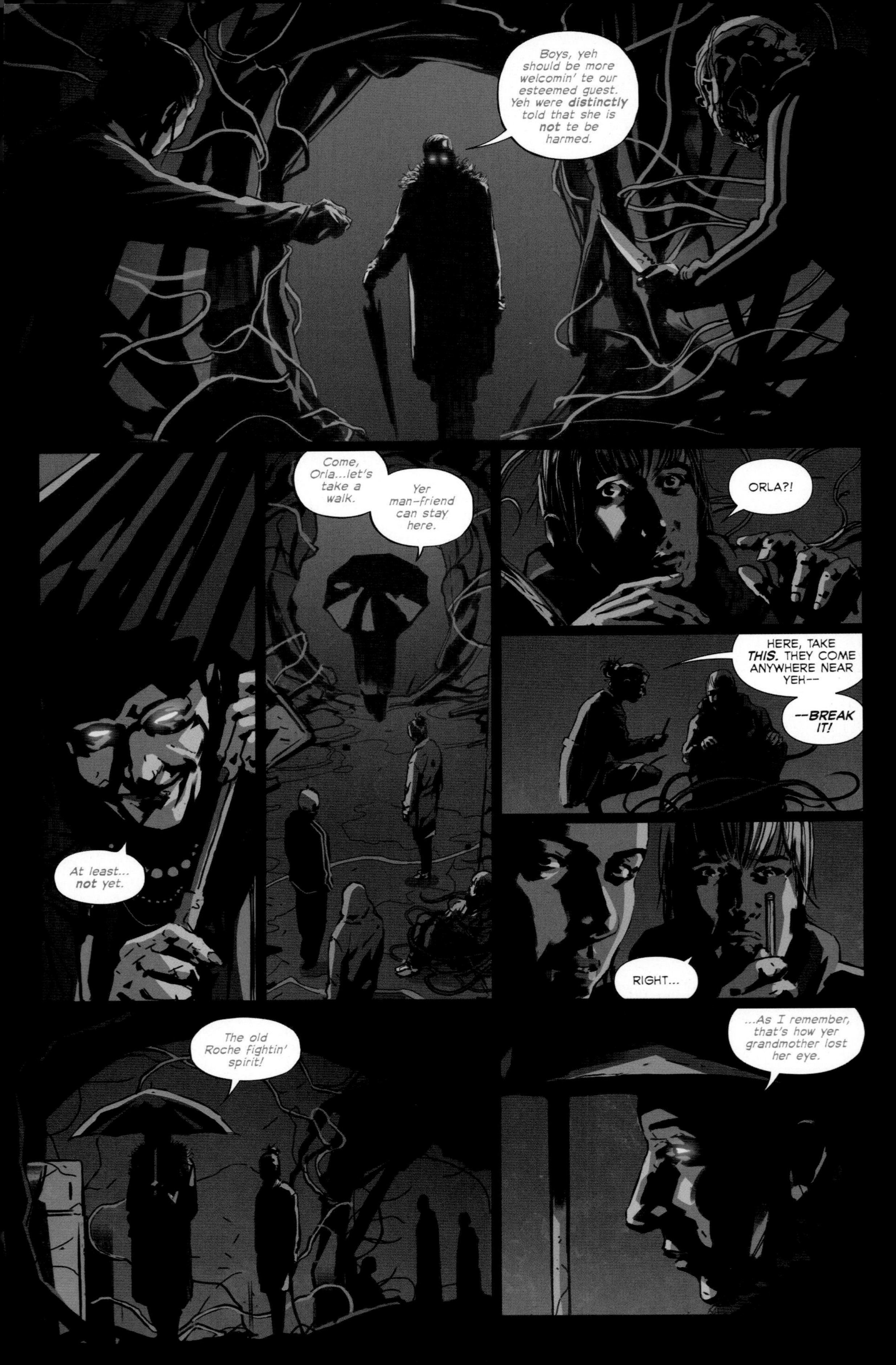
Boys, yeh should be more welcomin' te our esteemed guest. Yeh were **distinctly** told that she is **not** te be harmed.
At least... **not** yet.
Come, Orla...let's take a walk.
Yer man-friend can stay here.
ORLA?!
HERE, TAKE **THIS.** THEY COME ANYWHERE NEAR YEH--
--BREAK IT!
RIGHT...
The old Roche fightin' spirit!
...As I remember, that's how yer grandmother lost her eye.

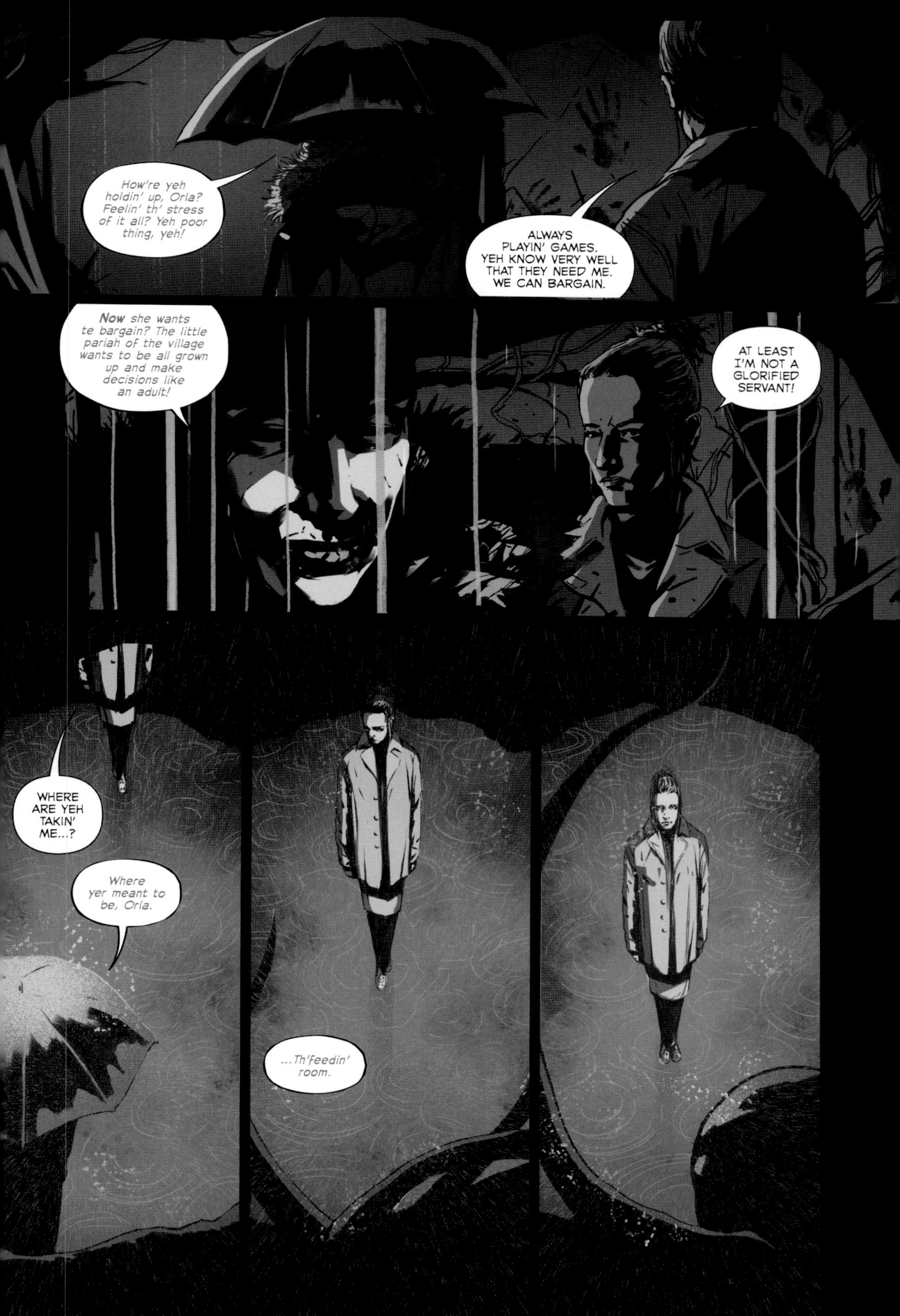
How're yeh holdin' up, Orla? Feelin' th' stress of it all? Yeh poor thing, yeh!
ALWAYS PLAYIN' GAMES. YEH KNOW VERY WELL THAT THEY NEED ME. WE CAN BARGAIN.
Now she wants te bargain? The little pariah of the village wants to be all grown up and make decisions like an adult!
AT LEAST I'M NOT A GLORIFIED SERVANT!
WHERE ARE YEH TAKIN' ME...?
Where yer meant to be, Orla.
...Th'feedin' room.

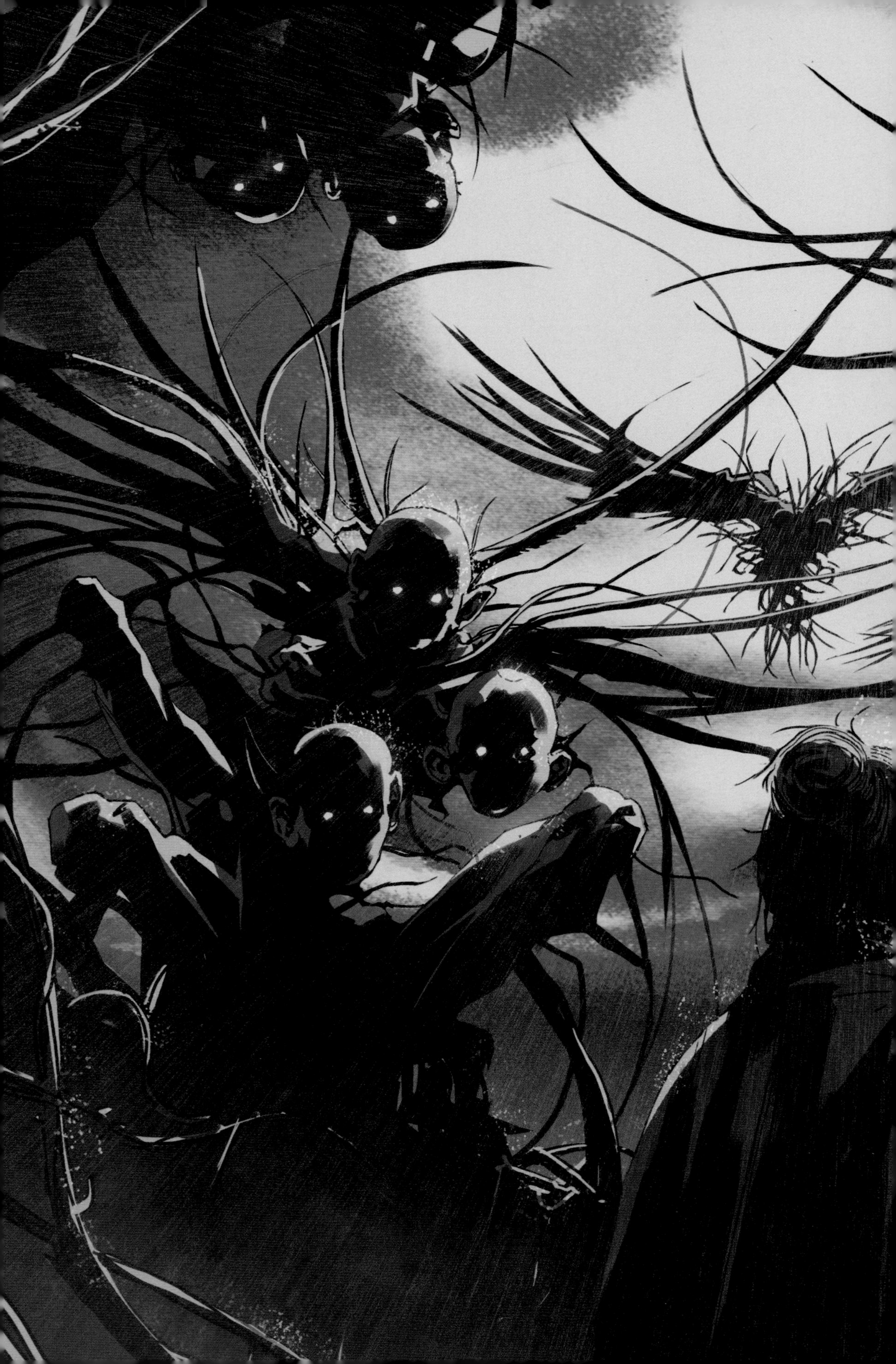

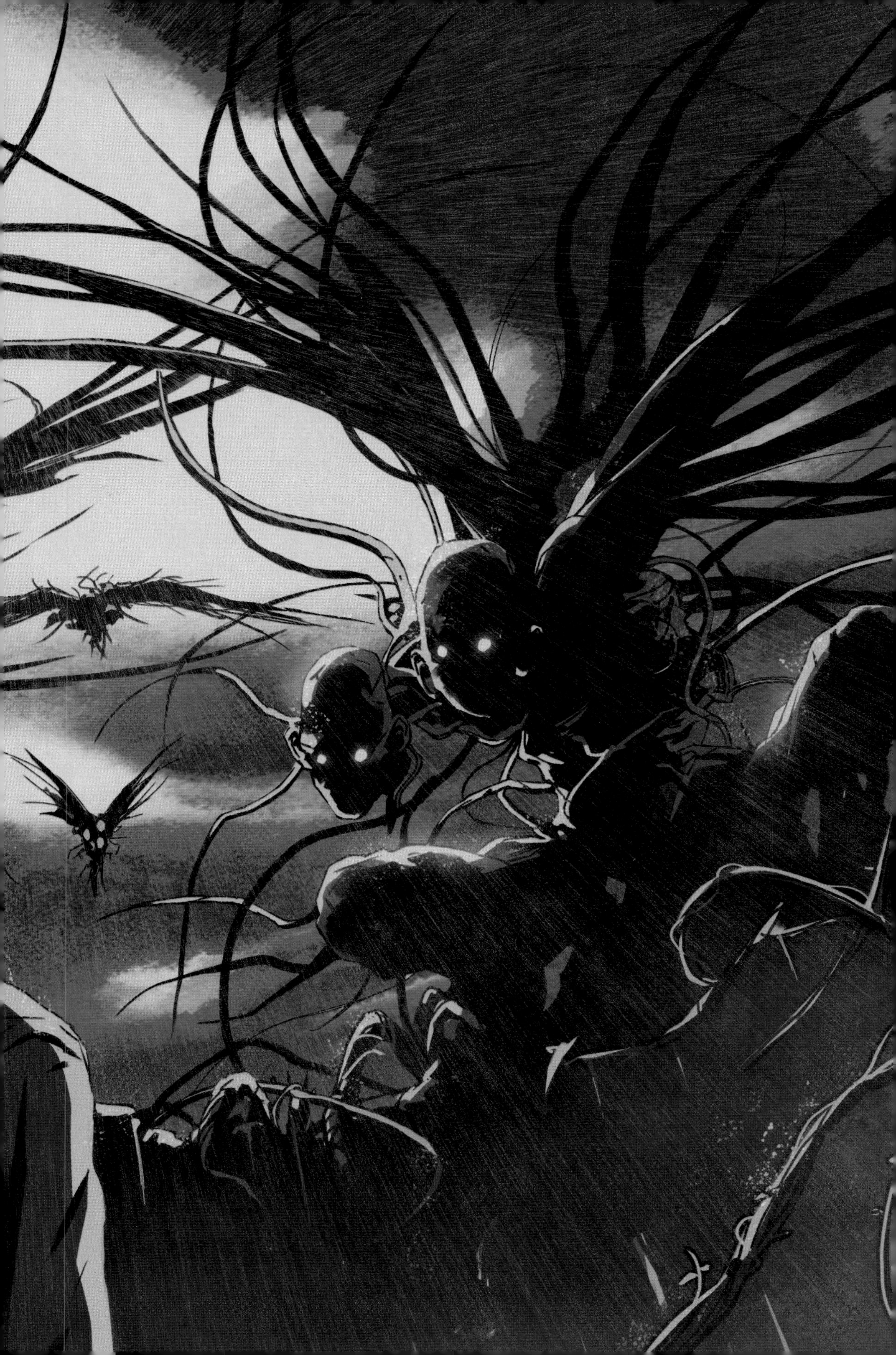

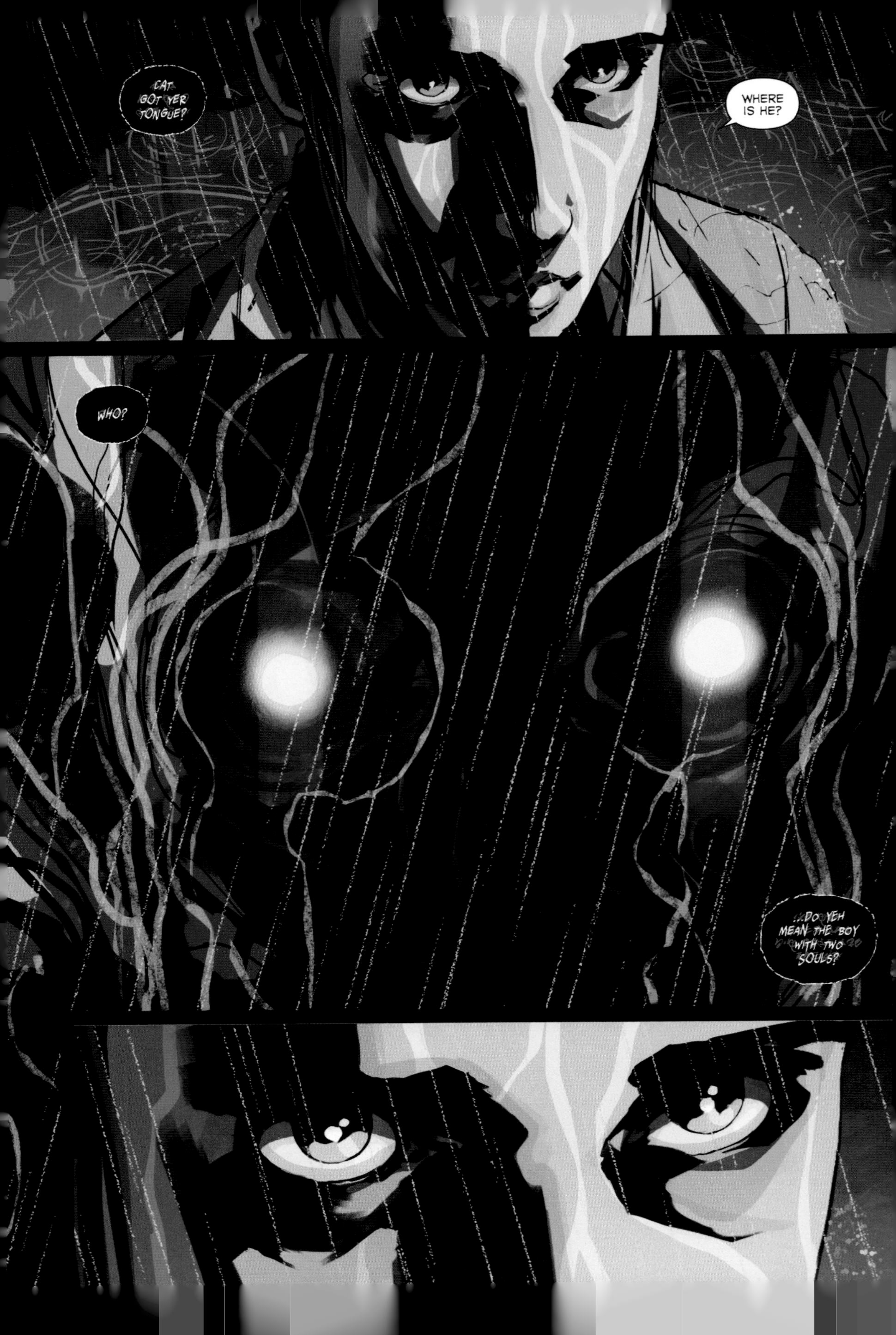
CAT GOT YER TONGUE?
WHERE IS HE?
WHO?
...DO YEH MEAN THE BOY WITH TWO SOULS?

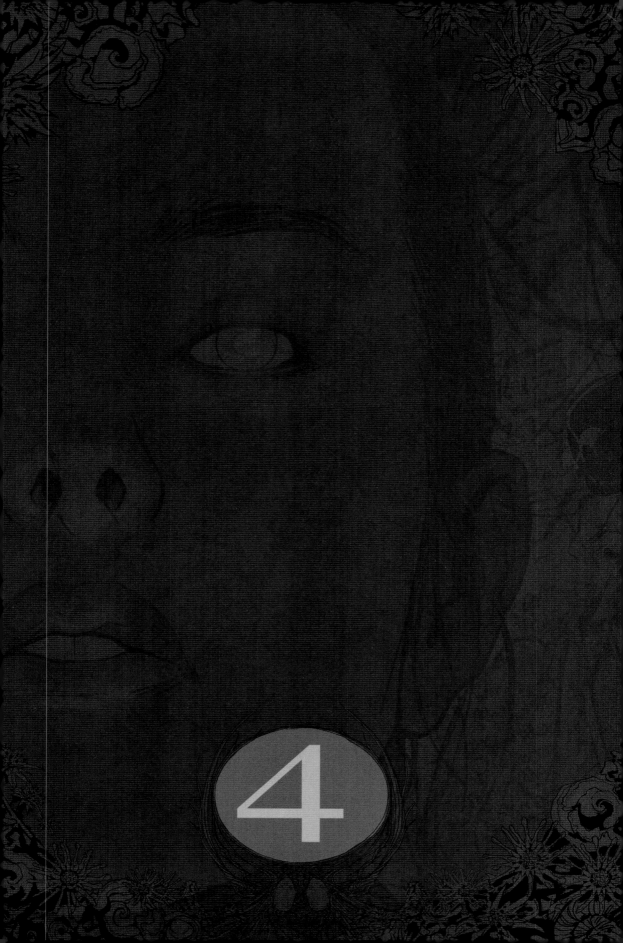

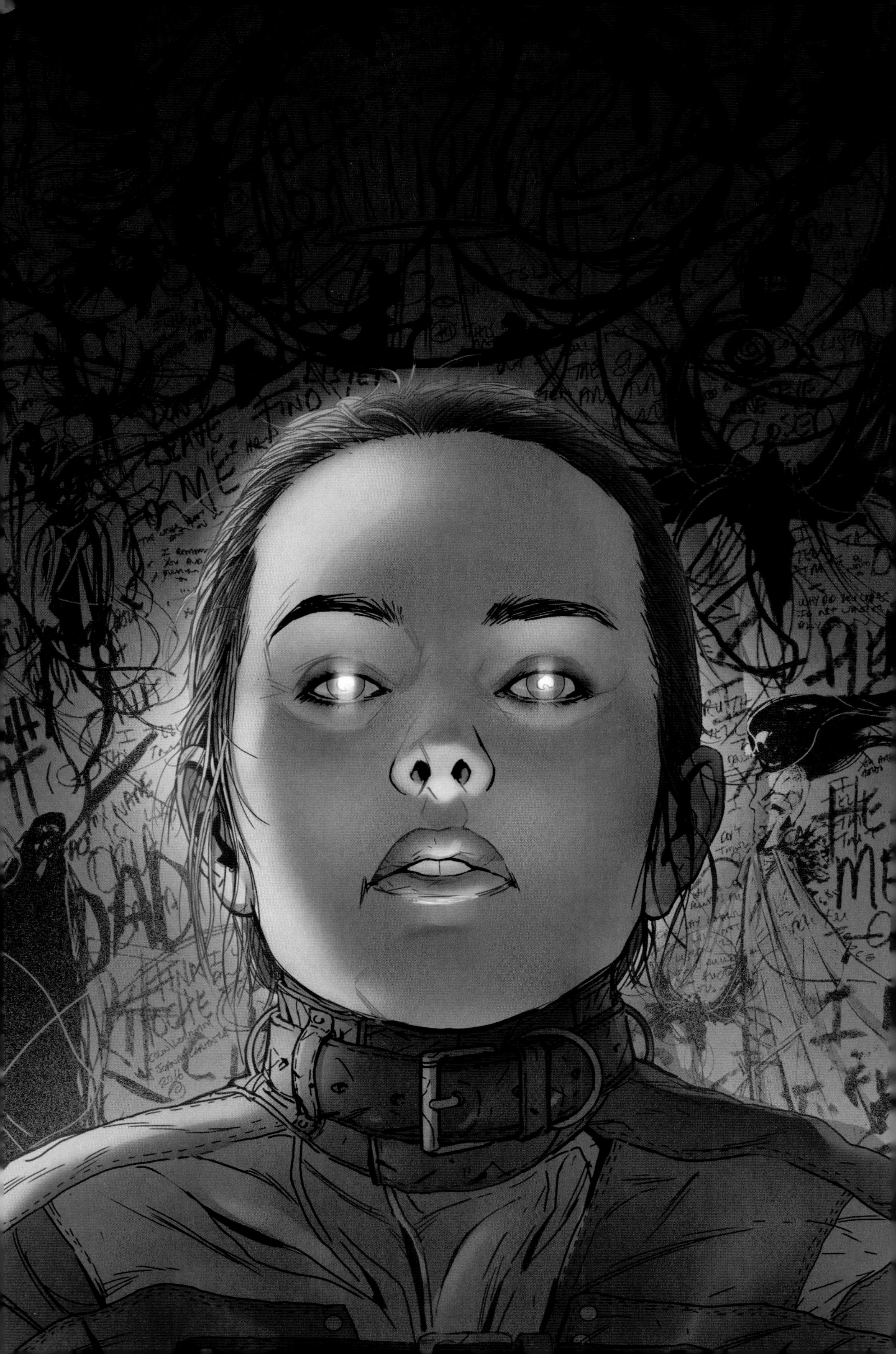

FIND
DAD

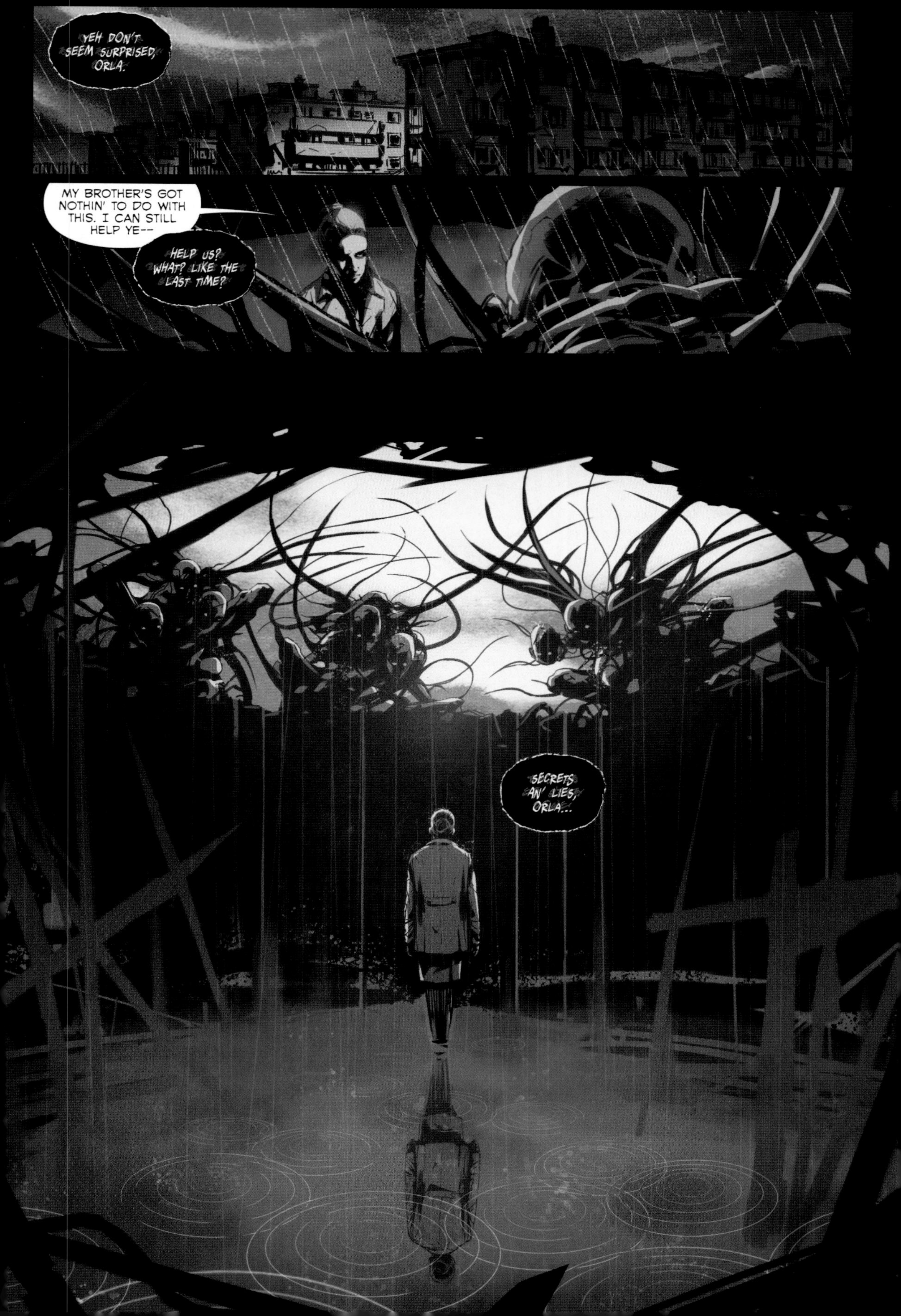
YEH DON'T SEEM SURPRISED, ORLA.
MY BROTHER'S GOT NOTHIN' TO DO WITH THIS. I CAN STILL HELP YE--
HELP US? WHAT? LIKE THE LAST TIME?
SECRETS AN' LIES, ORLA...

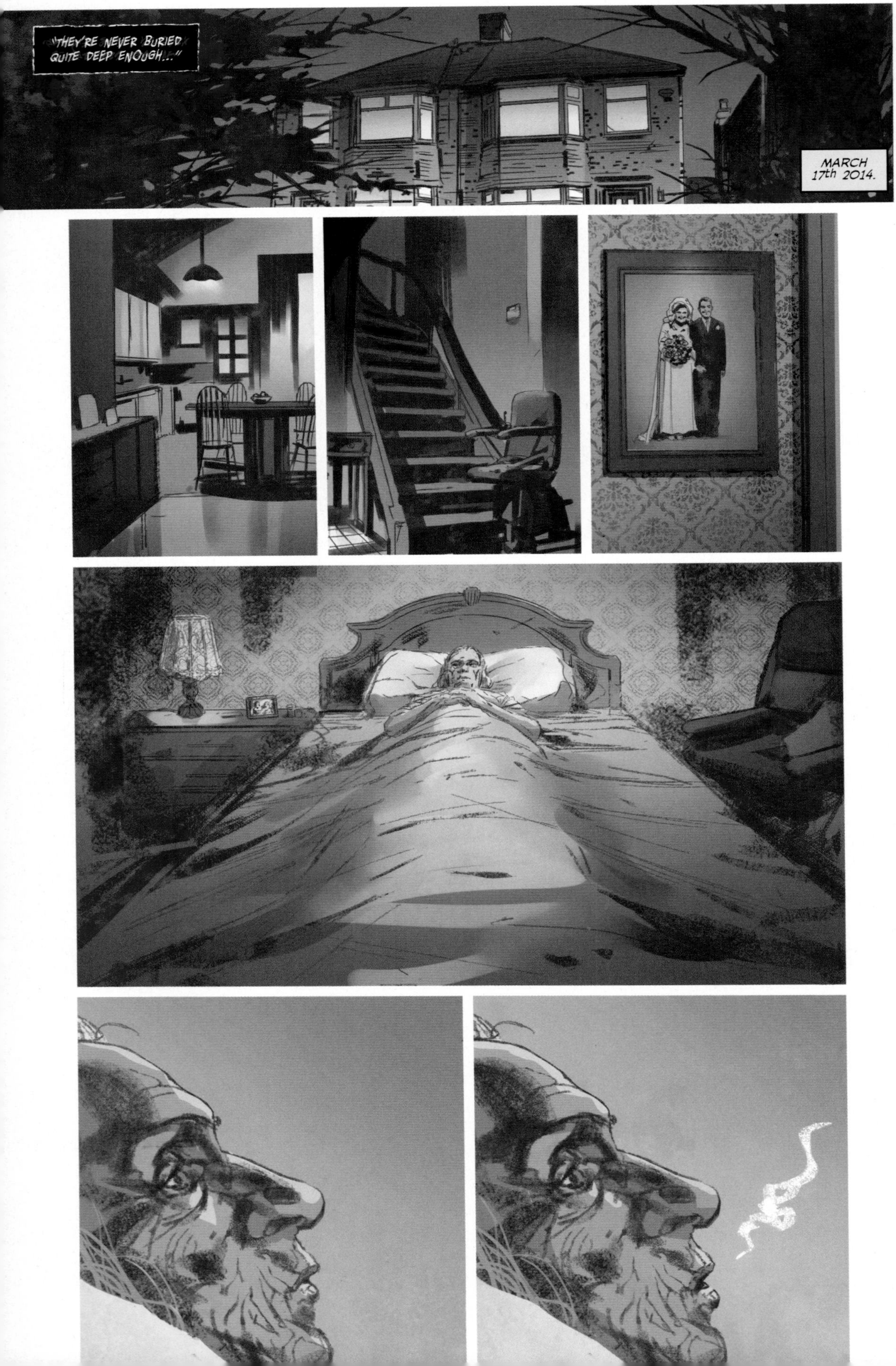
"THEY'RE NEVER BURIED QUITE DEEP ENOUGH..."
MARCH 17th 2014.

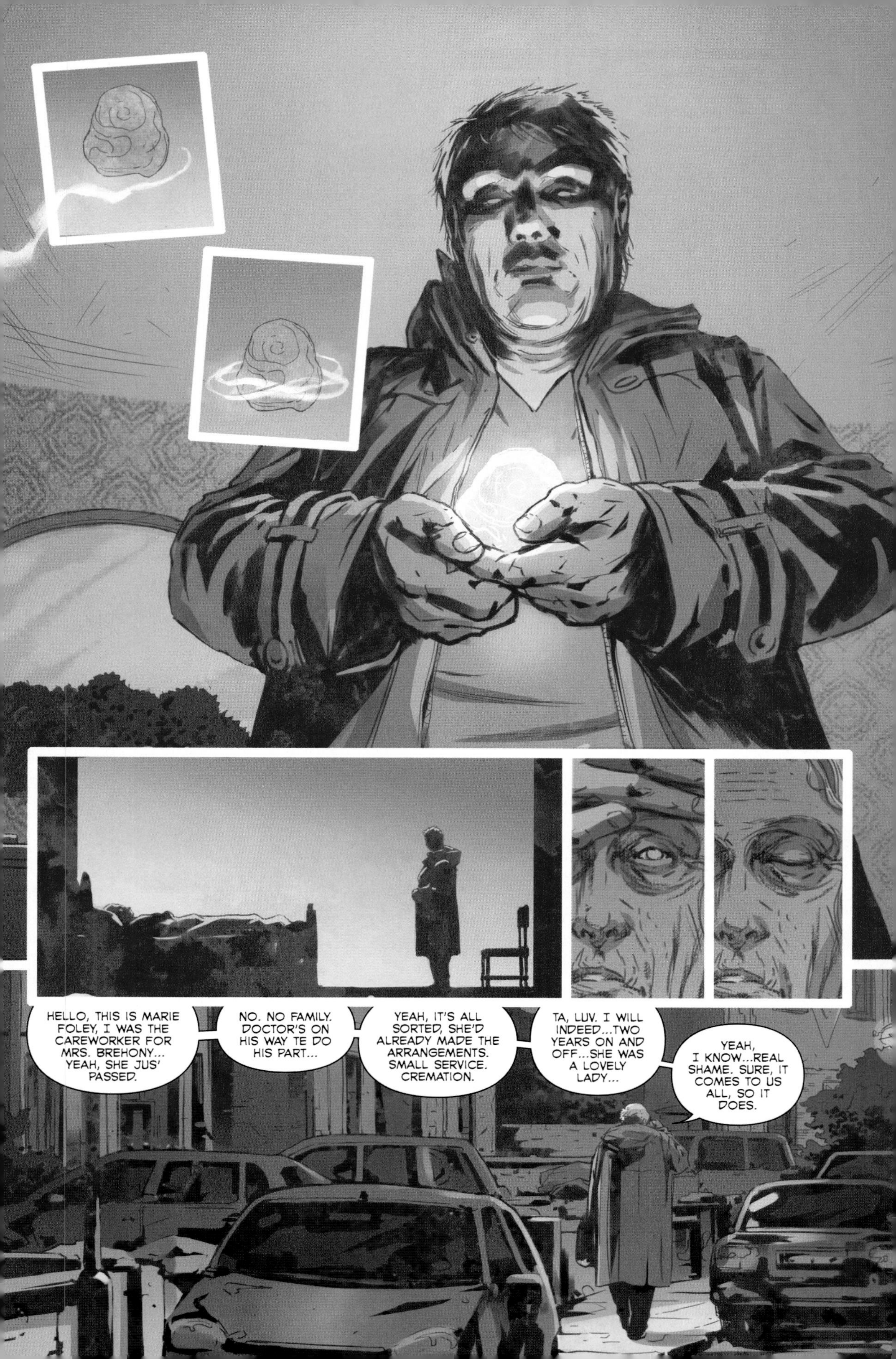
HELLO, THIS IS MARIE FOLEY, I WAS THE CAREWORKER FOR MRS. BREHONY... YEAH, SHE JUS' PASSED.
NO. NO FAMILY. DOCTOR'S ON HIS WAY TE DO HIS PART...
YEAH, IT'S ALL SORTED, SHE'D ALREADY MADE THE ARRANGEMENTS. SMALL SERVICE. CREMATION.
TA, LUV. I WILL INDEED...TWO YEARS ON AND OFF...SHE WAS A LOVELY LADY...
YEAH, I KNOW...REAL SHAME. SURE, IT COMES TO US ALL, SO IT DOES.

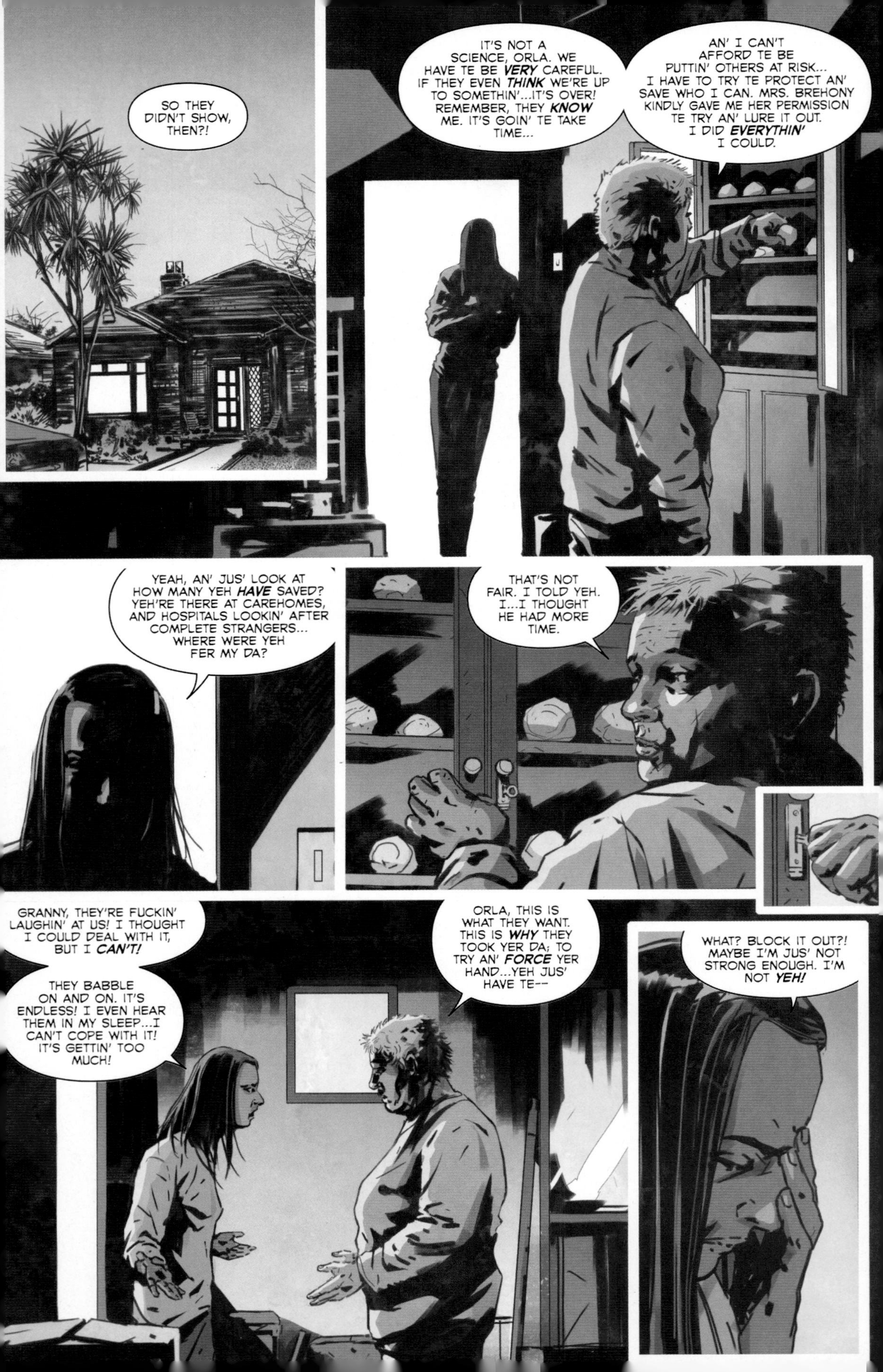

SO THEY DIDN'T SHOW, THEN?!
IT'S NOT A SCIENCE, ORLA. WE HAVE TE BE VERY CAREFUL. IF THEY EVEN THINK WE'RE UP TO SOMETHIN'...IT'S OVER! REMEMBER, THEY KNOW ME. IT'S GOIN' TE TAKE TIME...
AN' I CAN'T AFFORD TE BE PUTTIN' OTHERS AT RISK... I HAVE TO TRY TE PROTECT AN' SAVE WHO I CAN. MRS. BREHONY KINDLY GAVE ME HER PERMISSION TE TRY AN' LURE IT OUT. I DID EVERYTHIN' I COULD.
YEAH, AN' JUS' LOOK AT HOW MANY YEH HAVE SAVED? YEH'RE THERE AT CAREHOMES, AND HOSPITALS LOOKIN' AFTER COMPLETE STRANGERS... WHERE WERE YEH FER MY DA?
THAT'S NOT FAIR. I TOLD YEH. I...I THOUGHT HE HAD MORE TIME.
GRANNY, THEY'RE FUCKIN' LAUGHIN' AT US! I THOUGHT I COULD DEAL WITH IT, BUT I CAN'T!
THEY BABBLE ON AND ON. IT'S ENDLESS! I EVEN HEAR THEM IN MY SLEEP...I CAN'T COPE WITH IT! IT'S GETTIN' TOO MUCH!
ORLA, THIS IS WHAT THEY WANT. THIS IS WHY THEY TOOK YER DA; TO TRY AN' FORCE YER HAND...YEH JUS' HAVE TE--
WHAT? BLOCK IT OUT?! MAYBE I'M JUS' NOT STRONG ENOUGH. I'M NOT YEH!

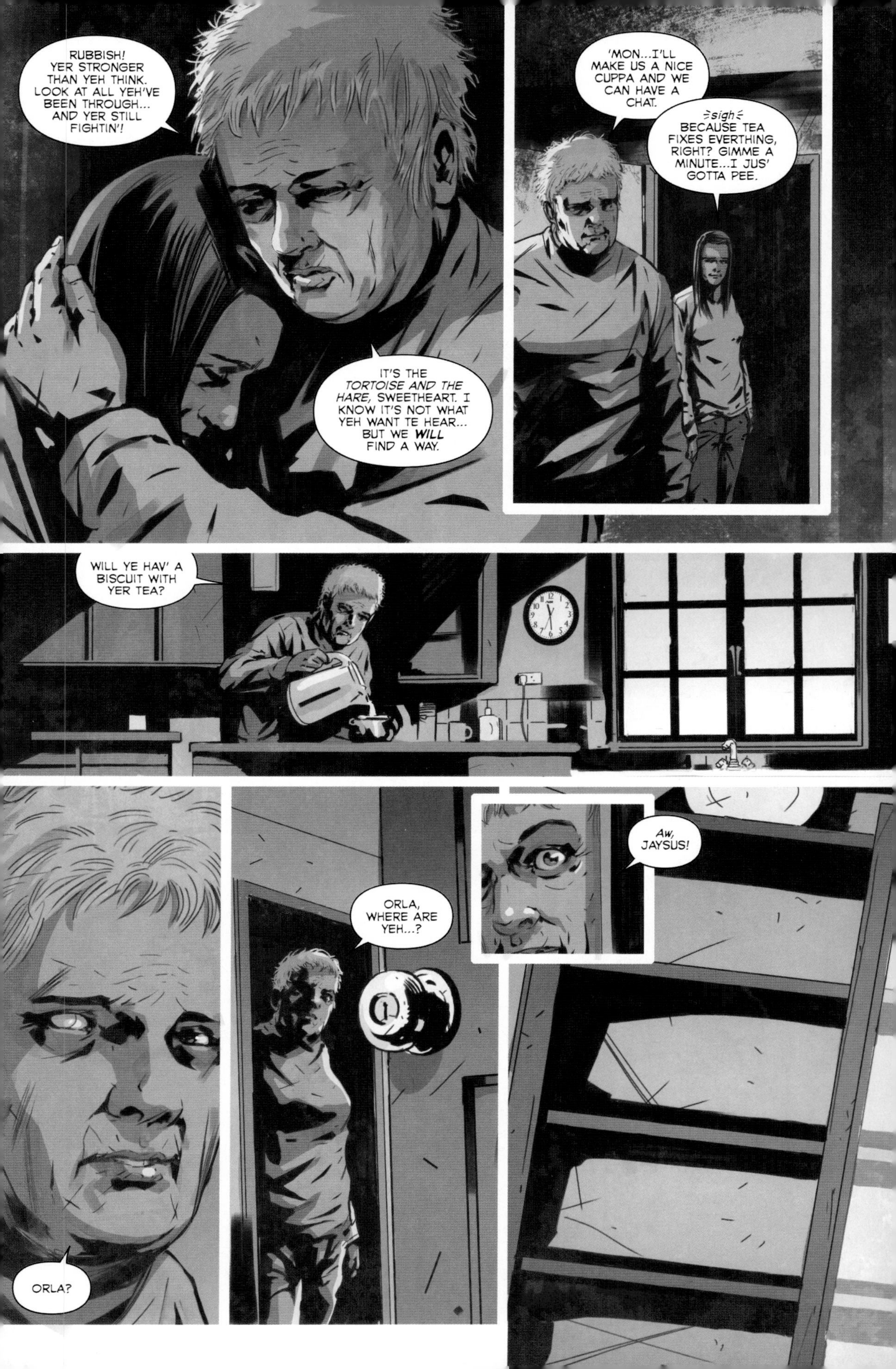
RUBBISH! YER STRONGER THAN YEH THINK. LOOK AT ALL YEH'VE BEEN THROUGH... AND YER STILL FIGHTIN'!
IT'S THE *TORTOISE AND THE HARE,* SWEETHEART. I KNOW IT'S NOT WHAT YEH WANT TE HEAR... BUT WE ***WILL*** FIND A WAY.
'MON...I'LL MAKE US A NICE CUPPA AND WE CAN HAVE A CHAT.
sigh BECAUSE TEA FIXES EVERTHING, RIGHT? GIMME A MINUTE...I JUS' GOTTA PEE.
WILL YE HAV' A BISCUIT WITH YER TEA?
ORLA?
ORLA, WHERE ARE YEH...?
AW, JAYSUS!

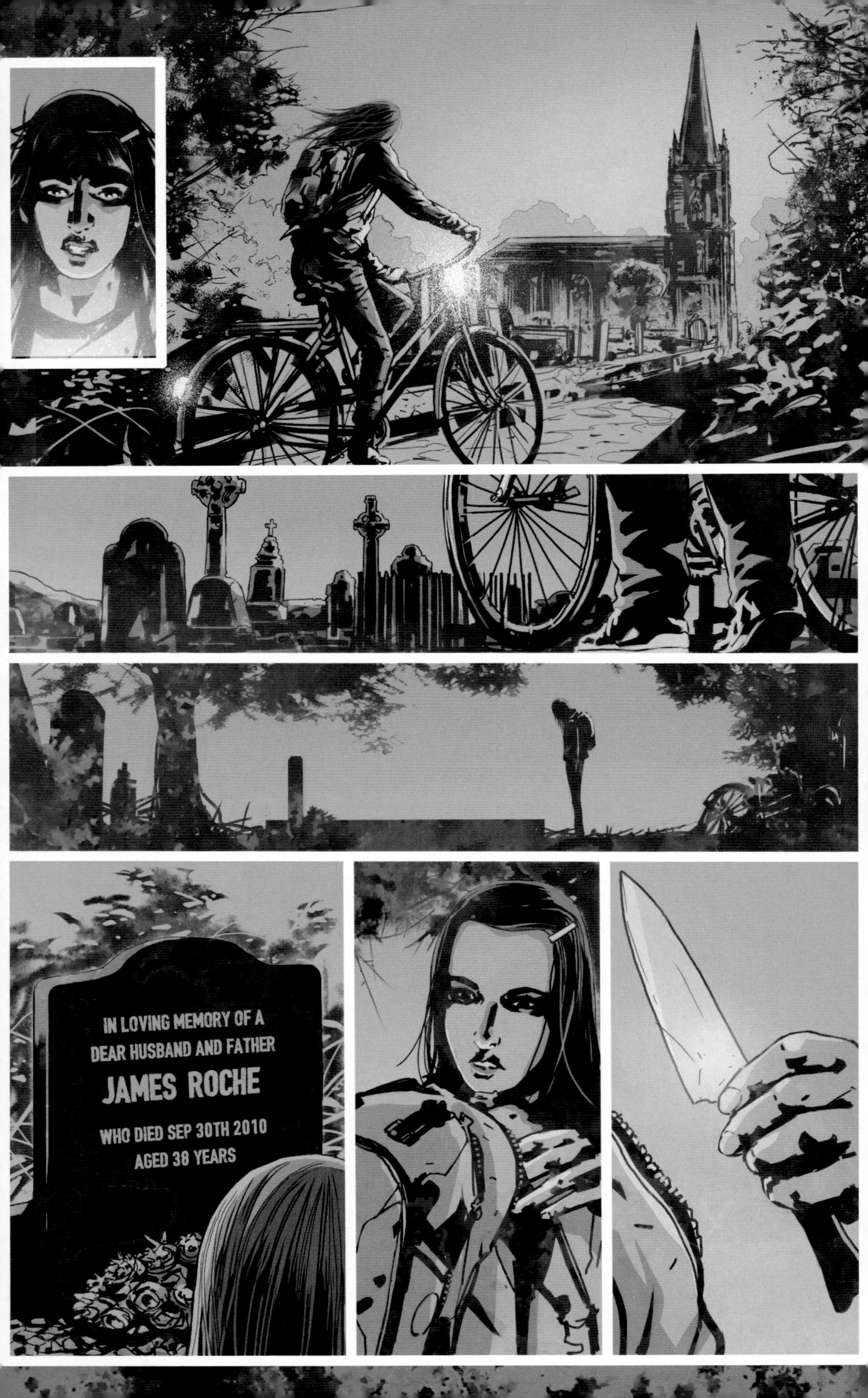
IN LOVING MEMORY OF A
DEAR HUSBAND AND FATHER
JAMES ROCHE
WHO DIED SEP 30TH 2010
AGED 38 YEARS

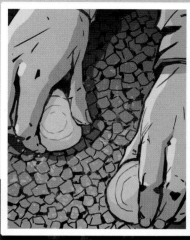

AHHHHHH!

EYE THAT HAS SEEN...

...CONJURES UP THE ONE REMEMBERED FROM INBETWEEN.

...AN OFFERIN' ARRANGED, FER THE PURPOSE OF EXCHANGE.

C'mon, c'mon...Where are yeh?

HOW KIND...YEH BROUGHT GIFTS.

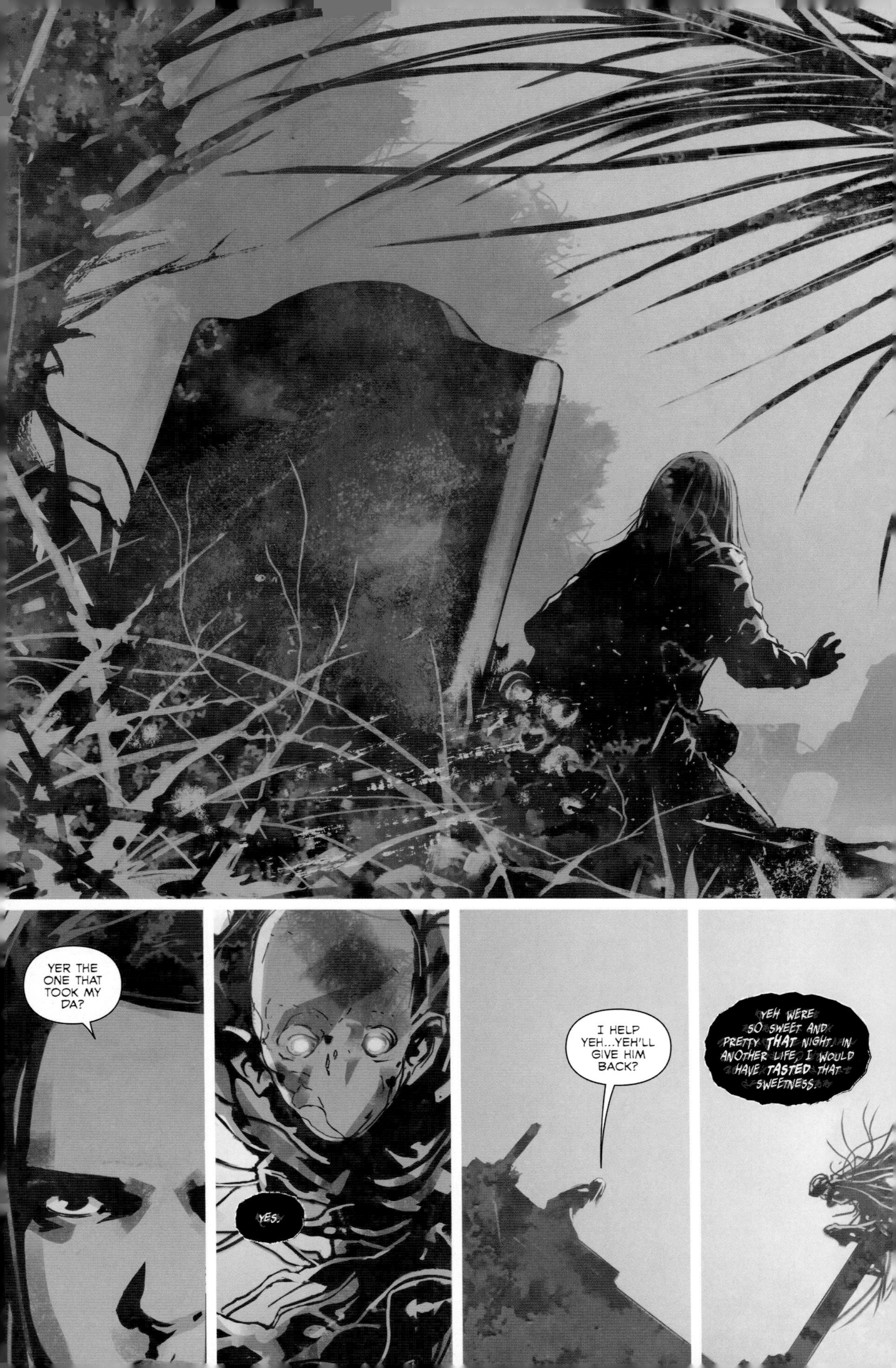

YER THE ONE THAT TOOK MY DA?
YES.
I HELP YEH...YEH'LL GIVE HIM BACK?
YEH WERE SO SWEET AND PRETTY THAT NIGHT. IN ANOTHER LIFE, I WOULD HAVE TASTED THAT SWEETNESS.

ANSWER ME!

YES

YEH HAVE HIM WITH YEH?

IT'S ALWAYS WITH US.

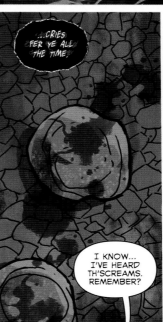

...CRIES FER YE ALL THE TIME...

I KNOW... I'VE HEARD TH'SCREAMS. REMEMBER?

WELL, NOW YEH HAVE THE CHANCE TE SILENCE THEM.

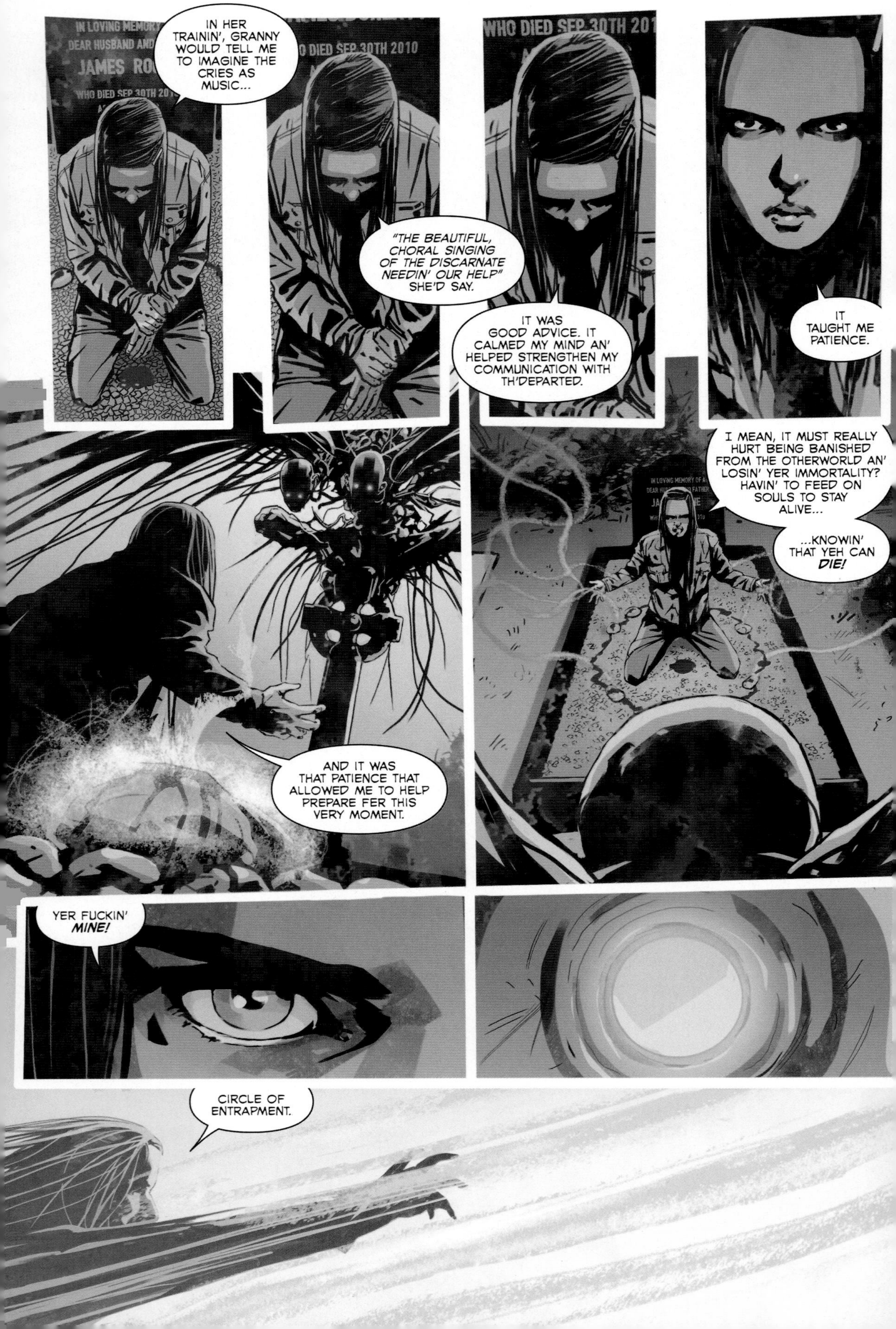
IN LOVING MEMORY
DEAR HUSBAND AND
JAMES RO
WHO DIED SEP 30TH 201
IN HER TRAININ', GRANNY WOULD TELL ME TO IMAGINE THE CRIES AS MUSIC...
WHO DIED SEP 30TH 2010
"THE BEAUTIFUL, CHORAL SINGING OF THE DISCARNATE NEEDIN' OUR HELP" SHE'D SAY.
WHO DIED SEP 30TH 201
IT WAS GOOD ADVICE. IT CALMED MY MIND AN' HELPED STRENGTHEN MY COMMUNICATION WITH TH'DEPARTED.
IT TAUGHT ME PATIENCE.
AND IT WAS THAT PATIENCE THAT ALLOWED ME TO HELP PREPARE FER THIS VERY MOMENT.
I MEAN, IT MUST REALLY HURT BEING BANISHED FROM THE OTHERWORLD AN' LOSIN' YER IMMORTALITY? HAVIN' TO FEED ON SOULS TO STAY ALIVE...
...KNOWIN' THAT YEH CAN *DIE!*
YER FUCKIN' *MINE!*
CIRCLE OF ENTRAPMENT.

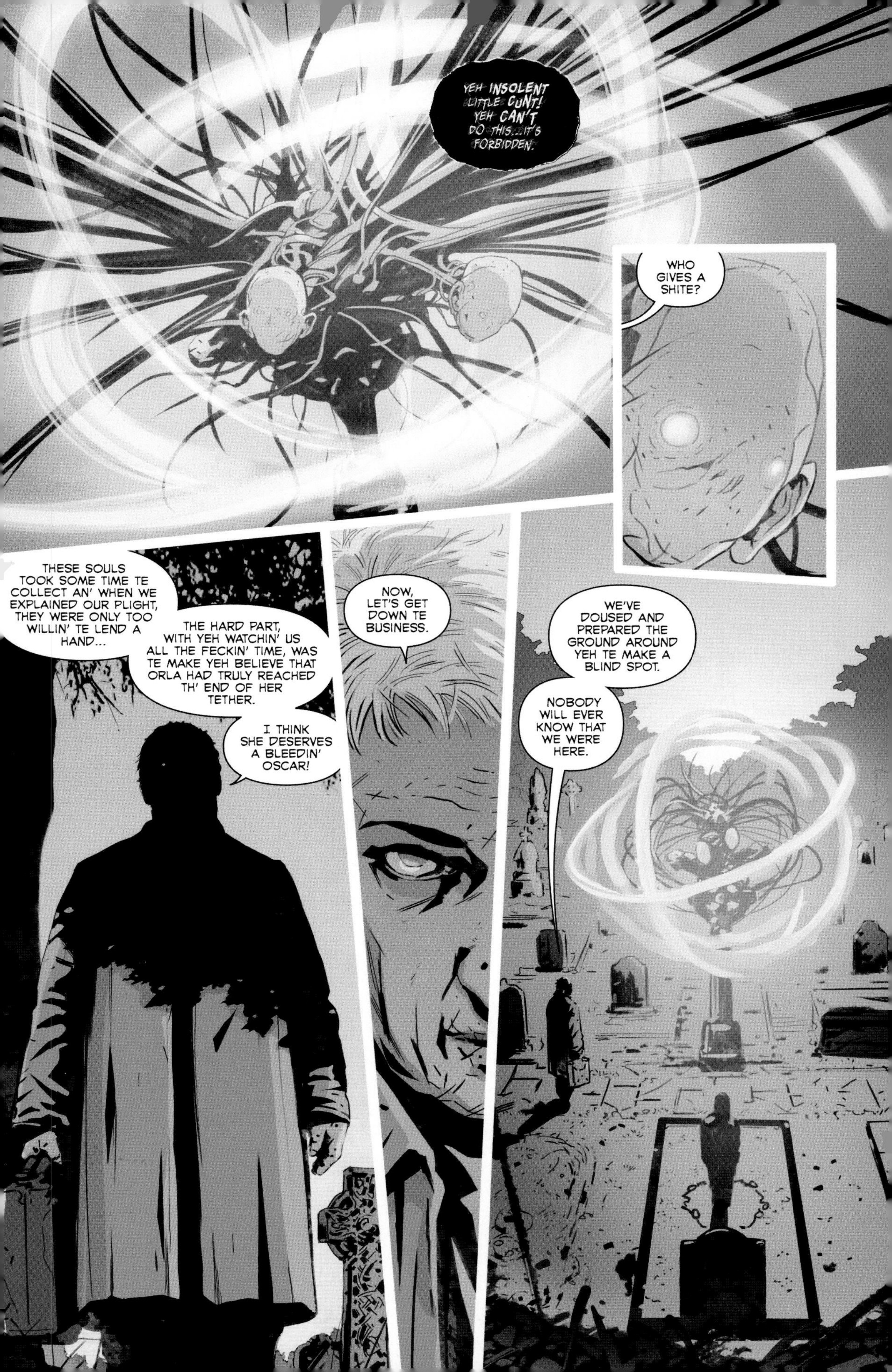
YEH INSOLENT LITTLE CUNT! YEH CAN'T DO THIS...IT'S FORBIDDEN.
WHO GIVES A SHITE?
THESE SOULS TOOK SOME TIME TE COLLECT AN' WHEN WE EXPLAINED OUR PLIGHT, THEY WERE ONLY TOO WILLIN' TE LEND A HAND...
THE HARD PART, WITH YEH WATCHIN' US ALL THE FECKIN' TIME, WAS TE MAKE YEH BELIEVE THAT ORLA HAD TRULY REACHED TH' END OF HER TETHER.
I THINK SHE DESERVES A BLEEDIN' OSCAR!
NOW, LET'S GET DOWN TE BUSINESS.
WE'VE DOUSED AND PREPARED THE GROUND AROUND YEH TE MAKE A BLIND SPOT.
NOBODY WILL EVER KNOW THAT WE WERE HERE.

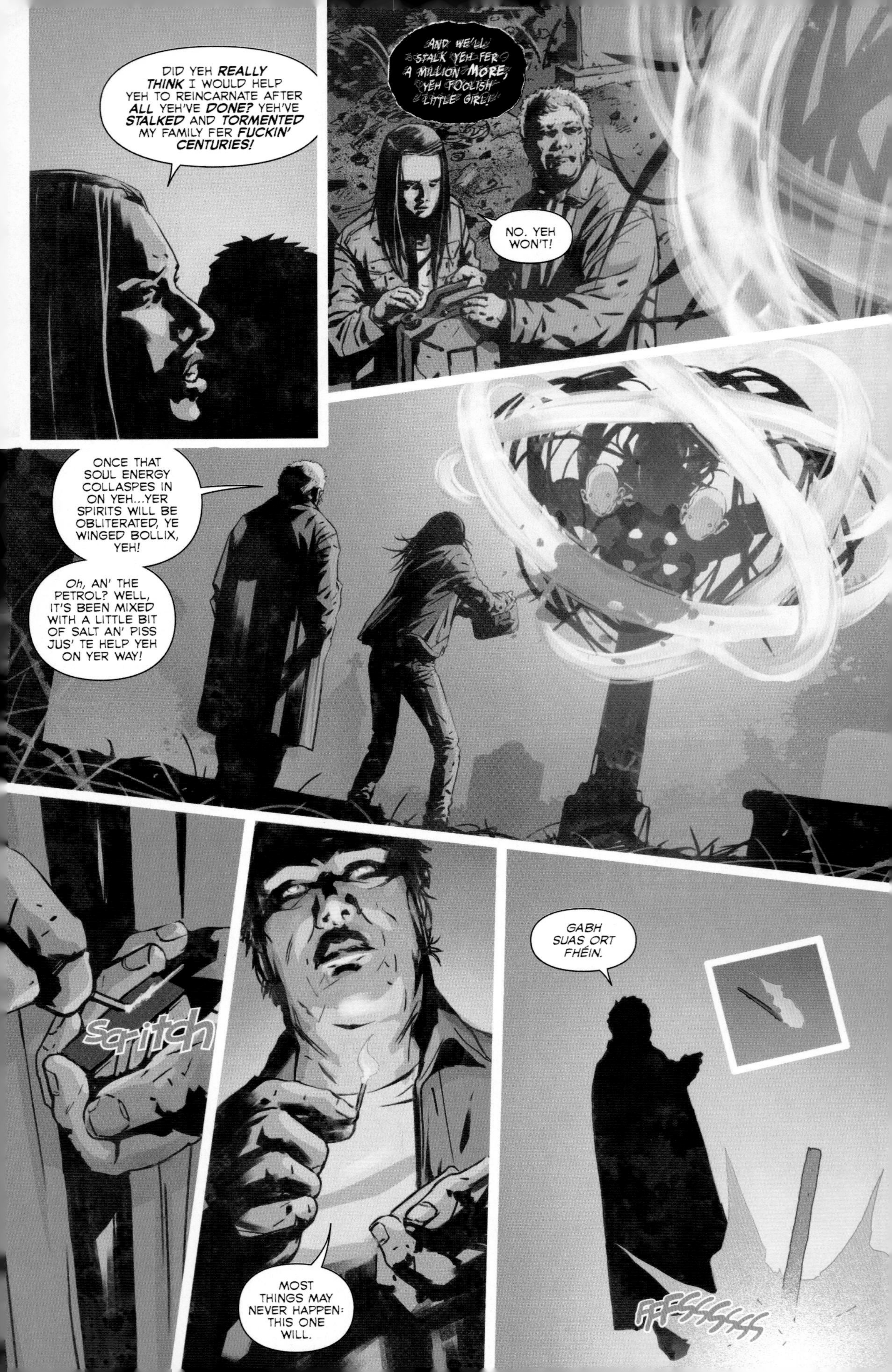
DID YEH REALLY THINK I WOULD HELP YEH TO REINCARNATE AFTER ALL YEH'VE DONE? YEH'VE STALKED AND TORMENTED MY FAMILY FER FUCKIN' CENTURIES!
AND WE'LL STALK YEH FER A MILLION MORE, YEH FOOLISH LITTLE GIRL!
NO. YEH WON'T!
ONCE THAT SOUL ENERGY COLLASPES IN ON YEH...YER SPIRITS WILL BE OBLITERATED, YE WINGED BOLLIX, YEH!
Oh, AN' THE PETROL? WELL, IT'S BEEN MIXED WITH A LITTLE BIT OF SALT AN' PISS JUS' TE HELP YEH ON YER WAY!
SCRITCH
MOST THINGS MAY NEVER HAPPEN: THIS ONE WILL.
GABH SUAS ORT FHÉIN.
FFFSSSSSS

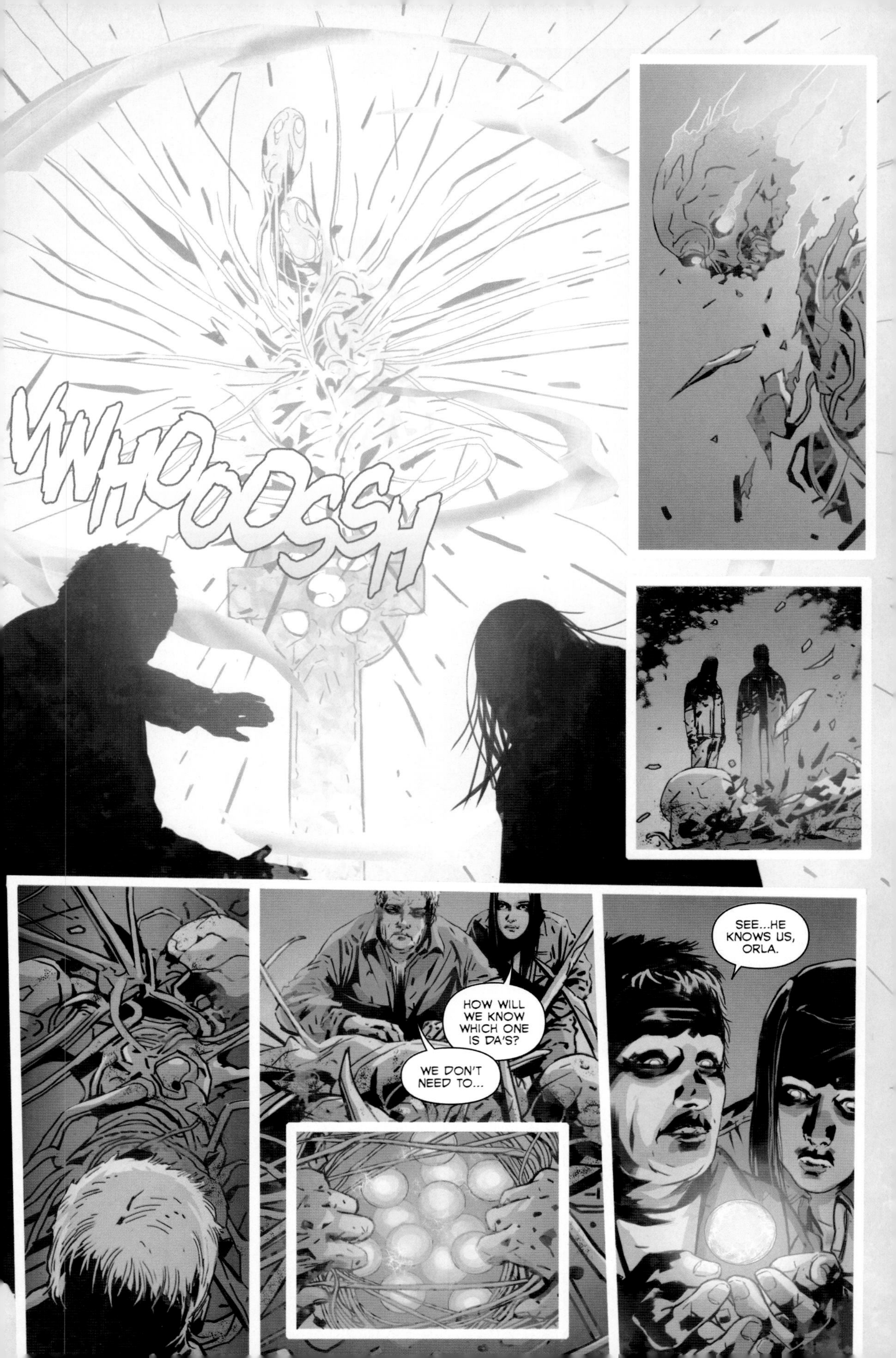
VWHOOOSSH
HOW WILL WE KNOW WHICH ONE IS DA'S?
WE DON'T NEED TO...
SEE...HE KNOWS US, ORLA.

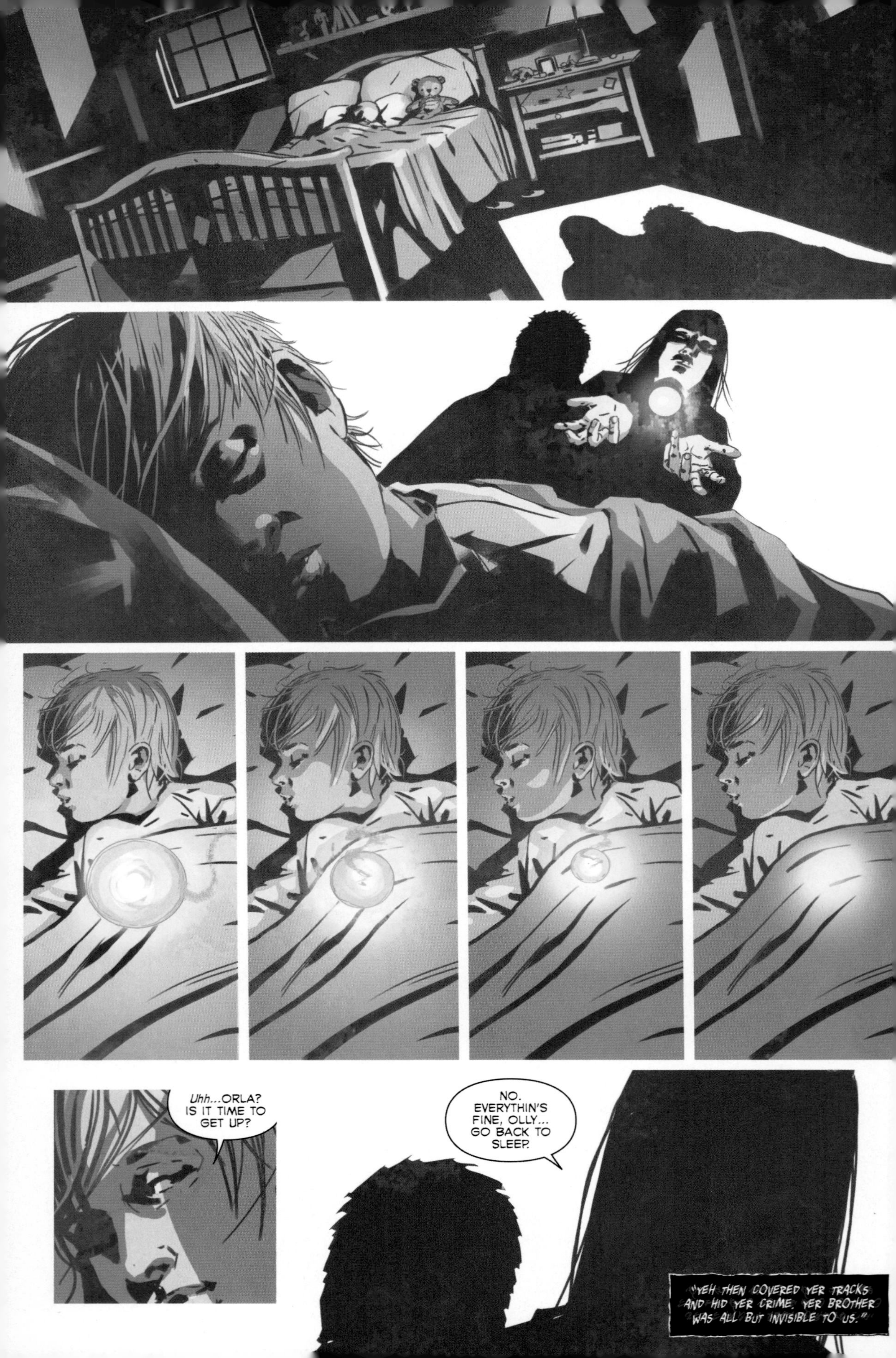
Uhh...ORLA? IS IT TIME TO GET UP?
NO. EVERYTHIN'S FINE, OLLY... GO BACK TO SLEEP.
"YEH THEN COVERED YER TRACKS AND HID YER CRIME. YER BROTHER WAS ALL BUT INVISIBLE TO US."

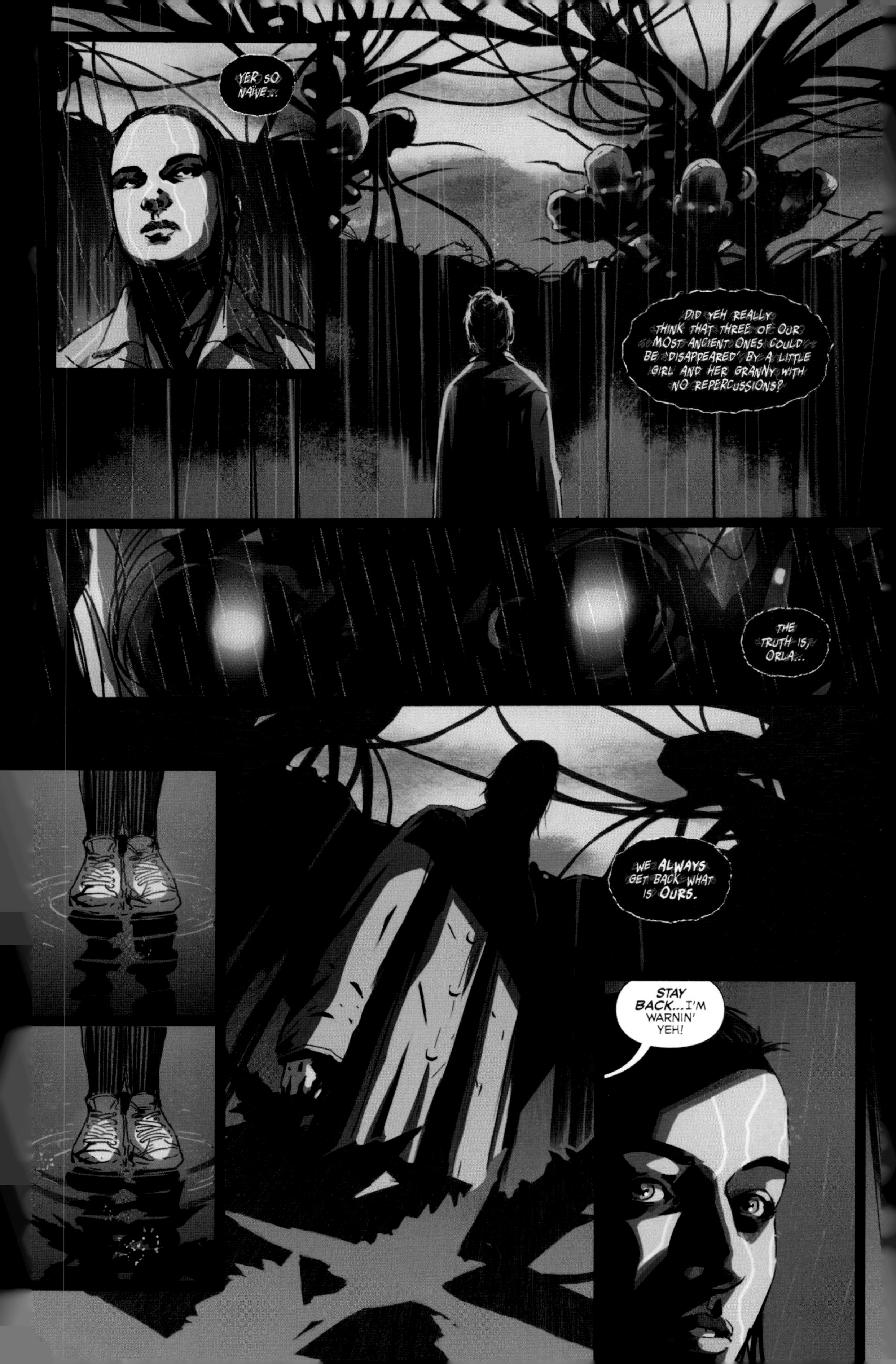
YER SO NAÏVE...
DID YEH REALLY THINK THAT THREE OF OUR MOST ANCIENT ONES COULD BE 'DISAPPEARED' BY A LITTLE GIRL AND HER GRANNY WITH NO REPERCUSSIONS?
THE TRUTH IS, ORLA...
WE ALWAYS GET BACK WHAT IS OURS.
STAY BACK...I'M WARNIN' YEH!

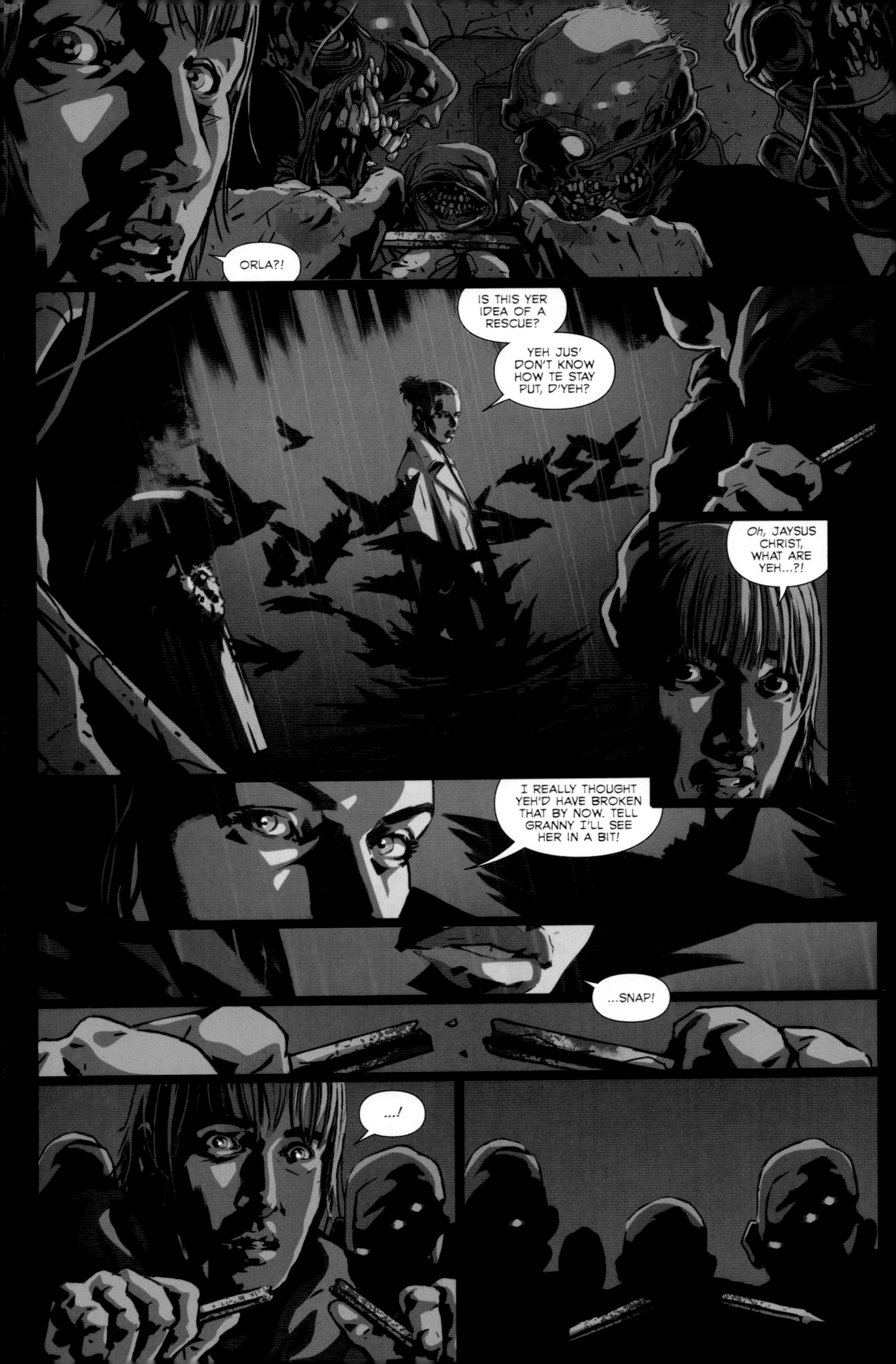
ORLA?!
IS THIS YER IDEA OF A RESCUE?
YEH JUS' DON'T KNOW HOW TE STAY PUT, D'YEH?
Oh, JAYSUS CHRIST, WHAT ARE YEH...?!
I REALLY THOUGHT YEH'D HAVE BROKEN THAT BY NOW. TELL GRANNY I'LL SEE HER IN A BIT!
...SNAP!
...!

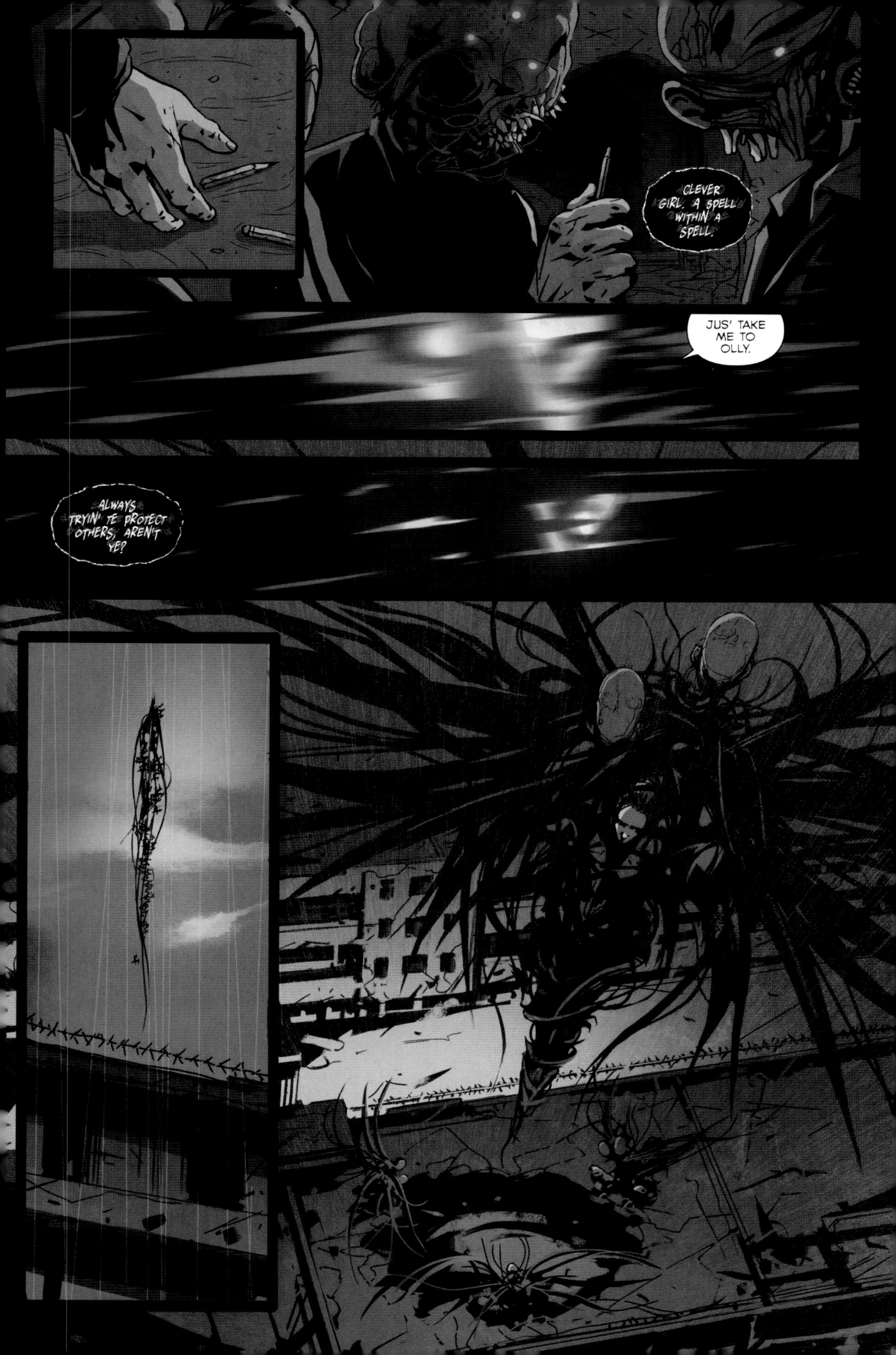
CLEVER GIRL. A SPELL WITHIN A SPELL.
JUS' TAKE ME TO OLLY.
ALWAYS TRYIN' TE PROTECT OTHERS, AREN'T YE?

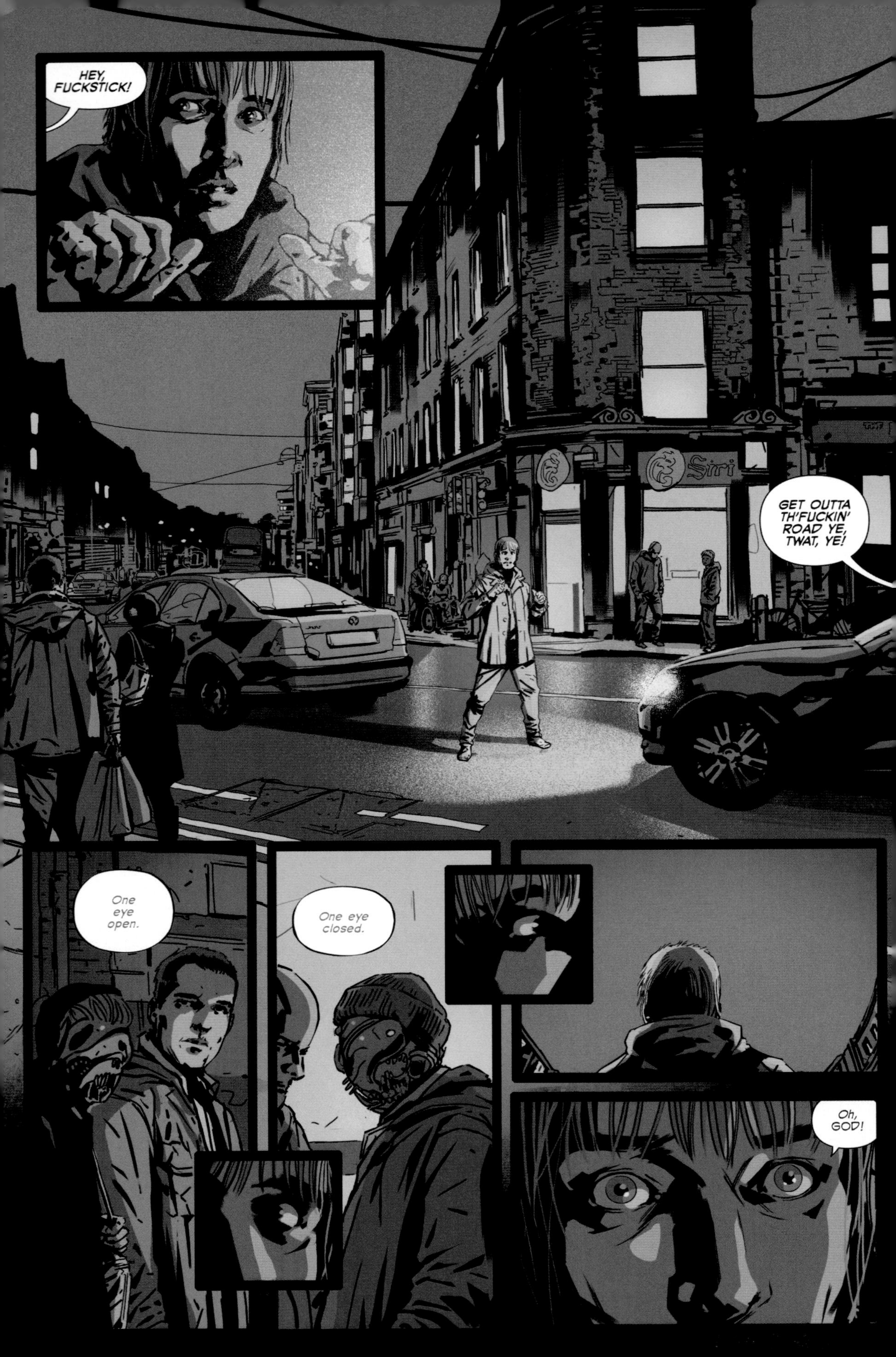
HEY, FUCKSTICK!
GET OUTTA TH'FUCKIN' ROAD YE, TWAT, YE!
One eye open.
One eye closed.
Oh, GOD!

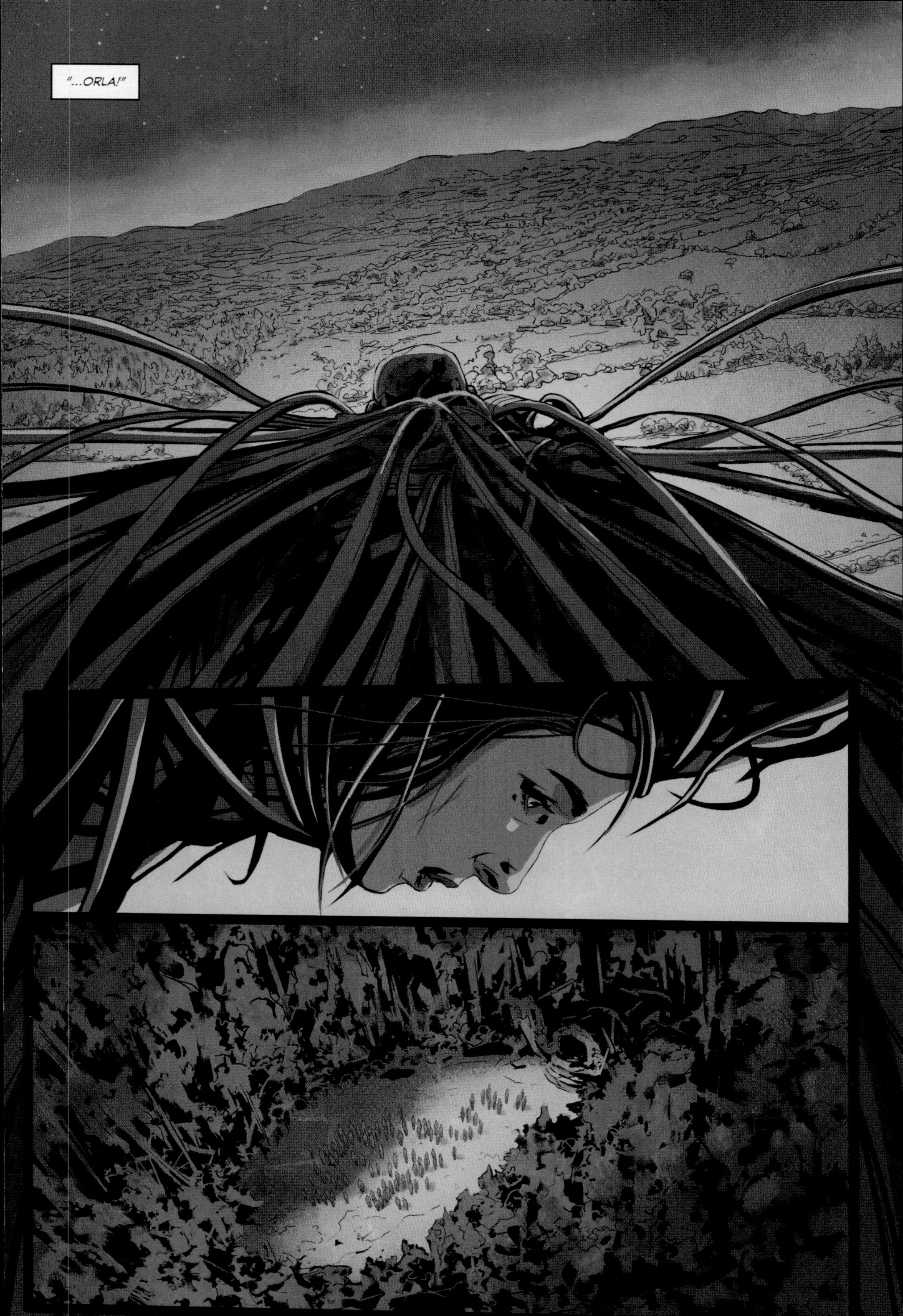
"...ORLA!"

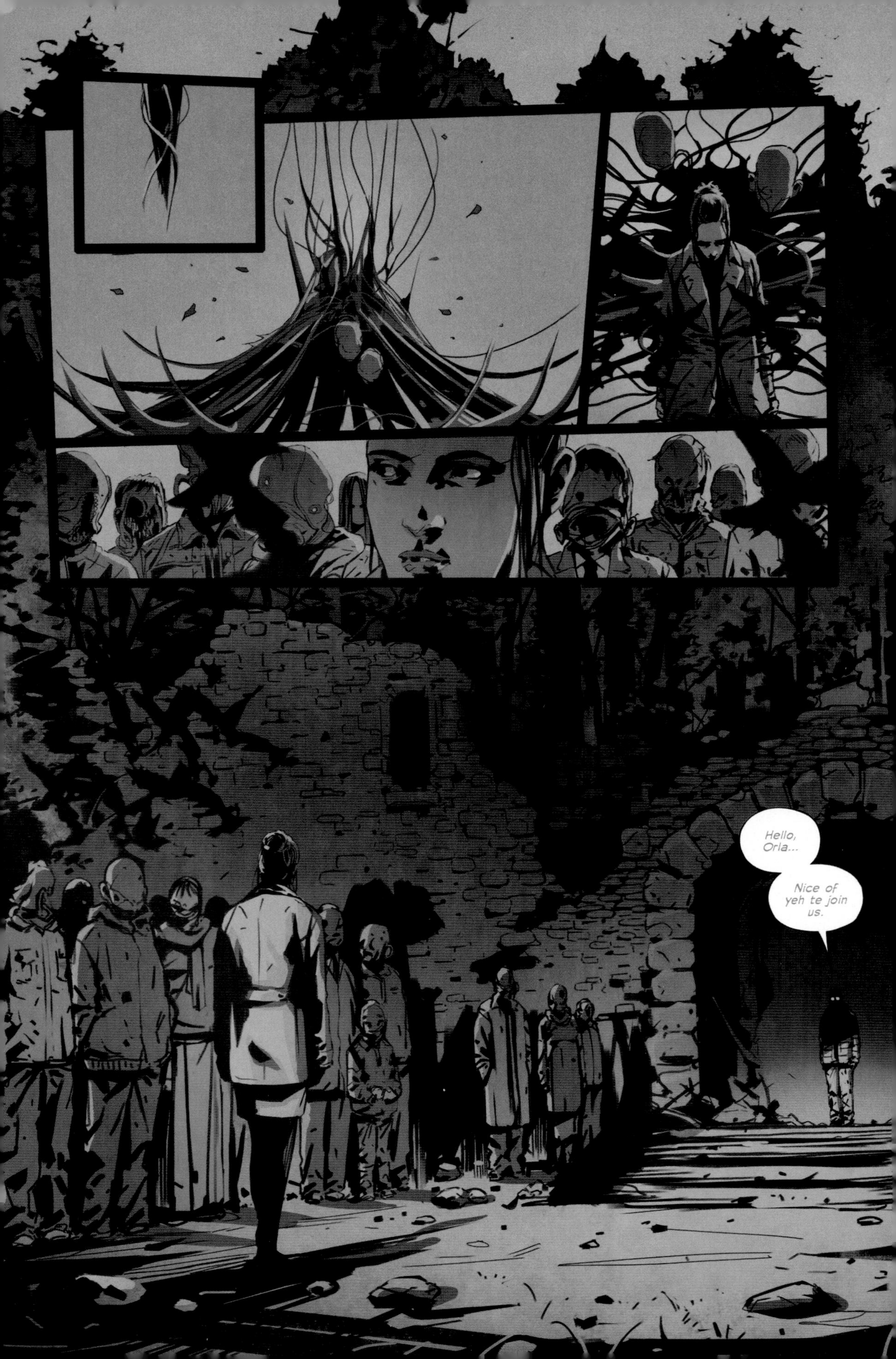
Hello, Orla...
Nice of yeh te join us.

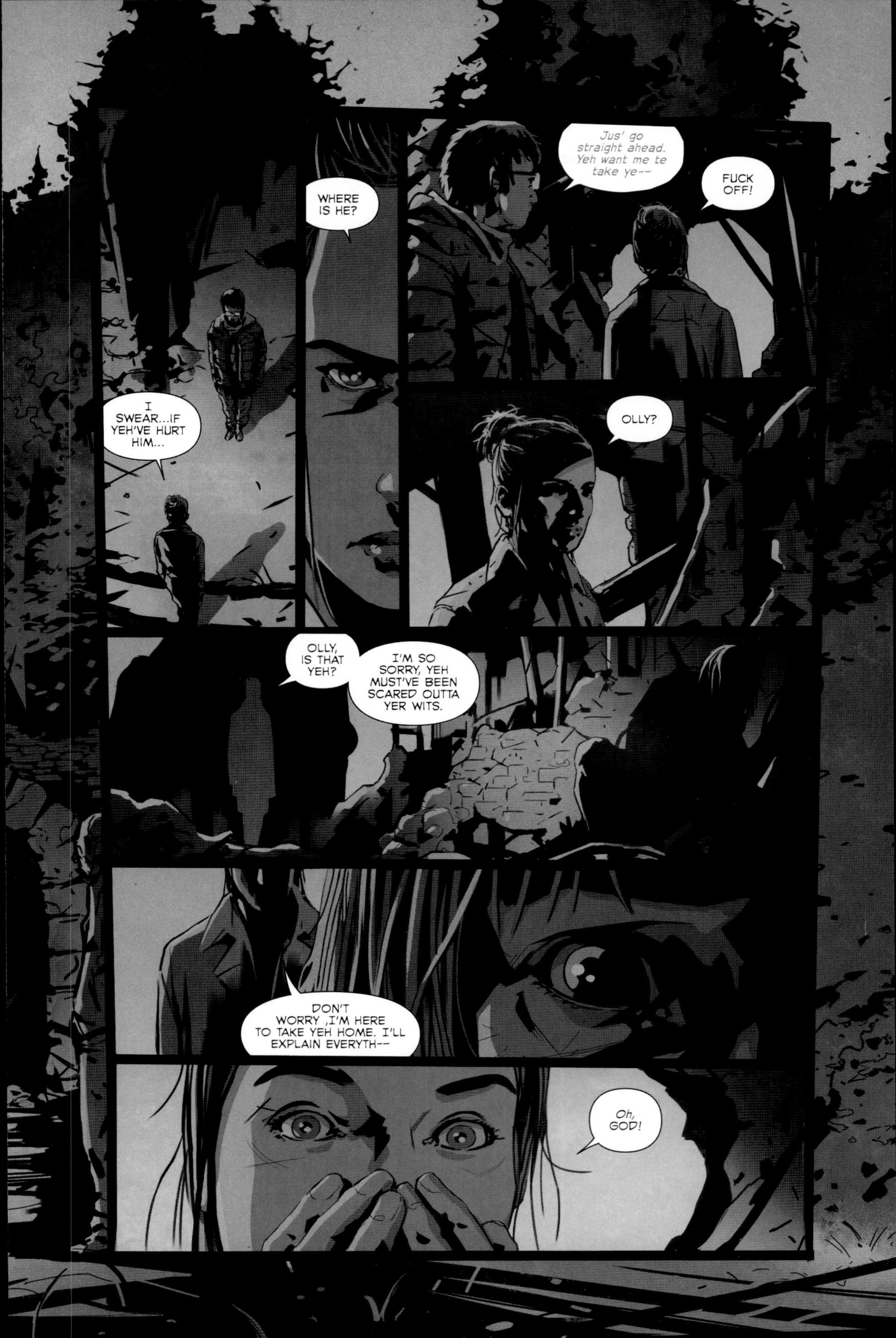
WHERE IS HE?
I SWEAR...IF YEH'VE HURT HIM...
Jus' go straight ahead. Yeh want me te take ye--
FUCK OFF!
OLLY?
OLLY, IS THAT YEH?
I'M SO SORRY, YEH MUST'VE BEEN SCARED OUTTA YER WITS.
DON'T WORRY ,I'M HERE TO TAKE YEH HOME. I'LL EXPLAIN EVERYTH--
Oh, GOD!

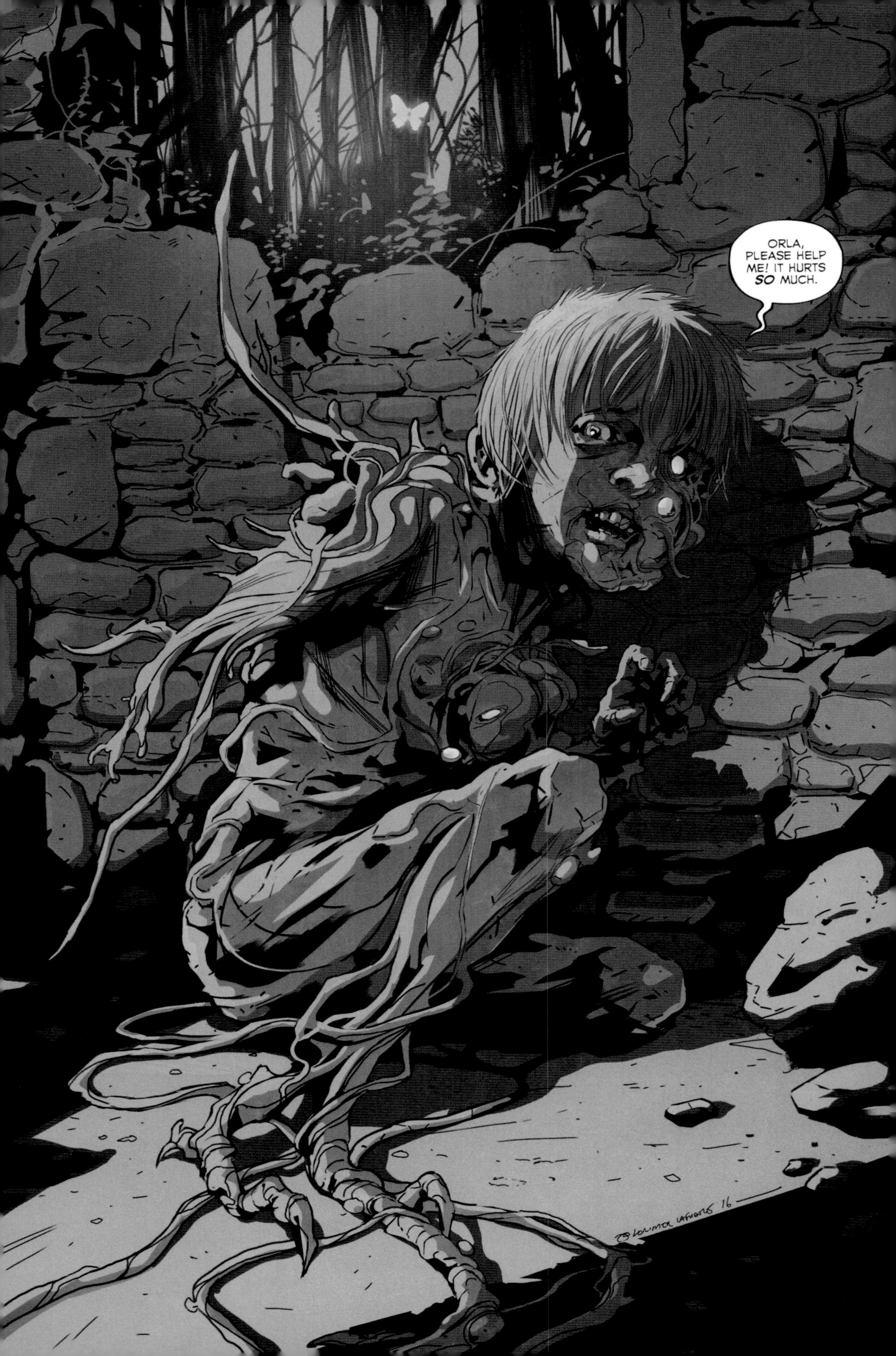
ORLA, PLEASE HELP ME! IT HURTS SO MUCH.

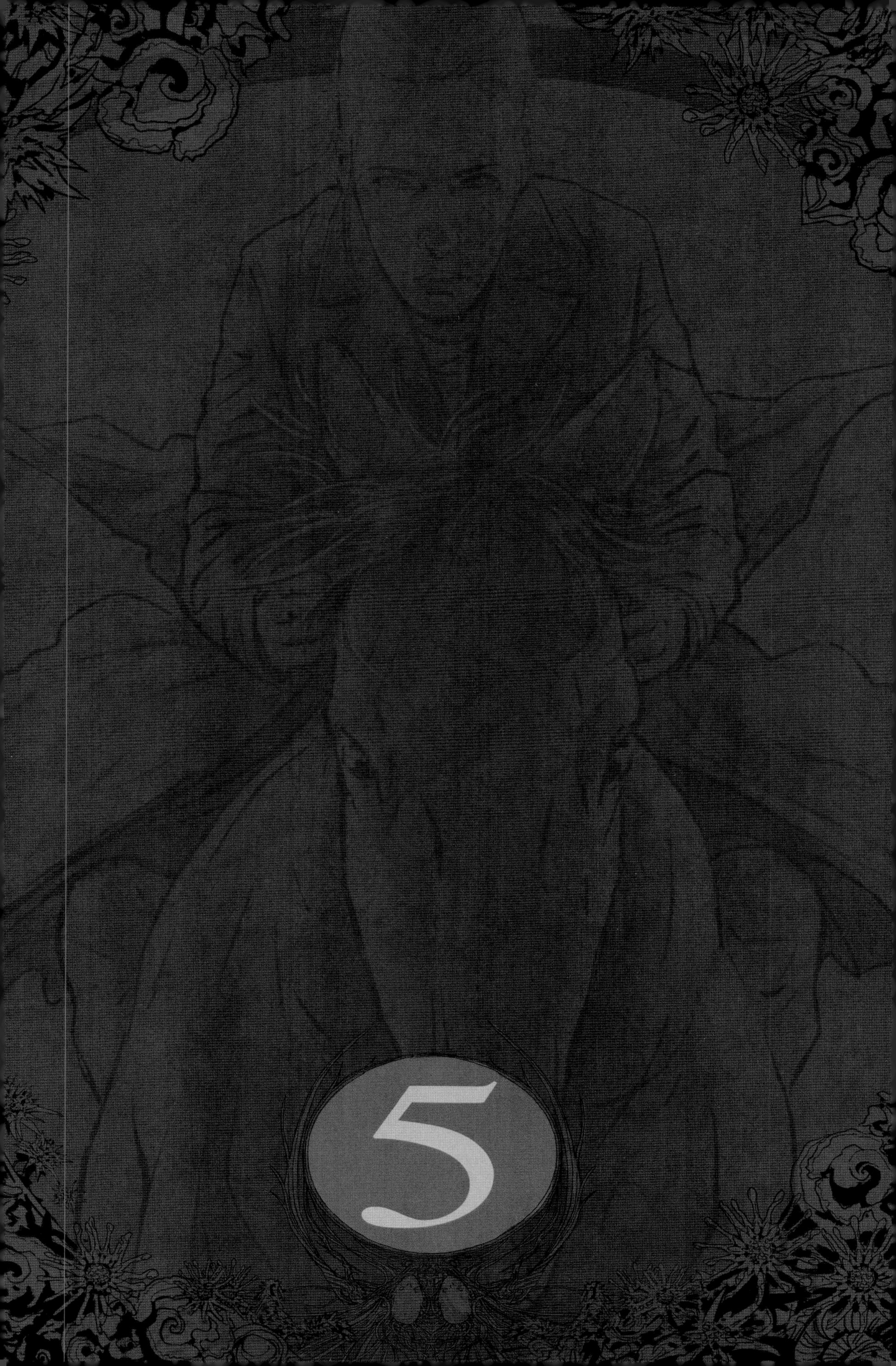
5

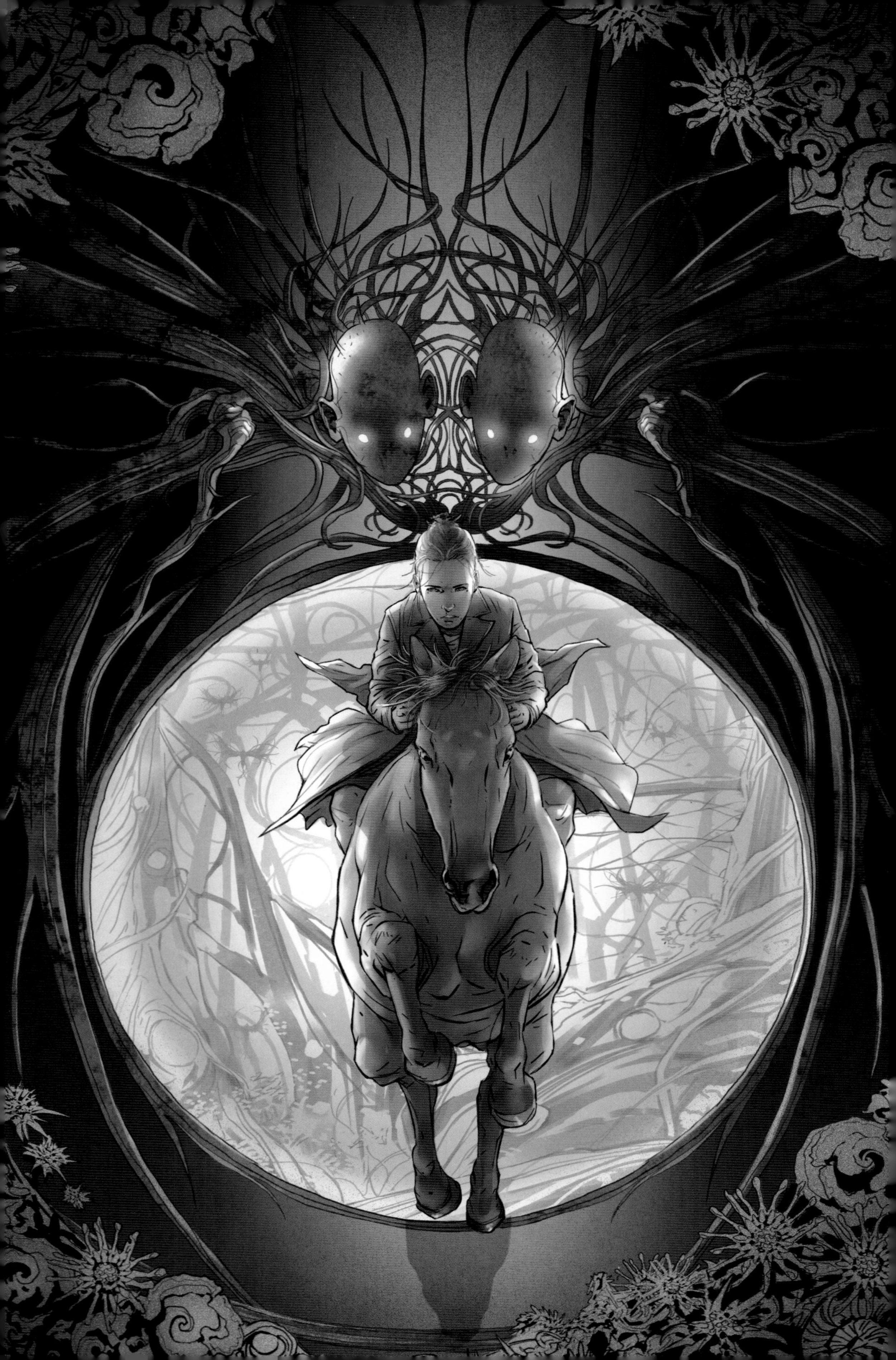

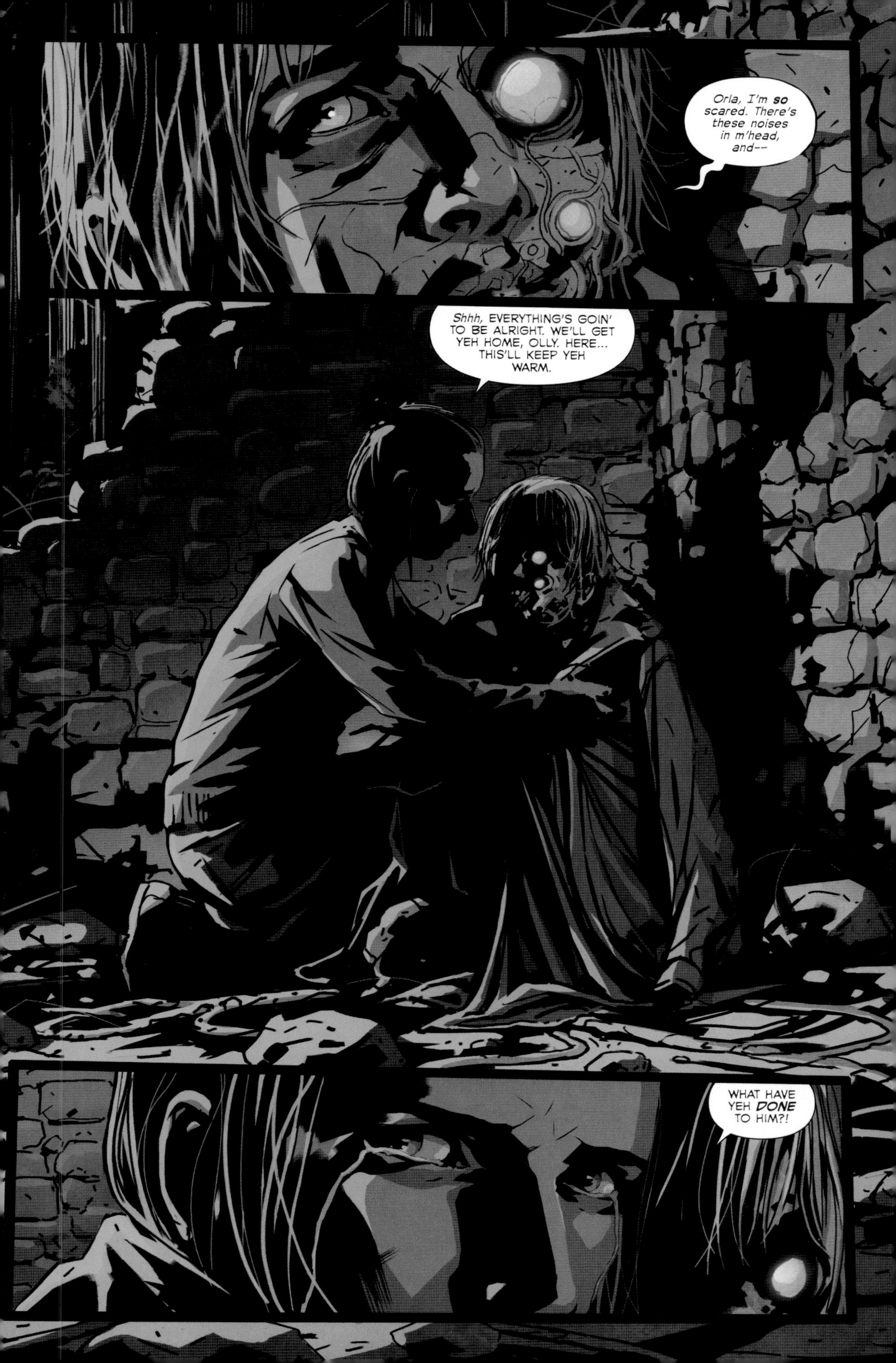
Orla, I'm **so** scared. There's these noises in m'head, and--
Shhh, EVERYTHING'S GOIN' TO BE ALRIGHT. WE'LL GET YEH HOME, OLLY. HERE... THIS'LL KEEP YEH WARM.
WHAT HAVE YEH ***DONE*** TO HIM?!

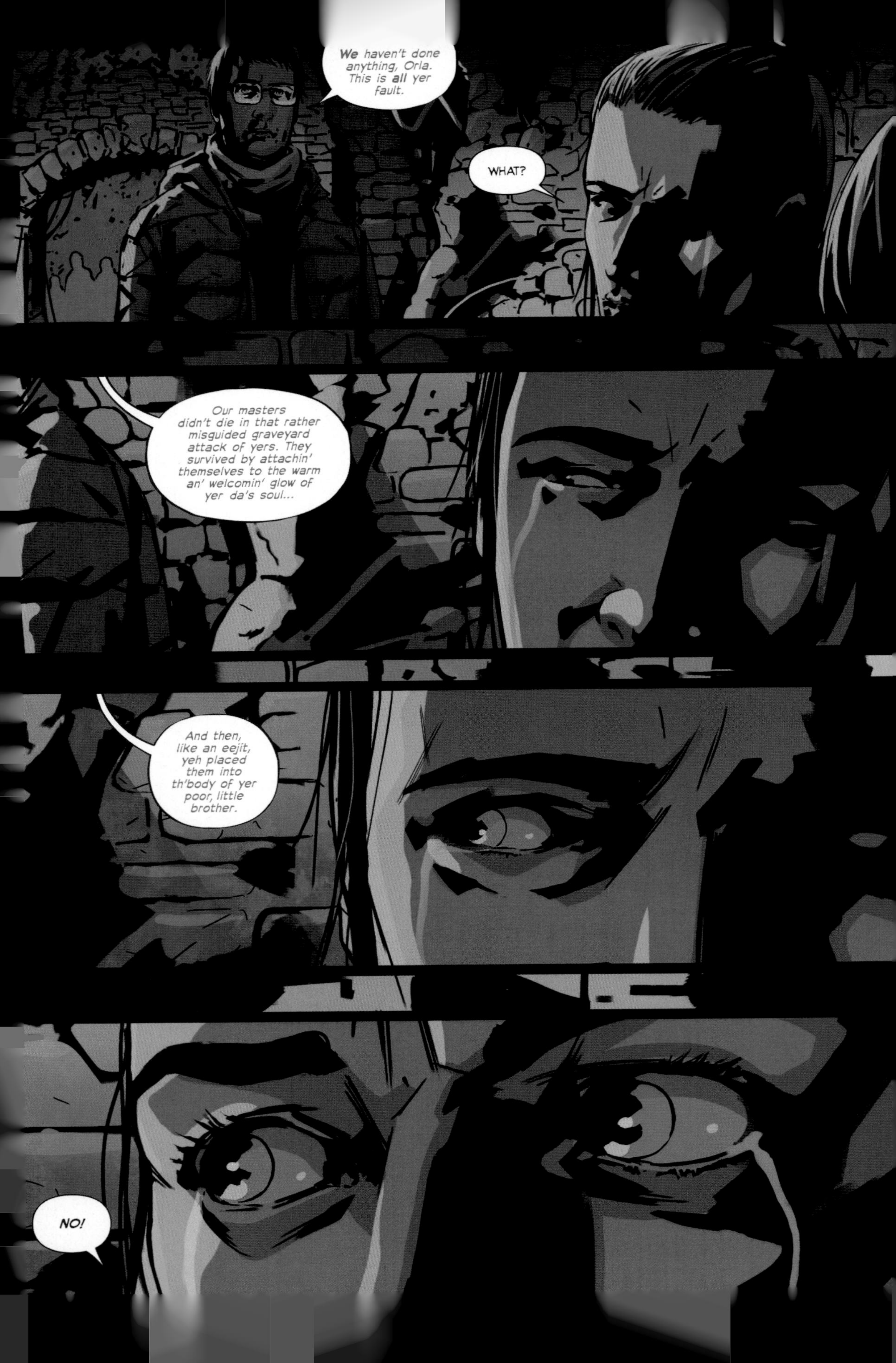
We haven't done anything, Orla. This is all yer fault.
WHAT?
Our masters didn't die in that rather misguided graveyard attack of yers. They survived by attachin' themselves to the warm an' welcomin' glow of yer da's soul...
And then, like an eejit, yeh placed them into th'body of yer poor, little brother.
NO!

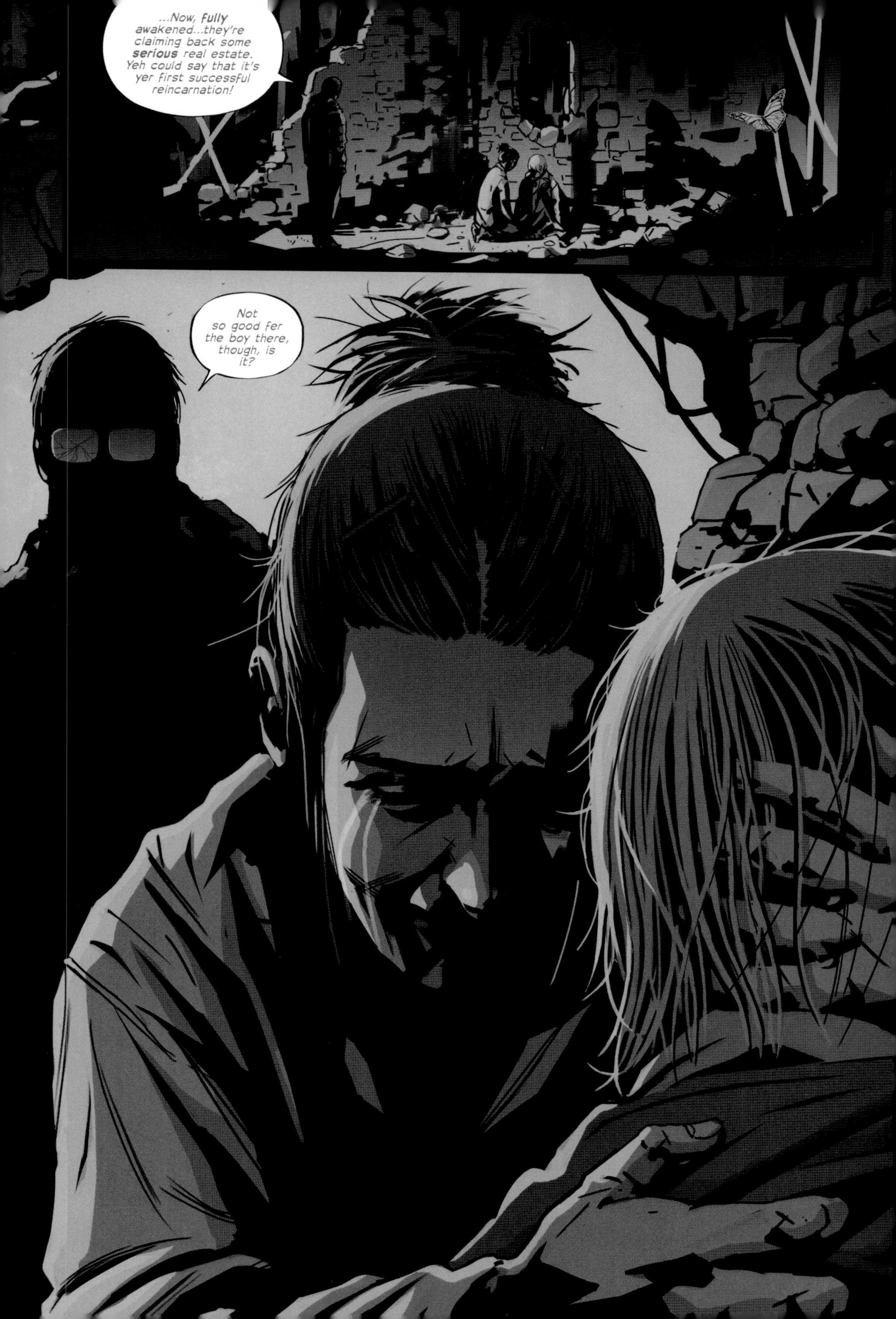
...Now, fully awakened...they're claiming back some serious real estate. Yeh could say that it's yer first successful reincarnation!
Not so good fer the boy there, though, is it?

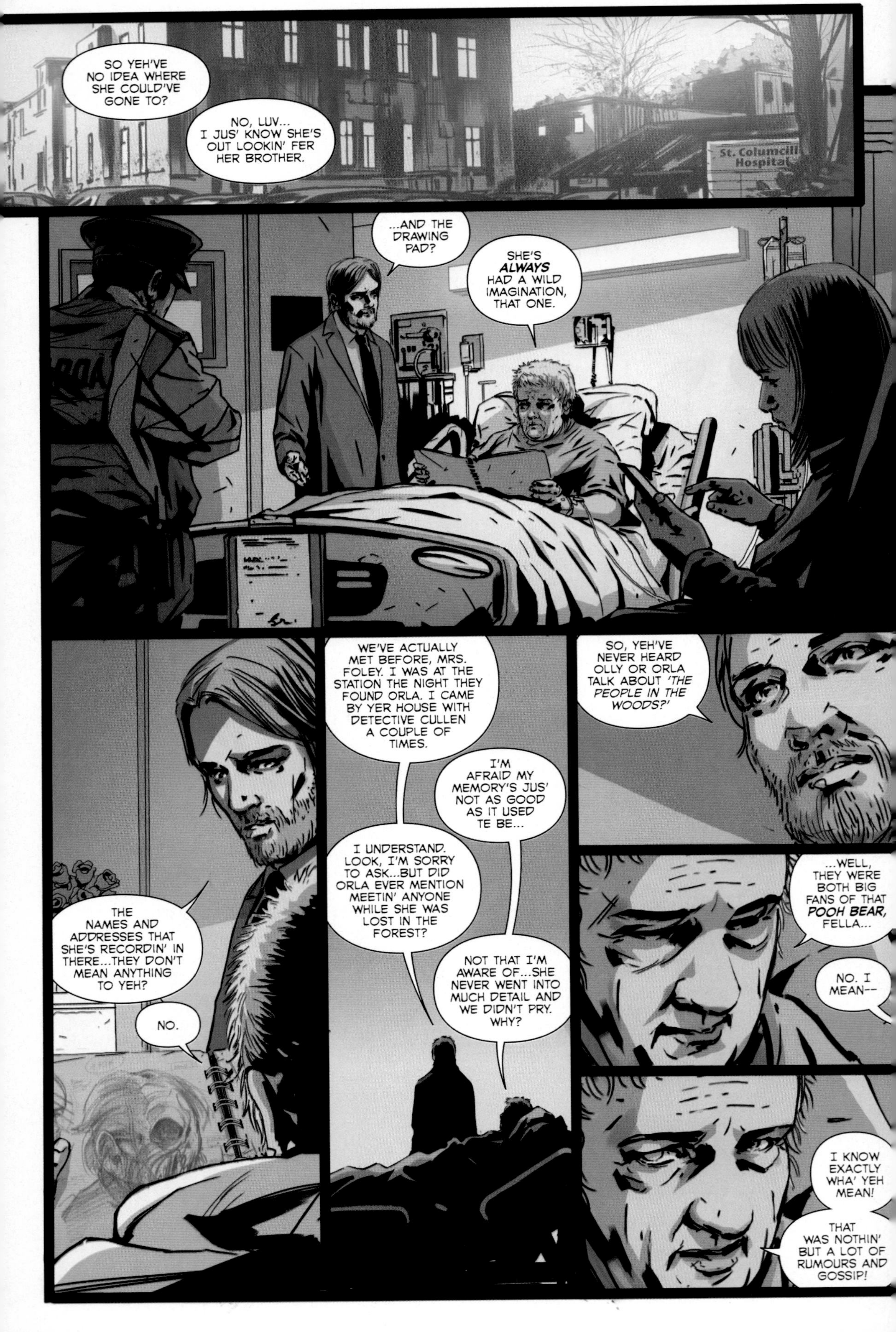
SO YEH'VE NO IDEA WHERE SHE COULD'VE GONE TO?
NO, LUV... I JUS' KNOW SHE'S OUT LOOKIN' FER HER BROTHER.
St. Columcill Hospital
...AND THE DRAWING PAD?
SHE'S ALWAYS HAD A WILD IMAGINATION, THAT ONE.
THE NAMES AND ADDRESSES THAT SHE'S RECORDIN' IN THERE...THEY DON'T MEAN ANYTHING TO YEH?
NO.
WE'VE ACTUALLY MET BEFORE, MRS. FOLEY. I WAS AT THE STATION THE NIGHT THEY FOUND ORLA. I CAME BY YER HOUSE WITH DETECTIVE CULLEN A COUPLE OF TIMES.
I'M AFRAID MY MEMORY'S JUS' NOT AS GOOD AS IT USED TE BE...
I UNDERSTAND. LOOK, I'M SORRY TO ASK...BUT DID ORLA EVER MENTION MEETIN' ANYONE WHILE SHE WAS LOST IN THE FOREST?
NOT THAT I'M AWARE OF...SHE NEVER WENT INTO MUCH DETAIL AND WE DIDN'T PRY. WHY?
SO, YEH'VE NEVER HEARD OLLY OR ORLA TALK ABOUT 'THE PEOPLE IN THE WOODS?'
...WELL, THEY WERE BOTH BIG FANS OF THAT POOH BEAR, FELLA...
NO. I MEAN--
I KNOW EXACTLY WHA' YEH MEAN!
THAT WAS NOTHIN' BUT A LOT OF RUMOURS AND GOSSIP!

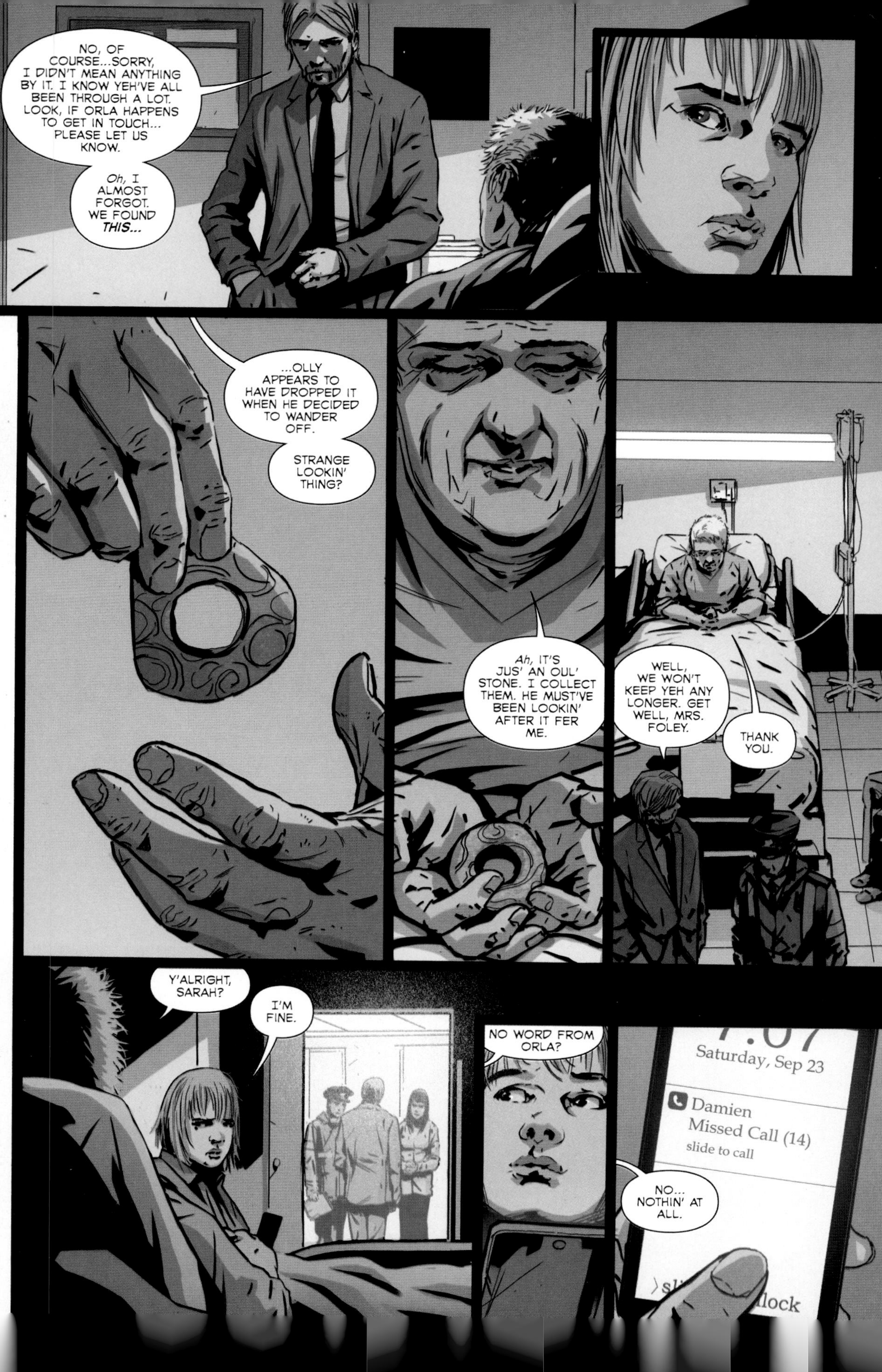
NO, OF COURSE...SORRY, I DIDN'T MEAN ANYTHING BY IT. I KNOW YEH'VE ALL BEEN THROUGH A LOT. LOOK, IF ORLA HAPPENS TO GET IN TOUCH... PLEASE LET US KNOW.
Oh, I ALMOST FORGOT. WE FOUND ***THIS...***
...OLLY APPEARS TO HAVE DROPPED IT WHEN HE DECIDED TO WANDER OFF.
STRANGE LOOKIN' THING?
Ah, IT'S JUS' AN OUL' STONE. I COLLECT THEM. HE MUST'VE BEEN LOOKIN' AFTER IT FER ME.
WELL, WE WON'T KEEP YEH ANY LONGER. GET WELL, MRS. FOLEY.
THANK YOU.
Y'ALRIGHT, SARAH?
I'M FINE.
NO WORD FROM ORLA?
Saturday, Sep 23
Damien
Missed Call (14)
slide to call
NO... NOTHIN' AT ALL.

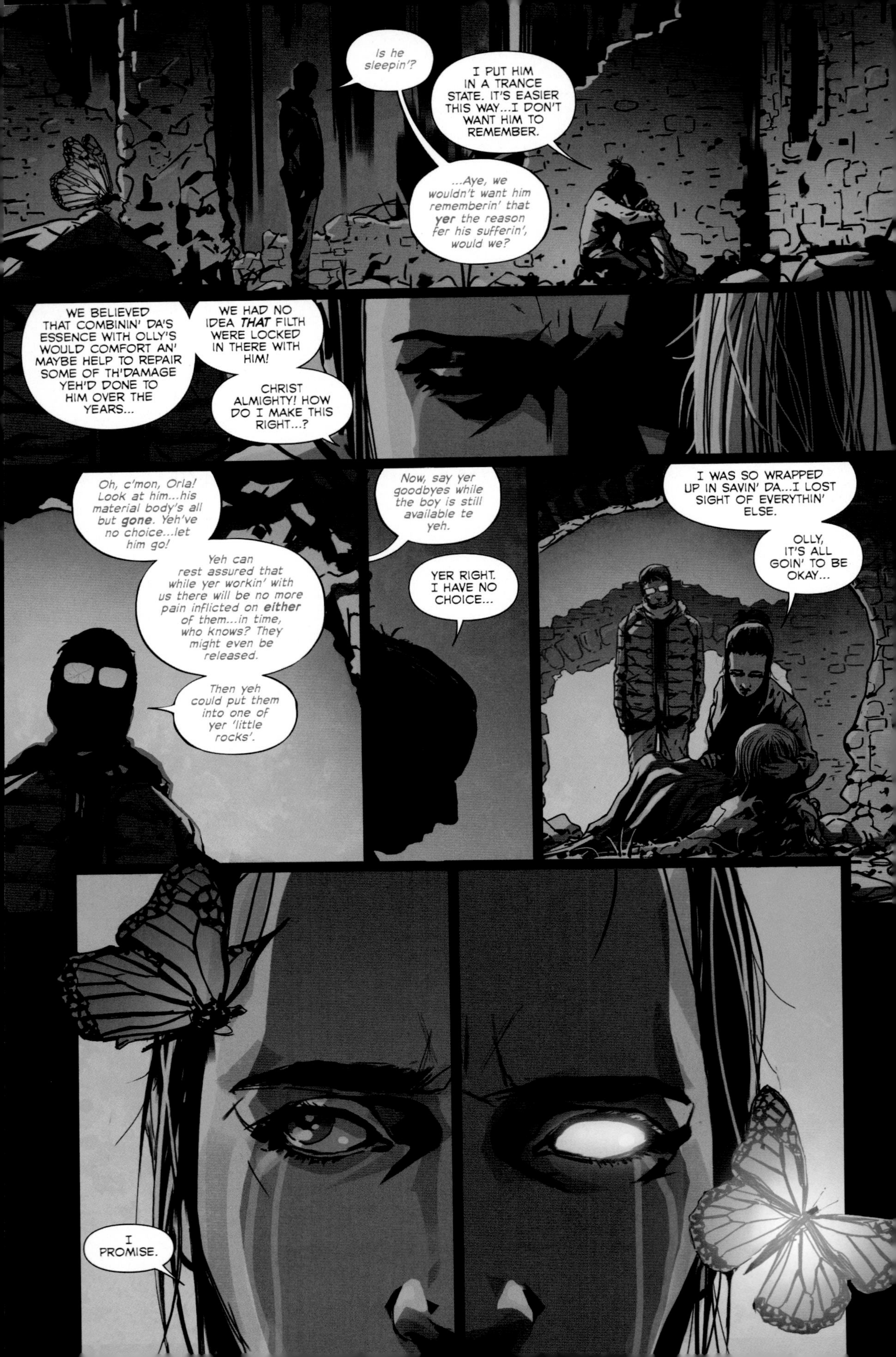

Is he sleepin'?
I PUT HIM IN A TRANCE STATE. IT'S EASIER THIS WAY...I DON'T WANT HIM TO REMEMBER.
...Aye, we wouldn't want him rememberin' that yer the reason fer his sufferin', would we?
WE BELIEVED THAT COMBININ' DA'S ESSENCE WITH OLLY'S WOULD COMFORT AN' MAYBE HELP TO REPAIR SOME OF TH'DAMAGE YEH'D DONE TO HIM OVER THE YEARS...
WE HAD NO IDEA THAT FILTH WERE LOCKED IN THERE WITH HIM!
CHRIST ALMIGHTY! HOW DO I MAKE THIS RIGHT...?
Oh, c'mon, Orla! Look at him...his material body's all but gone. Yeh've no choice...let him go!
Yeh can rest assured that while yer workin' with us there will be no more pain inflicted on either of them...in time, who knows? They might even be released.
Then yeh could put them into one of yer 'little rocks'.
Now, say yer goodbyes while the boy is still available te yeh.
YER RIGHT. I HAVE NO CHOICE...
I WAS SO WRAPPED UP IN SAVIN' DA...I LOST SIGHT OF EVERYTHIN' ELSE.
OLLY, IT'S ALL GOIN' TO BE OKAY...
I PROMISE.

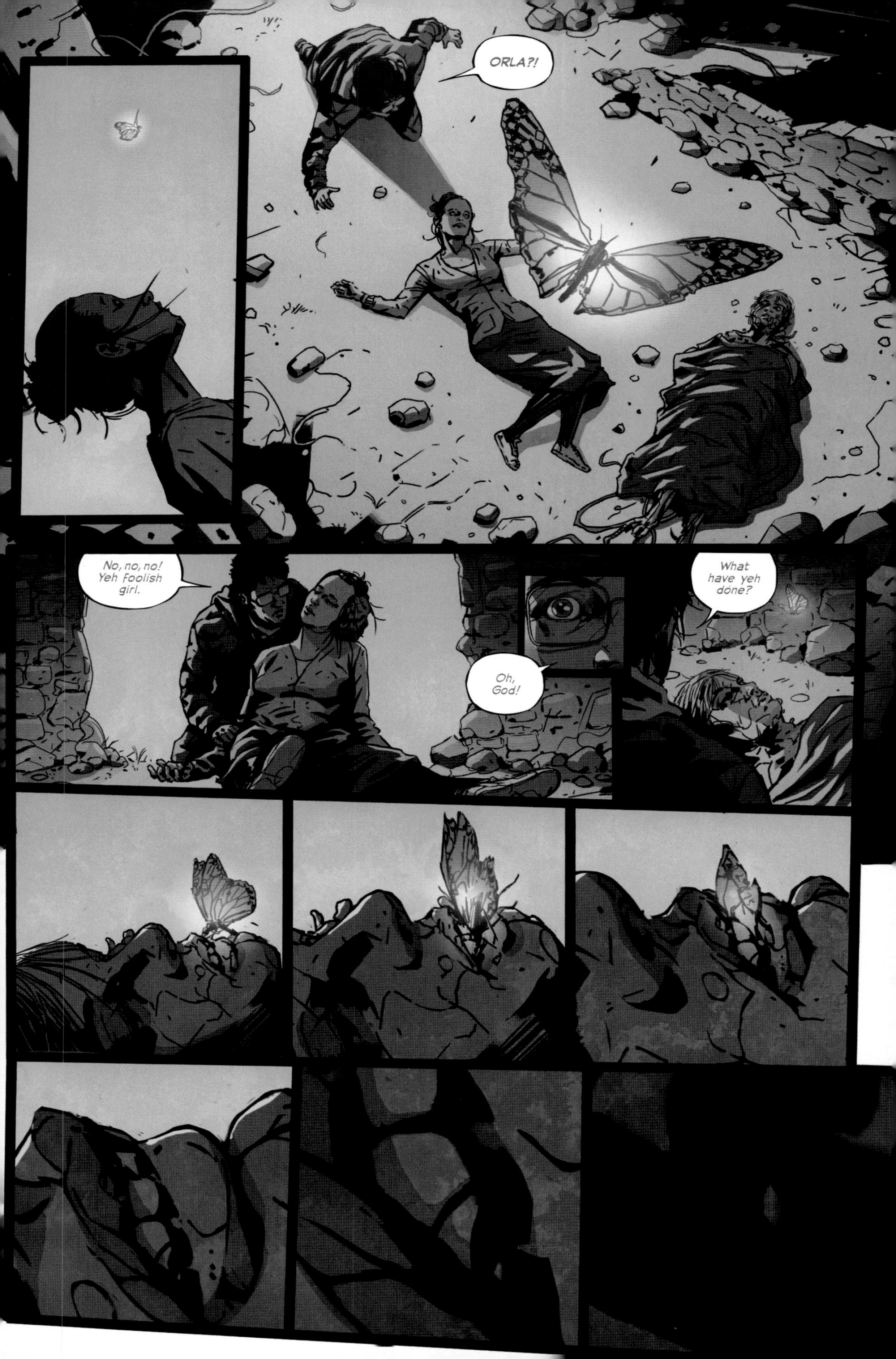
ORLA?!
No, no, no! Yeh foolish girl.
Oh, God!
What have yeh done?

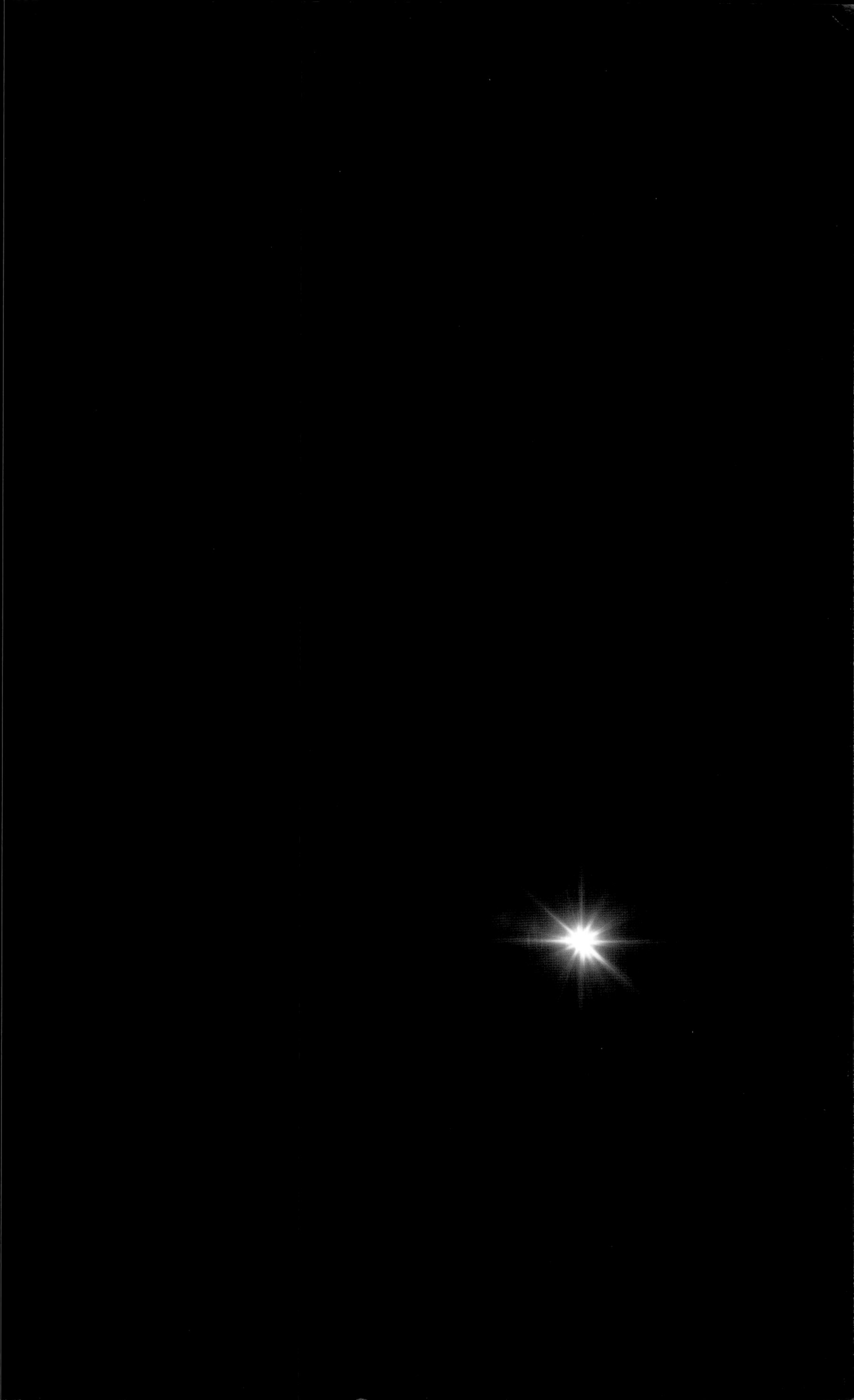

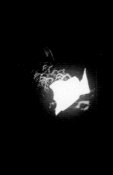

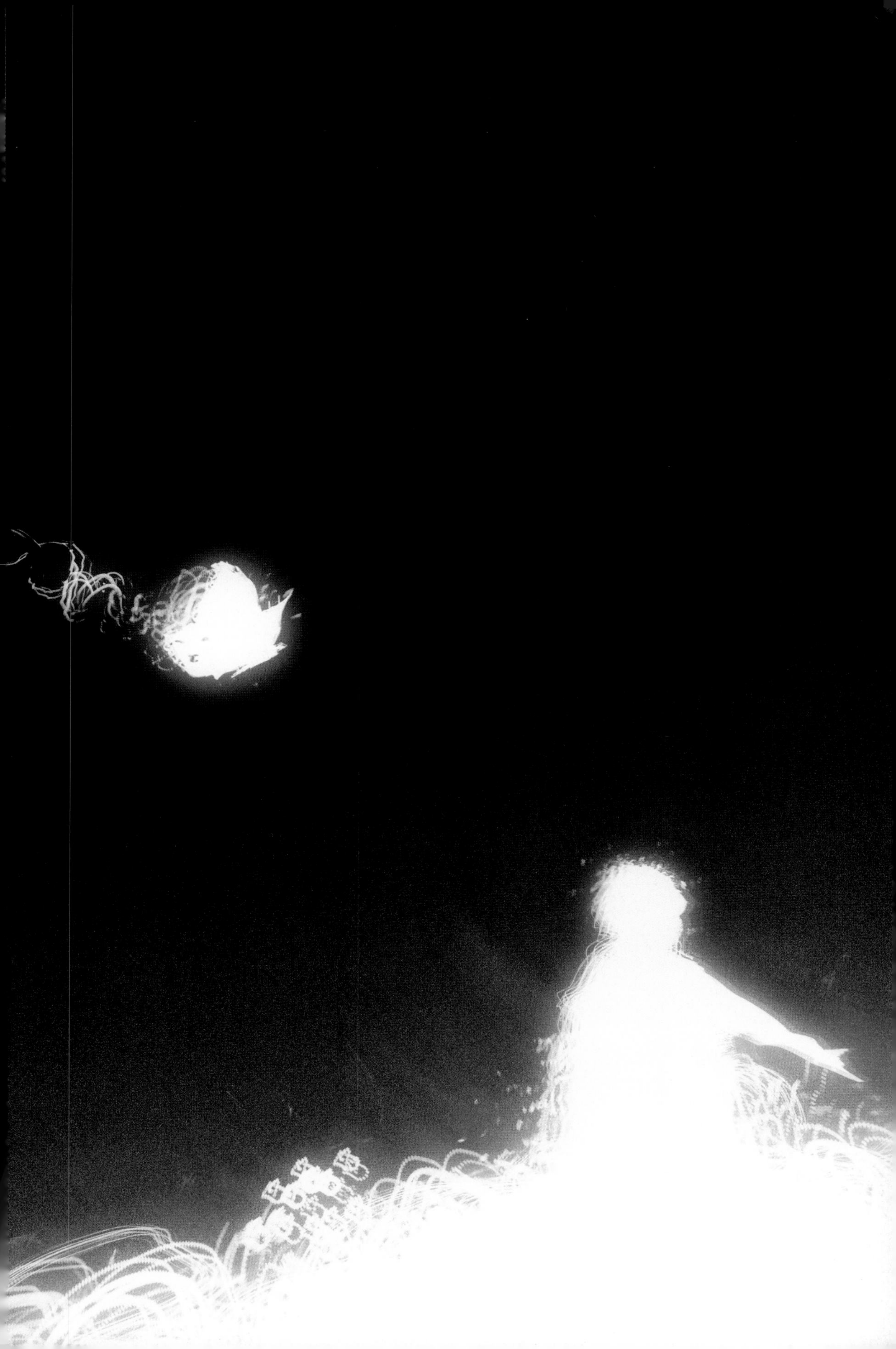

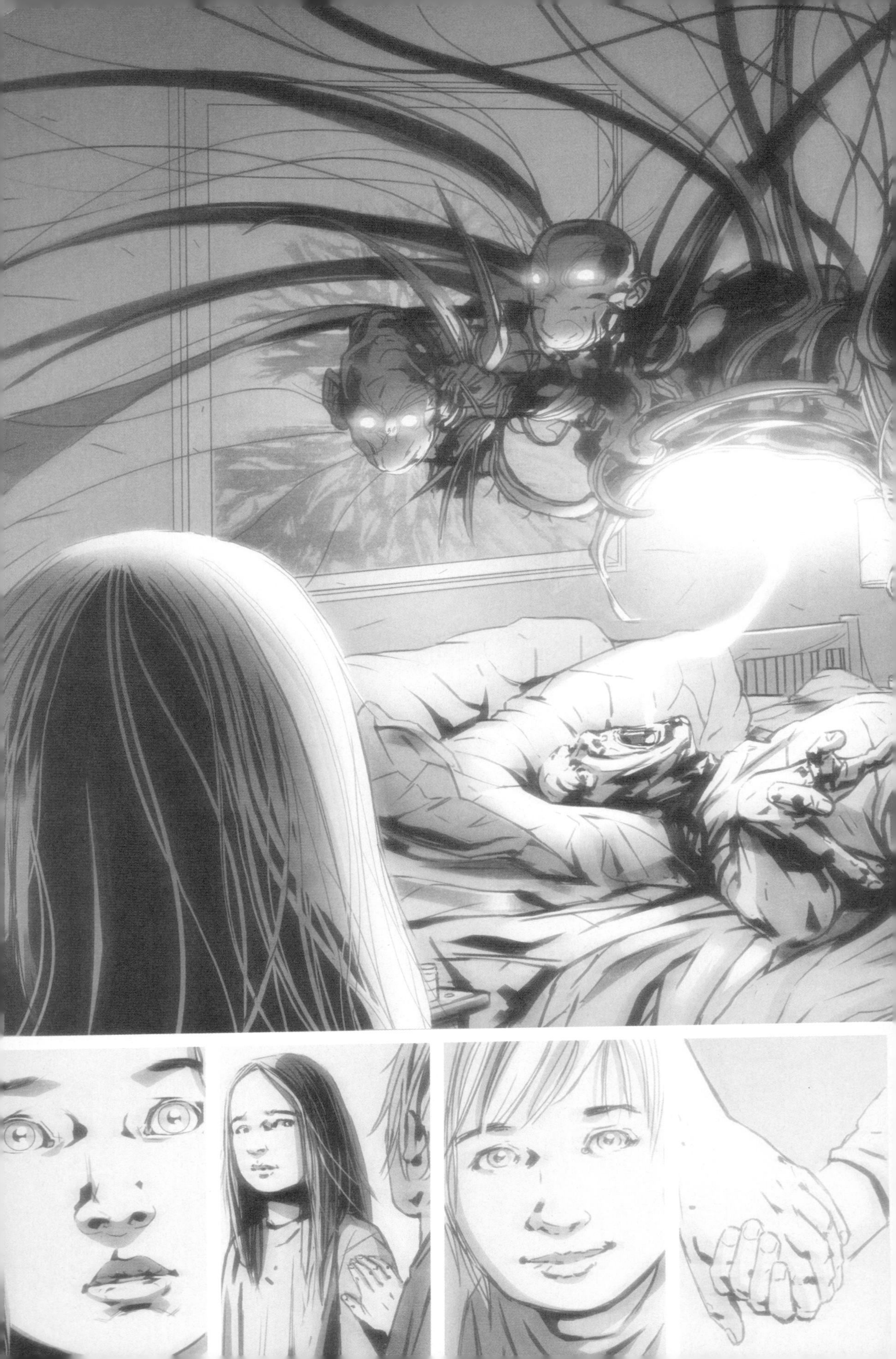

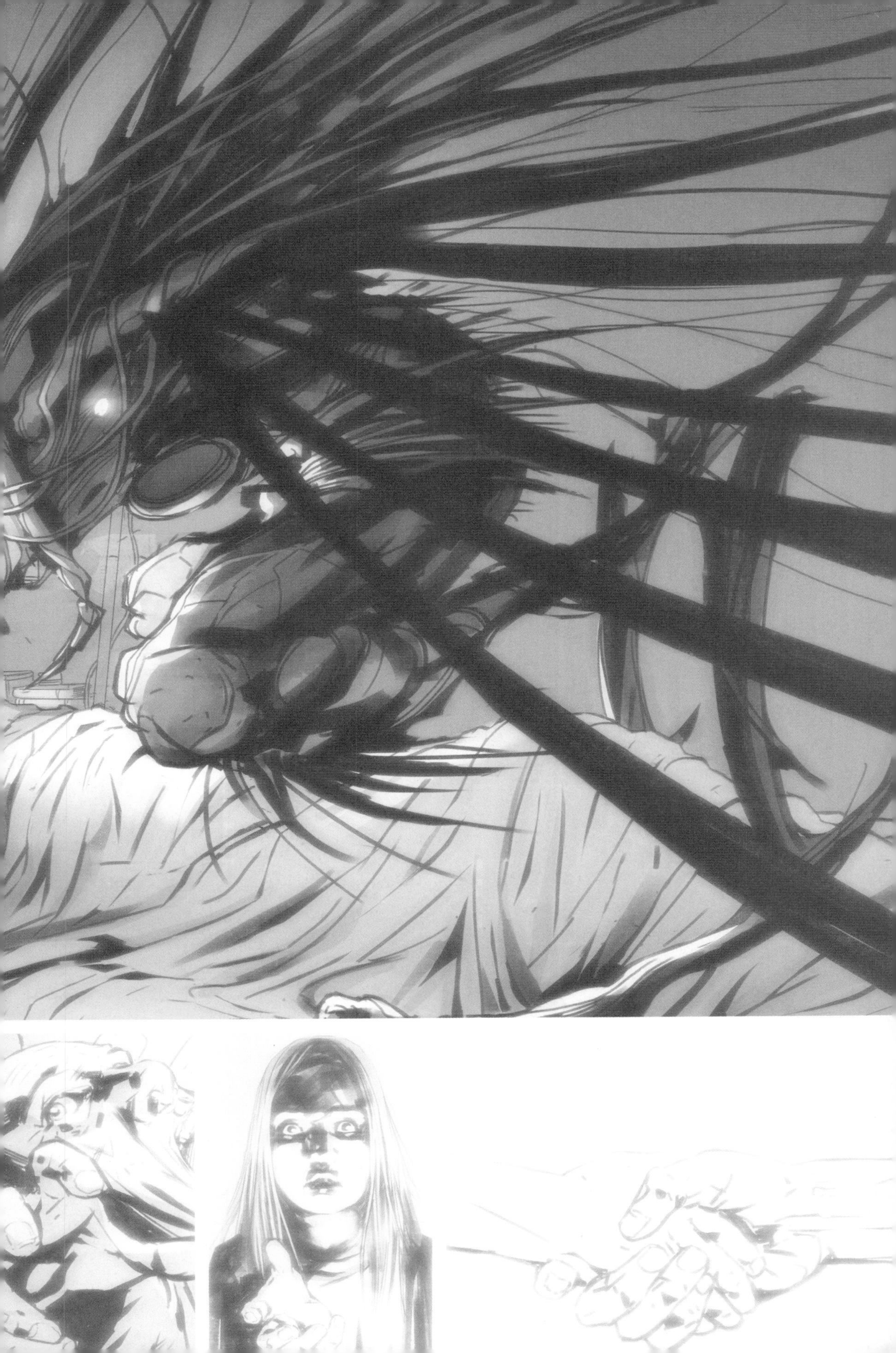

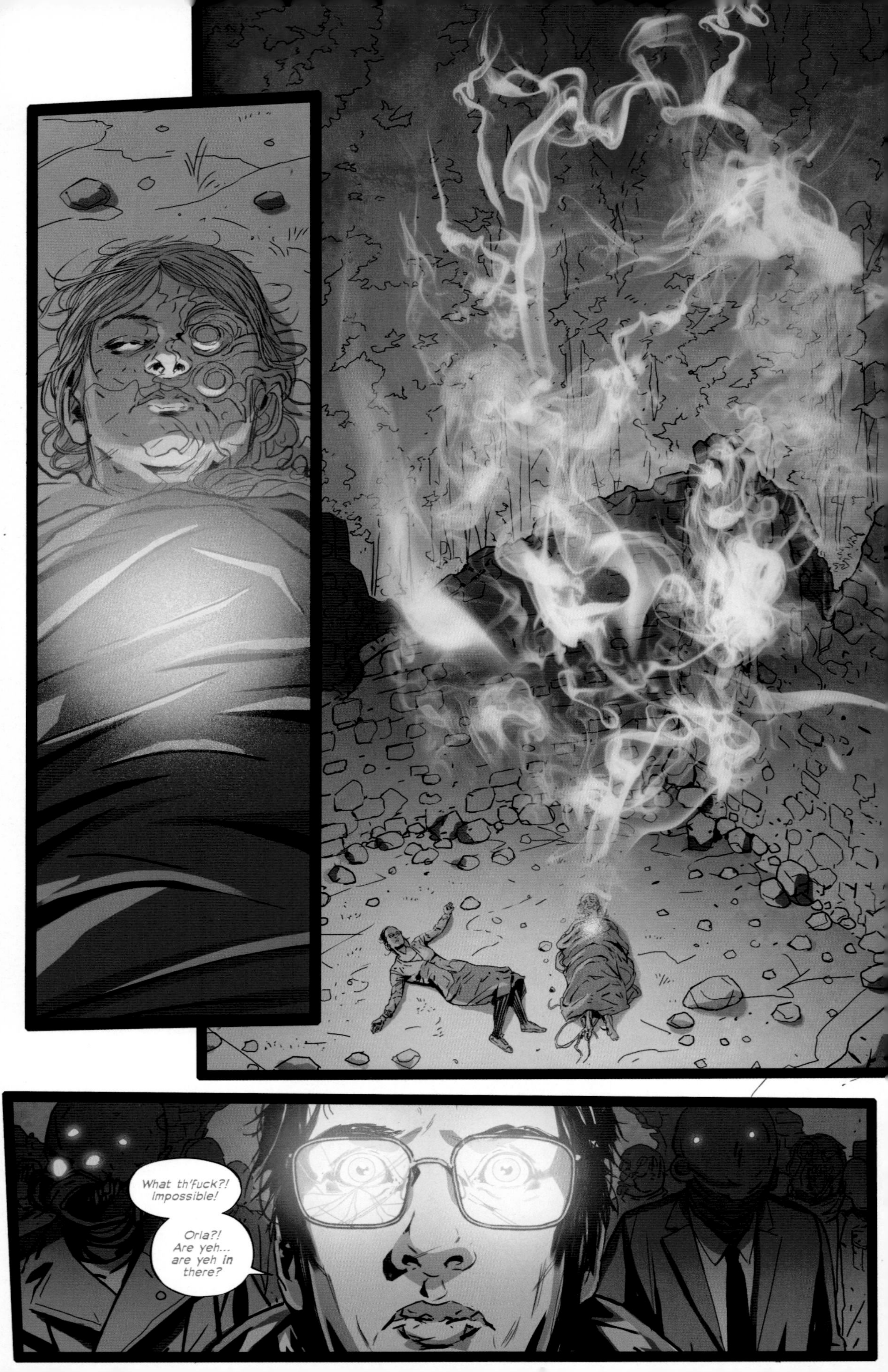

What th'fuck?! Impossible!
Orla?! Are yeh... are yeh in there?

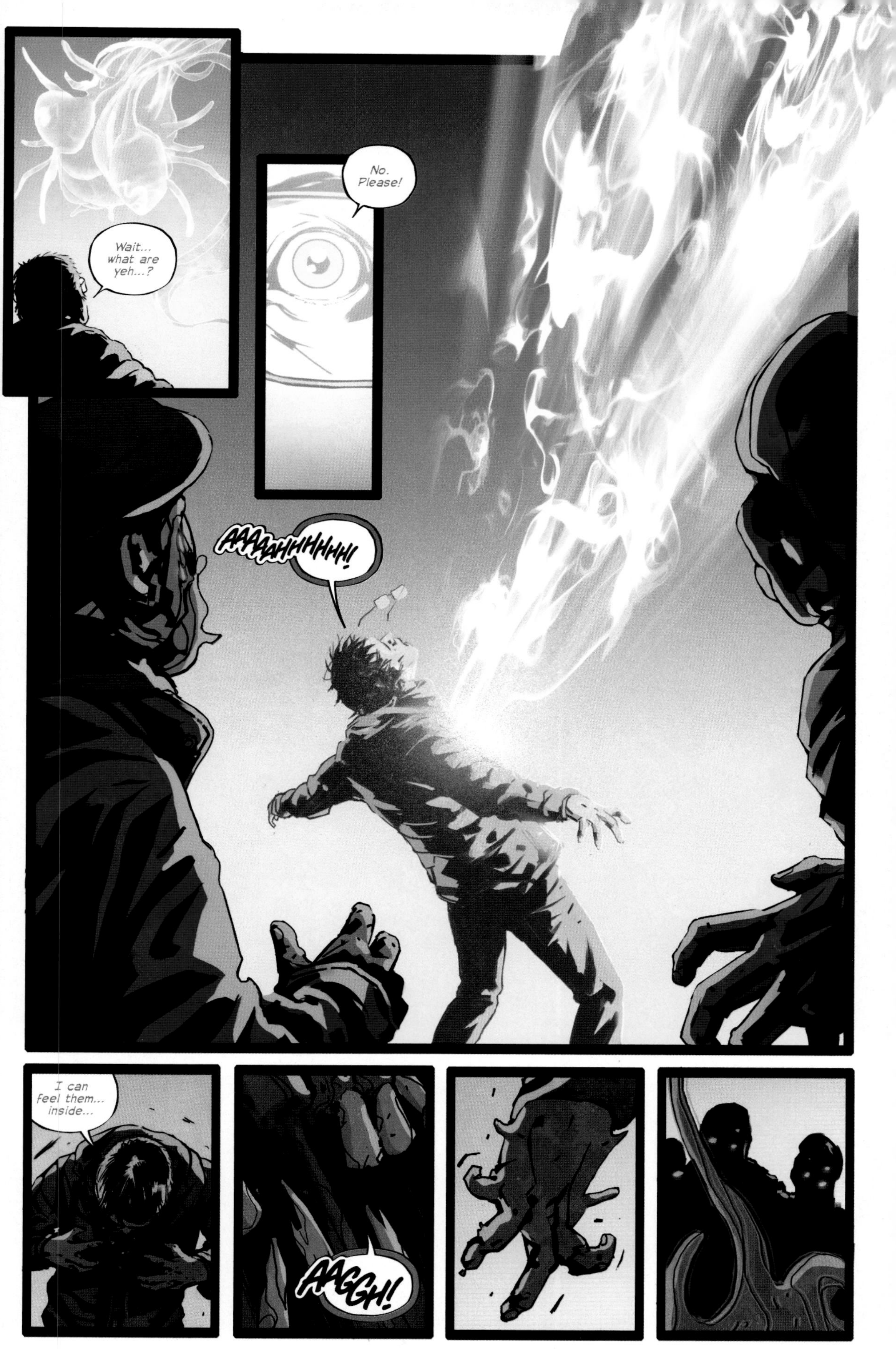
Wait... what are yeh...?
No. Please!
AAAAAHHHHHH!
I can feel them... inside...
AAGGH!

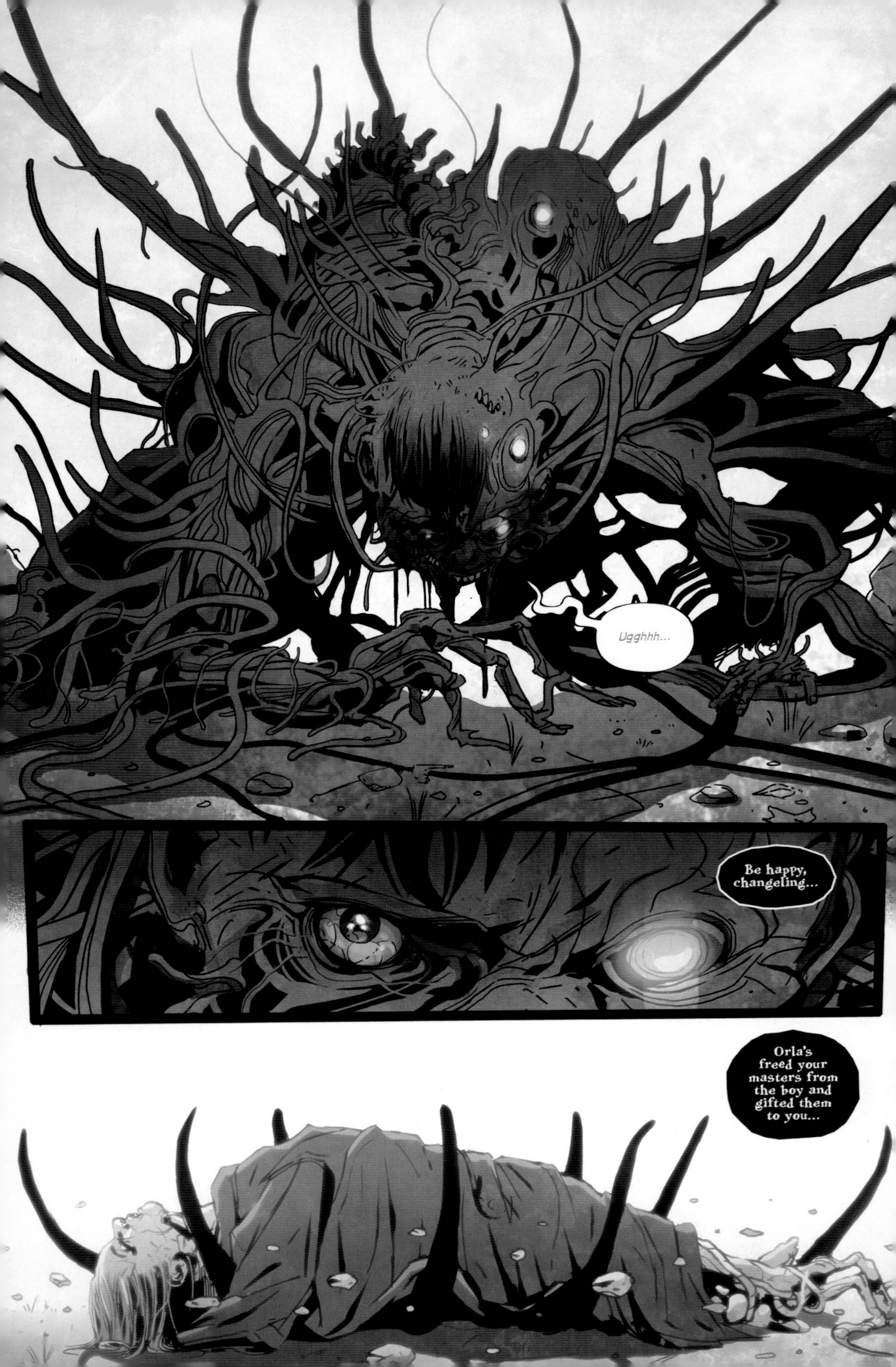
Ugghhh...
Be happy, changeling...
Orla's freed your masters from the boy and gifted them to you...

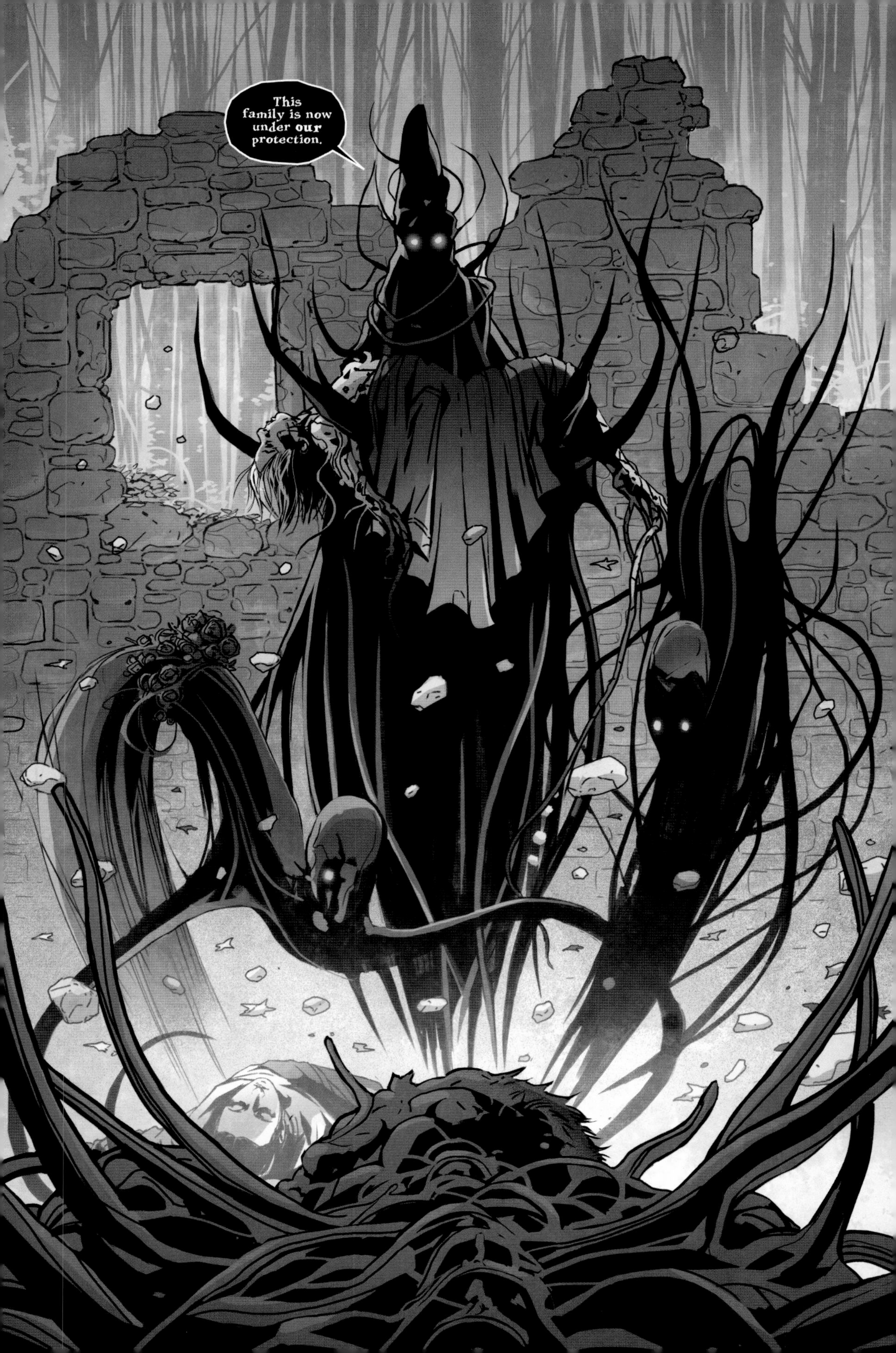
This family is now under our protection.

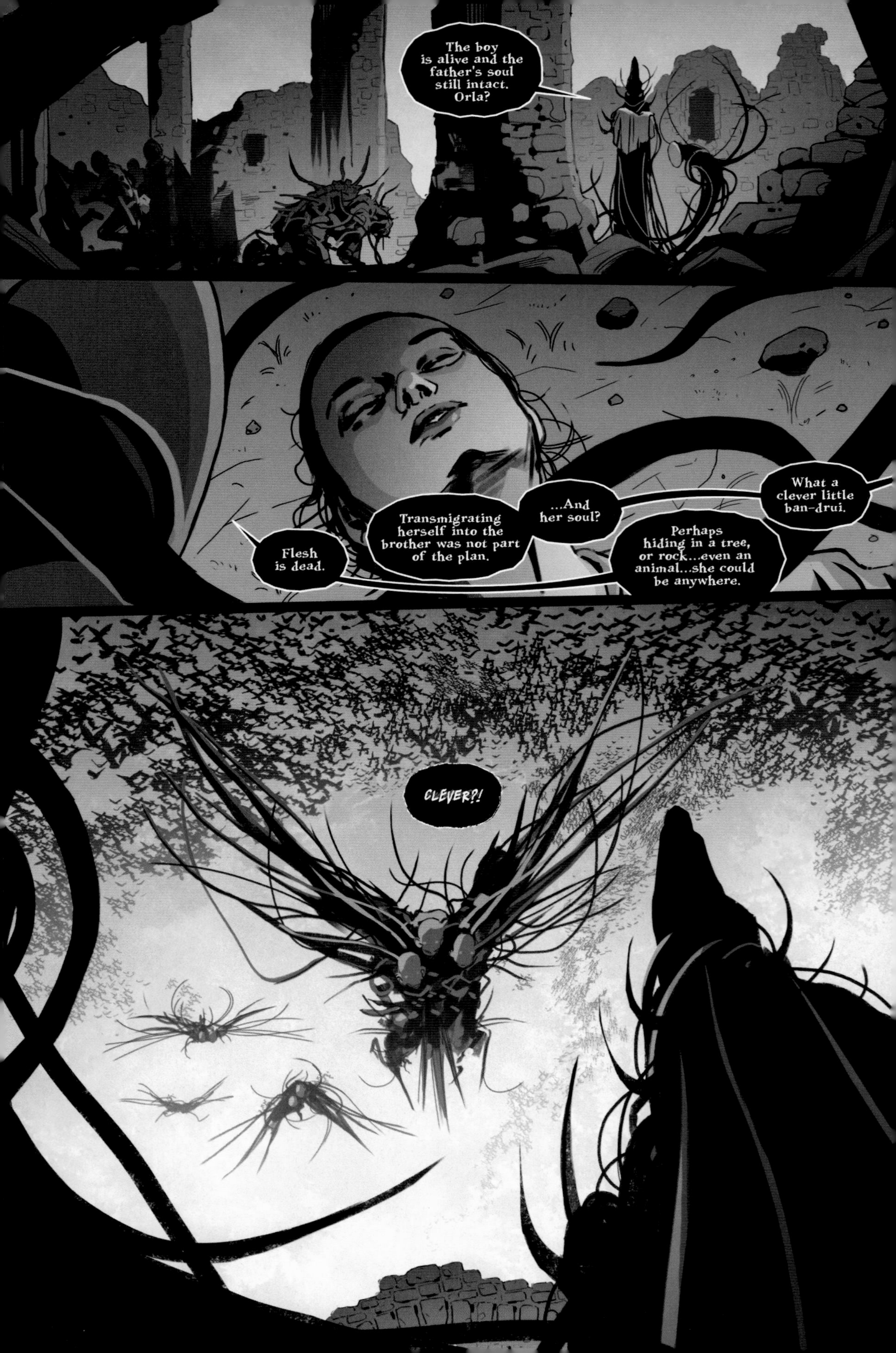
The boy is alive and the father's soul still intact. Orla?
Flesh is dead.
Transmigrating herself into the brother was not part of the plan.
...And her soul?
Perhaps hiding in a tree, or rock...even an animal...she could be anywhere.
What a clever little ban-drui.
CLEVER?!

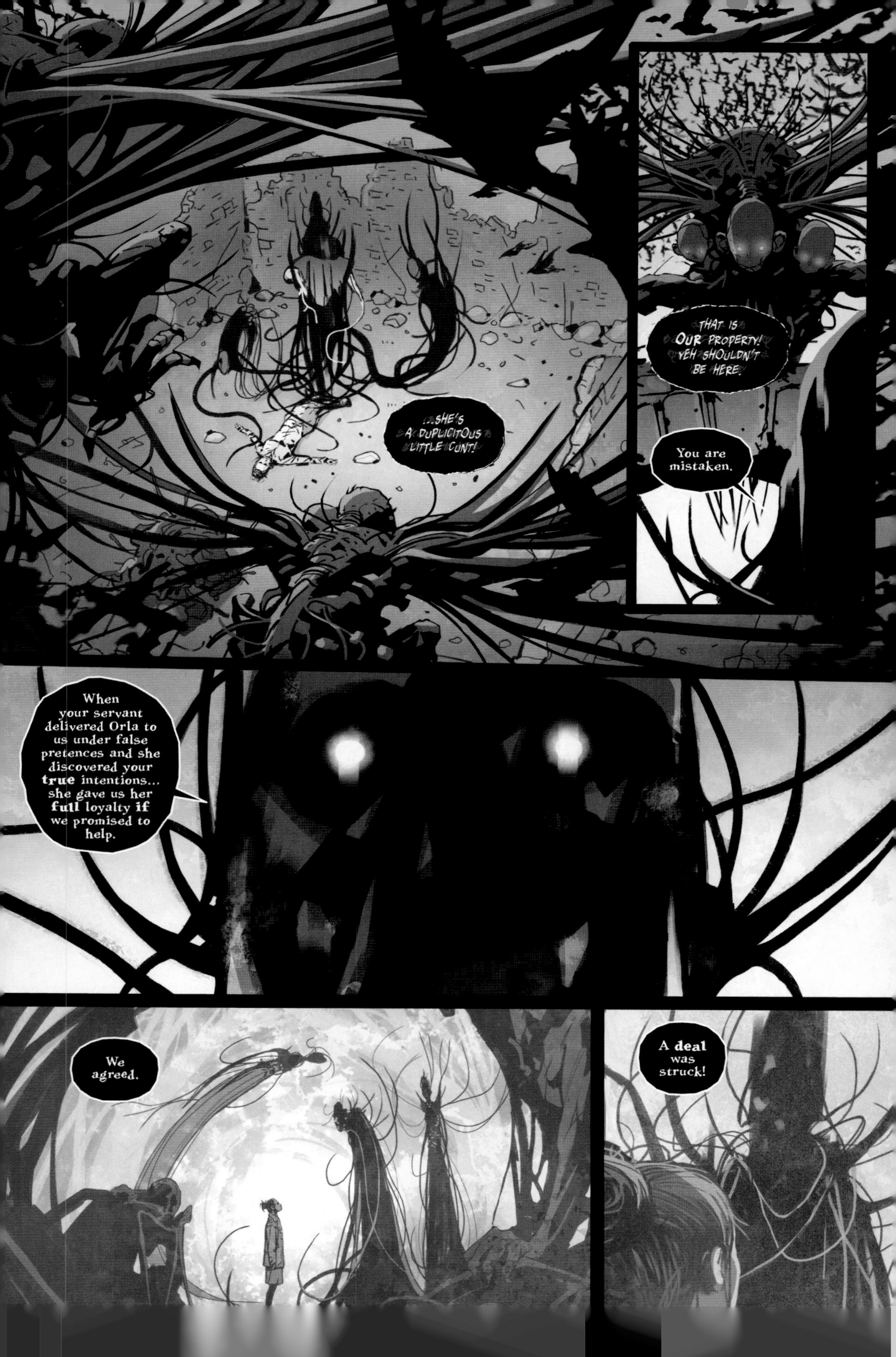
...SHE'S A DUPLICITOUS LITTLE CUNT!
THAT IS OUR PROPERTY! YEH SHOULDN'T BE HERE.
You are mistaken.
When your servant delivered Orla to us under false pretences and she discovered your true intentions... she gave us her full loyalty if we promised to help.
We agreed.
A deal was struck!

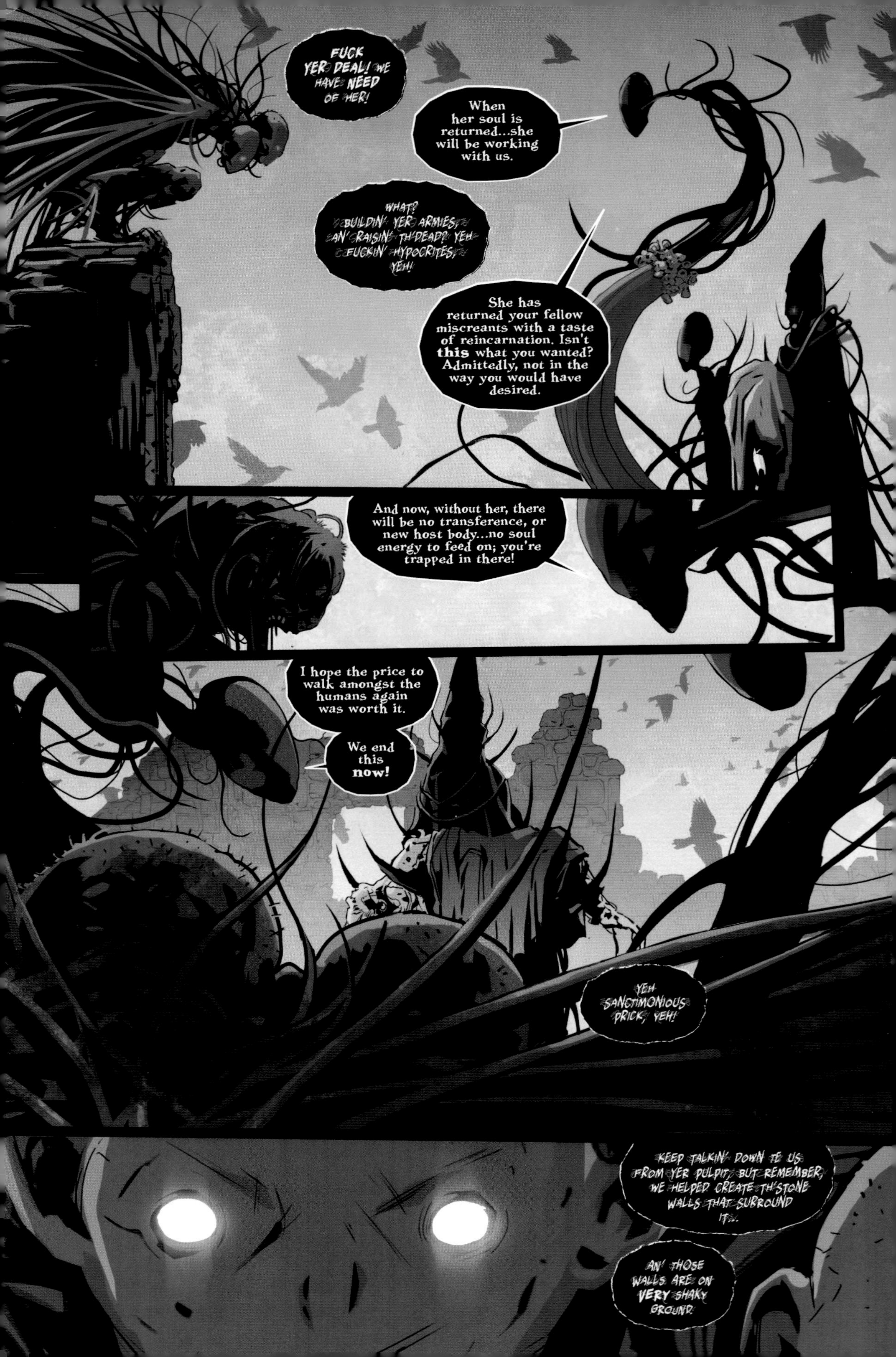
FUCK YER DEAL! WE HAVE NEED OF HER!
When her soul is returned...she will be working with us.
WHAT? BUILDIN' YER ARMIES, AN' RAISIN' TH' DEAD? YEH FUCKIN' HYPOCRITES, YEH!
She has returned your fellow miscreants with a taste of reincarnation. Isn't this what you wanted? Admittedly, not in the way you would have desired.
And now, without her, there will be no transference, or new host body...no soul energy to feed on; you're trapped in there!
I hope the price to walk amongst the humans again was worth it.
We end this now!
YEH SANCTIMONIOUS PRICK, YEH!
KEEP TALKIN' DOWN TE US FROM YER PULPIT, BUT REMEMBER, WE HELPED CREATE TH' STONE WALLS THAT SURROUND IT.
AN' THOSE WALLS ARE ON VERY SHAKY GROUND.

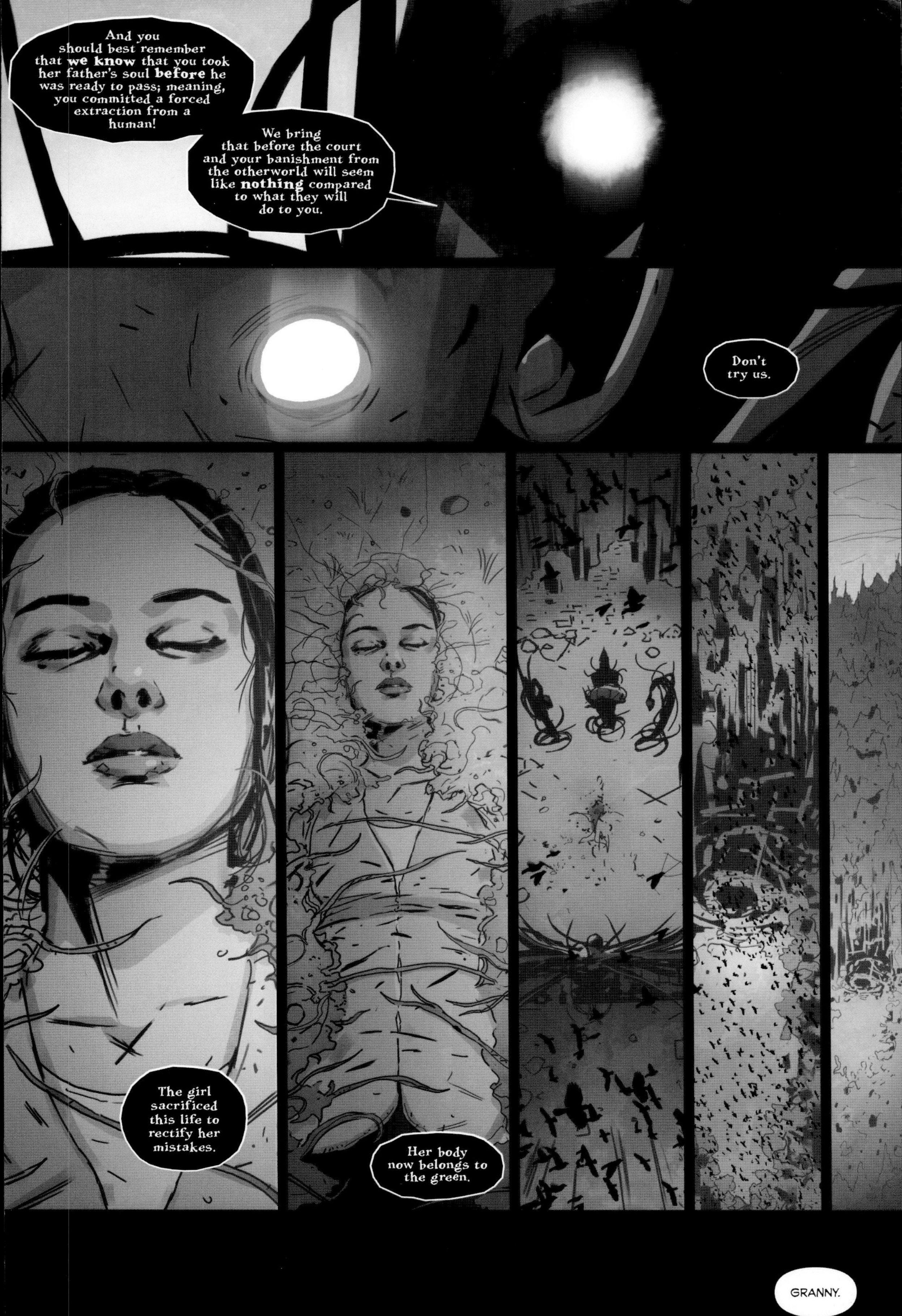
And you should best remember that **we know** that you took her father's soul **before** he was ready to pass; meaning, you committed a forced extraction from a human!
We bring that before the court and your banishment from the otherworld will seem like **nothing** compared to what they will do to you.
Don't try us.
The girl sacrificed this life to rectify her mistakes.
Her body now belongs to the green.
GRANNY.

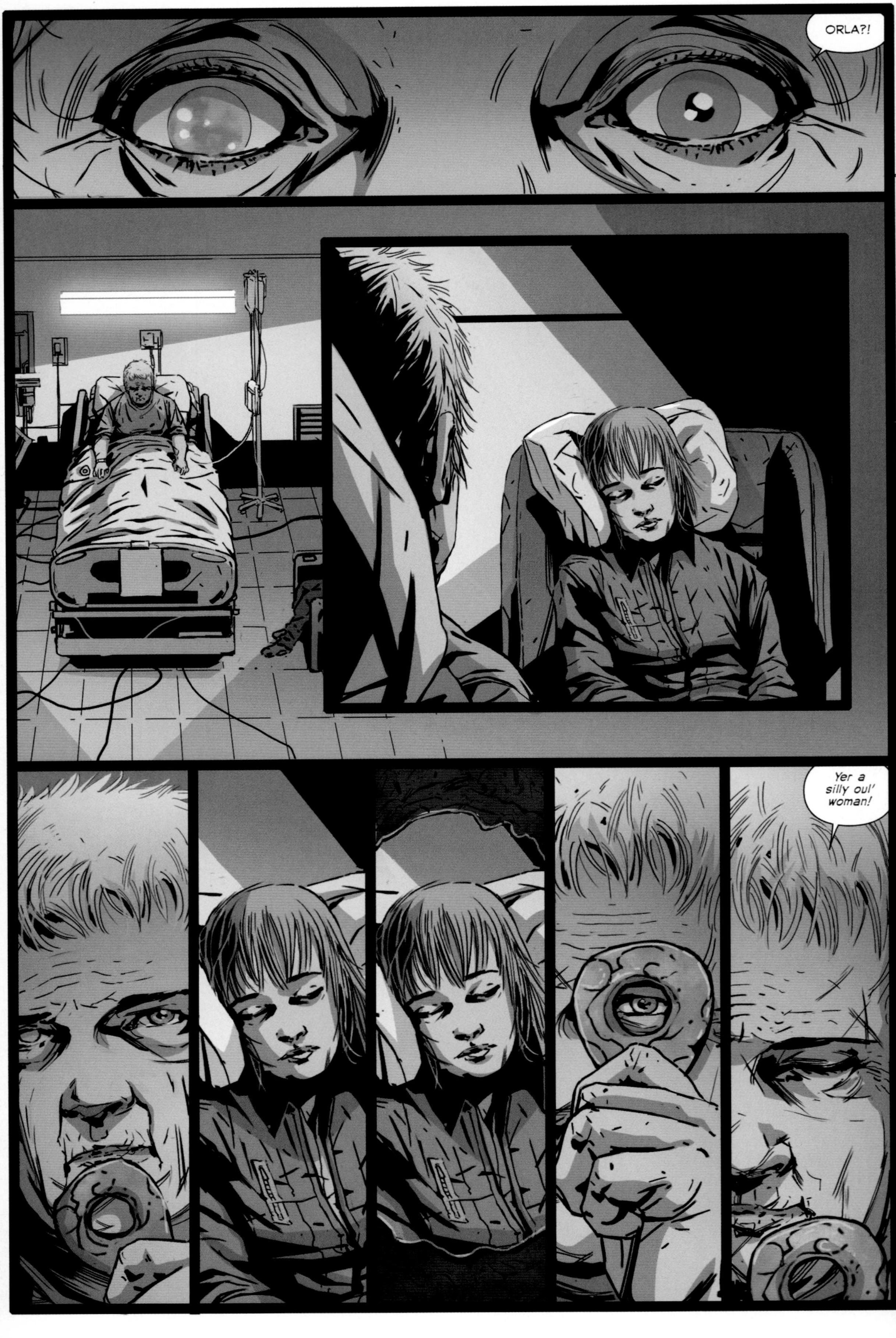
ORLA?!
Yer a silly oul' woman!

UGGHH!

C'MON, ORLA...WHERE TH'HECK ARE YE?

"PICK UP, LUV!

"I NEED TO KNOW YEH AND OLLY ARE OKAY..."

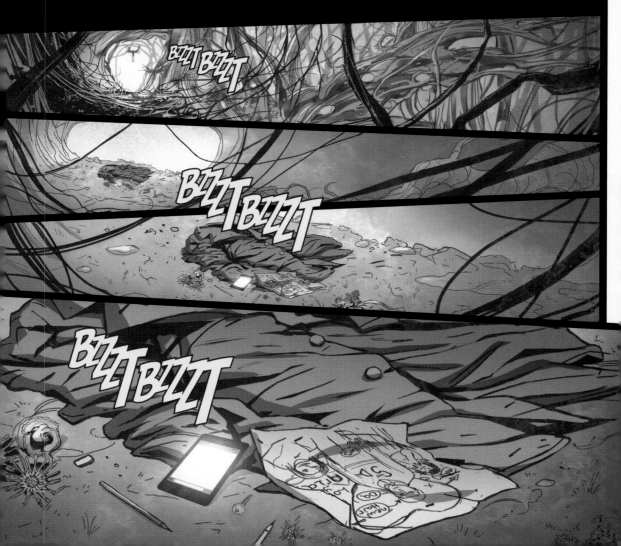

BZZZT BZZZT

BZZZT BZZZT

BZZZT BZZZT

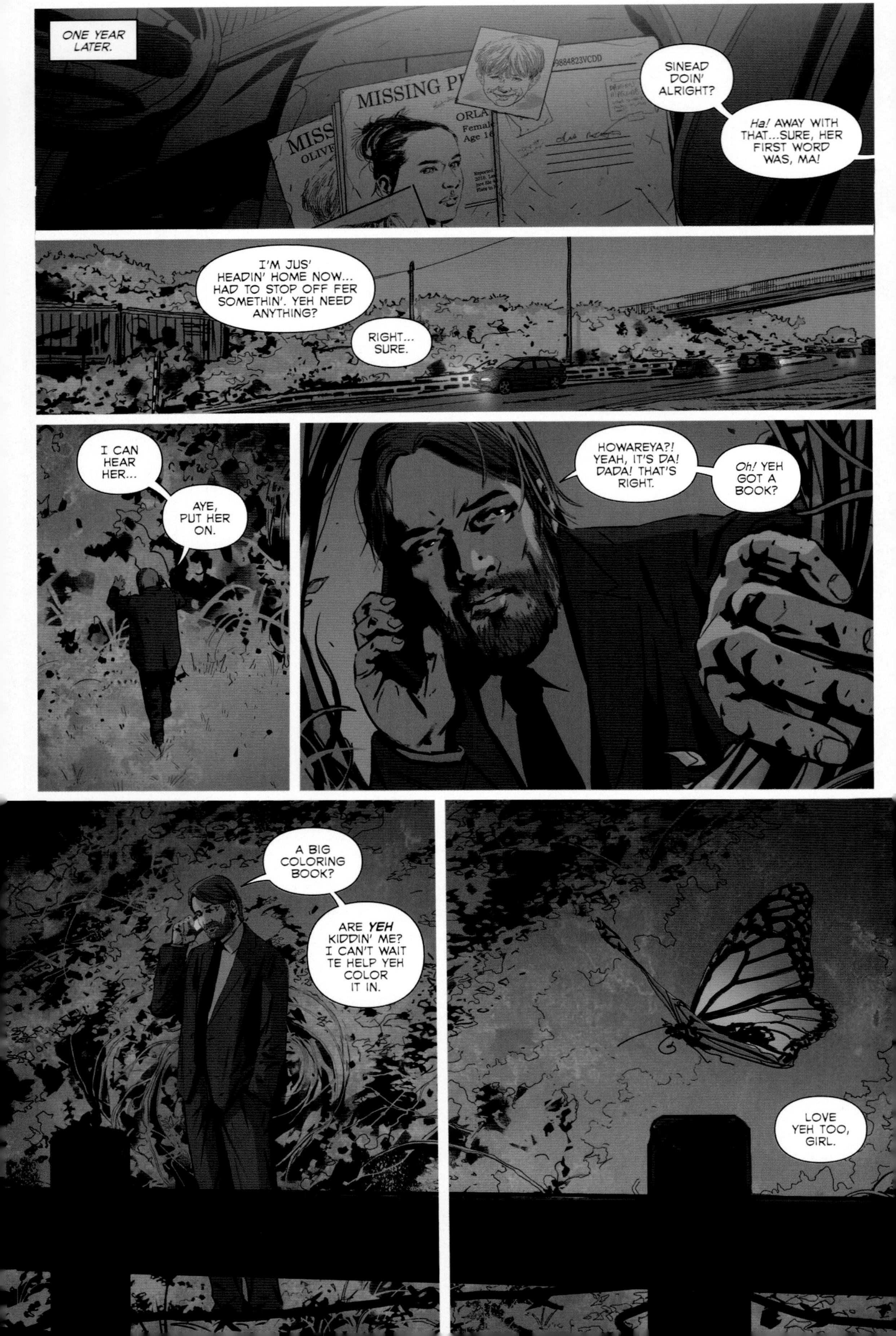
ONE YEAR LATER.
SINEAD DOIN' ALRIGHT?
Ha! AWAY WITH THAT...SURE, HER FIRST WORD WAS, MA!
I'M JUS' HEADIN' HOME NOW... HAD TO STOP OFF FER SOMETHIN'. YEH NEED ANYTHING?
RIGHT... SURE.
I CAN HEAR HER...
AYE, PUT HER ON.
HOWAREYA?! YEAH, IT'S DA! DADA! THAT'S RIGHT.
Oh! YEH GOT A BOOK?
A BIG COLORING BOOK?
ARE YEH KIDDIN' ME? I CAN'T WAIT TE HELP YEH COLOR IT IN.
LOVE YEH TOO, GIRL.

BONUS FEATURES

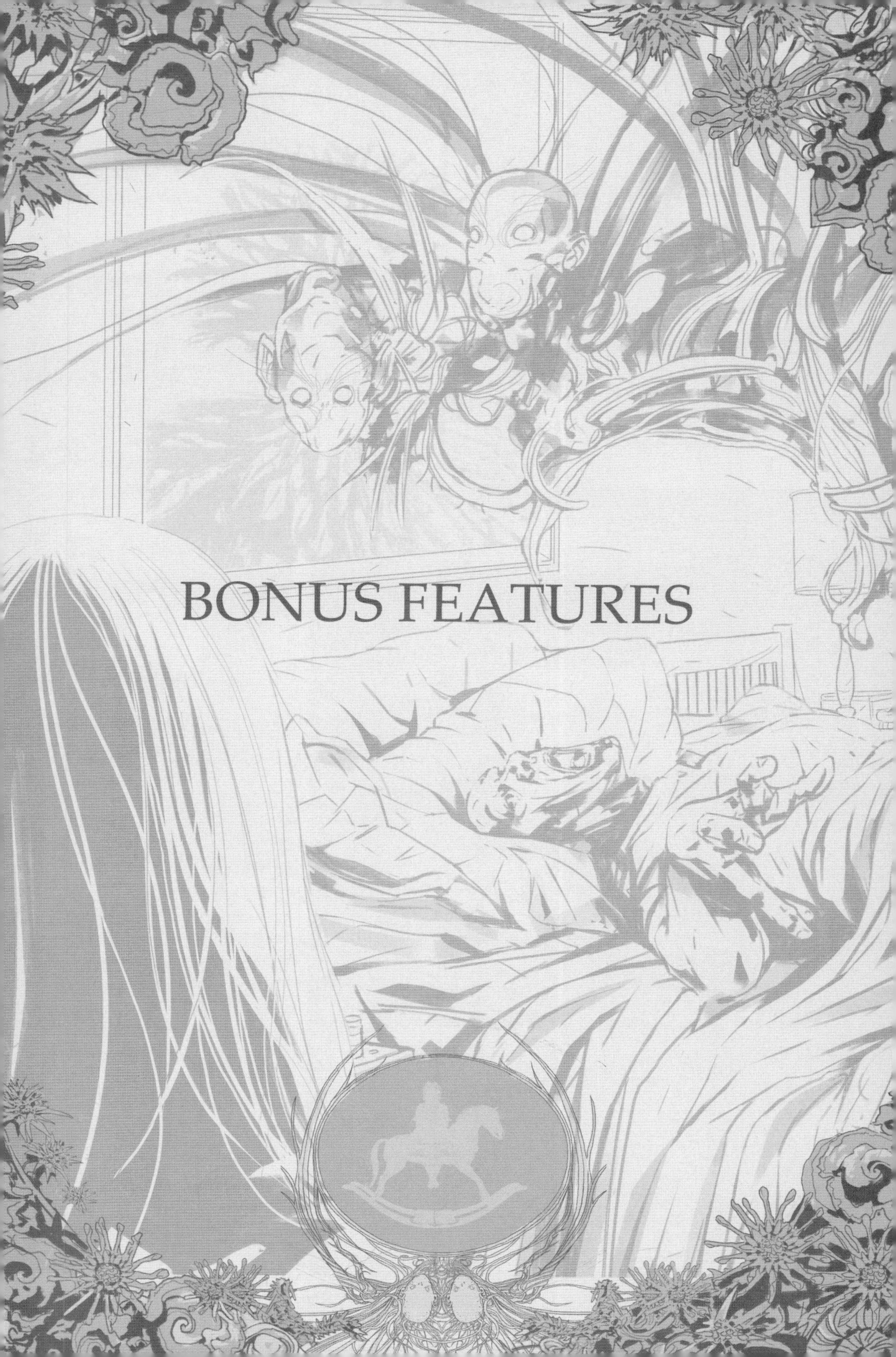

COVER IDEAS

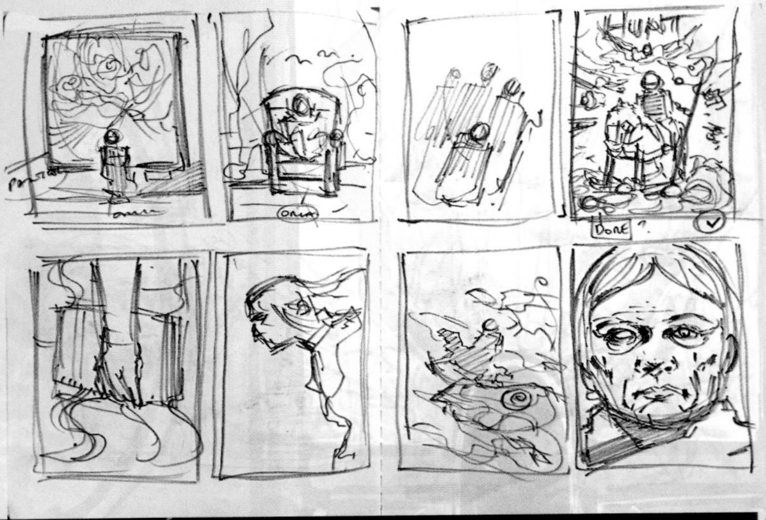
ORLA
DONE ?

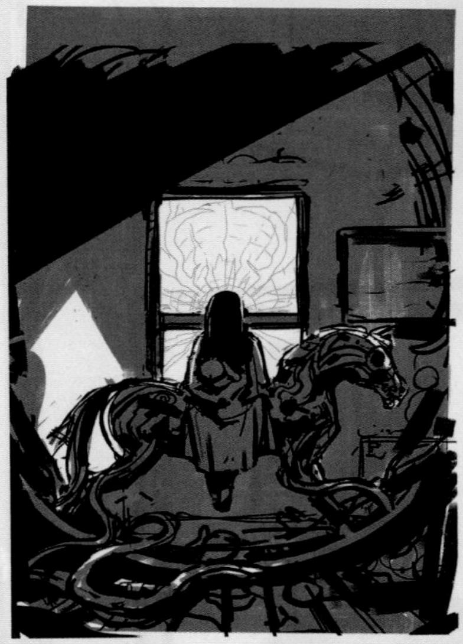

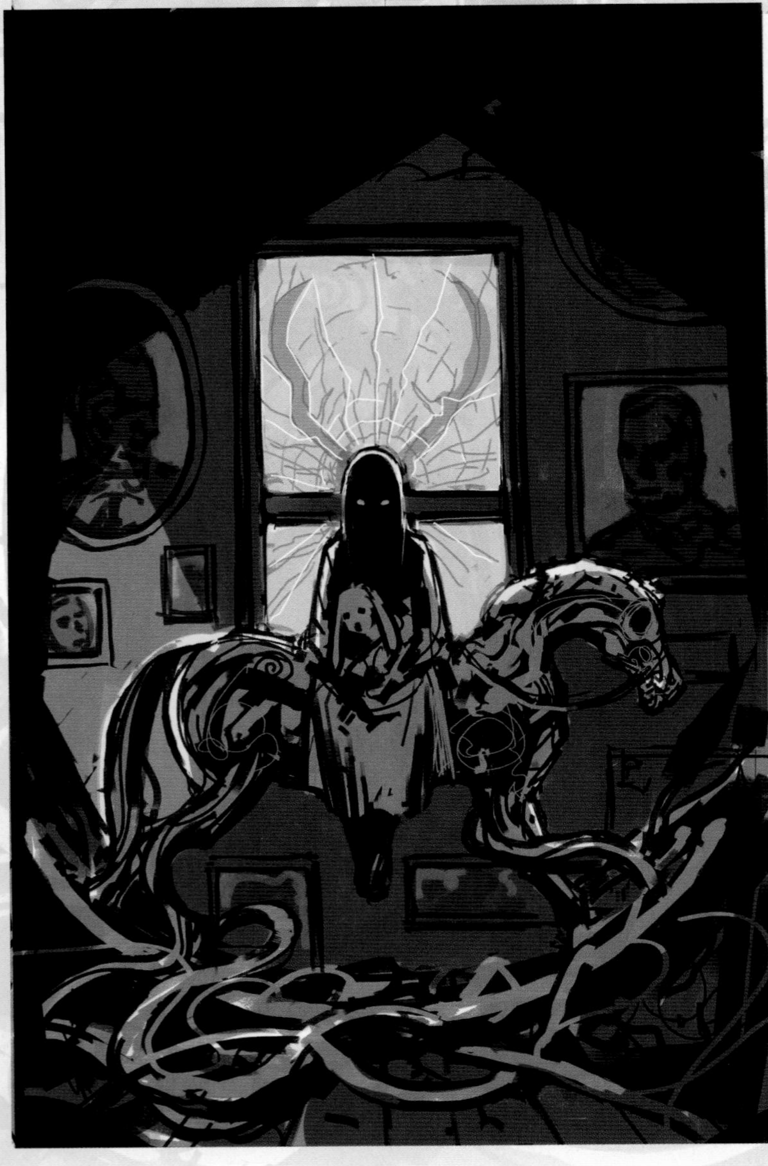

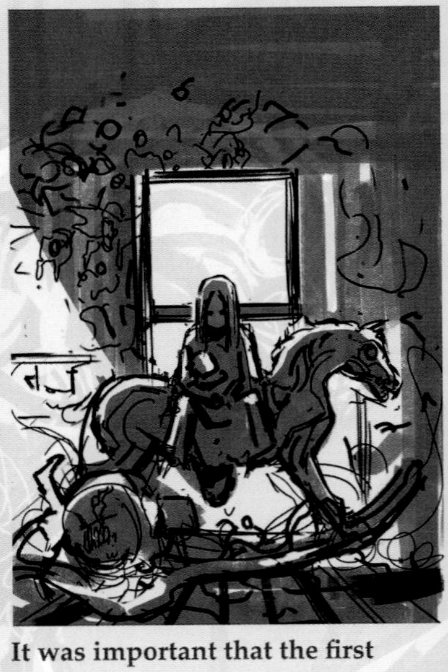

It was important that the first cover suggested the myth of 'The Wild Hunt' as those tales were the bedrock of my story. The initial sketches (seen here) were too dark in tone and didn't give that sense of 'fairytale' that it required, so I stripped out all the detail and just went with Orla on the rocking horse.

I then added some Harry Clarke type design and asked Joana to colour it green; we were thinking green, white, and gold but decided that it may be overdoing the 'Irish theme' a little too much.

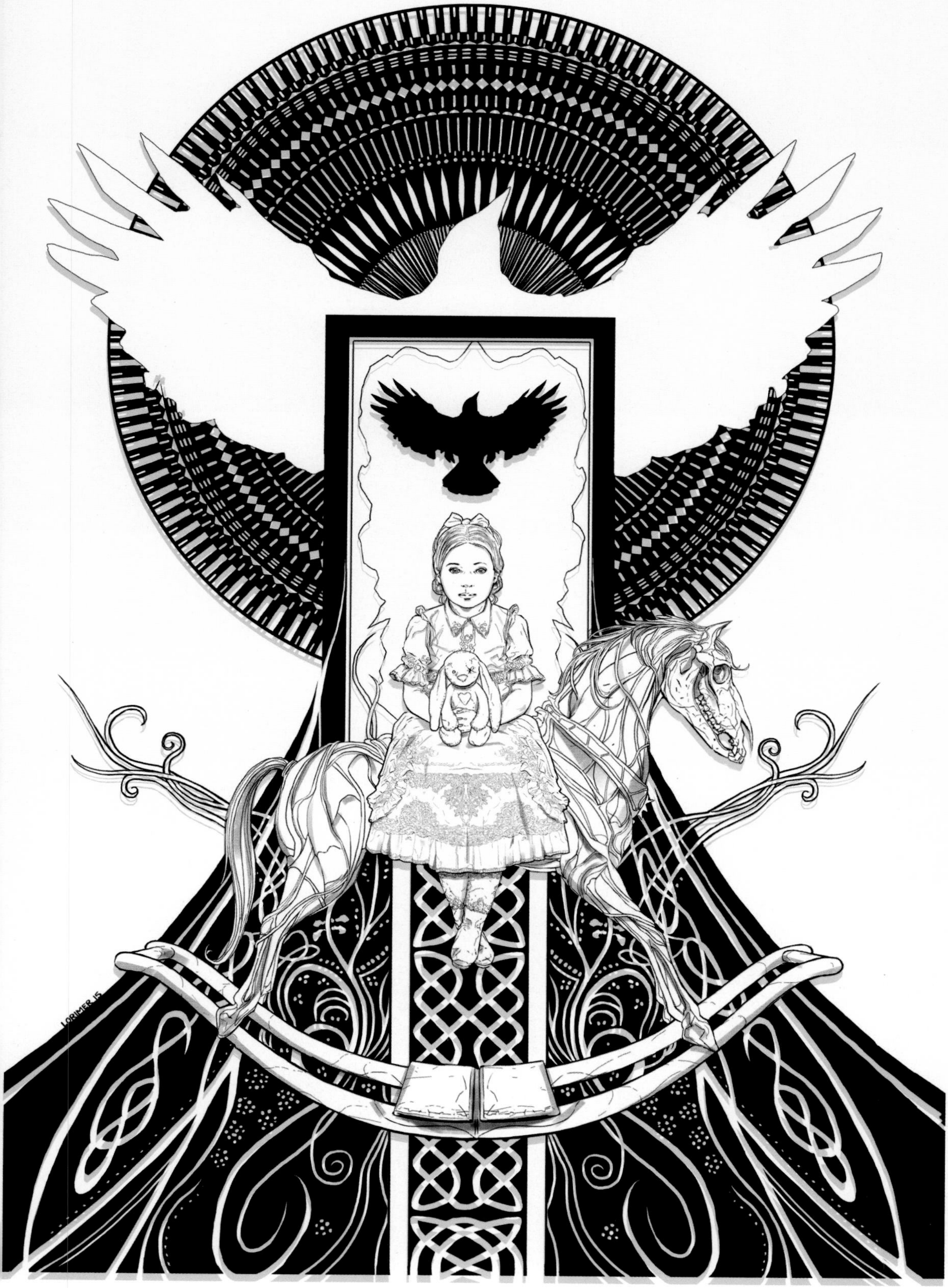
LORIMER 15

Final inks for cover #1

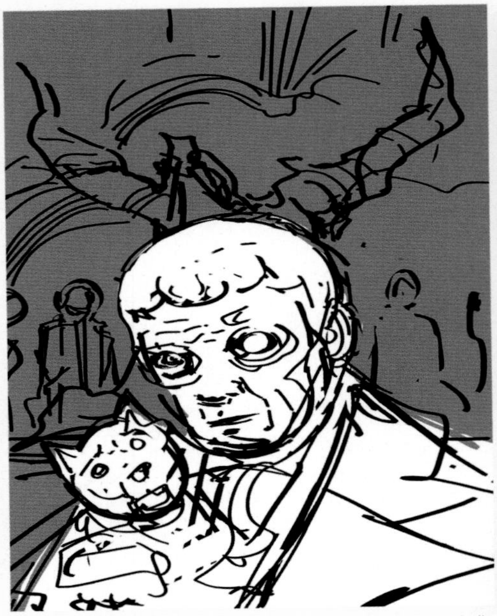

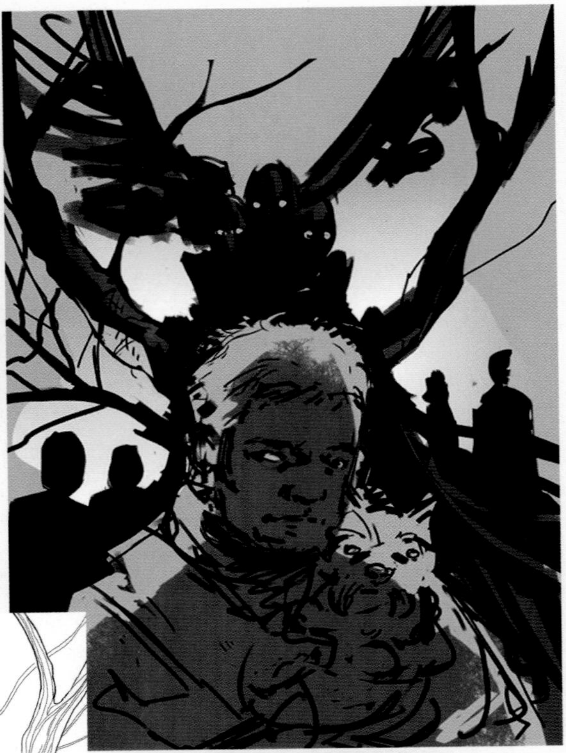

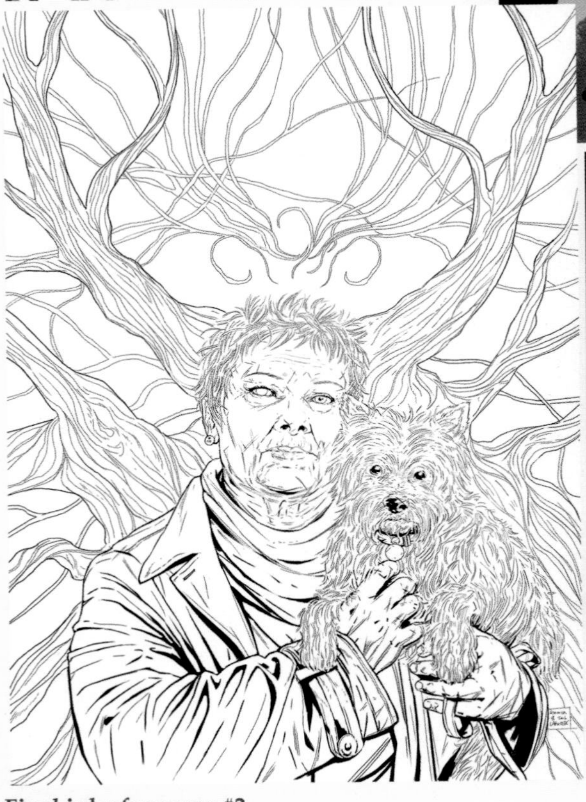

Final inks for cover #2

What could be scarier than a one-eyed, old age pensioner and her dog?

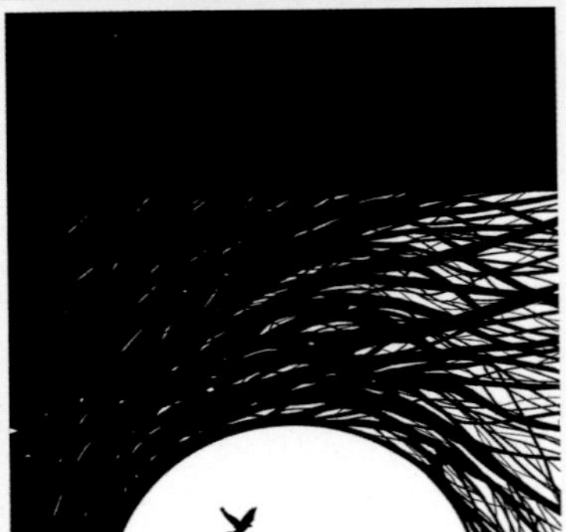

Cover idea for issue #3

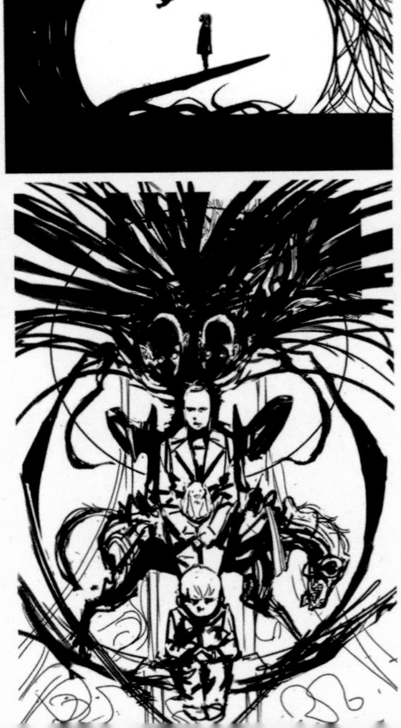

Cover idea for issue #5

CHARACTER DESIGN

I referenced a few actors as a starting point for the design of my two main characters. As I remember, the likeness of Sally Hawkins and Jocelin Donahue were considered for the role of Orla, and Dame Judi Dench for Granny.

Orla

Granny orla A 1

Granny

My friend Ciara Brehony's daughter, Finn (right) who not only happened to be the same age as Orla but looked just as I had pictured her, ended up filling the role perfectly and kindly allowed me to use her likeness.

I even kept to Finn's hairstyle as seen pictured in this reference photo.

FAERIES

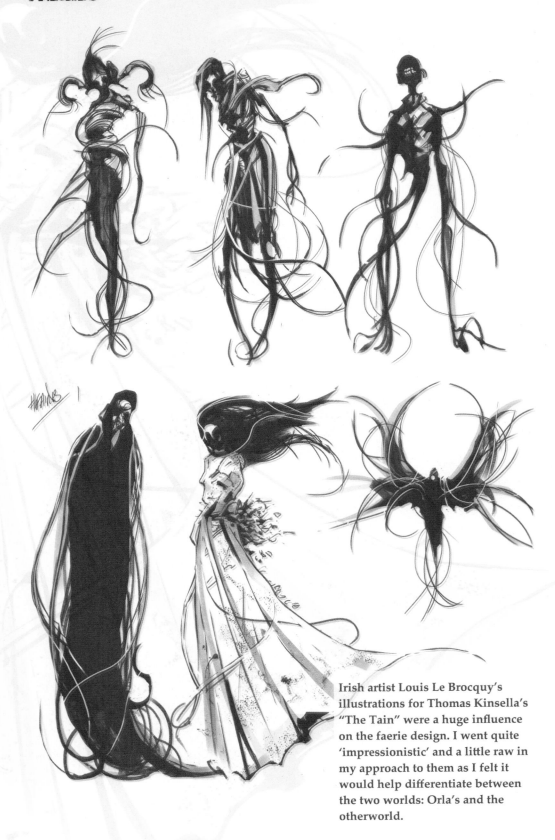

Irish artist Louis Le Brocquy's illustrations for Thomas Kinsella's "The Tain" were a huge influence on the faerie design. I went quite 'impressionistic' and a little raw in my approach to them as I felt it would help differentiate between the two worlds: Orla's and the otherworld.

PROCESS

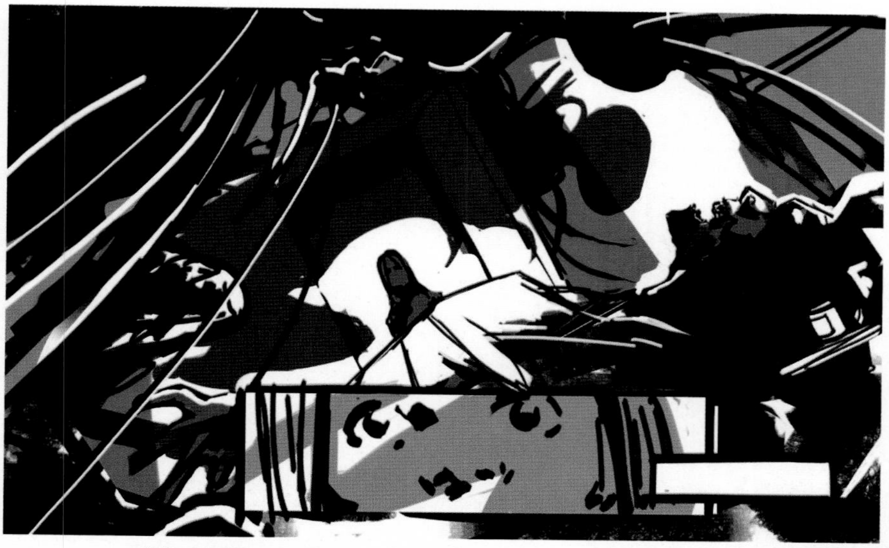

Here are some thumbnails from issue #1. You can see how certain panels were adjusted with some details being omitted and/or completely reworked. This is the fun part of the process: figuring out the staging, composition, general flow and pacing of the page.

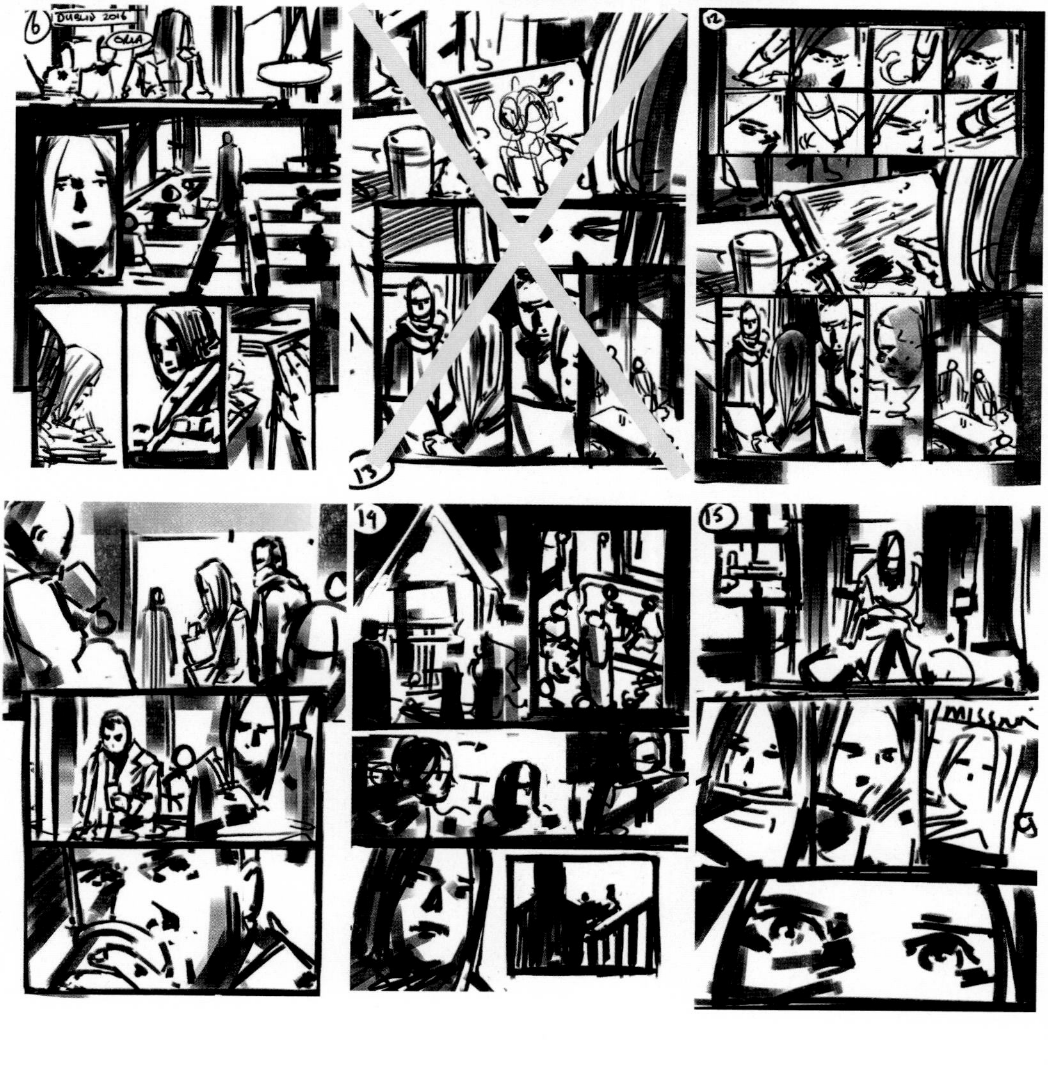

THUMBNAILS TO FINAL INKS

Once it's all working, I take the thumbs straight to inks. As I work digitally, I revise and refine the page as I go, making some last minute changes as required.

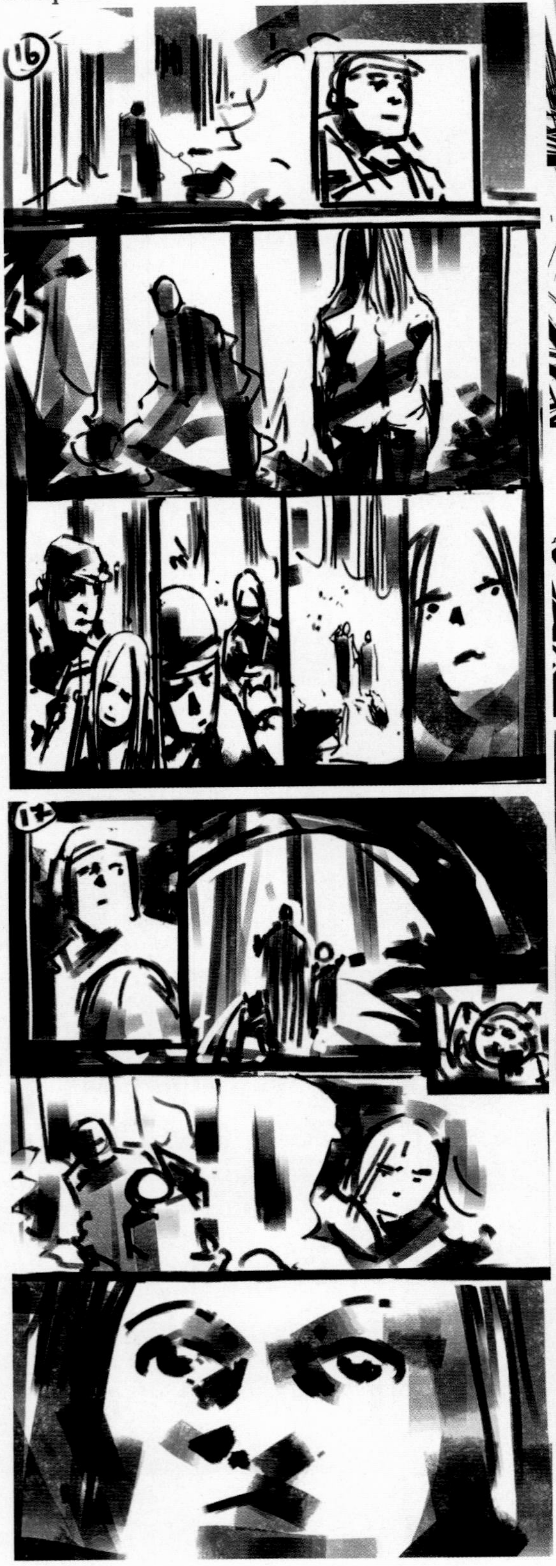

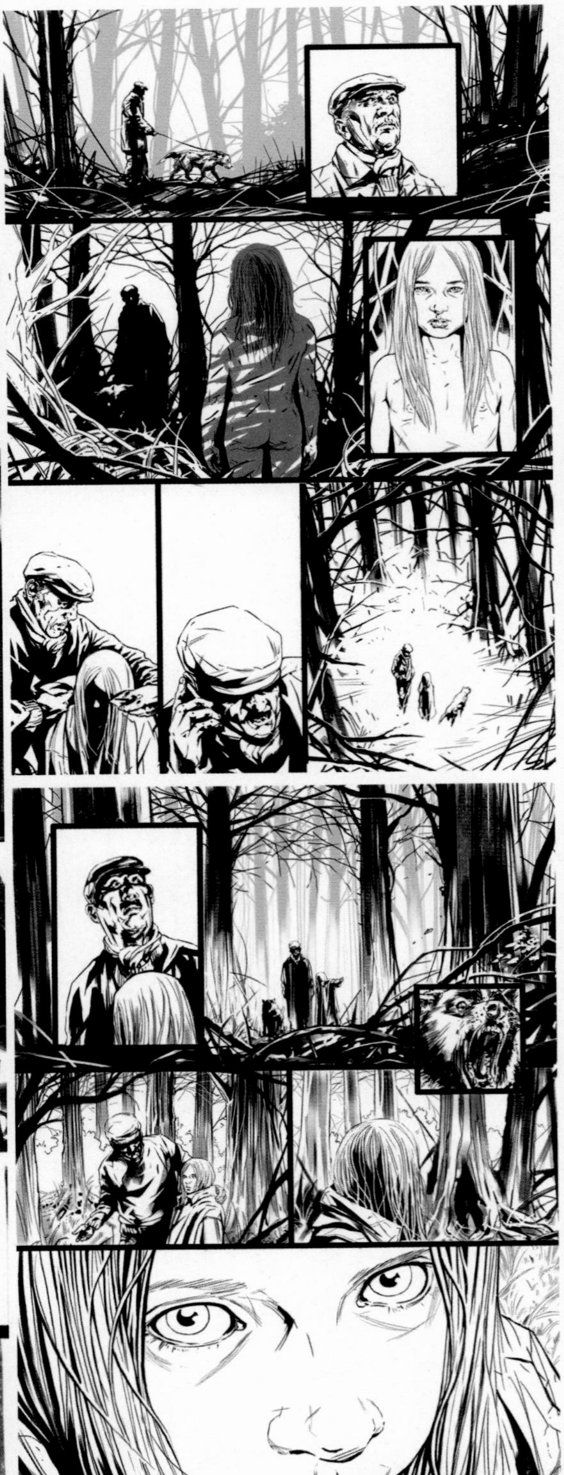

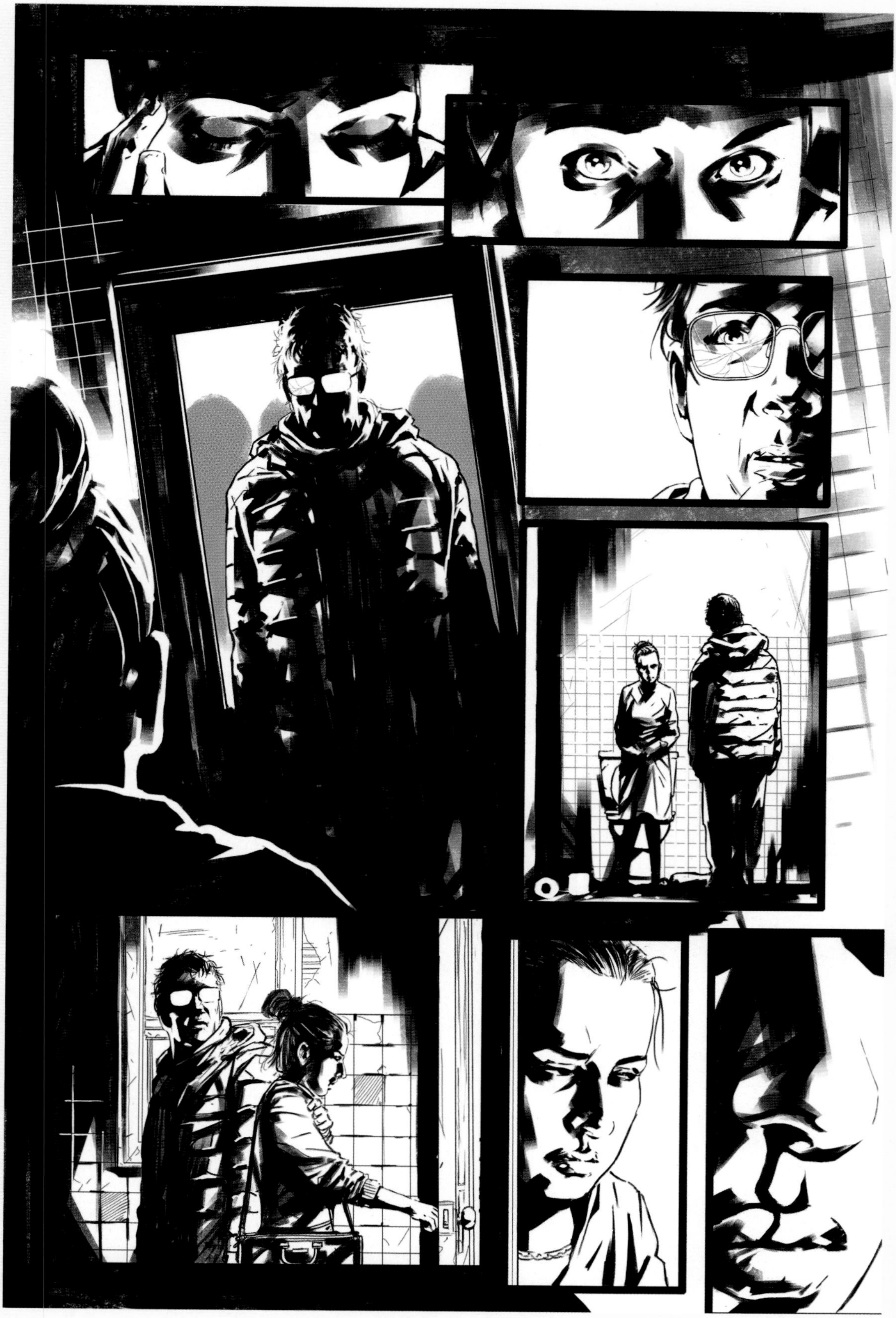

Final inks of page 17 from issue #1

Some early visual 'noodling' for issue #1. I had originally thought about introducing Olly in a forest witnessing a fight between some of his school friends, but due to a repeat flashback forest scene with Orla in the same issue, I decided to add him to the kitchen scene with his granny and mum. In the end, it was a much better choice as it helped Olly register more to the reader as Orla's brother.

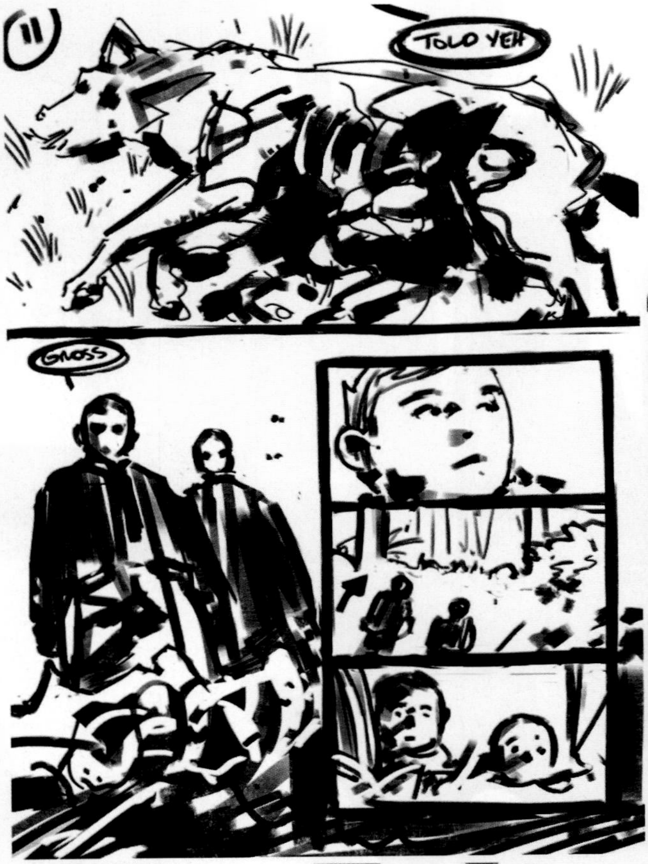
TOLD YEH
GROSS

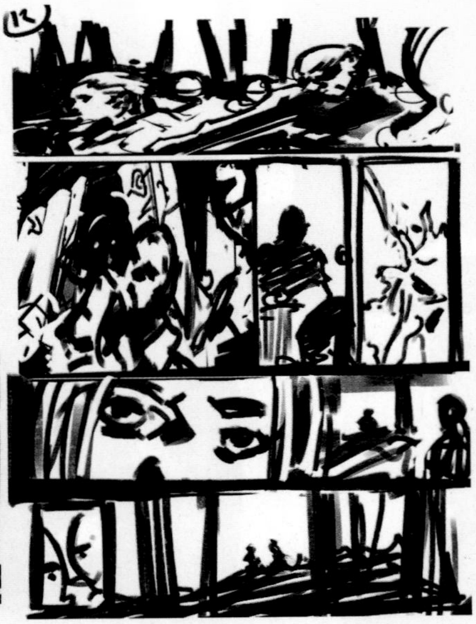

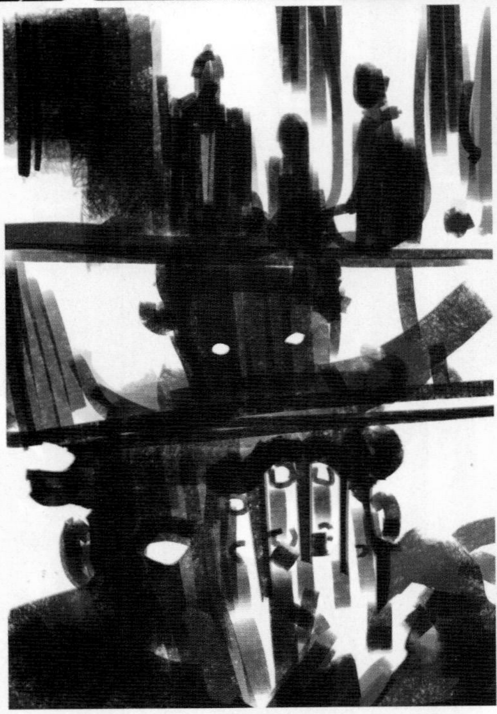

This was a potential flashback scene featuring 'The people in the woods.'

Below: Playing around with some 'alternate' takes on a few scenes.

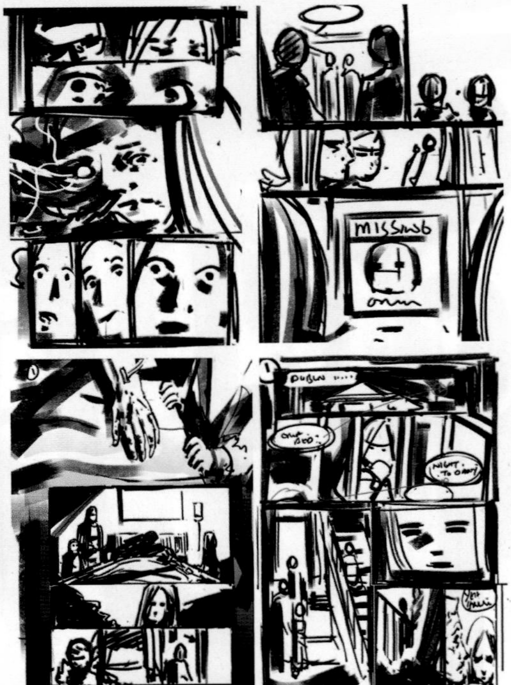

Acknowledgements.

Much love to my wife, Jacinta, and son, Olin who were there with me throughout this journey, listening to my story ideas and raising their eyebrows at all the appropriate places: changes were made accordingly.

Writing a book set in Ireland while based in Vancouver I was very fortunate to have the wonderful Ciara Brehony and Ian Lawton kindly supplying me with the odd bit of photo reference from the home country. They also took the time to read through early drafts of the scripts to make sure nothing seemed too out of place and that the Irish brogue all rang true.

A tip of the hat to Finn Roche, Donna Leong, Angie Palsak, Nate Smith, Colin Beadle, J Falconer, Ryan Cardinal, David Maclean, Albert Hughes, Johh Higgins, Joe Harris, Conor McMullin, Warren Scheske, and Declan Shalvey who either lent an ear or donated a kind word in support of the project. It was appreciated.

This book wouldn't exist without the participation of my partners-in-crime, Joana Lafuente and Jim Campbell. Their combined talents raised the bar at every turn and made for a very easy and pleasurable collaboration. And, of course, a sincere thank you to my publisher, Jim Valentino at Image/Shadowline, for having faith in the book and letting me run with it.

Finally, thanks to you, the reader, for buying it, and all you lovely comicbook retailers for stocking it.

Keep one eye open.

Colin Lorimer
Vancouver,
January 2017

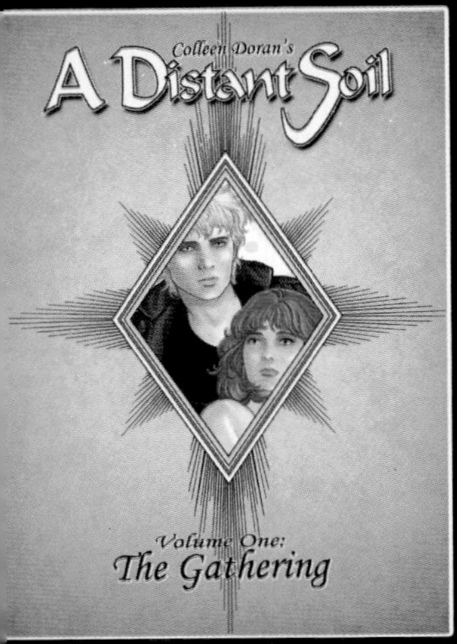
Colleen Doran's
A Distant Soil
Volume One:
The Gathering
COLLEEN DORAN

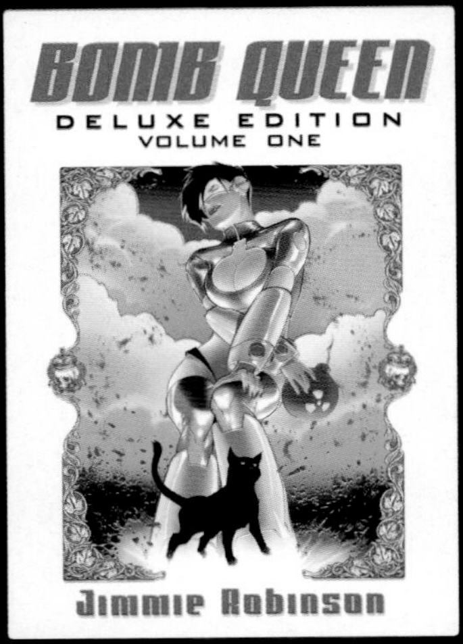
BOMB QUEEN
DELUXE EDITION
VOLUME ONE
Jimmie Robinson
JIMMIE ROBINSON

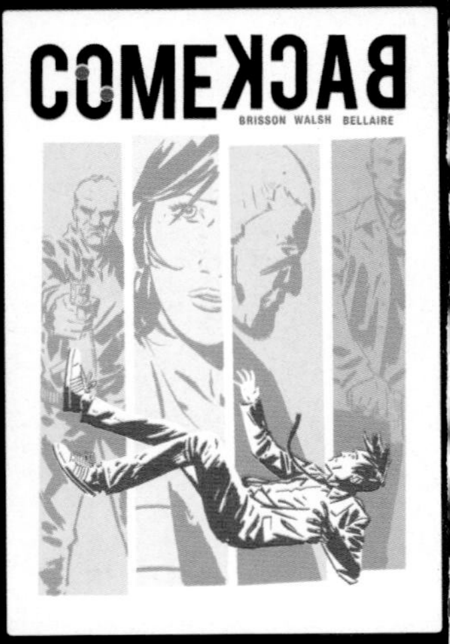
COMEBACK
BRISSON WALSH BELLAIRE
BRISSON/WALSH

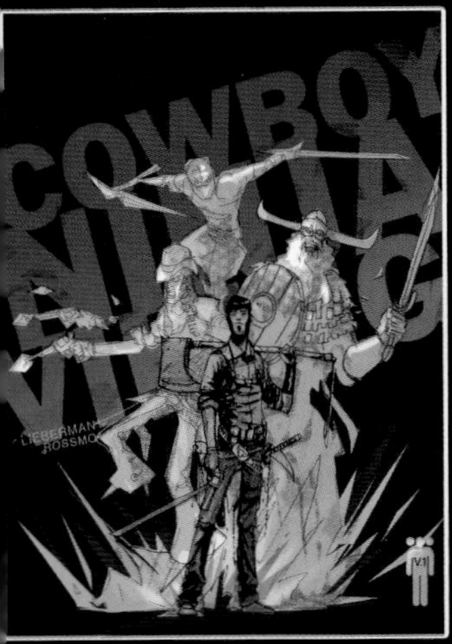
COWBOY NINJA VIKING
LIEBERMAN/ROSSMO

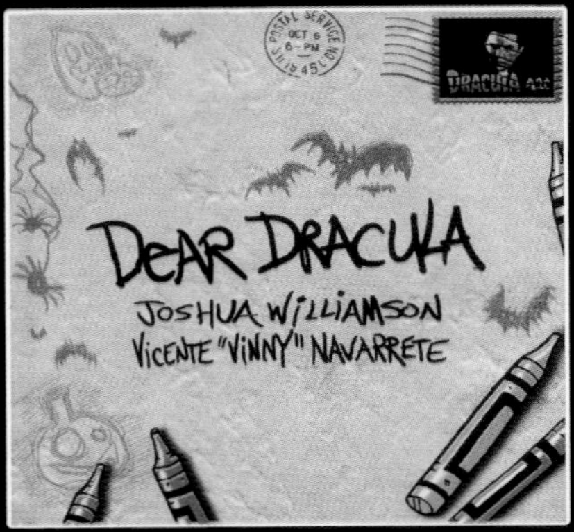
DEAR DRACULA
JOSHUA WILLIAMSON
VICENTE "VINNY" NAVARRETE
WILLIAMSON/NAVARRETE

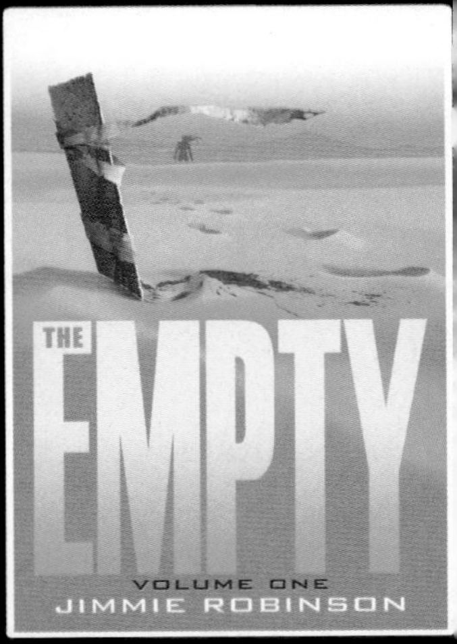
THE EMPTY
VOLUME ONE
JIMMIE ROBINSON
JIMMIE ROBINSON

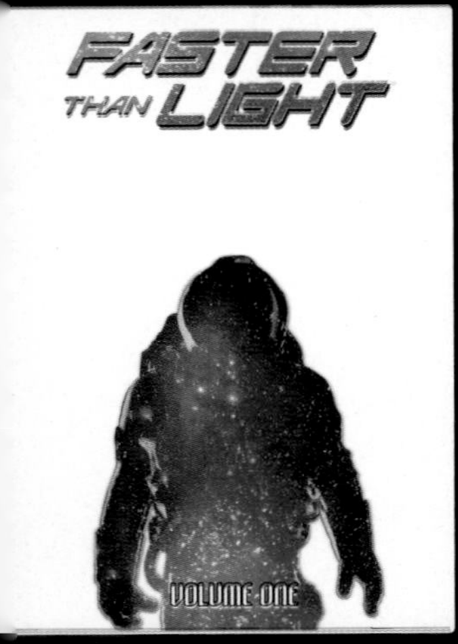
FASTER THAN LIGHT
VOLUME ONE
HABERLIN

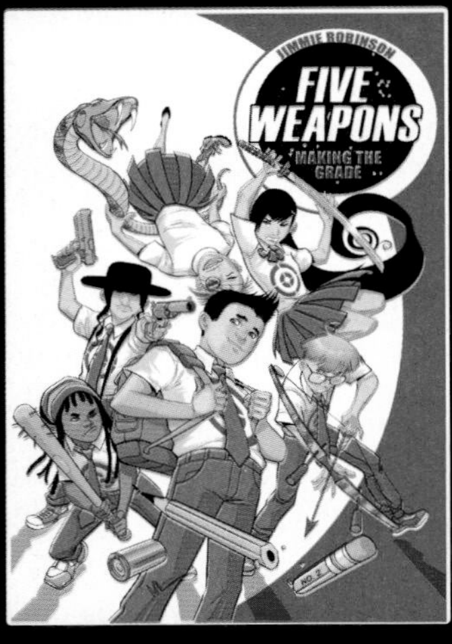
JIMMIE ROBINSON
FIVE WEAPONS
MAKING THE GRADE
JIMMIE ROBINSON

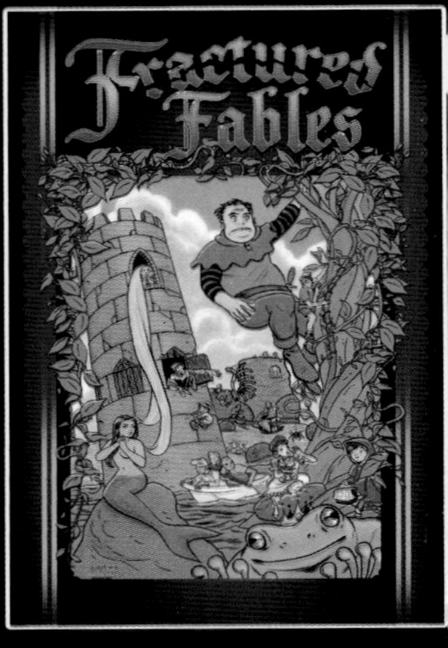
Fractured Fables
VARIOUS ARTISTS

THIS is Diversity... image® Shadowline®